**Praise for T...**

'A deliciously macabr...
**Abigail Dean**

'This is a sun-soaked page-turner packed with deliciously
terrible people and twist after twist. Loved it!'
**Ellery Lloyd**

'A mind blowing rollercoaster ride of a book!'
**Nikki Smith**

'A refreshingly unique story of layered
betrayal and revenge . . . I loved it'
**L V Matthews**

'Proving once again she's the mistress of "one two punch"
twists, Emily Freud's *The Cliffhanger* is a masterpiece'
**Lizzy Barber**

'The perfect book to disappear into . . . I really, really loved it'
**Emma Curtis**

'A killer hook, a stunning location and a fiercely compelling
mystery – this book has it all. I couldn't put it down'
**B P Walter**

'With its heady mix of toxic characters, sun-soaked backdrop and *Gone Girl* vibes, *The Cliffhanger* is irresistibly readable'
**Katherine Faulkner**

'Dark, twisty and utterly irresistible . . . And the twist, when it came, was the perfect blend of shocking yet inevitable'
**Jessica Bull**

'True to the title, *The Cliffhanger* kept me reading chapter after chapter'
**Sam Holland**

'Deliciously tense and twisty – this is a tale of ambition, betrayal and the darkness of creativity. I loved every page!'
**Lesley Kara**

'Unforgettable and a must-read for thriller fans'
**Charlotte Duckworth**

'A husband and wife writing team who are not what they seem, a gorgeous setting and some absolutely killer twists – loved it'
**Catherine Cooper**

# THE CLIFFHANGER

**Emily Freud** is the author of *My Best Friend's Secret*, *What She Left Behind* and *Her Last Summer*. She has worked on Emmy and BAFTA award winning television series including *Educating Yorkshire* and *First Dates*. Emily lives in North London, with her husband and two children.

Also by Emily Freud

*My Best Friend's Secret*
*What She Left Behind*
*Her Last Summer*

# THE
# CLIFFHANGER

## EMILY FREUD

QUERCUS

First published in Great Britain in 2025 by

**QUERCUS**

Quercus Editions Ltd
Carmelite House
50 Victoria Embankment
London EC4Y 0DZ

An Hachette UK company

The authorised representative in the EEA is Hachette Ireland,
8 Castlecourt Centre, Castleknock Road, Castleknock,
Dublin 15, D15 YF6A, Ireland (email: info@hbg.ie)

A CIP catalogue record for this book is available
from the British Library

PB ISBN 978 1 52943 815 4
EBOOK ISBN 978 1 52943 816 1

This book is a work of fiction. Names, characters,
businesses, organizations, places and events are
either the product of the author's imagination
or used fictitiously. Any resemblance to
actual persons, living or dead, events or
locales is entirely coincidental.

1

Typeset by CC Book Production
Printed and bound in Great Britain by Clays Ltd, Elcograf S.p.A.

**FSC**
www.fsc.org

**MIX**
Paper | Supporting
responsible forestry
FSC® C104740

Papers used by Quercus are from well-managed forests and other responsible sources.

# PART ONE

PART ONE

# CHAPTER ONE

We pull into a service station. We like French service stations. You can get a ham and cornichon sandwich for a couple of euros, and a black coffee that will burn the first layer of your tongue off. For some reason, I get a kick out of the culture shock from 'How may I help you, sir?' and 'Have a nice day' to the odd grunt and smirk at my barely scraped-together French, which is truly awful. Nothing is phoney here. People aren't going to overlace awkwardness with pleasantries and I like it. After fifteen years living in the US, I crave that European nonchalance I used to get back home. There is nothing like a British accent in Manhattan to open doors. People assume I'm cousins with royalty, not the son of a plumber. Yeah, my father runs his own successful business, but it's a far cry from Buckingham Palace, and I was never going to encourage all that & Son stuff. I knew I was destined for bigger things than ferrying one of Dad's fleet of lilac vans around Islington, showing up at every bored housewife's townhouse with a spanner. *I heard your pipes need cleaning?* The look on his face when I told him his only son wanted to be a writer. He couldn't get his head around it for a second. I'm from a long line of wheeler-dealers who all toed the line, taking on the role bestowed to them, the business falling finally to my senior, who grafted, turning the small firm into an empire. And I was just going to walk away from all that? To become a writer? I don't think Dad's read a book in his life, apart from instruction manuals. *Who's this John Steinbeck then? A new kid at school?*

Besides, New York is just … the place. You know. Stuff can happen in New York … New York … There are songs about that city. How many inspirational songs have you heard about London? Apart from the fighty, politically charged punk stomper, which is basically about burning the place down, I can't think of any. Zilch.

I get back to the car; the 1979 Fiat Spider convertible Emma arranged, newly buffed and hand delivered to us at the airport, is now devastated by a thin layer of dust. I think she imagined driving down country lanes with her silk scarf waving in the breeze. Like one of those foreign art-house films she lusts over. It's not, we have found out, the best car for high-speed motorways. Every time we're overtaken the tin can shakes, and every bump rattles through me. But I'm feeling rather delicate today.

I duck into the door, leaning across to hand her the coffee she ordered, before getting inside. I take a big toothy bite out of the chewy bread. 'I was half expecting you to be gone,' I joke, mouth full.

Emma peers across at me. 'You'd like that, wouldn't you?' Ah, a response. I've got a thread, maybe I can keep going, pull and pull and pull until I've released the deadlock.

I swallow the mouthful of baguette down. 'I just mean, a French service station on a swelteringly hot afternoon. Unbranded lorries.' I gesture to the large rusty white vehicles, a few pot-bellied guys in vests loitering around. 'Look at that absolute rust bucket.' I point to a creepy old-fashioned car with blacked-out windows that could easily stand in for a hearse. 'Gives me the shivers, doesn't it you?' I attempt. Her gaze follows mine and I think I may have caught something. 'Aren't you meant to get abducted on your way back from the bathroom? Isn't that how the story goes?' I ask, having another go.

She makes a little sound, a sigh, and crosses her arms, as if trying her best not to engage. But she can't help herself. 'Well, some guy did accost me to help with his car.' She puts on a fake French accent, and it fights over her New York twang. 'Madame, would you please help me reach in here to get my keys. They've fallen down, you see?'

I smile. *Yes, you can't help yourself, can you?* I know my wife. Too well. That kind of well that brings with it a knowledge of each other's faults so completely that the person you created in your head when you first met no longer exists at all. She turns her hand to admire her perfect manicure. 'But I'm too savvy to have fallen for that one. Sorry, honey, I ain't getting buried alive by some psycho.'

'Not today,' I muse.

'No. Not today,' she says, a tease of a smile on her lips.

I shift my body, turning towards her in the confined space. 'Well, that's a pity. I'd prepped myself to run in and demand to see the CCTV recording.' I grin, enjoying the humour embedded within this exchange. Our favourite kind of game, imagining the worst in every situation. It gets the juices flowing for whatever we turn our hand to next.

'It would be busted, wouldn't it?' she suggests. 'Didn't record a darn thing.'

I look up to the camera stuck on the corner of the square building. 'Yes, it doesn't seem to be working.'

'Well, ain't that a shame,' she adds with faux regret. 'Guess the cops wouldn't be worth a damn in this mess.'

'Oh, no. They'd think I was mad.'

'They'd be very dubious of you. You'd look guilty as hell.'

'Yes. Suspicious. I am the husband after all.' I nod in recognition. 'Statistically it's always the one closest to you, the one who loves you the most.' I hope she picks up on the sentiment in the last sentence, but I doubt it. She's been trying her best to hold on to the fury of the last twenty-four hours. But she can't be cross with me for ever – and she'll never be able to keep it up for six weeks.

'And once they look into your background . . .' She leaves that hanging in the air. It was a dig. The creeping menace within the sarcasm is close to tipping point, and I'm done. She's looking for a fight and I don't have the energy to weather one right now. The game is over. I toss the unfinished sandwich into the paper bag, chuck it into her lap, and start the car. *Bitch*.

An hour later we're still on the road. I look ahead at the scorched fields and the endless tarmac, the hills in the distance and the never-ending malaise of heat all around. I glug some more water down. That coffee did nothing but fasten the nausea presiding in my guts. Her eyes flick over at me, and she asks quietly, 'Still nursing that hangover, huh?'

'Just trying to keep hydrated,' I reply lightly, not wanting the conversation to turn down that highway of resentment. Instead, I take it to far more pleasant lands. 'God, it feels good to be away,' I muse. The journey to France has been a murky voyage. We left New York before sunrise, and I stumbled through Charles de Gaulle, rushing behind Emma to make our connecting flight to Montpellier. The first plane ride is a blur, as the previous night was not my most shining of moments. I can barely remember it, which is usually not a good sign. We were at a book launch – a much lauded over debut that had the whole town talking. The kind of shindig that is good to be seen at; it shows we pay our success forward and keeps us relevant, Emma says. I could have done without it to be honest. I must have drunk too much before we went out, because the whole evening disintegrated into vapour quickly. I've done something embarrassing, and shameful. I could tell the moment Emma violently shook me awake. The memory of the look on her face is etched on my frontal lobe. Disgusted, shocked and – most of all – disappointed. But God knows what I've done. I woke up in the guest room, which is a mark of something pretty terrible. I'm trying my best to file it under 'forget and move on' with all the other drunken half-memories of indignity, but it's sticking.

I managed to sort myself out by the time we landed, which

was lucky as Emma would never have driven the few hours it will take to get to the house. I'm still feeling ropey but haven't crashed yet.

Emma has been stuck to her phone the whole journey, glued to whatever is going on in the ether of mess back where we came from, and endlessly scrolling through our various social media sites, which is an addiction of its own, not that she'd ever admit it.

'Why don't you take a break? We don't have a book coming out, we deserve some downtime from all that,' I say, gesturing to the account she has open. 'Even Max promised he wouldn't bother us. Heads down and focus, remember?' She ignores me and I try again. 'Why are you doing it to yourself? Look out the window, we're in southern France. You've always said you'd love to spend the summer here.'

We travel a lot. For book tours and festivals, luxury holidays and trips to see the array of successful international friends we've collected over the last decade. But this time it's different. We're not here to relax or to bask in the fanfare of a new title launch, we're here to graft. Of course it would be France, Emma loves it here. Usually it would be Paris, or a chic beach town like Cannes. But we need time to think, to write, with no distractions, and the pin dropped in the map all the way out here.

'So, you don't want to know who they've cast?' she asks, a devious smile on her lips.

Okay, yeah, she's got me – I definitely want to know that. Fuck the scenery. 'They've cast Melany?'

'Yep. Rachel Headley!' Emma exclaims, elated. 'They got

her! I knew they could. They kept saying she wouldn't do a thriller, was focusing on Broadway, heart set on a Tony. But I knew she could be turned if she just read the script; that if she read Melany's part, she'd see it differently.' She sighs. 'Why do they always snub their noses? That's what I want to know. Twenty million folks can't all be off the mark.'

'Well, that's something worth celebrating.' Our third book is in the process of being turned into a film. We've been given veto at every stage; it was part of the contract, mainly because Emma is a massive control freak. She continues, 'Rachel has the range to nail Melany – only a few actors could really pull her off, elevate the whole thing. I still have no idea how they're going to film the asylum, and that twist. It feels like a stretch visually.' Emma sighs. 'Well, I suppose that's not our conundrum to grapple with.' She looks out the window, leaning her elbow on the side of the door, her hand cupping her mouth. The reflection of the scenery dances on her shiny black sunglasses.

I try to steady the ship of worry. 'It's written so vividly. My God, Emma!' I nudge her playfully. 'You wrote it as if you'd actually been there!' I laugh, but she doesn't react. Then I add gently, 'You did all the heavy lifting, Emma,' I say, hoping to deliver the olive branch we both need at this moment in time.

'I don't think I'll manage to sit through it,' she mutters, swallowing. 'What if I hate it?'

'You won't feel like that by the time the première comes around, and designers are queueing up to dress you. Come on, all that is the fun bit,' I tell her, but she looks glum. I reach for her hand and hold it, squeezing it supportively. She lets me.

'No one gives a damn about us authors when books get turned into movies, Felix. We get left in the dust.'

The satnav tells me to take a right and I indicate. 'Ten minutes,' I tell her, sensing this conversation is testing her nerves.

She sighs. I wish she'd stop doing that. I'm finding it rather triggering. There's a whole world of bitterness within that tiny breath of air. How unhappy she is, how unhappy I've made her. It makes the big ball of stress in my chest grow and bleed into my organs. 'I hope this works,' she murmurs.

'It will,' I reply. So much is riding on this summer, it's hard to even imagine the ending if we don't make it through. After eight books over nine years, not one word has been written of our long-awaited ninth novel. Our usual simpatico is ruined and it is all down to me. With every chasing email from our agent, Max, the guilt gnaws at me. I am the reason my wife can barely look in my direction. Barely focus. Let alone write a book with the hefty pressure of success dolloped on top. Writing is her escape and when she can't tap into it, she shrinks into herself and it's painful to watch. Especially as our success has been ferocious and unstoppable, to crash into this wall of nothingness is a shock to us both.

Because the trajectory has been an anomaly. We both knew, going into it, that finding true success in publishing is a nought-point-nought-one affair. Like trying to crack Hollywood or landing a number one pop song in the charts. It doesn't happen. It just doesn't.

But here we are: eight books sold in countless territories, constantly charting on bestseller lists, awards – you name it, we've done it. The Bram Stoker, the Goodreads Choice, a Reese's Book Club pick, and Barnes and Noble's Book of the Year (every year). Each of our books have been optioned, with the third likely to go into production later this year. The most acclaimed and lauded writers now fight to have their blurbs splashed across our covers. If there is a commercial fiction accolade, you can assume we've received it. It's beyond anything we could have dreamt up in those heady early days of writing together.

It's just a shame we're both so miserable.

But at least we're out of Manhattan, out of the state, out of the country. I felt like I couldn't breathe the last few weeks. Europe feels like another planet somehow. Back there, in those twenty-three square miles of high-rises, brownstones and bodegas, there is the eternal press forward. The glitzy parties and interviews, the photoshoots. The times I just want a quiet drink and I'm set upon by a baying fan (okay, that's a lie. I quite like that bit). The book events where I raise my Sharpie high before performing the elegant swirl: Morgan Savage.

No. Not my name. Ours. The name synonymous with our stream of very lucrative novels. The distinctive twisty thrillers that also feature quite a bit of gore. Emma likes writing about blood. She has written it every which way imaginable. Spewing from eyeballs, sticking to the soles of shoes like gum, dribbling delicately down porcelain cheeks, and popping like bubbles. I've never known anyone with the ability to capture the horror of pain and death so vividly. She expertly leads the reader on a journey into the unknown and then smacks them in the face with a heart-stopping twist. And by God, the readers love it. *When's the next one?* is the question shot urgently across trestle tables in bookshops around the world. I used to confidently be able to say. Now, not so much.

And it's all because of me.

Writer's block is a peculiar thing, and I never thought it was a problem we'd encounter. When I say we, I mean, well, Emma. Because it's my wife finding it impossible to compose the next book – and all the other titles were, even though it pains me to say, mainly down to her genius. A fact we rarely discuss. We are, after all, 'a team', and there is no 'I' in team. Though there probably should be in this case.

Public facing, Morgan Savage is the work of Emma AND Felix Larson. Behind closed doors, there is another truth entirely. But we don't dwell on that. It only makes us argue. And there is no answer to the question of what to do about it. I feel emasculated and imposter syndrome twists and turns with every compliment bestowed upon my name. Felix Larson, the great writer, and his wife, Emma, they all assume. Her name always secondary because I am the more front-facing member of the 'team' – and the inverted commas are very much necessary, let me assure you. 'The camera loves you,' Max is always quick to say. And I suppose my looks have always got me out of trouble. And into it.

Emma is stunning, don't get me wrong. But she has a coolness people naturally shy away from. A right charmer, my granny used to call me, with her East End accent and thumby cheek pinches. And that I am. I could charm a carrot off a donkey. But it is, of course, a cover for being totally devoid of any natural talent.

I used to think I could write a book; it was a dream of mine. It was why I headed to New York in the first place. Hung out in writers' cafés and became what I called a successful copywriter (a job I'd only done on five separate occasions) while I worked on my great literary novel. The book comprised of three sweated-over chapters that never seemed to grow, which wasn't helped by the addictive dating scene, the twenty-four-hour party people vibe and, quite possibly, the hefty allowance from my old man. Just when I thought I was destined to for ever loiter around Manhattan charming pretty girls with my floppy hair and posh accent stolen from my affluent public school, I met Emma, and we began a project together and, well, the rest is history.

The irony here is that I am the cause of the shuddering halt to Max and the publisher's gravy train. What I did has infected Emma's ability with so much force, I'm afraid it's terminal. If she can't find the headspace to work, we're both lost.

After years of holding steadfast to a book-a-year merry-go-round of bestsellers, we're behind in sending over a new outline and the publishers are jittery to say the least.

We're avoiding the discussion. But the weight of it between us is awkward and heavy. We cannot bring ourselves to say her name out loud, but with every silent moment it is whispered. Every look of disdain, every time a conversation becomes close, or jovial, Emma pulls away. And she is right to. I am a bad man, and I have hurt her terribly. I'm here to make it up to her. Make things right. Draw a line under it and revive our marriage and the career that hangs limply between us. Because if we can't scrape the first draft of a new Morgan Savage together this summer, it isn't just our career that will be buried, it will be our marriage too.

But here, I feel it's easier to breathe already. It is as though a pause button has been pressed on the never-ending race you feel as though you're competing in back home, in the city. Here, the remotest enclave of France seems to have just gone, 'This is good enough,' and chucked its chips in, no longer on the hunt for something better. And by God, it really is perfect.

The car begins to climb an incline. Trees appear around turns spun with foliage. Burnt orange rocks strike poses as we move past, slower now we're off the main road. We turn a corner, and a haphazard row of houses lines the way, pale blue peeling shutters closed, shrouded in sombre slumber, the inhabitants hiding from the breathless heat.

A few minutes later we come to the top of the hill, and large ornate metal gates end the road. The trees are gone, and I feel the sort of weightlessness that comes with being up high. I get out and open the heavy gates, which groan as I drag them against the gravel ground. Then I look up, transfixed.

Max found this place out of desperation and practically ran us out of town, told us to get out of the city for the whole summer, and write that elusive first draft. The last time I saw him I drunkenly vomited on his handmade Italian shoes, so I half expected a one-way ticket to rehab, but no, there is a book to be written first.

The house is quintessentially French – large but not quite a chateau. A bastide, Emma had called it when showing me photos. The elegant, large, rectangular building is made of finely cut square stone bricks. Vines grow recklessly up the frontage and the tiled roof is almost flat. The shuttered windows are thin and long. The inner sanctum is a courtyard, with two ground-level medieval-looking arches, and a wishing well to one side. Although it's obviously old, it's well cared for, and any restoration works seem to have been to conserve rather than modernise.

'Are you going to leave me here?' Emma calls, hanging out the car window. And I walk back and get in, driving the vehicle inside.

'Well, this is pretty nice,' I say, as I turn off the ignition, gesturing to the house, waiting for Emma to admire it.

She looks away from her phone for just a second. 'I suppose.' *Don't you dare*, I think, just as she lets out one of those loaded sighs. She can be so blasé it irks me rotten.

Irritation hits me and I fling my door open, but instead of getting out, I whisper furiously, 'Emma, are you going to be like this the whole time we're here?'

She turns slowly towards me, her jaw fused. For a second, I think she's going to erupt. But she softens and lowers her phone into her lap. She blinks a few times. Her mouth opens and I expect her to lead with a rebut, so am surprised by, 'You're right. This is beautiful, just how I imagined it.' She smiles at me, her pearly teeth a white flag.

I swallow thickly, relieved. 'I know I've been awful, and I take responsibility for that.' Her fingers curl into her palm

15

and squeeze. I continue, not wanting to dwell on that thought. 'I just want to start this on the right footing, you know? Set off on a positive note.' The subtext is obvious. I'm asking her to forget about last night and move on. None of the usual jibes, the underlying resentment threatening to unravel at any moment. Rewind the tape while we're here and get back to how it used to be between us.

She wipes her hand across her face, and nods. 'No point in being here otherwise.'

'Six weeks,' I remind her.

She peers up. 'Just us. Do you think we'll be okay?' There is a comforting tease to her voice. I move a strand of hair from her face. She sits back, leaving my empty hand suspended in the air.

'Yes.' My heart feels sore. 'I really do.' My reply is devoid of any humour, just pure hope.

'Let's go.' She pats my hand and twists to open her car door, and I join her. We walk to the front of the car and stare up at the house we'll be sharing for the summer.

'But will it really be any different here?' she asks fearfully. I wonder if she is talking about our relationship or writing the book. I suppose the two are interchangeable.

'All we can do is try,' I reply, trying to hide my own apprehension. I feel like this is a crossroads moment. Maybe we can get through this united, and with eighty thousand words. But mostly, with her forgiveness.

That is how this story needs to end. I just wish I knew how to get us there.

# CHAPTER TWO

Emma finds the key behind a glazed olive-green plant pot, as instructed. We enter the house, and the cool air trapped between the thick stone walls is a relief from the unsettling heat. I pace around the new space, taking it in. Having come from Europe and travelled around it from a young age, on villa holidays and school ski trips, the aesthetic isn't lost on me. The interior bridges the gap between elegance and simplicity, classic with that modern twist that most aspire to, and the French really know how to get right. The colours are muted with the odd flash of blue in the soft furnishings and details. The living area is full of antiques, beautifully arranged, as if passed down through generations, with each leaving a small collection, giving an eclectic feel. A wall must have been taken down at some point in recent history, as this main room is large, with a kitchen to one side that looks new. There are honed marble counters with bespoke off-white wooden cabinets hunched around a huge worn Lacanche cooker that looks as if it couldn't be moved, even if they tried.

Emma is beguiled. France – well, the whole of Europe – is

still a quaint oddity to her. I don't think she even had a passport until she turned twenty. She loves travelling, and we
come often. Vienna, Lisbon, Berlin – she moves around the
whole continent as if it is a living museum. I watch as she
picks up trinkets, and feels the fabric of the curtains, and
smells dried lavender in tiny ceramic vases. Wanting each of
her five senses to take in everything, as she does, so she can
store it for use later.

I walk over to the kitchen counter where a loaf of bread
has been left folded inside a red gingham cloth, an envelope
propped against it. I take out the note to have a read while
Emma gets her bearings.

Bonjour Morgan,
Welcome to Villa de la Falaise. We hope you enjoy
your stay. The fridge and larder are stocked, and I can
order you groceries to be delivered, but the *supermarché*
is only a twenty-minute drive, if you'd prefer. The
blue folder has all the owners' particulars. This is
my number: +33 6 39 98 88 33. I understand you are
here to work but if there is anything you need, do not
hesitate to contact me.
Juliette

'What is it?' Emma asks, walking up behind me. She plucks
the note from my hand and studies it closely.

'Funny how many people don't realise we're not Morgan.' I
chuckle. Readers are often unaware a married couple is behind

18

our bestselling books. The more successful we have become, the more this piece of trivia is enjoyed.

'I doubt she even knows who Morgan Savage is, Felix. You'd be surprised how few people have heard of Morgan, out here, in the real world. You're not as much of a household name as you fancy yourself.' She enjoyed doling that out. Have it.

'She's probably expecting some bespectacled, middle-aged professor type,' I say, looking at myself in an oval gilded mirror.

'You are middle-aged,' she shoots back.

I move towards her, using the moment to get close. I try to hug her. 'Yes, yes, we all know you're the younger, far more beautiful half of Morgan Savage.'

She flaps me away. 'Well, I'm definitely more mature,' she says.

Emma is five years younger than me, and we met when she was twenty-five and I was thirty. She's always been wise beyond her years; it has never felt as though there is a gap at all. If anything, she was far more responsible and prudent from the off. She used to joke that I was a classic Peter Pan. She doesn't laugh about that any more, she seethes.

Emma slides a hand over her perfectly managed hair, which is up and pinned. She undoes the knot of the small silk scarf she had tied around her neck and shakes it out. I watch her as she does this. Her movements still captivate me. How she works, how she functions. Getting to be the one to turn that face from controlled scrutiny to messy bliss has been a favoured pastime of mine. I'm the one that gets to see her at her most vulnerable, and I get a kick out of that. I've seen her cry, scream, bang on my chest in anger and frustration. I've seen her eyes glaze over with pleasure too. And not many people can say that.

She certainly is more mature, and more talented, I want to add. But I don't. We don't say things like that out loud. We only think them. Stew in them. The silence of those hissing thoughts causes the erosion of so many things.

But I know the truth behind the pearls and carefully selected designer clothes that make her seem a decade older. Emma is not as high society as she likes to project. Far from the gilded age, Emma grew up in one of those narrow wooden slatted houses in an overpopulated residential area of New Jersey. She won a full-bursary scholarship to Sarah Lawrence. People take her coolness as having come from money – that she doesn't need to try to make people like her, because she just doesn't need to care whether they do or not. They would be wrong. She is so tightly wound, because she has spent every second since she got out of there trying to be something she is not. Yes, my wife and I have that in common.

I saw through it quickly; I understood that need to belong. My father made his millions from the very bottom up. 'New money' they'd call me at school while I was surrounded by the sons of politicians and double-barrelled surnames that creak under the weight of a thousand years of British heritage. I'm what you would call a first-generation trust fund kid. This was sniffed at in all the circles I was surrounded by. Look, I'm not playing the victim, okay. Everyone is awful at that age, especially in the ultra-competitive culture we were deposited within. You had to rise to the surface and survive, just like in the real world, old boy. If you had a smidge of a difference, it was jumped upon, used to press your buttons, to garner a reaction. Never react. It's only a joke. It's banter – ha! Besides, I got rather good at giving it out.

Better than most, actually.

To them, I have done the seemingly impossible: carved a successful career from talent. But then, they don't know the truth, do they? Emma is the one who smashed past the hand she was dealt and achieved the impossible. She came from where she did and got into a prestigious university on scholarship, no less. Then moved to New York off her own back with no safety net. She is the naturally talented one; she is spectacular. Not me.

The thought makes me search around for some sort of alcoholic drink. There must be an alcohol trolley somewhere around here.

The sight of a painting disrupts this thought. A young girl, her face obscured by an open book. The rich redness of her dress and the cobalt blue of the cover create a striking visual. Funny that the artist omitted the face for a book, I think. But then once you open a book, what is your face anyway? You have left this place and emerged in another's body. Stories are the only way to truly escape. That's why I wanted to write. Whenever things got too much, and the bravado I was masking my true nature behind needed to catch its breath, I would escape into the American literary greats. And maybe I dreamt I could do that for someone else, too.

That is what readers say they love about Morgan Savage. Whatever they have going on in their lives, they pick one up and are transported away. No matter how dark or twisted it gets, it seems to be favourable to being in their own heads for a few hours. Unputdownable, they call them.

Emma walks over to the French doors and opens them, using the key projecting out of the lock. We step out onto the veranda that seems to be covered by another arch, the same design as the ones in the courtyard out front. The ceiling is a mesh of vines dripping from above. There is a table with metal chairs and soft cushions tied to their seat, and a cut-out metal Moroccan lantern hangs from above. *Yes, this is nice*, I think, as my fingers touch the hand-painted tiles fixed to the surface of the table.

I follow Emma to the top of the veranda and stand, staring at the extensive grounds laid out before us, glimmering in the sun. I hold the back of my neck as I stand there, stunned. Below is a wide lush-green lawn, with a chipped-stone swimming pool, a collection of loungers pointing towards it with yellow striped parasols turned down.

The view either side of the lawn is acutely different. On the left is a little stone pillared wall, over which is just blue sky and nothing else. On the other side is a uniform collection of trees, an orchard possibly.

'It's built on the side of a cliff,' Emma realises. Over the lip of the wall is a hazy shimmering veil of heat. She walks over, and I follow. We lean on the wall and look over the top – the sparkling blue sky hangs above an outstretched vista.

'Bloody hell,' I say. 'Well, if ever there was a place to inspire, it's here,' I tell her.

She remains quiet but then whispers, 'What if we've exhausted it all, and we're done for?'

'We'll get it done,' I whisper, stroking her back, and her body jolts with my touch. I continue anyway, hoping to feel her shoulders fall beneath my palm. 'One day at a time.' I give her the advice she has given me. *If you write every day, and move the plot along, you'll wake up one morning and have written a book!* She told me that, with excitement shining in her eyes, the first time we tried. It worked then.

'I'll get the bags out the car,' I say, as we turn back into the house.

As we enter the main room, I hear the sound of a bicycle bell from outside, and then a knock on the door. '*Salut!*' is cheerfully called before the door opens. A woman stands there smiling, a large bunch of flowers in her arms, her cheeks red from exertion.

'*Pardon!* I thought you weren't arriving until later,' she says, directing her words at me. They tumble out of perfect, plump lips. 'But then I saw your car.' She steps forward. 'I was meant to bring these earlier, when setting up the 'ouse.'

I feel the starkness of Emma's surprise, and she radiates coolness.

The woman's carefree smile begins to fade. 'I should leave you to get comfortable . . . I shouldn't 'ave disturbed you after such a long journey.' I look at Emma's face. Jesus Christ. What a horror show. The last thing we need right now, to be perfectly honest, is a beautiful French woman standing in the house with a bunch of flowers.

But Emma recovers quickly. 'It's okay, come in. Is it Juliette?' she asks.

Juliette nods. '*Oui*, I work for the couple who own the 'ouse.' She comes inside to greet us.

I hold out my hand and Juliette shakes it with a bemused smile. She is probably used to men like me leaning in for a double kiss. But I wouldn't dare. Not in front of my wife.

She could be Emma's age, or maybe ten years younger – it's difficult to age her. Her clothes are secondary to her striking appearance. She has long wavy dark hair with a knot at the top tied in a red velvet scrunchie. A loose T-shirt that hangs off a shoulder. A dangling silver necklace, with a shorter one tight against the flesh of her neck. Denim shorts, with torn edges. Trainers that have seen better days.

The difference between them is startling. Emma with her perfectly quaffed hair, pearl drop earrings. Her smart, minimalist clothes that exude quality and expense. Next to this woman, not a jot of make-up on, naturally pretty, tanned. She is the flip side of a coin.

Juliette looks between us, a tad confused. I realise she was expecting one guest, a man. '*Bonjour*, Monsieur Savage. I 'ear you are a writer.' She turns to Emma, 'And 'ello, Madame Savage.' Emma tries to hide the look of pure contempt, and I can't really blame her, not after what we've been through.

I shoot Emma a look – *Be nice* – and she laughs, stepping forward. 'No, you see, I'm Mrs Larson,' she explains with a hand on her chest before pointing in my direction. 'And this is my husband, Mr Larson.'

The woman's eyes widen. She looks between us, still on the back foot. I try again, 'This is Emma, my wife, and I'm Felix. Your boss may not have relayed it, or it got confused somewhere along the way, but our pen name is Morgan Savage. We write together, as a team.' She looks mystified, and I try again, 'Morgan Savage isn't a real person. We – my wife and I – write under that name.'

'Ah! You write together.'

*Together.* The word hangs in the air between Emma and me. This thing that has trailed us around all these years and hasn't got easier to rectify.

'Yes,' Emma cuts in. 'We write them together.' I look over at her, surprised at the confident stride of her words. I smile at her warmly.

'I 'ave no idea 'ow a person writes a book, let alone two as one. And married! You must 'ave a very strong relationship. Most married couples see each other a few hours a day and that's enough!' She laughs. 'May I?' She points to a large vase on one side of the living area.

'Sure,' Emma tells her. And Juliette walks across the room and picks up the item, taking it to the kitchen to fill with water before carefully undoing the paper and sorting the stems.

'Are they successful? The books?'

Emma and I look between us, unsure how to answer this without sounding smug. '*Excusez-moi!* What a rude question. I

'ave – 'ow do you say? – no filter! It gets me into trouble, a lot.'
She has such a nice way about her, it is hard to be annoyed.

'We get by,' Emma says, as bemused as I am.

'I'm afraid I don't really read,' Juliette says with a shrug. 'I like poetry,' she offers, looking up with a coy smile. 'I write it too.'

'Really? That's wonderful,' I tell her, impressed.

Maybe I'm a little too enthusiastic because Emma pipes in, 'Felix fancies himself as someone who gets poetry,' she says. 'But I bet you could school him,' she adds with a chuckle.

I give her a look of exasperation. I really don't want to get into a debate about my shortcomings, so I step away, and move back towards the painting on the wall of the girl reading.

'This is very charming,' I muse.

Juliette chuckles as she arranges the flowers. 'Charming,' she repeats. 'I don't think you would say that if you knew.'

I turn. 'Knew what?'

'*Oh là là!* You really don't know?' she asks. 'About the 'ouse? I thought that's why you'd come,' she says. I am impressed with her English; her accent is heavy, but her grammar and diction are practically perfect. I can tell she is smart, this one. 'It is of the sister of the owner of the 'ouse. When they were young, and their parents were still alive, she fell off the cliff.'

'The cliff,' I repeat.

Juliette smiles. '*Oui* – the cliff. Villa de la Falaise – Villa of the Cliff, I think it is in English?' She shakes her head. 'The girl, she sleepwalked and one night she made her way all the way out, to the cliff, and fell. Well, that is what they say 'appened. The father killed 'imself the following year, and the village 'as always been a-buzz with gossip about 'is – what is the word? – temperament.' An image shoots into my mind of a girl in a white nightdress falling. The dull sound of a body hitting rocks. And the eerie silence before the house awoke to discover the scene and screams echoed into the valley.

'That's awful,' I say.

'People say she still comes out at night, claws 'erself back up the cliff and tries to get into the 'ouse, back into 'er own bed.' She relishes saying this, a cheeky glint in her eye.

'What? They do not,' Emma says, with a snort.

I look back at the painting. *Max, you've really tried to create the perfect backdrop for our writing retreat*, I think, scratching my chin. 'Have you ever seen her?' I ask Juliette.

She shakes her head and laughs. '*Non*, it is just a silly – how do you say? – a rumour.' She dismisses the notion with a flick of her hand.

'Urban legend,' Emma whispers, as she comes up to the painting. 'Jesus. That's just awful. If my daughter sleepwalked and there was a cliff outside, I'd tie her to the goddamn bed.'

'People come to stay in the 'ouse because they like the idea of it being 'aunted,' Juliette says. 'That is why I think you 'ad come.'

'Not intentionally,' I tell her. 'Our agent must have thought it would be funny.' Bloody Max, always with the wisecracks.

Emma's long neck extends as she looks up at the painting.

'What a good story, though,' she says, her finger out, following the painted crease in the fabric of her dress.

'*Voilà!* Okay, I'll leave you. I live in the cottage on the other side of the orchard, on the far side of the *hameau* – the 'amlet. You will 'ave passed it on your way up.' I think back to the small collection of houses by the road. 'Do let me know if you need anything – I'm 'ere to 'elp all summer but I won't disturb you. I can bring up baked trays of food you can cook yourselves. I can 'elp with restaurant bookings, or anything you need really.'

'Thank you, Juliette. That sounds perfect. We'll let you know once we're all settled in,' Emma tells her gratefully. She watches her leave, her eyes pinned on the back of her slim legs. 'Well, what a way to make an entrance,' she says after the door has closed.

'She seemed nice,' I try.

'Very sweet.' The words are slightly clipped, as she agrees. 'I did like the story, didn't you?' She peers over at me. 'Maybe I will be able to write here,' she breathes, collapsing back on the plump sofa, a hand resting on her forehead. A shard of early evening light rests on her face, and as I stare at my beautiful wife, I wonder how I could have done it.

# CHAPTER THREE

Once our bags are unpacked, and we've showered and changed out of our creased travel clothes, we head out to the veranda to eat. The kitchen was well stocked, and we've made a little mezze dinner. Sliced cheese, salad, cold meats. Wine, there was plenty of that too. I uncork a bottle of the local stuff and smell it before pouring us each a glass. Emma takes hers and swirls the liquid around, then takes a sip. My mouthful empties half the glass. I've been waiting all day to do that. But stuck travelling with Emma, and driving all that way, there wasn't much opportunity. And I'm good at sniffing out an opportunity to drink.

It's very late by the time we sit down, and evenings here are just as mesmerising as the daytime, it seems. Festoon lights are hung generously, dotted about the place like floating orbs. The heady whine of crickets is the only sound.

'Anyway, we made it,' I say with a sigh, finishing my glass, pouring another.

'You keep saying that,' she says, knocking away my attempt at conversation. But then, 'I never get over your dedication to

29

miss a flight.' She leans in, cutting off a corner of hard cheese. 'It's as if you actively want us to have a stressful journey,' she says, placing the triangle of cheese in her mouth.

*Here we go.* She's been waiting until I've relaxed to bring this up. 'I think I had alcohol poisoning,' I tell her. 'That wine at the party was incredibly cheap.'

She raises an eyebrow and her lips fall into a sallow smile of bemusement. 'Funny how it's always you that's given the spoilt bottle.'

Maybe if you hadn't turned me into a shell of my former self, I think. But I refuse to rise to it. Nothing good will come of that, and I certainly don't want a big blow-out fight on our first night – they get out of hand quickly. The dark shadows of the previous evening begin to swirl, a distant scream ringing in my ears. I do my best to change the subject.

'So tomorrow we begin,' I say. The book – she'll want to talk about that. 'Any ideas? Have we definitely binned the island murder mystery idea?'

Emma stares out at the twinkling lights. 'I think so. No point flogging a dead horse.' She's used one of my British-isms there, and it bugs me. I'm guilty of picking up words from the States, having lived there over a decade. My family back home always laugh when I say 'store' instead of 'shop', 'sidewalk' instead of 'pavement' and accentuate the word 'vitamin' wrong. I'm a fully embedded Americanophile, I even read the weather in Fahrenheit and use a twelve-hour clock on my phone. But for some reason when she picks up on my sayings and proverbs, I feel as though she's making fun of me.

'I had an idea on the journey, Felix. Eight books in and we need something fresh to keep us afloat. The usual tricks just aren't cutting it any more, you've got to admit.' She looks at me expectantly.

'Okay . . .' God, what is she going to say? I like the routine! I know what I have to do with the routine!

'Don't panic.' She touches my arm. 'We'll still do our usual: my morning pages, that you will follow. But I thought instead of spending the first week or so thrashing out ideas and plotting, we'll just . . . wing it,' she says with an excited smile.

'Wing it?' I repeat, my heart sinking. 'But what about the spreadsheet?'

She shakes her head. 'We've tried that, and it's come up short,' she says forcefully. I wipe my face. I need that spreadsheet of carefully mapped-out chapters, so I know what to write. Without it, I'm completely lost. These last six months, we've sat around in the basement of our Manhattan apartment, our hallowed 'writing room', a laptop between us, fighting over rows and columns – invariably ending in an argument, with me screaming, 'I can't work like this!' Emma shouting, me slamming doors. I'd end up storming out, on the hunt for a dive bar to get wrecked in. Leaving Emma before I did something I'd regret.

'I reckon this time we oughta just dive in blind,' Emma says, looking at me tentatively.

I laugh. 'You're joking.' I check her over. 'You're not joking.' A tugging feeling in my stomach: fear, vulnerability. 'But if we don't know what's coming, how will we write it?' I swallow.

'Authors do it all the time, Felix. I know historically we've been plotters, but discovery writers seem to knock out a book. How many times have we had to listen to them gush on about the magic of letting an idea grow organically? And we need a bit of magic right now. What do we have to lose? Come on, it'll be fun.'

It doesn't sound very fun to me. I usually rely heavily on that embellished spreadsheet we work on together. Well, I type as Emma paces the room dictating ideas. With me desperately thinking of something clever to add that she'll agree to. I'll tap away, adding my thoughts into the mix of ideas, knowing deep down they'll be mysteriously cut when we come to write the first draft.

She leans forward. 'Look, don't stress. I'll take care of the first chapter. Felix, this approach might just be perfect for you. Maybe you've been a pantser all along, and we never even knew it.' She chuckles.

'What do you mean by that?' The tart burn in my stomach digs deeper.

'I didn't mean anything, Felix.' She sighs. 'You're so defensive.'

'I'm not!' I say tersely, trying very hard not to sound defensive. *Come on, Felix, show Emma you're not the man she calls you out to be.* I sit back in my seat. 'Okay, sure. Why not.'

'We can give it a shot. If it doesn't pan out, we'll pivot. But we have to do something different.'

'I said yes, Emma, let's do it,' I say, the tight frustration in my chest building.

She breaks into a relieved smile. I stare into the balmy darkness. 'Maybe it was New York . . . maybe here . . .'

'It wasn't.' She shakes her head quickly. 'Moving geographically isn't going to miraculously help us write a novel, no matter what Max says. He doesn't have a clue what it takes to write a book, Felix. It's down to us to fix this. It's down to . . .' Her sentence peters out. I know what she means. She means her. It's down to her. I guess I need to do whatever makes her comfortable. That is my part in this. Be the cheerleader, and the encourager, while she does all the hard work.

'Okay. Let's try this new magical organic way to write.' I lean in and stroke her hand. I notice her fingers shake slightly with my touch. Is she repelled by me? Doesn't she even want my skin to touch hers?

Emma grins, moving it away, using the excuse of another sip of wine. 'Great. This could give us the new energy we need to get this train back on the rails.' I look at how happy this decision has made her. God, that sight on that pretty face is rare these days. There was a time I would jump through hoops to make her happy. When did that change?

'Whatever helps get you there,' I tell her. She smiles at me. That sort of lazy, untarnished smile of a hundred years ago. Back into the depths of our past. When we'd idle in bed for entire mornings with toast crumbs and adventurous sex. Back when we held hands wandering in Central Park. She'd lie back on my chest as we lolled on a picnic blanket pointing out the different shapes we'd see in the clouds. Back when

I'd say something stupid, and she'd laugh lightly, instead of looking repulsed.

Emma's face jolts in the direction of the trees below. A sound, screeching, or crying out. As though someone is in pain. 'Do you hear that?' she whispers. It goes away, then reappears – more guttural, an urgent whine.

I slap the linen napkin on the table as I stand. Another eerie pained shriek which rises into the tops of trees, causing a flock of birds to flee into the sky. I take a step towards it.

'Felix,' Emma warns, the word crackling in the back of her throat. She gets up too and feels around for my hand. She must be scared. She attempts to pull me towards the door. I'm delighted to have been given this role in the unfolding drama and stand taller, detaching myself from her grasp and walking towards, not away from the sound. 'Felix,' she says again. 'Let's just go back in.'

'It's okay, I'll just check it out,' I tell her forcefully.

Another sound lingers in the air as I step off the paving and onto the grass.

'Jesus, Felix, be careful,' Emma says, swallowing.

I wave her back, my heart pounding. The story of the girl crawling back up the dirt-packed path towards the house rings in my ears. My mind embellishes the tale: her long dark hair wiry about her face, her mud-filled broken nails bleeding onto her white cotton dress. Her eyes chasms of nightmarish pain. My heart thumps as I walk to the bush.

A rustling sound now, mingling with the horrible screeching. *Jesus Christ.* I look back at Emma. Her hand is over her mouth.

It's nice to see her intimidated for once. I have a chance here, to save her, to take the lead. Be the one to get us out of a mess, for once.

I look around for something, anything, to take with me. There's a spade stuck in the flower bedding, and I pull it out of the dry mud. I look ahead to the trees. There is something in there, something hurt. I'm glad I had that glass of wine.

'Stay back, Emma,' I tell her as she attempts to step off the veranda.

The whine of pain permeates the air. *Fucking hell*, I think, as I move towards the trees shrouded in darkness. Sweat licks my neck as I get closer, and I'm suddenly awash with regret at my initial bravado. We should have gone inside and locked the door.

A bustle of movement and then bang, out stumbles a bright red fox. It looks up at me, terrified, with red veiny eyes. Its mouth dangles open and crooked to one side, hanging uncomfortably as it makes the gargled rasping sound. I remember the ghastly sound of foxes mating in London, a noise more akin to assault. No wonder what we heard was unearthly. It does it again, and I see its agony as the noise screeches out from its throat, broadening into a wail as the pain hits its jaw. There is blood on its chest and a front leg curled up and dangling.

'Felix!' Emma calls from behind. 'What is it?' My frame is obscuring the view.

'It's okay, just a fox. It's hurt,' I call back.

It wobbles towards me, and then to one side. Looks like its jaw is broken, and most probably its leg too. My shoulders relax, the spade falls to my side. 'Hey,' I whisper, but fear grips it and it scampers back. 'It's all right, boy,' I tell it. It's shaking, and I realise it is terrified of me. 'Let's get you some help.' Then it collapses onto the ground and curls into a ball.

I walk slowly back up to the house, to Emma.

'It's hurt, that's all.' I scratch the back of my head. 'What do we do?'

'I'll shoot a message to the owners; they might have a contact for a wildlife agency or something.' She looks down the lawn towards it. 'I thought . . .' she begins. I know exactly what she thought. I thought the same thing.

But I laugh. 'Oh my God, Emma. You thought some dead girl was going to crawl out of there?' I chuckle, and she looks foolish. I pull her into me for a hug. 'Your imagination knows no bounds, does it? Don't worry, darling.' And she lets me hold her.

'Poor thing,' she breathes. 'This place,' she starts. 'There's something about it.'

I look above her head at the stars which seem to float in a blaze of space dust. It is otherworldly here. But I don't want to stir the pot of unease. 'It's all in your head. You always look for things to worry about,' I tell her softly. But she's right. This place is giving me the creeps.

# CHAPTER FOUR

I wake up. The previous day hits me in a flash: the journey, arriving at the bastide. The old guy who turned up in the middle of the night in an open-back pickup to take the poor thing away. He said it was most likely hit by a car and ran into the trees, before stumbling up to the lights of the house. We didn't ask what would happen to it, but I noticed a shotgun in the back. The fox had looked up at me with glassy-eyed fear as I'd smashed the tailgate up and walked away, feeling conflicted.

The horrific way the animal's jaw hung to one side in an ugly grimace rings in my mind, and the pain attached to it hits my stomach and I want to gag. Why do we write about such horrible things? On paper it feels so distant, almost cartoonish. But there in front of me, it pierced into my soul, and I feel nauseous. Was it fear, or was it because I liked it? So raw, so real. My pounding heart and the wave of adrenalin it unleashed. I'm so numb to feelings these days, to have something tangible was a relief. I found it exhilarating.

Jesus, what the hell am I saying?

I'm hungover. My mind is playing tricks on me. Why did I

drink that second bottle of wine. Why do I always take it too far? Why can't I just stop after a couple?

The first went down a treat but didn't quite satisfy me. It never does. I've always liked a drink. At school and university I was the one you could rely on to know where revelries were taking place. I could handle it then, wake up bright-eyed and bushy-tailed, regaling my pals with the previous night's antics. Good stories have currency, I learnt that early on. And the more anecdotes I had up my sleeve to serve out, the better. Hangovers were minor. I still got my work done. Yes, I only scraped through, but once you have a degree from Cambridge, no one asks for the finer details.

I can't pinpoint the exact moment it got out of control – it seems to have risen in perfect symmetry with every number one bestseller.

I had a great upbringing. My parents love me, I love them. They didn't have anything growing up, so they threw the lot at me. I had a great time, I was popular. I could talk to friends' parents, and they loved having me hang around. But I worked hard for every laugh and slap on the back.

I was embarrassed showing friends around our rather opulent new-build mansion with Mum's tacky oriental fountain in the hallway and her penchant for leopard-print soft furnishings. The way she'd arrive in heels, full-on make-up and a hair-raising blow dry to a countryside invite where everyone was in Barbours and wellies and a half-forgotten string of pearls. My parents would say the wrong things politically, and their social cues were all off. It was maddening.

I'd laugh them off. Get in there first, joking that money didn't buy taste and whatnot. And then I'd feel bad that I was making a fool out of them too. I even bought a little signet ring, signifying that I belonged, which I still wear today.

I took that boy over with me when I moved to America a few years after uni. I didn't want to end up working for my dad. I would probably be in the back office rather than the trenches with a spanner, but following in someone else's footsteps isn't who I am. I wanted to carve my own path, impress people by doing something impossible. So, I took that foppish Cambridge University-educated boy with the signet ring, that the girls all loved, to my loft apartment that I didn't tell anyone my dad was paying for. And wore glasses I didn't really need to wear and had shelves and shelves of books which were only really for show. Because all I've ever wanted is to be taken seriously.

And now they do. But it's not real either, is it? It's as phoney as those glasses and that signet ring.

I should see my parents more. But I find it painful. I guess I feel like they see me for what I truly am and look on quizzically when I put on a show. They laugh at me and take the mickey, rather than becoming instantly charmed like the others do.

No. I'm not sure why I drink so much.

In the last few years, it is as if I can't feel relaxed in reality unless I've had a couple of glasses. And then, once I've had a few of those, I can't seem to stop, and I'm thrown into a chase for oblivion.

It's like I can't be *me* unless I'm not.

But that's because who I am isn't real. I'm still a fake. Like those Gucci and Louis Vuitton bags they sell on the pavement on Canal Street. All those words people write about me, the admiration, it isn't for anything I've done, is it? But there is this need in me to play the game, live up to whoever that person is. Give them what they want and who I wish I was.

I rub my face; the whole thing is a mess. Rolling onto my side, I groan. Light flows through the window, landing on the bedsheets, already hot from a few hours of roasting. The other side is empty, where Emma slept and absconded long ago.

Emma has always been an early riser. She says she's more creative first thing. She does morning pages and likes to write with the birds, a coffee steaming by her computer. Emailing her chapter as I wake. Me, on the other hand, I need my sleep. A night owl is my excuse. But really, we both know that my late-night benders are the reason. Emma doesn't nag. Her preferred tool is silence. Or the odd dig. She told me once it is better to let people work things out for themselves. She isn't a meddler. She would find that demeaning. So, I crawl into bed bombed where Emma has been sleeping peacefully since ten.

Her first chapter will be on my phone to read now. I have no idea what to expect. Usually, I'll know the basic premise and story arc. And then we'll email over each of our chapters, and the nuance and the intrigue will grow into a book. But this time is different. Emma's prolific track record is frozen back in a time before what I did.

This new route we've agreed on, to discover as we write, terrifies me. It is as though she is setting me up to fail, forcing me to wallow in my lumbering prose day after day.

First drafts are hell. I've regaled audiences with my preferred metaphor for it, a microphone in hand as they hang on my every word. I pause dramatically as though it has just occurred to me: this part of writing is like running around a dark house opening all the doors and windows. A myriad of possibilities, any number of which might deliver us to the moment where all the threads tie up in the end. And during the edit, with a better understanding of the blueprint, we'll shut some doors, leaving others wide open. Unlocking the ones we had no idea were there the first time around.

I've given this pithy speech many times, on socials, at Q&As – readers look at me as though I'm a wizard, and I like that. Even though it isn't something I said at all – Emma did. She doesn't seem to care I stole it; she's never mentioned the plagiarism. That isn't her style. What is good for me is good for us and good for Morgan. And Morgan wins every time.

I winch myself up, leaning back on one of the opulent white square pillows, and reach for my phone. It is time to find out what world Emma has flung us into for the summer.

Morgansavage@infinitymail.com
10.07.2024
**Subject:** Book 9 – First Draft

***CHAPTER ONE – HER***

*Can you picture it? The peaceful suburban neighbourhood with its south-western-style houses that, outside of a few aesthetic* variations, are much the same. Surrounding the residential area are red rocky mountains and block-blue skies. The weather is kind of seasonal: pleasant in winter, and hot as hell in summer, they say. The cacti stand, watching the population as they mill about their business. Driving to the mall, which is still a hub, even though it opened in 1961. They religiously gather to watch the high school football team on a Friday night: Go Rattlers! And have neighbourly barbecues where the children go feral with excitement, bashing piñatas and diving for sweets.

It is in this quiet corner of Arizona, just outside Phoenix, that we meet Hanna. Let's find her, shall we? If we zoom in, tighter and tighter – right a bit, keep going. Yes. That house, that one just there with the aluminium mailbox at the end of the drive. You can see her in the window of the kitchen, with her yellow Marigolds on, humming as she does the dishes. She looks nice, doesn't she?

Shall we go inside and meet her?

Hanna takes off the gloves and admires her work. All Hanna has ever wanted is this. The perfect house on the perfect street. The all-mod-con kitchen. The baby sleeping peacefully in the crib. She wants to do the ironing, and cook the three-course meals. All prepared and ready for him as he comes home and delights her with the highs and lows of his very busy day, with very important people, with deals that she couldn't possibly understand. With clients and colleagues so hard to manage, only the most Machiavellian survive.

Her job is to make sure he can handle all that, shirts starched, stomach fed, ready for the day. And if she plays her part in all of that, he will play his.

That is the deal. Every marriage has one.

She happily ties the apron around her waist, and puts on her lipstick, just so, and busies herself with shopping for groceries at Trader Joe's and picking up his dry cleaning and then popping into Walgreens for his shaving foam and whatnot.

Some women want it all. They want the power suits and the jobs and kids and the husband. But that doesn't work. Hanna knows. Marriages can't survive that. And it's usually the child that is left to deal with the fallout, their lives littered with the shrapnel of that explosion. She knows the darkness that lingers between the broken cracks of a family. It is down to the mother to keep the family together. Whatever the cost, however she feels about it. To be selfless in her destiny. That is the answer to all of it.

She wakes up early every day, and heads downstairs to do an hour of Pilates in the garage. Then she showers and gets herself dressed before making a start on breakfast. When she hears Ivy's little blabberings coming through the monitor, she wipes her hands dry and rushes up the stairs.

Ivy. Oh, Ivy! The most precious thing she's ever held in her hands.

The eighteen-month-old is standing up in her cot, a great big cheery smile plastered on her face, which is red from the cocoon of sleep. Her eyes light up when she sees Hanna. 'Mumma,' Ivy says, her hands reaching forward.

Never in her life did Hanna think she'd have all this. Never, never, never. Not after . . . Her head rings. 'Don't think of it,' she whispers to herself.

She straightens the front of her apron and takes a deep breath before rushing to the child and picking her up with both arms. 'My darling! My darling girl. Did you sleep well? You look like you did!' she cries. The child gurgles in her arms. Little hands touch her face. Hanna's eyes well with happiness.

She changes her nappy, taking her out of her cotton night-time onesie, printed with quacking ducks, all the time talking and laughing and tickling her rotund tummy. 'The cleverest girl, the most wonderful little chick,' she coos as she changes her.

She sees movement and turns. There he is, her Sebastian. The man. Her one and only true love. She grins at him. And he grins back, as he knots his tie. 'Oh, honey, let me have a go at that,' she says, picking up Ivy and handing her to him, so she can perfect it. She stands back and looks at Sebastian with Ivy in his arms. Picture perfect. Flawless.

'Busy day?' he asks.

'I thought I'd run some errands, and then I thought I would make a start on the basement; it really needs a spring clean. And we're having meatloaf for dinner.'

'You really are wonderful,' he says, leaning forward to kiss her. 'The best wife a man could ever hope for,' he adds. Yes, she thinks. I am. Pride filling her up. 'But do have a rest. Maybe call Clementine and arrange a playdate with her little one. I don't want you getting lonesome here all day.'

Hanna's smile freezes in place. There is always some way he finds to fault her.

He hands Ivy back to her. 'Listen, I might be late tonight. Big deal going down and I think I'll need to take the team out to celebrate if we clinch it.' Hanna's eyes narrow. 'I'll try and sneak away back to you both as soon as I can,' he tells her, kissing the end of her nose.

The ringing starts then, the ringing that makes her head jerk. And she tries her best to keep the smile plastered on and her face straight. 'Of course, darlin',' she sings, stroking Ivy's face, 'I completely understand. You need to show the team how much you appreciate them.'

He is going out; there will be drinking involved. And women. She's seen those sluts he works with, on the little jaunt she took into the office, with Ivy in tow. As they cooed over her Hanna could see them sneaking looks at Sebastian, thinking, Oh, what a dream guy.

No. Sebastian wouldn't do something like that. He wouldn't cheat on her, he couldn't. He isn't like the others, is he? But the kernel of doubt has been sewn. And she looks around for something to tidy, or sort, to take her mind off things.

After breakfast she watches him back the Tesla out of the drive. He gives her a final wave as he reverses into the street and rides away. She feels dizzy and grabs on to the side of the porch.

They moved here six months ago. The scenery earthy and arid, very different from urban, rainy Chicago. But she likes it. There is a tidy uniformity to it. And it is so very far away from where she came from.

*Hanna has run from mess her whole life.*
*She hopes she ran far enough this time.*

I look up from my screen. Even in this heat and with a sweaty hangover I am frozen by it. The emotions she has chosen to explore make me nervous, and I am overwhelmed by what it means and what could be languishing between the lines.

If Sebastian turns out to be a cheating cad, well, we all know where she came up with that, don't we? Did I think she could just forget about it? The biggest, darkest thing between us.

Everything is up for grabs when we write. Emma mines dark experiences and puts them into our books. Her disastrous upbringing: book two – *The Hiding Girl*. A friend that was hurt during a hazing ceremony that went wrong at college: book four – *Nobody Can Hear You*. That time she was stalked after our debut novel hit the number one slot in twenty territories: book six – *If Looks Could Kill*. Our relationship seems to have come through unscathed, until now.

Pissed off, I chuck my phone down, putting my head in my hands. Is nothing sacred around here?

I think back to the night before we left to come to France. I promised I wouldn't make a fool of myself. I promised I would get back and have a good sleep before our flight. I can't seem to help myself. A snatch of a memory that causes a physical reaction in my bones. The feeling of someone's nails slashing, trying to get at me. I touch my face where I saw a cut in my reflection the previous day, a scratch I have no idea how I got. The sound of a scream and a guttural groan. Then darkness.

I blink it away. It must have been a dream. I was drunk – maybe Emma was shouting at me, slapping me for letting her down again. I shake my head. No wonder she barely uttered a word to me on the plane. I was a mess.

I get out of bed gingerly and walk over to the open window. The white lace privacy curtains attempt a waft with a feeble snatch of breeze. God, it's hot. I look down to the pool. I can see her there, lying on one of the loungers. A big straw hat and a new monochrome swimsuit I've not seen before. As if feeling my presence from above, the view of the hat is replaced with her face, staring up at me. She doesn't smile, but instead lowers it down, to the book she's reading.

Emma must write what she is feeling. Or it just sits in her stomach and bleeds into her veins. But am I able to explore my part in this marriage breaking down this summer? I had thought, hoped, it was something we could leave in New York. We could drift back together in the smouldering heat, wine and cheese softening the fall.

It doesn't look like it's to be that way, after all. It is going to be darker. And if there is anything Emma loves, it is darkness.

# CHAPTER FIVE

I wander down to the pool, and perch on the edge of Emma's lounger. She looks up from her book, her thumbed copy of Dennis Lehane's *Shutter Island*, only for a second. A novel she's always said she'd love to emulate. Emma is always reading. She says if you're writing, you should be reading. Once she'd finished studying English at Sarah Lawrence, she went straight into a training scheme at one of the top five publishing houses in the city. She climbed the ladder, becoming an assistant to one of the commissioning editors quickly, even building a small list of authors of her own, honing and amplifying the works of others way before the name Morgan Savage was even a whisper. But this work never quite fulfilled her.

The book. The elusive book that we'd both grown up dreaming of writing, and that only emerged once we came together. And now we're tied to this joint venture, is it what we wanted? Or are dreams an illusion? Are humans ever really content? Maybe people like us never are. There will always be something further out of reach.

'I can't believe you're reading that again. What do you like about it so much?' I ask.

She rests the book, open, on her chest as she settles back with the sun in her face. 'Mmm . . . I like how the protagonist has no idea what's going on. How deluded he is. And the ride the reader takes with him, it's genius. I find it infuriating,' she says with a sigh. 'What did you think of the chapter?' she asks, nonchalantly, eyes still closed. But she cares. Oh, she cares very much indeed.

'I love it. Very unnerving. Perfect setting.'

'For some blood to be spilt?' she says, with a wry smile.

'Suburbia has always intrigued me. Pretty anti-feminist, don't you think?' I ask. 'You're going to subvert it, in some way. Turn it inwards, I assume.' I look at her with a side-eye, wondering if she is really letting go, really relinquishing control to the process. She must have some sort of plan as to where this is headed – she always does.

'We'll see,' she says.

I look out at the apple orchard beyond the pool. The homogeny of trees, low hung, brittle, with dusty green leaves. A wind chime moves in the breeze, performing a dingle.

Emma looks up for a moment, to find the source of the noise. I know it will irritate her. She doesn't like infiltrating sounds or smells. They bother her. If she'd hung the chimes, that would be okay, or cooked some particularly pungent fish, fine. But those she didn't command to be, they press on her. It's a control thing.

'Hanna,' I mutter. 'Why?'

49

Emma opens her eyes and sits up, surrendering to having to converse with me. 'Well, she's no palindrome, that's for sure. She doesn't loop back where she began. She's unpredictable. Adrift.'

'And what is she running from?' I ask her. 'That line in the chapter, "She hopes she ran far enough this time."' I look across at Emma for clues.

Emma thinks a moment. 'Not sure yet, I haven't worked it out.' The whole thing makes me feel anxious. If Emma doesn't know where this is heading, what hope do we have? She slaps my leg and leans forward, laughing at me. 'Felix, don't look so troubled. It's part of it. We just need to stew in it, let it percolate, let the magic happen. I've given you a great set-up here, you just need to run with it.'

'I see.' I stroke my chin. 'She is, well, damaged by . . .' I can't say it out loud. 'Are you sure you want to write about this?' I ask gently. 'Isn't this meant to be a chance to get away from that? All those feelings. All that regret. I thought, I'd hoped, we could clear a path to find, you know, forgiveness.'

A pregnant pause. 'Maybe this is how we get there,' she replies simply.

I look up at her hopefully, but she manages to crush me just as quickly. Lifting her hand away. 'Seriously, Felix, what else do we have to write about?'

'I see,' I murmur. Understanding. This is part of my punishment. We are now to spend the summer dwelling on that, and the damage I have caused. I get it now. Her very own version of couple's therapy.

She has been silent on the subject this long. And now I will pay. She always waits for the perfect moment. Clever, nasty Emma.

She often does this, in front of friends, waits until she has the whole table's attention at a dinner party at the house in Amagansett, in the Hamptons, or on a friend's boat in West Palm Beach. She'll reach a crescendo of conversation where everyone is looking directly at her. And tell them something about me she promised she wouldn't tell a soul. That I puked in the toilet the previous night, or I said something vulgar to our publisher's CEO, or that she had to go to the police station to bail me out of another DUI. Everyone will laugh, delighted at my antics, thinking that because she is, they are permitted to, too. And, of course, I have to make a show of not caring as they berate me, joke along, while inside I am dying. My ego raging, kicking up dust and screaming into the air. But I take a sip of my drink and laugh with them all, hoping my good-natured smile doesn't look stung.

She undermines me, slowly removing any respect I have for myself, and other people have in me. I see how our friends look at me with bemusement now, or a slight eye roll when I start a discussion. I am a laughing stock. Secret by secret. It is powerplay, a need to be above me. She pushes me into the limelight, and then removes the floorboards, one by one.

My hands twist in my lap. 'You got this, Felix. I know you do.' She looks out at the view wistfully. 'This is how we save Morgan. Use it. Put it into the work.'

'So . . . What is the inciting incident going to be, to break down the world we've entered?' I ask, trying to get as much detail from her as possible before I begin my shift.

She sighs. 'You got this, honey. Everything you need is right there in the chapter. Just pick up on those cues and go with it.' And my frustration builds. I know I won't, and she'll come up with something perfect, as usual.

I get up and stretch.

'Wait,' she orders, getting out her phone and gesturing me to move to the left. I hold in my stomach as she takes a photo. She admires the picture. 'It looks so pretty,' she whispers, before fiddling with the screen. Probably putting on a filter and drafting a post to put on our socials.

'Are you going to write your chapter?' she asks coolly, without looking up.

'I thought I'd go for a walk, get the lay of the land.'

She's annoyed. 'You're putting it off.'

'Emma, we've just got here, give me a break,' I snip back, although she is right. 'Besides, you know walking helps me write.' I think I see a smirk cross her face. But maybe I imagined it.

I want to go and check out this cliff. There is something about the story of the girl. The morbid side of me, that same side that gets a kick out of the darkness of our books, wants to see it. How high it is and to imagine the fall. I climb over the low stone wall. The cliff isn't right below; there is a short walk down the slant of a hill. The grass is no longer tended to on this side, and it is yellowing and sad. The ground is so cracked and dry that dust lifts with every step. A few minutes later, I come to it. The raw edge of red clay stone with hairy tufts of dried grass sticking from it. From here you can really see the view unhindered by anything else. The rest of southern France out there, patched out by agriculture.

I tentatively inch forward to get an idea of the drop. I am a total coward and crane my neck forward, so I don't have to get my body any closer. The descent sways in front of my eyes. *Yep, that is quite a drop.* All that is below is hard burnt orange soil. I shudder at the thought of blood seeping into the gritty dust. Could she really have sleepwalked out here? In the darkness, picking her way down. Bare feet caught on rough stones. The whole thing gives me the heebie-jeebies and I shake off the feeling and turn around.

Emma gives me a hopeful look as I walk back past the pool and up to the house. *Yes, dear, I'm going to write.* My teeth clench together at the thought of it. She has a notebook and a pencil raised; she'll be brainstorming ideas for her next chapter. Something startling and spine-tingling she'll drop in that'll make mine look like a toddler's drawing in comparison. I know what she's like. She says she wants this to grow organically, but her mind will be whirring, reeling until we type *The End*.

Sometimes I wonder why she bothers me with this at all. Why keep up the charade of my chapters if she'll just alter them anyway? But if I stop, if I own up to it, then I really have nothing. She tells me, over and over, that she could never write without me, and she needs my input. Maybe she likes me to do it, so when it comes to the flashing lights of promotion, which she hates, I have a handle on the story. I can go and play my role, out there, having been with her every step of the way.

Thrillers, they were just never my thing. I'm just not good at writing them like she is. I'd always wanted to write something with purpose and weight. Something pondering and life affirming; less about plot and more about thematic exploration and lingering prose that will stay with you for life. Not this throwaway piece of entertainment.

I scruff my shoes against the mat and walk into the little room off the main living area we're using as a study this summer. Emma likes to have a base to work from. At home we have our study in the basement with two desks that face each other (not that we are ever sat behind them at the same time) and a large whiteboard. The walls are solid books, with shelves and shelves dedicated to our many editions and translations.

In this smaller room, yellow Post-it notes are stuck to a corkboard. We're so early on in the process, there isn't much up there yet. But they are all clues to consider as I write. *Revenge. Adultery. Who is Hanna running from?* The words glare at me in Emma's looping handwriting as I take my seat in front of the laptop.

I've written – co-written – all of our hits on this laptop and it looks it. It takes an age to load, making strange gargling noises as if gearing up for use, and I worry that this summer will be the last time I write on it.

I open the browser and wait for the internet to warm up before logging on to my email and finding the first chapter.

54

Next, I do my usual dance of procrastination. Get up for a forgotten glass of water. Retweet a few nice reader reviews. Check the headlines of the papers. Before rereading the first chapter and beginning my own.

I drum my fingers on the wooden desk. *Come on, Felix, you can do this*, I tell myself. I imagine being Sebastian. Meeting this woman and falling in love, having a child with her. But Hanna is so odd, I'm finding it tough. But then, Emma was very different when we met. She was easy to love. When did that change? Did that change for Sebastian and Hanna too?

Could Emma be right, and writing about this dynamic will clear the arduous writer's block – and free us from this locked-in nightmare we seem to have found ourselves in? Purge us from the past and fling us into the future?

All we can do is try.

I begin.

### CHAPTER TWO – HIM

*Sebastian is in a taxi. He sniffs his suit; does it smell of perfume? He can't tell any more; his nostrils have been invaded with it all evening. Hanna is paranoid, and acting so bizarrely since the move, she'll be all over any little thing in an instant. He takes his jacket off in the back of the cab, opens the window to allow a cleansing breeze. Then he decides to go the whole hog and puts his face out the window. He could do with sobering up a little, too. It's late, two a.m. Far later than he'd promised Hanna he'd come back. But he was having such* a good time, and home has become pretty, well, unbearable lately, and it wasn't a tricky draw to stay out, laughing with his young and vibrant colleagues, over returning to that bloody house that stinks of bleach.

At least Hanna will be asleep. Unless she's had one of her insomnia attacks and is waiting for him at the kitchen table. Drinking herbal tea, staring at the clock, looking insane.

How did they get here? Hanna was not like this at all when they met. Sure, her apartment was orderly, and she had a Pinterest board for everything, but nothing like this. If he puts something down even for a second, it is whipped up and put away. He wipes his face. His leg shakes.

All he ever wanted was this – a family. But now he's got it, he's not sure he wants it at all. It doesn't make sense, none of it. How did they go from that utter bliss to this? Hanna has taken to wearing a fucking apron, for God's sake! Like some sort of trad-wife. He never wanted that, and she thinks he should be grateful.

It's like she's been invaded by body snatchers or something. So uptight and obsessed with perfection. He wishes she'd just relax.

She gets this look in her eye, like she's in hyper focus, a feverish zone that he can't pull her out of. And then this new job, jeez. The pressure to perform. The team of people looking up to him for answers. You gotta fake it 'til you make it! his dad used to say, and he feels like he's been doing a hell of a lot of that recently. Pretending to be strong, pretending to have everything together, fake, fake, fake.

He quietly opens the door to the house. Slips off his brogues and neatly lines them up by the door, just so. Hang on, should they go there? Or does she prefer the other side of the wall? This is madness. He uses the guest bathroom to shower and get rid of the pungent floral scent left on him from the spontaneous laughs and interesting conversations that he didn't want to leave.

He comes out the shower and opens the door. 'Argh!' he shouts, adrenalin pumping. Hanna is standing there, right in front of the door, wearing that infernal Victorian-looking nightdress. She hasn't reacted to his scream. And he waves his hand in front of her face. This gives no reaction either. She's sleepwalking. This started a few months ago, and he gently leads her by the arm and folds her into bed.

'Don't take Ivy,' her gravelly, sleepy voice proclaims. 'Please don't take her.'

'You're dreaming, Hanna,' he whispers, and she moans softly and settles into her pillow.

He lies awake, staring at the ceiling. How can something that began so perfectly have turned into this waking nightmare?

I sit back in the chair. I did it. I feel a rumble of pleasure in my chest. I think it's quite good, actually. The sleepwalking element came to me as my fingers searched the keyboard, as if out of nowhere. But it didn't. Everything is in preparation to write. Every anecdote, every film, TV show, book. It's all lodged in there, waiting. Every life experience is a toy in this game.

My smile shifts as I run over what I've written. The emotions Sebastian has for Hanna are too real, too honest. The stress and anxiety that built up and finally drew me to do the unthinkable to our marriage. How I've felt going home to Emma – sniffing my dinner jacket, full of shame. For us, it wasn't house cleaning and babies that were her obsession. It was her obsessiveness around our brand, and our books. And her one true love: Morgan.

I can't send her this. Am I mad? It would be like writing a letter containing my true feelings. My finger hovers over the delete button.

I think back to my old apartment in the city. The one at the top of a brownstone in Brooklyn that cost the earth that I pretended to pay for myself. It even had a little bookshop in the commercial unit below. One of my favourite things to do was hang out there on a Monday afternoon, coffee in hand, 'browsing' the fiction section while eyeing the door for the next young woman to come in, who would invariably select the same hot-ticket female empowering commercial hit. But I knew what they really wanted. I'd play a game with myself. The 'meet-cute' game. I'd try to think up an original introduction every time. It was like a creative workout for my brain. That's what I told myself anyway.

Because deep down what they were desperate for was a funny, romantic anecdote to tell their friends, that read like it was straight out of a David Nicholls book.

I met Emma in that bookshop. I'd scoped her out as I pretended to read the latest Martin Amis. The little bell rang signifying a customer, and I looked up to see her in these big glasses shaking out her hair, having come in from the rain.

I watched as she entered, and as the smell of books hit her, she instantly relaxed. Like a weight had lifted. She ran her fingers over spines and looked at which titles were displayed on the tables. I noticed her tote bag, which had the logo of one of the big brand publishing houses emblazoned on it, and a manuscript poking out the top, littered with Post-it notes. Maybe that was the reason she made me nervous. An actual insider from the industry I was desperate to crack.

I was wracking my brains for a good ice-breaker, something clever and funny that would make me look intellectual and in the know, but before I had the chance she came over.

'Excuse me, have you got the new Stephen King? I can't find it.'

I cracked a smile. Wonderful. I took her over to the 'K's and crossed my arms. 'Ah, yes, King, one of my go-tos. I met him once at a talk in Boston, he was charming.' And she blinked at me. I couldn't tell if she was impressed with the lie.

'You're British.'

'Guilty.' I raised a hand. 'There don't seem to be any.' I point to the spot where the book should preside.

'Yes, I know. Can you check on the computer or something?' she asked, turning back to point at the dusty desktop at the counter.

'I would, but they might call the police, seeing as I don't actually work here.'

59

'Oh.' And I got a laugh out of her. 'I'm sorry,' she said, just as the owner stepped out of the back office.

I gave her my hand. 'I'm Felix, the resident struggling writer around here.'

'You're an author?' She looked at me with new respect.

'Well . . . trying.'

'Ah, I see. Unpublished?'

'So far. I come in here in the hope that inspiration might strike. Or maybe to make a few new contacts,' I told her brazenly, pointing to her tote bag. I'd learnt by then that Americans like it when you are straight, and there was no shame in being forthright about making contacts to achieve what you want.

She smiled. 'Well, I'm embarrassed I thought you worked here. I'm sorry.'

'Yes, I'm mortified.' I scratched the back of my head, in that way that makes my hair flop forward. 'Maybe I could buy you a coffee next door to smooth it all out.'

That date was followed by another, and another. Hours of talking and laughing. I found out about her career and told her about my dreams of becoming published, which to my surprise she didn't gawp at and call me a cliché over. Instead, she sat down at my desk, opening her laptop, telling me her secret: that she didn't just want to edit books, she wanted to author them too. She unlocked a life I could never have achieved on my own. I owe her this.

I owe her writing this novel.

Even if it kills me.

# CHAPTER SIX

I skulk around in the study for a bit, messing with Twitter, commenting on posts, and getting excited replies from readers after I've 'made their year!' by interacting with them. My ego bolstered, I leave the room. When I come out, evening is setting in. To my surprise, Emma is standing in the hallway all dolled up. Red lipstick, her hair down and sultry, and the faint smell of freshly sprayed perfume. 'I'm bored, I want to go out.' She leans into the mirror and fixes a smudge. 'I've looked up the local town online, and there are a few restaurants I'd like to check out.'

'Really? I rather fancied another crusty bread meal and a bottle of Châteauneuf-du-Pape on the veranda.'

She gives me a look. 'Felix, I'm still shaken after that fox last night, and could do with putting a bit of time between ravages.'

I slide in behind her, kissing her neck as she arranges her necklace in the mirror. 'Really? Surely enough time has passed between ravages?' I ask her suggestively.

She watches me in the mirror, as I kiss her tender skin. I

slip her strap off her shoulder; she doesn't stop me, so I reach around the front for her breast. Her hard nipple catches my inner palm and a longing to be close to my wife takes hold. For intimacy, to look into her eyes and whisper I love her, and all the other stuff will just blend into the ether.

But she moves away, pushing my hands off her body.

She takes the car key out of the marbled ceramic bowl perched on the antique French sideboard. 'Come on, if you drive there, I'll let you get *sloshed*' – another British bit of slang she's learnt from me – 'and I'll drive back.' She dangles the key, and I'm sold.

We get into the car. The sun makes its way below the horizon as we descend the hill. The landscape is pretty in this light. Pink and yellow tint the wispy melting clouds. It's still boiling, even this late in the day, and we take the roof down, so the flailing breeze can cool us down.

She hasn't mentioned the chapter I sent her earlier. I know the definition of insanity – but I still hope for that little gleam of respect, a nod that says, *That was pretty damn good, Felix, well done.*

Usually, I'm happy with what I've written, until Emma's edit comes back, and it is so riddled with changes, the red marked-up paragraphs sieving my work down to a crumble. The book that had been two-dimensional has become nuanced, and clever. Devourable in a way it wasn't before.

I try to dismiss the feelings of inferiority that swell. Emma always tells me I care too much. People buy into a package. And Morgan Savage is this fiendishly gory writer, who is, in fact, a married couple? No way! I'm buying that book.

The truth is, Emma's better at holding a plot in her head. She is excellent at twists; one'll come to her at the most random of times and she'll dart at me, eyes blazing, when it's caught her. Like a hound on heat, it follows her around, waiting to pounce. And when it does, a look of euphoria explodes onto her face as she explains it. Falling into a chair with orgasmic relief that she's finally worked it out. Papers tumbling out of her hand as she relaxes back for the first time in months.

And I've just stood there. A lopsided grin of regret on my face. That I didn't think of it – yet again. And I am just a pound of flesh in the room with no reason to be there at all.

There are things I tell myself that help. We wouldn't be the bestselling success story if I wasn't here. The one with the microphone talking up our latest books, with the cheeky grin they all love, and amusing quick-snap responses to the most tedious of questions. It's not my fault people assume I am the creative force behind this. And if she has grown resentful because of that, how can I be to blame?

*Liar.*

'Felix!' Emma cries, and I blink.

*Shit!* I quickly turn the wheel to the right, away from the edge, where the road ends and a tumbling hill begins. 'Sorry, I . . .' I start. My concentration went there for a moment, I was so caught up in my thoughts. My head just doesn't stop. Going over it all, again and again, trying to find a route out of it. My fingers squeeze the wheel, and I readjust in my seat.

\*

After about ten minutes we make it onto the main road. Surrounding us are fields of sunflowers and golden wheat. In the distance, buildings emerge. The town is old, and medieval spires break through the disjointed roofscape. We slow down as we navigate the narrow streets, finally parking under a tree. The buildings are made of the same pinkish stone as the bastide, crumbling at corners like a biscuit. We get out of the vehicle and a light breeze drifts past, bringing with it the smell of jasmine as we wander, following Google Maps to the square.

Arriving, we stand there a moment, taking in the pretty spot. There is a smattering of olive trees, and tall narrow buildings with shutters, colourful overflowing flower boxes dangling. A few old guys are playing boules on a rectangle of gravel-topped terrain. The men in their flat caps talk in clusters as they clutch their steel balls. There is a fountain in the middle with children playing on one corner, parents sipping wine chatting and laughing, on the edge of a collection of tables belonging to one of the restaurants. I look over at Emma. She is watching the children, with a soft look of curiosity, and I squeeze her hand. She shifts her gaze as she feels my touch, and points to one of the three restaurants. 'It's that one.' And we walk towards the cluster of tables parked on the uneven cobble stones.

'*Monsieur!*' I shout over at a guy in a T-shirt with an apron around his waist. '*Deux.*' I hold my fingers up.

'*Ici,*' he says, scooting over and banging the backs of two chairs away from a table, and patting them as he rushes away.

'I guess he wants us to sit here,' Emma says.

'Looks like it,' I reply, taking a seat, and lighting a cigarette.

'Let me have one of those,' Emma says, picking up the crunched packet of Gauloises. I bought a box at the airport – when in Rome. She removes a cigarette, putting it between her fingers, taking a drag without lighting the tip.

The food in the restaurant surprises us both. It is simple, fresh, rich – utterly delicious. And we sit back in our chairs satisfied, enjoying the cheap full-bodied wine and the unpretentious luxury of the square – which is perfect for people-watching.

I often watched older couples in restaurants when I was younger, thinking how depressing it was, not a word passing between them, staring ahead as if consumed by the abyss. And now, that is me. We've told all our stories; we've said all there is to say about everything we think. All there is left are the things we would never say to one another. I get it now. Now, I look at the couples in the throes of that early pink cloud. And I want to run over and tell them, grab them by the shoulders, as they look at me with the same pitying eyes I once owned, *I was like you once!*

Finally, she speaks. 'I thought your chapter was great, by the way,' she tells me, as if she can tell I need it.

'You read it?'

'Of course I read it. It's brilliant. Well done.' I beam at the compliment, although I don't quite believe it.

'Really?' I ask.

'Yes, it's excellent to have something to work with.' Hope fades. I take another sip of wine. She leans forward. 'But

Sebastian, he's a bit too much of a good guy, isn't he? He's meant to be cheating on her, I thought that was pretty clear.'

I snort. 'I thought we were discovering the story, and the characters, as we go.'

'But Hanna needs a reason to blow.' She looks up at me, eyes wide.

I take a drag of my cigarette. I feel protective of Sebastian, even after one chapter. And here Emma is, trying to meddle with him.

'Why does the guy always have to be in the wrong? Hanna seems like she's hiding something. Why do his actions have to be the precursor for that bubbling over?'

Emma sighs. 'There needs to be a reason for the conflict. The inciting incident.'

'Her past can be the reason. Backstory is everything in this genre. Complex characters in extreme circumstances – why are they there in the first place? It's always backstory. You say that all the time!' I'm frustrated. I already know I'm in a battle I can't win. 'If you want to do this discovery writing bullshit, you are going to have to let it happen.' Then I choke a laugh, remembering her phrase. 'Let the magic happen, Emma,' I say, leaning in, taking my chance to mimic her this time.

'You're so cruel,' she whispers.

I swipe a piece of ash off my leg. 'Don't you want to write something else? Aren't you bored of it?'

She sighs. 'Not this again.' The sound comes out in a groan.

'I just think the reason I'm not feeling fulfilled is that I'm not writing what I want,' I tell her. 'What I'm good at.'

66

'Jesus, Felix.' She stubs out the unlit cigarette until it breaks in half in the ashtray.

'I just don't get a kick out of it like you do. And you see it yourself. I mean, you change half of what I write!' I lean in. 'If I could work on what I am passionate about, what I want to write, then maybe I won't feel like this any longer.'

'Felix,' she hisses. 'Do it then. You've talked about it for years, it's all I've heard about.' She raises her hands in the air gesticulating. 'This great book you have locked inside you as you belittle what we've worked so hard on. Just do it! Write it! After this summer take a hall pass and go to the Catskills and write the thing,' she says, frustrated.

'We're always so focused on Morgan. I've never had the chance to—'

'That's bullshit. If you want to write this goddamn book of yours, I am not standing in your way. You're the only one doing that.'

'Maybe I will, go away after the summer,' I tell her stubbornly. I wonder if I could find the courage.

'Fine. Do it.' She is unbothered, as if she knows it will never happen.

Silence falls over us and she leans back in her chair, taking a sip of wine as she stares out at the square. The children have gone to bed now most probably, it is past ten. But she stares at the lip of the fountain where they had been playing. Emma said she doesn't want children. She said creatives can't have both, and that's why men have been able to take the lead in so many avenues for so long. They had someone else doing the cooking and the cleaning and the child rearing, so they could sit in their office and create new worlds undistracted, never letting go of the flow. I agreed, at the time. But I do regret it. I often wonder if she does too. There is still time, but she's never brought it up, and I fear it is a topic that would incite friction if I were to.

'I loved the sleepwalking stuff,' she says finally.

I shift up in my seat. 'Really?' I smile, take another drag of my cigarette and nod along. 'Yeah, I thought that worked well, it felt really . . .'

'Instinctive?' Emma finishes for me.

I look over at her. 'Yeah, exactly.'

'Emma . . . it's too . . .'

'What?'

'It's too honest.' I sigh. 'I've said things . . . I don't want to . . .'

'Hurt me?'

I nod. But she shakes her head stubbornly. 'This is what I want us to do. Brutal honesty. It could be the closure from that whole nightmare we need.'

'Don't you care?' I whisper.

She gives me a startled look. 'What the hell, Felix? It's all I care about,' she adds, with her east-coast no-nonsense tone.

'Morgan,' I state flatly. Knowing that is what she means. The brand is all she cares about. Not me.

'Us,' she corrects. And I choose to believe her. In that moment, I do. Even if she's lying. 'Listen, I'm sorry you're feeling so dissatisfied. If you want some time to work on your own project, after we've finished this, you can have as long as you want.'

'Thank you,' I tell her, already feeling fidgety about how much I'd have to prove, and Emma's knowing face when I come back empty-handed.

'But book nine – we need to add some new characters. I'll work on that tomorrow. Someone to turn Sebastian's head and to play with Hanna's – the antagonist.'

I nod, thinking. 'Yeah, definitely.' I swallow. As I blink, the memories flood. Hurried illicit sex, lying about my whereabouts, quickly deleting messages on my phone. No, Sebastian isn't like that. He isn't like me.

After we pay the bill, Emma stands up and gets out her phone, snapping away at the pretty scene. She fiddles around for a bit, looking at the pictures she's taken, before grabbing me and forcing me into a selfie with her. She then uploads these to our public Instagram account, and onto our Twitter feed. As notifications ping, I have a look at what she's posted.

*A Very French Affair – having a self-imposed writing retreat in Europe to carve out book nine. Six weeks, just us – hopefully we don't kill each other before we write THE END. Hold on to your hats, it's coming! X*

She's added a carousel of photos, including the one of me standing by the pool earlier with my shirt undone. I'm smiling. Only I can see the pain in my eyes. We look like we're having a great time. There is no hint of the darkness that lingers.

# CHAPTER SEVEN

As we walk out of the square, we pass a bar with tall stools and tables outside. Music is pumping and a gaggle of people are smoking, picking at olives and gesticulating wildly.

I pause, and peer through the entrance, staring at the bar, wishing I could sit there alone, with a glass of something strong.

A figure walks towards me with a waving hand: Juliette. 'Felix! *Salut!*' she calls, coming out, wiping her hands on a tea towel as she heads over. She is in front of me before I know it. Emma turns around sharply at the sound of my name. 'Emma!' Juliette cries, delighted. 'It's so good to see you both 'ere. Did you eat at Le Cirque?'

'Yes, yes, we did. It was very good, we were impressed. Do you work here?' Emma asks, examining the establishment for the first time.

Juliette nods. 'Only when they're short. I 'elp with some 'oliday rentals in the area too, and I deliver bread and cook meals some days.' She shrugs, laughing. 'You cannot get away from me around 'ere.' She grabs on to my arm. 'I'm like a letch!' she jokes.

'Leech,' Emma corrects, looking at her hand on my arm.

''Ow is the book?' she asks.

'Hard to tell at this stage,' I say. 'Eight books in, it doesn't get any easier.' I feel Emma stiffen. Having to talk about previous success when we're stuck in a rut is hard.

'Ah!' Juliette is impressed. They are always impressed. Usually this would be my cue to lean in and impress her further. But I am a reformed character. Besides, Emma is here.

'I looked you up. You are very famous.' She tucks a strand of hair behind her ear, revealing a pretty line of tiny hoops that hug her delicate lobe. 'I feel silly that I didn't know before. I can't believe you 'ave come to our little corner of France to write your next. We are so 'onoured.'

'Thank you, Juliette, that is . . . erm . . .'

'*Une minute!*' she shouts, remembering something and running back inside. She comes back armed with a copy of one of our books. It's the one that sold the most: *Meghan's Wrath*. She hands it to me, and I examine it. I've not seen this cover before. A dagger covered in blood – how original. The title has been translated into *La Colère de Meghan*. She holds out a pen, as I flick through the pages. 'Would you?'

'Sure – I don't think we've ever signed this version before.' I use the biro to do a swirling Morgan Savage and Juliette is thrilled.

'Is it very scary?' she asks us. 'Will I get nightmares?'

'If we've done our job,' Emma replies.

'I didn't realise there were murderers staying at the 'ouse.' Juliette laughs. '*Merci* – thank you so much for this.'

'It's our pleasure,' Emma says.

'Come in.' She smiles at us both. ''Ave a drink, on me!'

'We really should get back,' Emma starts.

'Come on, Em,' I tell her. This looks fun.

She sighs. 'Okay, just one. I want to get up early and get back to the book.'

I take a stool at the bar as Emma looks around the joint. The walls are filled with old French shop signs and movie posters. Emma dusts off the stool next to mine and sits down. The bar is quietly busy with people chatting around small tables in corners. Juliette places some glasses on the bar and pours us each a drink, along with a shot of something strong.

'I'm driving,' Emma says, moving her shot glass towards me.

I'm distracted as an older man wearing a police uniform knocks back the entrance door, and comes in. He strides over to the bar and leans in to speak to the young man behind it, who nods profusely and turns the music down so he can hear the lecture. They proceed to have a heated discussion. Emma leans towards them, trying to listen. I bet she desperately wishes she spoke French; she loves earwigging on police conversations. I wonder if this time next year we'll be working on a police procedural set in the south of France. '*Oui, oui, ça ne se reproduira pas*,' the barman says, sounding annoyed and harassed, and the policeman leaves.

Juliette notices the interest on Emma's face. 'The local capitaine. 'E 'as the easiest job in the region.' Juliette laughs. 'Nothing better to do than to blame us for a drunk driver in a ditch.' She laughs. '*Marco! Monte le volume!*' and he does as requested.

French rap blares out of the speaker. Emma nods her head softly to the beat, with a quizzical look. Emma likes all kinds of things, from Charlotte Brontë to John Grisham, slasher movies to romcoms. Opera to Drake. She bites her bottom lip as she works out how she feels about this.

'Rap sounds so much better in French,' I shout over the music towards Juliette, who is leaning over the bar towards us. 'Something about it – even though I have no idea what they're saying, it just seems more . . . more evocative, more profound.' I glance to see Juliette's reaction. Not that I'm trying to impress her or anything. I'm just trying to make conversation.

'Much like poetry,' Juliette mutters. Then she stands, leaning over to lower the music before she recites:

> 'La tombe dit à la rose:
> – Des pleurs dont l'aube t'arrose
> Que fais-tu, fleur des amours?
> La rose dit à la tombe:
> – Que fais-tu de ce qui tombe
> Dans ton gouffre ouvert toujours?'

We clap along with the barman, and she bows with a flourish. 'Wow, that's beautiful. One of yours?' I ask.

Emma gives a laugh, designed to make me feel thick. 'No, Felix! It's Victor Hugo. One of his most famous.'

'Oh, well . . . It's beautiful,' I tell Juliette.

'It is a trick. It is about death. A rose on a tomb. Is there anything more devastating than a gift left to rot on a grave?'

Then Emma pips in, her voice husky and wise. 'Devastation is a vital ingredient for creativity. Without the pain of loss, do you think we'd have anything of worth? Suffering is part of life – and the only way of absolving yourself is to channel it into something useful.' I feel a yawn coming on. I almost crack a joke – thanking her for her Ted Talk. But that wouldn't go down well.

'Love does too. What music would be made without that?' I add.

'Nothing inspires more than the pain of love,' Juliette says quietly. She stares, as if thinking of something else.

Emma downs the rest of her wine. 'Come on, Fe. We need to scoot.' I've already finished my drink; I was planning on another.

'But—'

'Come on, we said one,' she says swiftly. 'Thank you, Juliette. That was very generous of you,' Emma says, smiling at her kindly. I nearly push for more. But decide against it. Juliette smiles and waves as we leave.

We walk back to the car in silence.

'She's pretty,' Emma says, thoughtfully. Emma is well versed in excited women approaching us and aiming every word in my direction.

'Is she?' I ask, pretending to be naive to her looks. 'I hadn't noticed.'

We get in the car and Emma starts the engine. 'Felix. You were practically frothing at the mouth,' Emma mutters.

'I was not,' I say quickly, looking away. Was I? 'Is this going to be our life now? You picking at me every time I talk to the opposite sex?'

She doesn't answer, just leans forward and fiddles with the radio. We interrupt a forlorn song, just a guy and a guitar. He's hitting all the high notes, which hang in the air, reverberating with desolation.

She starts the car and drives away from our parking spot.

'Be careful,' she warns. It lingers.

# CHAPTER EIGHT

I wake up. A rotten dry mouth and a banging head greet me. The bottle of whisky on the veranda began to disappear as if someone else was pouring it. I freeze for a moment, thinking of Emma in the kitchen, making her wholesome matcha from the powder she brought with her from home, and turning her nose up in disgust at the empty bottle left there.

I blink as the dregs of my dream curl into my memory. It's left me with an amplified feeling of shame. Someone grabbing on to me. Or was it me grabbing on to them? The sound of someone screaming *'STOP!'* woke me up with a bang. I wipe the greasy sweat off my forehead. I'm hungover and can barely let a thought finish before giving up. A distraction, that's what I need. I pick up my phone.

It is ten a.m. and Emma's chapter has arrived.

Morgansavage@infinitymail.com
11.07.2024
**Subject:** Book 9 – First Draft

## CHAPTER THREE – HER

A moth sits on the wall, its back legs rubbing together, still wounded from hitting an exposed light bulb on its last expedition. It doesn't like this room. It feels exposed. There is no dust or cobwebs – its fellow insects have been picked off, one by one. Its antennae can only sense a strange acrid odour, nothing familiar or comforting. It is too scared to move, in case it is detected, and taken to wherever the others have gone.

Hanna's eyes flick up and narrow, noticing the dark blur on the grey barren wall. She blinks at it, having been lost in her own head. It is an interesting place, that head. She's spent the evening, while Sebastian is out, sitting at the dining table paralysed by thought. Blood careering through her cheeks, as she thinks of his fingers itching towards flesh. Of quivering lips tentatively brushing, before sighing, and tongues pushed through lips. She can see it all so clearly. It is like she is there, in the room.

But he wouldn't leave her, would he? That would mean he'd have to leave Ivy, and he couldn't do that. Ivy is her only bargaining tool in this whole deal. Ivy is what keeps him here, not her.

Because he knows, he can never have another.

Sebastian doesn't know that Hanna has all his passwords. She's read between the lines of the cheerful, overly enthusiastic messages and emails he sends these women he spends all day with.

Hanna stands up. With the dust cloth still clutched in her

hand from her frenzied housework earlier she whips the wall. The bug falls onto the grey carpet, and she treads on it. 'Drat,' she whispers, removing her foot. She has inadvertently made a mark on the pile. Unease spreads, and she goes to fix it. Moths. What had her mother said about those? A bad omen, she is sure of it.

At midnight precisely, she gets into bed and pretends to sleep. At some point, without meaning to, she drifts off.

So consumed by her anxiety she is the next day, she looks down during an extensive washing-up session and realises she hasn't cleaned one damn thing. 'Darn it,' she whispers. Shrugging, she wipes her hands on her apron.

A flash of Sebastian in a dark room kissing someone that isn't her. And she holds her head tightly. 'No, no!' she tells herself. 'No, no.' She was able to keep up the pretence of sanity so well at the beginning. She was able to be the woman Sebastian wanted – carefree and fun. But since they moved to Phoenix, and he's been so busy with other things, her head is just not as good at behaving itself.

Hanna hears a truck outside the front of the house and pulls her gloves off as she walks to the front window. There is a removal van parked outside the opposite property.

She squints at the people milling around, trying to pick out the owners. Two children shout excitedly as they run into their new home. A boy and a girl, they look around ten years old. Hanna's pupils dart, looking for the friendly face of a woman, someone she could befriend. Sebastian would like her to have more of a social life. It's been stubbornly on her to-do list for weeks.

*Then she sees her and is instantly let down. An older woman, not pretty or fashionable. Not how she had imagined in her head. Hanna sighs. The husband looks similarly boring. Oh, well. At least that means she can focus on her housework.*

*Then her eyes narrow as she sees a young woman, drastically different to the frumpy mother. Early twenties. Long blonde hair. Big plump lips. Slender figure. The little girl runs up to the young woman, who quickly encases her in a hug. Then the mother comes over and talks to the young woman, as though gently giving orders.*

A nanny! How disgusting!

*Hanna would never in a million years hire someone to look after Ivy.*

*Her lips twitch, and her mouth downturns. But then the woman notices her at the window and waves, and Hanna smiles, and she waves back enthusiastically. She'd better not introduce herself now, she isn't perfectly presented. And that is extremely important when meeting new people.*

*Hanna steps back from the window. The image of the young woman is lodged in her mind. How she wishes she could tear that alluring smile off her face with her bare hands. She finds herself back in front of the sink. In a sort of trance, she adds bleach to the washing-up mixture and scrubs and scrubs until her fingers prune and her nails begin to bleed.*

I throw the phone down. It's good. Emma is a master at layering tension, slowly, meaningfully. But there is something about being with Hanna for those few pages that has made me feel queasy. There is something familiar about her. Emma can be a perfectionist, too. I cough the thought away. Of course, Emma is going to use her own defects, embellish them, grow them exponentially in a jar, before laying them out on a page for readers to dine on. It's what we do.

After a quick shower to freshen up, I go downstairs and find Emma on the edge of the veranda. A yoga mat is laid out on the lawn with a few of her latex Pilates resistance bands dotted about the grass. She has had a full morning before I've barely woken up. A book is resting on her lap and a coffee sits on the floor next to the chair, a peaceful look on her face as she basks in the slice of sunlight that hits that spot. Hearing me open the door, she turns. A devilish grin appears.

'It's good, isn't it? I'm so enjoying writing Hanna,' she says with glee. 'You know, I think you're right. She should be the baddie, through and through. How fun.' I'm pleased at the admission. 'Your turn,' she says quickly. As if it comes as naturally to me.

My chapter. How will I follow it? What shall happen next? Is she enjoying watching me suffer like this? No, Emma just wants what's best for the book. I must stop sliding into resentment all the time. It's a weakness, and I need to control it.

'It will come to you. Your instincts will kick in,' she says. 'You're a writer, after all.' Was there a side edge to the comment? I glance across at her, but she just smiles supportively. It's just my ghastly head, making things up. Again.

# CHAPTER NINE

I take a coffee into the study, having sneaked a thumb of spirit in there to stop the unnameable panic rising. All I can think about is Emma's clever, insidious ways of belittling me, which are so easily refuted as sensitivity, or paranoia, if I were ever to bring it up. I am tightly wound and irritated by the time I stare at the blank page on my desktop.

Right. Sebastian. I've got this.

**CHAPTER FOUR – HIM**

*Sebastian drives home from a long day at work, dreading it. He often works late to avoid being there, and his late nights at the office have become even later recently. Hanna is always standing in the hallway, looking at him expectantly, as if she's been waiting most of the afternoon. The meals have become elaborate, and there are these long monologues that are so perfectly executed about her filled day, performed as if she'd been practising in the mirror. Which is a ridiculous thought. Hanna wouldn't do that. Would she?*

He swallows down the discourse. Hanna just needs to make some friends. He keeps telling her that. Then she wouldn't be so obsessive about keeping the house clean. She gets agitated when he mentions this, so he's tried not to go on.

At least he'll get to see Ivy. Ivy, Ivy. The most perfect little thing he's ever laid eyes on. Sebastian always wanted to be a father. Yes, the career is great and everything. But having a child to watch grow. There is nothing he's ever wanted more. But Hanna gave him that ticket, and now, he wonders if it was what he wanted, after all.

He pulls into the street. There is a large truck on the other side of the road. Robert's Removals, From A to B, Stress Free, it says on the side. He's seen the estate agent going in and out of the empty property with various prospective buyers for months. Sebastian pulls into the drive and watches in the rear-view mirror as removal men hop into the cab of the truck and drive away. A nice-looking couple, slightly older than them, wave them off, flanked by two middle-school-aged children.

Sebastian goes to open the car door, but his hand freezes when he catches sight of a younger woman. She's grinning and looks light and happy. She starts to tickle the young boy and the whole family join her, laughing hysterically.

He stares at the scene, mesmerised. That's what he wants. That family. Like the one he had growing up before his brother died and sent them all into the darkest of places, never to recover. He wants a piece of that sunshine.

Coming to his senses, he gets out of the car. The dad notices him first, and waves.

'Hello there.' Sebastian strides over. 'I'm assuming you are the new owners unless you're planning a squat.' He laughs at his own joke. Luckily, they join him.

'Yes, I'm Hank, and this is my wife, Jolene – our kids Chad and Ashley. And this is Nancy, our nanny.'

Nancy grins, and waves. 'How ya'll doing?' she asks in a slow, sweet Southern accent. Sebastian shakes Hank and Jolene's hands and rustles the hair on Chad's head. The little girl hides behind Nancy, who calls her a doofus for being so shy.

'We've just moved out here from the city. Decided the 'burbs were better for this stage of life. We both work at the university,' Jolene explains.

'Great. About time we had a few brain cells around here,' Sebastian says good-naturedly. People usually warm to him quickly. 'We've only been here six months. My company relocated me,' he explains.

Jolene's distracted by something over his shoulder. And Sebastian turns to see Hanna bowling out of the house, Ivy on her hip. Newly applied lip gloss. 'Ah! Here she is.' She joins him, parking herself directly under his arm. Jiggling Ivy around.

'Hello,' Hanna whispers.

'This is my wife, Hanna. And Ivy,' he tells them.

Nancy reaches over, a big grin on her face. 'Oh my gawd! Hello, little one.' She takes Ivy's hand and begins to make adorable popping noises with her mouth. Sebastian can feel Hanna moving into his side further, causing him to buckle slightly.

83

'If you guys ever need a sitter, I'd love to help out – if Hank and Jolene don't need me, of course.'

Hanna interrupts her. 'No, no, thank you. We don't need any help.'

'Oh. Sure,' Nancy says, dropping her hand, rather abashed at the speed of rejection. Jesus, Hanna, Sebastian thinks. Can't you just be normal for once?

'You know what? That might be great. We could do with getting out more.' He doesn't need to look at Hanna's face to know the thunder she'll be unsuccessfully masking. 'Well, we'd better go in. Nice to meet you all. And if you ever need a cup of sugar or anything, feel free to knock on our door, any time.'

He takes Hanna's hand, and they walk over the road to their house. As soon as the door closes, he knows what she's going to say.

'I'm not having that girl look after Ivy!' she spits.

He sighs. 'But why, Hanna? You were fine with it in Chicago. What the hell is going on with you?' She clings on to Ivy, refusing to reply. 'You need to get out of this house. Have some fun for a change. You literally never leave! You spend all your time with a baby. Don't you want to do something for yourself, for us, for a change? That's what parents do!'

'I've got to go put her down,' Hanna tells Sebastian crossly. Then she stops, turns, and with that insane plastered smile on her face says, 'Fine. If you want a babysitter, we shall have a babysitter.' And she leaves with a flourish.

Sebastian goes to the fridge and opens a cold beer. How did

*he get caught up in this? What the hell is he going to do? He's never felt so stuck in his life.*

I did what Emma always tells me to do. Moved the plot along. I sit back, pleased with the scene. I've introduced characters, and I've given Nancy a genuine reason to get involved with the family that doesn't feel clunky. The prose could do with some work, but that isn't what first drafts are for.

After making a drink I walk down to the pool, where Emma is reading on her phone. It must be my chapter. My pace slows. More cautious. I put my free hand in my pocket and wait for her to finish. She looks up, noticing me briefly, and then looks back at her phone to finish.

'Well?' I ask with trepidation.

'You put your brother in there?' She is surprised. I don't talk about my brother. Let alone immortalise him in print. 'Are you sure?'

I shrug. 'It just felt right.' My older brother died when I was fourteen. He was only seventeen. He was this really cool guy that everyone loved, who seemed to walk through life with this authentic confidence – he was just him, through and through. Self-deprecating, hilarious. Confident. He was brilliant at every sport he tried his hand at. He never made a fool of himself or got too drunk or stoned – like teenagers usually do. He didn't have a speck of that macho nastiness used to weaponise the upper hand I'd experienced from other boys. He was caring and emotionally intelligent, but also firm and resolute when he felt there was some sort of injustice.

Mum and Dad loved him the most. I always knew it. He wanted to join my dad in the family business after uni, but first, he wanted to prove himself outside of that and get into Sandhurst and have a stint as an officer in the army. My dad was thrilled by this plan – he'd heard it was the best training a young man could have, with a multitude of transferrable skills and an assiduous work ethic instilled.

It was all set out and, to be honest, it was a relief I didn't need to worry about that pressure of taking on the role. But I guess there was part of me that has always been jealous. It's a resentment that has sat there for years, keeping me away.

Emma says I have rose-tinted glasses, and he can't have been as perfect as I recall, and no wonder, I was barely a teen. She says I am lucky to have such wonderful parents, and I've built it up in my head to be something it probably isn't. But she wasn't there. She could never understand what a great guy he was. So much better than me.

And then he was just – gone. A cycling accident, his head hit the edge of the pavement, and his helmet wasn't fastened properly. You see, he wasn't perfect after all.

And my parents were stuck with plan B. Me.

I sometimes wonder whether the reason I had such an adverse reaction to working with Dad, and staying in the UK, was that initial implied rejection. And if I had turned around and stepped into my dead brother's shoes, my dad would spend the whole time comparing everything I did, every fuck-up, every disappointment, and wishing it was him there and not me. His ghost would dictate everything I ever did for ever more, and I just couldn't listen to the constant stream of *not good enough* everyone would be thinking, even me.

Emma beckons me over and pats on the side of her lounger. I do as commanded and sit down. She must be happy with the chapter. Either that or she's about to deliver a scathing under-hand attack. Instead, she sighs. 'I got the numbers through for the last book. The hardback bombed and they're saying the paperback retailer slots won't be what we're used to.' She stares into the distance as she says this.

I barely get involved in the business end; our books have always sold well, and it's just been one piece of good news after another so I've slowly stopped paying attention, and assumed it would just trundle along much the same. 'Maybe people are getting bored of Morgan finally,' she whispers, a panicked twinge to her voice. 'A lot is riding on this book, Felix, it needs to be our best yet.' I wish she hadn't said that. The pressure is already suffocating.

'It will be. It's going to be,' I tell her confidently, hoping to mask my inner doubt.

'I hope so,' she says, her fingers on her temple. Then she reaches down into her little bag and takes out a small brown plastic bottle. It rattles as she opens the lid and picks out a white tablet. She swallows it with water and sighs as it makes its way down her throat, leaning back on the lounger and closing her eyes.

# CHAPTER TEN

'She needs to die.' Emma walks up to me holding a tin of anchovies, an excited look on her face. It's the next day and we've driven into town to stock up at the local *supermarché*, having eaten and drunk our way through what was left for us when we arrived. *Die.* the word triggers something in me, and I blink.

'Nancy?' I ask, swallowing. The image I've created of the young woman rocks in my mind. Her sweet face now splattered with blood. It causes a gut reaction, a smash of something dark and disturbing. Like something is lodged in my brain, and I can't get it out.

'Yes. All that youth, innocence.' She puts the tin in the trolley we've loaded with our French spoils. Emma continues walking, eyeing up the foreign goods on display. The variety of cheese makes her stop in her tracks. 'All this Comté is going to make me fat,' she says, before slipping a greaseproof paper-wrapped wedge into the trolley and staring at the Roquefort longingly. 'Hanna's gonna dump all her crap on her. Every bit of her paranoia, all that hate for her own kind. Nancy doesn't even know the mess she's stumbled into. She's in way over her head,' she adds gleefully.

Therapy. That's what writing is to Emma. She needs to work through things. If this book is interrogating the failings of our marriage, in its own crazy way it will heal her hurt. It will be cathartic for her, killing Nancy.

I follow her down the aisle, pushing the trolley as she talks. 'So, in this morning's chapter, Nancy babysat, right? It did not go well; we also find out that Sebastian isn't Ivy's real dad, which is the first head-turn for the reader.' She looks quite pleased with herself when she says that. She turns, looking at me, eyes shining. 'Isn't this fun? I haven't felt like this about a story for such a long time!'

'What if they're both suspects?' I say, trying to think of something else to add. *Come on, brain. Think, think. Impress her.* 'Maybe it's an accident while Nancy is with Sebastian, and Hanna helps him cover it up.'

She turns to me slowly, and I hope for a second that she is entertaining it, but of course, I am wrong. 'Helps him cover it up,' she repeats. She pauses, thinking, and then looks across at me curiously. Did I crack it? 'Needs more thought,' she says quietly, frowning, biting her thumbnail. Glancing over at me, before moving away. *Okay, Emma, we're just brainstorming. Got to get out the bad ideas to get to the good ones and all that.*

Ah, the wine. I begin lifting bottles. They're so cheap compared to the imported ones in the US. After shifting a few into the trolley I notice the look on Emma's face. 'What? We're on holiday.'

89

'No, we're not,' she says briskly, as she walks towards the vegetables. I ignore her and grab a bottle of my favourite whisky.

I can't get the chapter Emma wrote this morning out of my head. The story is getting dark. It replays in my head over and over. The way she describes Nancy – she reminds me of . . . someone else.

Her blonde hair in a ballet bun, her heart-shaped face and the cluster of freckles dotted about the bridge of her nose. So young and so very ripe. Her unsullied laugh and the way she waves her hand, gesturing that nothing is too much trouble. Hanna feels old, and ugly in comparison. What must Sebastian think looking between them both?

She wonders how it would feel to take a kitchen knife and slice through that pretty neck.

That line had sent a shiver through me. Emma is exceptional at this. And this is only her first pass at Hanna – by draft three or four she'll be rampantly more terrifying.

We come out of the modern square building on the edge of town. The heady heat curls around us as I push the overfilled trolley towards the car. Once we've loaded up, Emma looks across at me. 'Right, well, over to you, I guess,' Emma says, smiling with the anticipation of the next chapter.

'Let's go and have a coffee,' I say, pointing towards the old town.

'It's late afternoon,' she mutters. 'The chapter.'

'I will, I will . . . Come on, you know I work better at night

90

anyway.' I'm putting it off, she's right. 'Come on, we've come all the way here.'

'The food . . .' She gestures to the boot.

'We'll be half an hour, it'll be fine. There might even be a few nice boutiques.' Her impulse mellows as this thought piques her interest.

We wander up the ancient streets. Emma finds a few small shops to potter around. She buys some wicker baskets and lavender-infused soap. I step into a cave-like record shop and sort through the vinyl – and find a scuffed Françoise Hardy album. She was one hot lady, back in the day. I haggle with the owner, which gets rather fiery.

'Felix,' Emma whispers, embarrassed.

'They like it,' I assure her.

We meander down a road and realise we've hit the square we had dinner at a few nights ago. It's crowded, and jubilant music is played by a band in one corner. People are dressed in finery. There is a couple in the centre garnering all the attention, with a girl in a white dress. 'A wedding,' Emma breathes as we observe the scene. The band starts up again and the joyous couple hold hands, and begin to dance. The guests clap and whoop as the bride blissfully lays her head on her new husband's chest.

'What a pretty place to get married.' Emma sighs at the scene. 'So many promises you make, with absolutely no idea what they mean. For better, for worse . . .'

'Emma,' I whisper. But she's right. Marriage is hard, they tell you that. Those vows you say through grinning cheeks, a smile a mile wide – but really, you're too naive to understand it. How being with one other person can be so gruelling.

'Come here,' I tell her, pulling her in. Forcing a hug between us. Kissing the top of her head.

As we part, I hear a cry and look up. The bride is coming towards us, dragging her new husband behind her. 'Morgan Savage!' she calls out, stopping in front of us. She says something in French, which her husband translates, with laughter in his voice. Shining eyes from the euphoria of the day.

'She says she is your biggest fan,' the handsome groom says. Shaking my hand and Emma's. The girl continues the hurried conversation we don't understand, and he translates. 'She says she 'eard zat you were staying in ze area and couldn't believe it. She's, umm, read all your books and 'oped zat we might bump into you. It must be lucky zat it was today.' Emma and I exchange bemused glances.

Suddenly the bride hugs Emma with such force she is nearly knocked back before moving on to me for the same. Emma laughs in surprise. '*Pardon*, she is *très* excited today!' the groom says. *And already a bit drunk*, I think.

'*Il nous faut une photo. Éric!*' the bride shouts over to the wedding party, and a photographer rushes through the crowd.

'I don't think—' Emma starts, already pulling her fingers through her hair.

'You must! You must – it will make 'er day.'

And before Emma can protest, they have rallied around us and pictures are being taken. 'Congratulations,' I tell them both, shaking hands as they laugh with delight.

'Join us! Please,' the groom says, gesturing at the party.

'Oh, we'd love to,' says Emma. 'That's so kind. But we have work to do.'

The groom explains to the bride, and her eyes widen. '*Un nouveau livre?*'

'She is asking if you are writing a next book.'

'Yes, yes, we are,' Emma says. And the bride whoops with joy and shoos us away, laughing jovially. 'Lovely to meet you! Have an amazing day!' we call as we leave them to it.

I feel Emma's hand and look down to see her fingers searching for mine. They entwine as we walk back to the car, in silent thought.

'Remember our wedding day?' Emma says quietly.

'How could I forget? That lilac dress.'

'I'd found it in that vintage store in Greenpoint, more tulle than I've ever seen.'

'You paired it with your favourite leather jacket. The looks we got on the subway.' I shake my head, smiling at the memory of Emma clinging to a pole on the train, laughing as everyone dotted around on plastic chairs haloed by graffiti admired her. Emma's style has matured; she used to be a little quirkier: more Williamsburg than Upper East Side.

'We were so late for the appointment at City Hall. I nearly twisted my ankle sprinting down Broadway crashing into tourists. When I looked at the bouquet of posies, there were barely any petals left, they were scattered all the way down the sidewalk,' she reminisces.

'We were all hot and sweaty when we got there, heaving

at the receptionist like we'd just run the marathon.' I laugh, squeezing her hand.

'But we didn't care. We were so happy,' she adds wistfully as we stop at the car.

'Yeah,' I say, swallowing. We were so happy. Deliriously happy.

We stare at each other across the roof of the car, the thought of happier times binding us together.

'Felix, listen. Whatever you've done, I'll stand by you. No matter what happens.' She jerks open the passenger door and gets in. And I am left to wonder, what the hell did she mean by that?

# CHAPTER ELEVEN

On our return, everything is quiet and still. Emma yawns. 'I'll whip up a sandwich for you, and you can eat while you work.' She's desperate for my chapter. I can't get out of it, so I make my way into the study. I cast my eyes across the Post-it notes.

The breakdown of a marriage. Secrets and lies. What is the inciting incident – a death? A missing person? S & N get closer. N joins them for a family dinner?? Sebastian isn't Ivy's real father.

So much to get my head around. I reread Emma's morning chapter.

The chapter ends with the couple going on a date, Hanna grabbing Nancy's hand:

*'If anyone comes to the door, don't answer it, promise me,'* *she whispers feverishly at a confused Nancy. 'Please, if anyone* *comes to the house, don't let them in.'*

95

There is an interesting sub-plot emerging, but without any knowledge of where it is leading, I have no idea how to lean into it for Emma. I'm as much in the dark as Sebastian. If Sebastian isn't Ivy's biological father, then who is? And who is Hanna hiding from?

What is the reason? I drum my fingers on the desk. Backstory. The answer is always in the backstory. In the draft, it says Sebastian always wanted a family. I remember something then and scroll back through Emma's chapters – *Because he knows he can never have another.* It's right there, isn't it? The answer. Sebastian can't have children! I feel like cheering. Just got to search for the breadcrumbs dotted between the lines and paragraphs.

Right, my turn. I bring up a blank page and give her what she wants. I try to get into Sebastian's head. To my surprise, it isn't that hard.

*Most guys would have bolted. But not him. Sebastian was told at a young age he wouldn't be able to have children. And he'd always longed for a family. He thought if he could do it right, maybe it would fill that void that emerged when his own family disintegrated after the terrible accident.*

I stare out the window, building an image of Sebastian cleaning his car in my mind. Nancy out front playing basketball with the kids. A scene played out in every suburb across America. Phoenix – hot sunshine. A sprinkler going possibly. Sebastian watching the picture-perfect view of the kids playing as he cleans his car. The pull of his longing. I pick at the dry skin on my lip. Sebastian needs to confide in Nancy.

The basketball rolls into the road, and Sebastian strides over to take it, a perfect incentive for an encounter.

Nancy meets him halfway. 'Thanks.' She smiles as he hands her the ball.

'Hey,' he says, as she walks back, and she stops. 'Thanks so much for sitting. I'm sorry about Hanna. She's quite an anxious mother.'

'That's okay. I get it.' She laughs. 'Are you guys in witness protection or something?'

'What? No. Why?'

'Just something she said.' Nancy shrugs.

'I think she's finding it tough. New town, all that. It's really affecting her.' He scuffs his shoe on the ground. 'We're not having the best time at the moment.'

'It will get better, I'm sure. And honestly, don't worry. I get it.'

'She never . . . she wasn't like this before.' What he doesn't say is that he can't help but feel Hanna lied about who she was, to get him, and now he is trapped. Is that a fair analysis of the situation, or is he just a terrible person? He's not sure he can tell any more.

'If there is anything I can do to help, just message me. Happy to sit for Ivy again. If there is anything I can do to make her more comfortable about me coming, y'all just let me know.'

97

*A smile breaks out over Sebastian's face. 'Thank you, I really appreciate it.'*

*She smiles too. 'No worries.' Her ponytail swings as she runs back to the kids.*

*Sebastian watches her leave. He feels this creeping longing to find another reason to get close to her. She is an antidote to Hanna, and he feels all the stresses from his marriage shift away when Nancy is near. Almost as if Hanna is forcing his hand. No, Sebastian would never cheat on his wife, no matter how crazed she makes him feel. He shakes the thought away. He promised her he would stick by her – no matter what.*

I put my head in my hands. Shame descends. I've put that last part in to wind Emma up. To tell her she is the reason behind my behaviours. My own little attempt at a dig and it doesn't feel good.

I scroll back through the chapter. It reminds me of my own encounters. How far I took newfound friendships, born of intimate confessions of loneliness. Telling them things I never should have about my wife. It's not just the sex, it's the emotional cheating too. It's the way I described Emma. I betrayed her twice. While Emma was at home working her arse off, where was I? Licking my wounds, feeling sorry for myself. Distracting myself from my own inadequacies. And then running away once their feelings got out of hand.

Because to lose Emma would be to lose Morgan.

*Pathetic.*

I leave the small claustrophobic room. Emma's gone to bed.

I look at the baroque wooden clock on the wall. It's past midnight. I've been in there sweating for hours.

Instead of going upstairs, I grab the neck of a bottle of red and make myself comfortable in a chair on the veranda. The view is shrouded in darkness, apart from the pop of festoon lights, and the glow of the moon. I sip wine, getting lost in thoughts of the past and the future.

A noise from inside jolts me upright. I get up slowly and peer into the house through the window. I duck quickly when I see Emma. I don't want to converse with her right now, while I'm like this. I wait for the sound of feet on the stairs, but there is nothing. And after a few minutes I peer inside again. Her back is to me, facing the wall, where the painting hangs of the girl and book.

I hide again, but then check a few minutes later, and she's still there. Her stance is peculiar – unnatural. I wonder if she's all right. Maybe I should go in, drunk or not. She turns, and I brace, expecting a flash of anger at my late-night drinking, a breathtaking look of pity before sweeping back up the stairs.

But her face is devoid of any expression at all. Her eyes are open, but blank. She steps forward and moves onto the veranda. 'Emma?' I ask. But she doesn't reply. She simply steps onwards, slowly, as if in a church procession. Her thin silk nightie ruffles around her shape as she steps off the paving and onto the grass. 'Emma,' I try again, softy, not wanting to shock her into waking suddenly.

She stops in the middle of the lawn. And then turns to the left, towards the cliff. It is at this moment I walk briskly towards her and take her arm gently. 'Come on, darling. Let's go to bed,' I whisper. There is a moment of resistance but then she lets me guide her back into the house, up the creaking stairs, through to our room where I lovingly tuck her into bed.

I stare at her face, as the room spins around me. Emma has never done that before; she usually sleeps like a log. 'I love you,' she mumbles. I stroke her face. That's all I ever want to hear from her, all I ever want to know. 'Morgan,' she breathes, turning over. And I drop my hand. Of course.

# CHAPTER TWELVE

I haven't slept. All I've done is watch her, the hissing anxiety that she could get up again playing on my mind. Emma in her flimsy nightgown, and the nauseating sound of a thud, played over and over, taunting me. It's all mixed up with my inebriation, and the story of the girl and the cliff. Finally, light breaks through the curtains and I almost cry with relief that it's over.

Not long after sunrise Emma begins to move. She yawns, and stretches. She turns and notices I'm awake, and she smiles. 'Felix. This is . . . new,' she chuckles.

I wipe my eyes. 'I haven't slept very well,' I say quietly, unsure whether to tell her what happened last night. She gives me a concerned glance. 'You look awful.'

'Thanks,' I say sarcastically.

'I didn't mean . . . Felix, you know what I think. But it seems like you're not really listening.' She shakes her head and gets up.

'No, I don't know what you think,' I reply hotly.

She sighs, turning back to face me. 'You're drunk all the time! Look at yourself! You can barely remember anything,

101

clueless about the consequences.' She shakes her head in frustration.

'That's . . . I am not,' I scoff, irritated. I want to tell her the reason I lay awake all night but don't want to spook her. Emma doesn't like being out of control. 'I had a headache, that's all,' I say as I touch my head.

'All right then. I need to get going,' she says, fishing her feet into sliders. 'I didn't even get a chance to read your chapter last night it was so late.' She walks over to the window and stares at the view. 'Maybe we should make this a summer tradition, get away to write. Next year, we could hit up the Bahamas or Bali.' There is something comforting about hearing her talk about the future.

'Yeah, yeah. That sounds great.' I try a smile at her.

'If we make it.' She stares, a dull look of fear in her eyes.

'What do you mean by that?' I ask, my stomach plunging.

'Well, if we don't get this book off the ground, will there be any point?' She searches around for her bag. Noticing the straps hanging from the end bedpost, she rummages inside it, and gets out another one of those pills. They're meant to be for occasional use, she'd said. She's been popping them like sweets since we arrived.

'It's going to be okay, Emma. You know that, right? We always pull something out the bag,' I tell her softly.

She just nods, pausing at the door frame before leaving. 'You catch up.' And she softly shuts the door, and I lie back on my pillow, drifting off to sleep.

*

I wake with a start, blinking. Everything comes into focus quickly. Where I am, what we're doing here. Emma's chapter will be lodged in my emails like a cyst. I don't have the energy to look at it yet.

My phone rings and I scramble around on the side table to find it. I knock it, and it smacks sharply at the contact with the stone floor. I groan, and leap down to retrieve it. Our agent, Max's, name lights up the screen. I wonder why he's calling me directly. Usually, he goes through Emma. It's rare to call me out of nowhere, especially recently, with all the headaches I've been giving him. He's been good to me, Max. Often taking the heat for my indiscretions to protect me when I need it the most. He's like a stoic uncle driving in to save the day when I least deserve it. Acting like I'm one of his rebellious daughters, whom he loves to death, but let's get away with far too much.

Fear grips me. I know instinctively this isn't good. I almost don't take it, but if I don't, he'll call Emma and I'd prefer to hear the unedited version of what he has to say. I lick my dry lips and prepare to put on a show.

'Felix,' he says, his voice booming. I imagine him in his office on Park Avenue. He'll be wearing a sharp grey suit, his reading glasses lodged just below his hairline, ready to shift over his eyes when he needs them. His white hair carefully combed to one side as he absent-mindedly drums his fingers on his teak mid-century desk, which is always cluttered with papers, refusing to fully comply with the technical advances of the last few years. The view of the city in the window behind. When we first went with him, he had an office in the same building. But lower down, smaller and pokier. His view of the city has become more impressive as we rose to success, pictures of his bestsellers framed around the room. He has been with me and Emma from the early days – a contact Emma knew from her career in publishing. She'd commissioned one of his authors, in the early years of having her own list. It was quite a coup as there were other, more experienced editors chasing it. Emma had all the ins; we would have just been another manuscript in the slush pile if it weren't for her.

'I thought you were blackballing us for six weeks to *get our asses on with the job*,' I laugh down the phone, mimicking him. I expect him to enjoy that, but he doesn't. Max is an all-in New Yorker – from an Italian family, he grew up in Hell's Kitchen and uses that authenticity to bluster his reputation of going balls deep to get what he wants.

'Hey, you by yourself? I gotta have a private chat.'

'That sounds ominous and rather chilling,' I joke. Max does not take the bait and I'm left with a sort of fragile, floating feeling. 'What is it?' I swallow.

'That girl, Robyn Avery, has gone missing.' A hammering starts in my chest. Robyn. 'It's not in the press. Just got word from the publishers. This is quite concerning because we don't need any of that mess leaking out. All it would take is a bit of digging to uncover the legal action she brought against the publishers 'cause of . . . well, you know.'

'What?' I croak, unable to take it all in.

'Look, the cops aren't takin' this seriously. There's gotta be a reason for that. Just wanted to give you a heads-up before we talk to Emma about it.'

'How long?' I ask.

'Not entirely sure. Got a panicked call from the team earlier. The mom's being real vocal, emailing everyone who's ever dealt with her daughter. She sent an aggressive note blamin' the publishing house for how they treated Robyn.'

'Right,' I mutter. 'Her poor family.' *I have* read (and co-written) enough stories that begin with this scenario to understand the murky conclusions of incidents like this.

'Just wanted to loop you in – since these things tend to leak. We might need to prep a statement. Show a bit of leg to keep 'em happy. I can talk to the publishers again, and they'll be hashing it out with their legal team. I'm sure Emma will have some thoughts.'

'But they can't do that, can they? What about the NDA?'

'We were in the process of getting that signed, Felix,' he tells me. 'And I ain't legally trained, so I got no idea how that would even come into play in a situation this serious.'

It is as if a ton of weight has been lowered onto my chest. 'In the process? You mean, she hadn't signed it?' The out-of-control feeling swirls.

'Look, this could all be arbitrary – she could be crashing at a friend's place or have skipped town. She could be living in Tent City for all we know! I mean, she wasn't exactly stable.'

I close my eyes for a moment. A flash of her soft lips and her giggle, which sounded like the first day of spring after a long and treacherous winter. But then the nasty look of betrayal when I refused to continue the affair – there was too much at stake. She didn't get it.

'Now, I'm giving you the opportunity to tell Emma before we call a meeting about it.'

*Hell, no.* 'Wait. Max . . .'

'Listen, she wouldn't want to stumble on this mess online,' he cautions. 'I was gonna ring you both up for a sit-down, but I figured I'd let you handle it first, y'know?' Whenever Robyn's name is mentioned, Emma is thrown into a terrible mood that lasts for weeks. 'Let's give it a minute. I mean . . . as you said, it may be nothing.'

'Felix, I reckon we gotta get her ready for this,' he pushes.

'But Max, we're writing, we're actually writing! You know how all this business derailed her.'

Max sighs. He wants that book more than anything. 'All right, sure. We'll keep it tight between us. But if anything shifts, we gotta figure out a plan, pronto.'

'Sure. Great. I'm sure it's nothing.'

After I hang up, I stand, and proceed to vomit in the toilet.

Robyn Avery. The whole thing was utterly stupid. It should never have started, but once it did, it was like a train I couldn't get off. Emma had become this brittle, horrible person to be around. All she cared about was the writing, and Morgan, hiding away in the office all day and night. Everything I did seemed to irritate her.

We had this huge US-wide tour to get through together and I was dreading it. Then Robyn turned up at the airport, our press girl for the tour, and she was so friendly, so interested.

Nothing was too much trouble. She made me feel . . . good about myself. When I'd been in the worst fug imaginable.

Then the tour finished, and she wanted more from me. She thought what we had was bigger than it was; she thought I would actually leave Emma, leave my career for her! Morgan is so ingrained in who I am, it's not something I can just drop like that. So, I did something I'm not too proud of. I blocked her number and ignored her. But she was always around, CC'ed into emails with the publisher, at events. Trying to grab me for a quick word or to plead. Emma was noticing. So, Emma did what she always does, she sorted it out. She had a quiet word with Max, and he took care of it.

And suddenly Robyn didn't work for our publishers any more. The problem had been removed. Until the legal papers landed on Max's desk, and that long arduous process began to try and make it go away to save the brand. I didn't think it could get any worse. But, it seems, I was wrong.

# CHAPTER THIRTEEN

I go down to the pool. Emma is lying on a lounger, that colourful sarong she bought on holiday in Tulum draped around her. She waves. 'Afternoon!' she calls over. She's in a much better mood than this morning. She must have let her anxiety out on her chapter. It is good to see her wrapped up in a story again.

Why does everything have to fall apart just as we're getting over this bump in the road and finally writing again? I swallow down the lingering bile in my throat. 'Hello!' I call over, attempting the same cheer.

'What did you think?' she asks as I get closer.

*Shit, her chapter.* I haven't read it. The news about Robyn is banging between my ears.

'What?' I call, pretending I haven't heard her, inching towards the path at the end of the lawn to go on a walk. The last thing I want to do is discuss anything. She'll be able to tell something is off, and the questions will start. I put my hands in my pockets as I wander away.

'Where are you going?' she calls.

'Just for a walk,' I reply.

To my dismay, she gets up and feeds her feet into her sandals. 'I'll tag along! Dying to hear what you think.'

I swallow. 'Great!' I say, as she slaps her book down on the lounger and ties the ends of her sarong together. She wanders over, linking an arm through mine.

'So . . . ?' she asks.

'It's great. Hanna is such a brilliant character . . . Very twisted.' I keep to what I know.

'Isn't her crazy meltdown in the supermarket hilarious?' she laughs. 'I love the idea of her being this mother, looking after something so vulnerable, and the reader knowing how close she is to breaking.'

'Yes, that really ups the suspense.' I cough. I realise Emma is taking us through the trees, around to the left, towards the cliff. 'Shall we go the other way?' I ask.

She ignores me. 'Last night I had the most intense dream.' She speaks quickly, almost relishing it. 'I dreamt that I fell off the cliff, like the girl in the story. I could feel the grass on my feet, it was so vivid.' She is tugging me along, towards it. 'Come on.'

We come to the cliff and Emma lets go of my arm. I feel that same sense of danger. The horrible image of the girl in the white nightie and that imaginary thud that replays on a sickening loop. 'Have we ever used a cliff in our books?' she asks.

I cough. 'I don't think so.'

'Such a clever device, you know? No real proof if someone was pushed, or if they jumped. Like the story Juliette told us. Everyone's still convinced the father could have done it.' She looks over the edge. 'If she was asleep, I wonder what happens when you die like that. Do you think she woke up, as she was falling? Like you do in dreams, you know? And for a split second she expected to open her eyes and be in bed, and have that relieved feeling that follows? But instead, she just smacked the floor?'

I swallow. 'Emma, what a horrible thought.' The smell of blood hits my nose and I can't work out where it has come from. Emma enjoys this game, pacing around, coming up with the worst ways to die, which usually end up in our novels. We started this when we first met – letting our imaginations run wild. They've become braver and darker – more twisted as time has gone on. But for some reason it all has more texture in my mind. A high-pitched scream rustles through my aching, tired head, which forces me to look around as if it were real. I touch the scratch on my face again.

Emma gives me a look. 'Anyway, not sure how we'd get that in this book. Maybe save it for number ten?' She looks at me hopefully then. 'I'm loving it here. I feel so alive, like the magic I thought I'd lost has come back.'

She takes a few pictures of the cliff, and the view. I see her typing something. 'The perfect scene for murder,' she mouths as she types, posting the pictures up. 'They'll love that.' She grins, talking about our followers.

'I'm glad you like it here,' I tell her. But I can't quash the foreboding thoughts and the trouble I feel is heading in my direction. 'Emma, I need to tell you something.' I'm going to do it. I'll tell her about Robyn. It will be hard, she'll be furious, but she is so good at fixing things, it will be for the best.

'What's up?' she asks, distracted by the 'likes' popping up on her phone.

I open my mouth to speak but bottle it, and grab on to the next possible thing I can say. 'So, you . . . I caught you sleep-walking in the garden last night.'

'Huh?' Her eyes lock mine in shock.

'I took you back up. It's why I couldn't sleep.'

Her head jerks. 'I don't sleepwalk. I never have.'

'I know. I'm sure it was an anomaly. You're so suscep-tible to stories, and this place, well, it's so atmospheric and all-encompassing.'

She stares at me. 'Was I walking towards the cliff?' she whispers, strained.

'No!' I cry. Not adding that before I stopped her, she could have been.

She stares towards the edge, deep in thought. Then she looks up. 'Felix, you know what to do.'

'What?' I ask, perplexed.

'You know,' she repeats, taking a last look over the top. I think I see a look of excitement dancing in her eyes. She takes a step closer, far too close for comfort.

'Emma,' I say. And she picks up a stone and chucks it over. We watch as it bounces off the ground below. Then she turns quickly away. The back of her heel licks the edge and my heart thuds in my chest.

*

111

'Want anything?' I call up the stairs after lunch. I'm feeling shaky and strange, and I need to get out of here to wallow in the news about Robyn undisturbed.

'Your chapter!' she shouts down from our bedroom, frustrated I've chosen to delay work again.

'I won't be long!' I call back in irritation.

She has no idea what is bubbling away in the wings – threatening to derail us this time.

I get in the car and drive over to town. My wife and I are opposites. Emma tackles problems head on, whereas I put things off until I absolutely need to. The king of procrastination, she calls me.

I park the car in the dusty car park and get out my phone, feeling strong enough to read her chapter now. My eyes glance over it. The scene in the supermarket is good. But another line about Sebastian and Nancy distracts me:

> Sebastian is very charming, he is putting on a show, and Lord, by the sounds of it, he desperately wants to impress this beautiful young thing.

God, I feel sick. I can see myself in this so clearly. I hate myself, but at the same time, I don't regret those experiences, not nearly as much as I should. I felt like Emma deserved it somehow.

I wipe my face; memories of Robyn slide into my mind. The way she looked at me in wonder like I was somebody. How

112

she'd brought me her manuscript and I promised to critique it for her, and she was beside herself with joy that me, Felix Larson, 'the great writer', was looking over *her* manuscript. I hadn't meant it to last more than a few nights but the affair seemed to span a whole summer in the end. Far longer than any of the others. All I really wanted was for Emma to look at me with that same respect.

I toss my phone on the passenger seat and sit there in silence, pressing my head against the steering wheel, wishing I could somehow turn back time. To when? When could I go back to change all this? To before I met Emma? To when she started fiddling with my work, eradicating my creativity from our output?

I should have known when she forced me to take her name instead of taking mine. *Brown?* She'd turned her nose up at it – never in a million years. I could see it dancing in her eyes. *How are we to stand out from the crowd with a name like that?* Larson is far more distinctive, she'd explained when pitching the idea. And I had to agree, it did have more flair. I felt it too; it would elevate that American literary greatness I was desperate for. *Emma and Felix Brown* just didn't cut the mustard in her eyes. I was on cloud nine about the publishing deal and didn't think it through. My parents didn't get it at all, of course they didn't. And the wedge between us grew.

I'm sure I would never have behaved how I did if she hadn't taken that away from me.

I get out the car and decide to walk off the restless, anxious energy the phone call with Max inflicted on me. The town seems to be deserted in the height of the heat. The little restaurant in the square is open but empty, and I order a beer and sit in the sun. The panama hat I nabbed from the boot room shields me from the stifling rays. I get out my book and lay my cigarettes on the table.

I blink. Robyn. Where could she be?

She was fairly obsessed by the end. Sending texts so long I'd have to scroll down and down, getting more uneasy with every warped word. I blocked her, she was out of control. Those messages would send me into a spiral of shame and hate. For a while I managed to forget about her, and I thought I was free. But then the legal letter arrived on Max's desk and the pain amplified, rebounding into every cavity of our lives. The secret no longer mine alone.

I fidget, needing an out from the washing machine turns of my mind. I pick up the book I've brought with me: *American Psycho*, by Bret Easton Ellis – that usually gets the juices flowing when I'm feeling stuck. Patrick Bateman is a type-A psycho killer. And the writing is a treat. My personal favourites are the crazy musical monologues he launches into, critiquing the latest CD release just before wielding an axe. It takes me a while to look up from the scorching insanity of the prose. I am all at once out of the chaos of 1980s-set Manhattan and back in the balmy stillness of southern France. I take a sip of beer which calms me. Patrick Bateman rings in my ears, his delighted glee of contempt making me wish I could be similar. Just not *care* about the nightmare I have created. *Be* more of a psychopath.

Then, smash. Another one of those murky memories I just cannot place. Someone grabbing at my face, the sound of a guttural wail.

I get up quickly, downing the rest of my drink. I need to keep moving. That is the only way to stop my head from taking over.

I slap a few euros down and look around. Maybe it's time to head back. Get lost in Sebastian's head, which is a much more pleasant place to be right now as at least I have some control over the way he is perceived. I stop when I see another person sitting on one of the tables, also reading. It's that policeman from the other night in the bar.

As I walk past, I dip slightly to see what he's reading. My heart skips when I see the name Morgan Savage below the French title. I trip on the cobble, having taken too long nosing at his book. He looks up as I recover. '*Vous allez bien?*'

'Sorry, I don't—' I begin.

'Are you okay?' he asks in English.

'Yeah, fine. Late night.'

'Be careful,' he says, licking a finger before turning a page.

'Yeah . . . stupid really.' I can't help but linger. I'm trying to work out which book he is reading. He peers up at me when he realises I've hung around. 'Good book?' I ask, pointing at it.

He shrugs. 'A bit – 'ow do you say? – dramatic for my liking. A kidnapped woman, locked in a tower.' Ah, yes. That one. I nod along, waiting for a compliment to lift my spirits. 'The writers are in town, Americans,' he explains with a French blow of the mouth and a shrug. 'My wife bought the book with the excitement. I picked it up and 'aven't been able to put it down.'

I smile. Yes, there it is. 'Ah, I'll have to check it out. Can I?' I ask, wanting to hold it.

'*Oui.*' He hands it over and I touch the cover.

'It is the 'usband,' The policeman sighs. This one is set in a penthouse in Manhattan, a woman is kidnapped on page one. The reader is led to believe the son may have something to do with it, but the big twist is that it was the husband all along. Nobody ever gets it, and I'm surprised he has.

'How do you know?' I ask.

'Monsieur, in my line of work, you know, it is always the 'usband.' He laughs. I chuckle along and hand the book back.

'See you,' I say.

'Enjoy your 'oliday. *Bonne journée,*' he says with a wave, picking the book back up, and finding his page.

I get into the car, and with *American Psycho* still playing on my mind, I put Patrick Bateman's favourite killing-spree soundtrack on, Phil Collins, and strike the steering wheel as the drum solo kicks in. The song fades out. An image of Robyn creeps into my head and I'm left with that same sobering feeling of a distant missile getting closer. 'Fuck,' I spit, banging on the wheel.

As I reach the end of the A road, I take the left that will take me to the *hameau*. I turn, slowing, as I notice a figure, and an upturned bike. Ah, Juliette. I stop and roll my window down.

'*Bonjour!*'

She looks over, a smile spreading as she recognises me. '*Ah, salut, Morgan,*' she jokes.

I point at her bike. 'Broken?'

'*Oui.*' She lifts it up and back on its wheels. 'I can walk it.'

'Let me give you a lift,' I suggest.

Her long legs have been swiped with black oil from the tyres, and she's tied her mass of hair in a haphazard bun, with that same red scrunchie. 'It's okay.' She shakes her head. 'Your car is tiny! It will scratch,' she says, as I get out the vehicle.

'I'm sure we can sort something,' I tell her, walking to the back of the car and opening the boot. 'Here, let me,' I say, picking up the bike and manoeuvring it inside. Half of it sticks out the back. I scratch my head and look over at Juliette, who is wiping her hands on the grass verge.

She turns around and laughs. 'Oh, Felix! This is silly. I can walk it.'

'No bother, I'll drive slowly. It isn't far.'

'If you're sure,' she agrees, and we get back in.

'No bother.' She laughs, mimicking the way I talk. I smile at her sweet-natured audacity as I turn back onto the road.

'So impressive you're writing a 'ole book 'ere.'

'Well, just a first draft. If we died tomorrow, we'd be mortified if anyone found it. And besides, Emma will probably . . .' I stop myself. 'It will be much better after an edit.'

'But still, a book. Creating something like that. Well . . . I feel very proud to have met you!' I get that usual lick of pride, followed by a sick feeling. 'And to get to come somewhere

117

like this and do what you love. Isn't that what people dream about?'

I snort. 'I don't love writing.'

She looks at me, astounded, 'But . . .'

'I hate it. It's abysmal. You sit and write and write and your head is giving you a running commentary of how horrific you are. It's like wallowing in self-pity for months and months until finally you sort of scrape something together.' And then someone else buffs it up to make it palatable. I managed to stop myself saying that last part out loud.

'Then why do you do it?' she asks, intrigued.

'Because if I don't, I feel worse.'

She blinks, no idea how to reply. She doesn't understand. No one does.

'Life terrifies me.' The words come out before I can stop them. I have no idea why I'm confiding in her. This woman from France who knows nothing about me, about my life. Maybe that's why. 'It's my only way of finding a release from it. If I don't write, how will I know I'm feeling anything?' I look at her. 'That sounds incredibly wanky, doesn't it?'

'Wanky?' she repeats. 'What is this word?'

I laugh. 'Pretentious.'

'Ah. I think you should just quit. *Voilà!*' she says with a shrug.

'What? Just like that?' I snap my fingers.

'If something isn't making me 'appy, I just stop, move on. Life is short, right?'

'So, you're happy hanging out here, working in people's houses, in bars?'

118

She frowns. Maybe I've gone too far. 'For now. But when it stops being fun, I'll leave. That is what I have always done. It works for me.'

'But what do you want to do? Don't you want to achieve something tangible with your life?' I ask and she just smirks.

'If I am 'appy, then I will 'ave lived well, don't you think?'

The simplicity of this idea renders me speechless. I've always been striving, always.

'My mother died a very painful death after spending most of her adult life looking after me. And just when I was old enough for 'er to be selfish for a change, she died. I was with 'er those final months, in 'er little cottage, 'olding her hand, feeding 'er, changing 'er. She made me promise I would live every moment, every second of it. Life is short, Felix.'

I glance over at her. She's staring at the view, a bittersweet look on her face.

'I'm so sorry.' I'm terrible at conversations like this, and it's the only thing I can think to say.

She turns to look at me. 'Don't be,' she whispers as our eyes lock. Then she realises where we are. 'This is me,' she says, pointing to a little house on the edge of the *hameau*.

'It's lovely,' I tell her.

She grins. 'It is perfect for what I need.'

She gets her bike out the back, refusing my help, and walks over to her cottage. She seems so different to the girls I encounter back home who are waiting for their big break in the big city. Juliette doesn't think like that, and I like it. She's older than them, I suppose, but there is something pure-hearted about her candidness. I can imagine her in her sixties with that same riot of hair, streaked with grey, in some surfing town in Morocco or something.

'Hey!' I call out as she walks away with her bike. She stops and turns, waiting for me to speak. 'So, you really think I should just jack it all in?' I ask, my arm hanging out the window.

She shrugs. 'What 'ave you got to lose?'

'My career, money, status . . . you know, everything.' I humour her.

She shrugs. 'Money, status. *Mon dieu*, Felix, you're really fucked up, you know that? They've trapped you and you don't even know it,' she says with a wide smile that lets me know she's playing. I nod and wave her goodbye. Her skirt lifts with the breeze and I grin. I haven't thought about Robyn the whole time I was with her.

Maybe all I need is a new distraction.

# CHAPTER FOURTEEN

'You've been gone for what feels like for ever,' Emma says, walking out of the main door as I park. She must have heard the tyres on the gravel and been pacing irritably in the hallway for my return. She opens the boot, then slams it shut. Comes over to the passenger door and opens it, putting her head inside. 'Where is all the stuff?' she asks. I'd made up some stupid excuse to get out, which I'd completely forgotten about.

'Oh, I had an epiphany about my chapter and wanted to get back and get on with it,' I say quickly. She'll like that.

'What's that smell?' she asks.

'What smell?' *God, do I stink of booze?*

'Roses,' she states. 'Was someone else in the car? It smells like perfume.' She stares at me.

'No!' I look around. 'You must be imagining it. I can't smell anything.' The lie came effortlessly, I have no idea why I said it. It seemed easier, I suppose.

She looks perturbed but closes the door. 'Come on, time to get on with it!' she calls as she heads back into the house.

I sigh and do as I'm told and walk into the study. I sit down behind the desk. New Post-its have emerged since I was last in here. I cast my eyes across them, then put my head in my hands. I need to make the reader believe in Sebastian and Hanna as a couple. Hanna had a small baby, that's a lot of baggage to take on. He must have fallen hard and fast. And Emma stated in a previous chapter that they moved to Phoenix six months ago. So, before Ivy turned one, they met, fell in love, got married. All very fast. Like Emma and me, I suppose.

Our honeymoon period was writing our first book and when we got our deal, I was so blown away by it all I asked her to be my wife. I didn't have a ring or anything. I just blurted it out without thinking whether I meant it. It was one of those halcyon midsummer days when we felt impossibly young. We were walking along Brooklyn Bridge holding hands. Max phoned, and our whole world was ripped apart. We'd screamed joyously at the gaping sky as I spun her around. Our dreams had come true. It just felt right to whisper, 'Marry me.'

These thoughts permeate as I take my seat and reread her chapter. I need to get Sebastian and Nancy to the point where Hanna is forced to act. I wipe my face. *Right then.*

*He met Hanna in a café, one of the ones with a kids' play area in the back. It was the closest to his apartment, so he was there most mornings, grabbing a caffeine hit before the day began. Hanna had been laughing with the guy behind the counter. She'd lost her phone and was discussing all her clumsy antics with such mirth, he was drawn in. They got talking too. It was only after a while that she said she'd better get back to her baby, who was asleep in the pram. Sebastian had searched her hand for a ring, but she didn't have one. Then she made a self-deprecating joke about being a single mother and he thought, Wow. To have all that responsibility and still be thriving, what a gal.*

*And there was this beautiful woman, and this gorgeous baby, just there. Like Ivy had been sent down especially for him. Hanna was so easy to fall in love with. So full of life and relaxed with Ivy. It is only since they moved that she's changed. This need to be perfect all the time. And hermitting herself away, with Ivy. It's infuriating. Although he hates to say it, it isn't what he signed up for.*

I swallow, my fingers tingling from what I've written. It came out easily. And I know why, don't I? *Like Ivy had been sent down, especially for him.* I slam the laptop screen down in disgust. *Fuck this.* I get out the chair, and then sit down again. If I stay in here, under the guise of work, I can go back out and Emma will be in bed, and I won't have to look into her eyes knowing I'm keeping something from her: Robyn.

I open the laptop again and pull up Twitter, typing *Robyn Avery*. My mouth goes dry as a Tweet pops up:

*HAS ANYONE SEEN ROBYN AVERY?*
*LAST SEEN 8th JULY 2024 –*
*PLEASE CALL 555-0100 WITH ANY INFORMATION.*

The photo depicts Robyn on a night out. She's wearing a sparkly top and her face is turned over a shoulder, with her

123

usual neat bun at the top of her head. She looks happy. I wonder where that face is now. I blink as an image of her hanging from a tree or floating in the Hudson pops into my mind. *No. She couldn't have, could she? Did I hurt her that badly? No, come on, Felix. This is nothing to do with you.*

The tweet hasn't got much traction yet. It seems to have been posted by a family member and hasn't broken through to the wider consciousness. I really should tell Emma; this is about to spill over, I can feel it. My fingers shake as I type her name into the main search engine. My shoulders fall as I realise there is nothing, the story hasn't hit the press yet. There must be a reason the police aren't taking this seriously; I console myself with that. Usually when a pretty blonde goes missing you can't get away from it.

I pull up Robyn's Instagram account. We'd blocked her from everything but I can still see hers without logging in. She doesn't look like she's depressed or having a hard time. She's in the gym, out with friends. Even standing next to a handsome guy holding hands. Her boyfriend? My lips grimace as I feel a stab of jealousy. I study her posts, her excited exclamation marks, and comments from friends. She doesn't seem like she's about to pack her things and head to skid row. But social media lies, we all know that. I bang the screen down and spark a cigarette, listening for Emma's footsteps on the stairs on her way to bed, so I can avoid her before leaving the room and heading out to my usual spot on the veranda.

*

Finally, an hour or so later, hearing the creaking stairs, I make my way into the living room. Emma has left me some food on the counter which I ignore, instead heading for the fridge and grabbing a bottle of something cold, I walk outside, taking a seat at the table, and sigh as I pour a glass. Robyn's face nags at me, the sound of her voice ringing in my ears as if I heard it yesterday. She's probably already home. It must be some huge misunderstanding. My leg jiggles as I think of it getting blown out of proportion, our affair splashed across every paper from New York to London. Oh, what a horrific nightmare. I keep drinking. More urgency to it now. I crave oblivion, anything, to get me out of my head.

I think of Juliette and how free she is here – her life a simple barefoot summer with nothing harrying her, no deadlines to meet, no people to perform for, just simple tasks easy to accomplish. Maybe she is right. Maybe I could just walk away from it all.

I hear something inside. I stand, swaying slightly with the effects of the drink, and peer through the window. There Emma is, in the middle of the room. That same glazed look. My first instinct is to go to her and lead her back upstairs. But then, another part of me is intrigued. How far will she take this?

She crosses the room, and joins me on the veranda. A breeze catches the ends of her hair as she stares soberly towards the wall, and the cliff. Emma steps robotically off the veranda and onto the grass. I hang back as she lingers in the centre of the outstretched green lawn, her whole body turned towards the cliff. Then, like some sort of angel, or effigy, she raises her arms and tilts her face up to the moonlight.

I follow her down, circling her, taking in every inch as the evening breeze licks at the fabric of her nightdress.

Then she moves, with those same considered steps, and I follow her to the left. When she reaches the edge of the lawn, where the wall is, she stops. She wouldn't climb over it. Surely not.

But I watch, aghast, as she calmly ambles over. I follow her over clumsily, trying to walk in her straight line, but I stumble. The horizon is bent out of shape and woozy through my inebriation.

She stops again, as we make it to the cliff, my breath scant as she moves towards it. She stops about three metres from the edge, and I walk towards her. 'Emma?' I say softly. I should wake her gently or pull at her arm and force her the other way.

But then other thoughts appear. Could I . . . just let her go? What would happen if she were to step off the lip? Would all my problems go away? Would eradicating Emma from my life actually make it better? Would I be free? I wouldn't have done anything wrong, if I just let it happen, would I? She moves again. One step, two . . . My heart thuds in my chest. They wouldn't believe me, would they? They would think that I pushed her, surely?

*What am I even weighing up here?*

*Jesus.*

I come to my senses and stride towards her, grabbing her arm. 'Come on, Emma, let's get you back to bed.' She tries to pull away, moaning as she attempts to struggle towards the cliff. But I hang on tightly. 'Come on, it's this way,' I tell her forcefully, and she gives in, allowing me to guide her back to the house.

With every step I try to dislodge my terrible thoughts, and give a last glance back to the cliff, shuddering at the man that I know dwells within me.

When we get into the house, I lock the back door, bolting it at the top and bottom, guiding Emma from behind as she places one foot in front of the other up the stairs. She dutifully lies down on the bed and I throw the sheet over her, tucking it gently under her chin. I lay my head on the pillow next to hers and stare at her face. The grim idea floats through my mind that had I not been there, she could be dead.

My eyes are red raw and gritty, dehydrated from my booze-filled system. I'm scared to sleep in case it happens again. In case I must listen to my head debating things it shouldn't. Emma's wild and overzealous imagination has been provoked. All the stress of writing this ninth book, with the threads of our marriage in flux, must have caused it.

The room spins, the nausea overwhelming. I am desperate to let my eyelids drop, but I am too afraid. My eyes fall on the olive-green strap of her robe. And an idea, poorly formed, appears. I glance up to the iron bars of the bed frame and think of her dainty wrists. Could I tie her to the bed? Is that crazy? Then I think of Emma's words to Juliette when she told us the story – *I would have tied her to the damn bed*. And then later, when I'd told her about her night wanderings – *You know what to do*. She'd want me to do it. She's given me permission to.

I get up and retrieve the robe strap. I knot the fabric to the bed, shaking slightly, the fabric burning my skin as I forcefully tighten it. I yank it, testing its strength – there is no way she could break free or untie it in her sleep. Then I leave enough slack so that her arm can comfortably fall by her side and pick up her other slender wrist and lace the opposite end of the strap beneath it, before knotting it twice. It puckers her skin at first, and she whimpers. I loosen it and try again. Once satisfied, I stare at the tether I have created. She won't be able to get up, not shackled there like that.

Now I can sink into oblivion.

# CHAPTER FIFTEEN

I wake up, with the frantic sense there is something amiss. I feel about on the other side of the bed. Nothing. Emma isn't next to me. I get up quickly, stars flooding my eyes at the swift movement. I rush to the window, the bright sunlight hitting my retinas, and I wince. Recovering, I peer down. My shoulders relax as I see her swimming lengths in the pool. She's fine. Memories of the previous night feel like the dregs of delirium.

I return to the bed frame, and hold the robe strap in my hands, letting the silk fall limply back to the post. It was real. It did happen.

I tied my wife to the bed.

I sit down on the edge of the mattress, staring ahead at the motes of dust in the sunlight. Robyn was in my dreams. She was crying out, asking for help. There is no escape. She has invaded my senses again. There was a time when all I could think of was her: when I discussed work with Emma or made dinner. Or sat in a boring meeting about marketing campaigns. My mind was invested in a different story, a fantasy. Of pushing her body against my desk, of bowing between her legs and biting her knickers. Of teasing her with a kiss and making her moan. I thought after it happened once that urge would go away. But it lingered and grew until it got out of hand.

I swipe my phone. Maybe Max has contacted me with news. But there is nothing. I debate asking him. I even start drafting a message but delete it. He'll pester me to tell Emma and I need more time. 'No news is good news,' I remind myself. I swallow. What happened between us wasn't that bad, was it? It didn't make her want to hurt herself, did it? I remember in one of Robyn's messages she told me someone had poisoned her name to every publishing house in the city, and she was unemploy-able. I'd dismissed it as a guilt-tripping exercise. Was it true?

I remember Emma watching us both in the car, on the way to an airport. My exchanges with Robyn were friendly by then; we'd found how to make each other laugh, and were enjoying the ease with which it was possible. I hadn't muted it for Emma's presence. Maybe part of me was desperate for her to react, for her to care. For her to fight for me, instead of her constant indifference.

I see what it was now. I was angry, and I wanted to get my own back. I wanted to show her what other women saw in me. But she just continued looking out the window, occasionally turning to glance, a bemused look on her face, as if watching a puppy playing with a dustbin lid.

I pick up my phone, ready to do some scrolling to get out of my head. But I see Emma's chapter and sigh. I may as well see where we're up to.

Morgansavage@infinitymail.com
14.07.2023

**Subject:** Book 9 – First Draft

## *CHAPTER NINE – HER*

The unvarying hiss of white noise is the soundtrack as she battles the thorny bush in the yard with clippers. Hanna started using it to get the baby to sleep. But now she likes it in her ears as she works, turning it up high, so the damaging thoughts cannot fight through it. Hiss, hiss.

'Ouch,' she mutters, looking down at a finger, squeezing the flesh with her nail so a solitary drop flowers up on her skin. An earbud falls and the comforting sound disappears.

She stands, and hears a car in the distance, a plane overhead. She puts her hands over her ears, trying to stop it, but they come for her.

Cheating. The thing about that is that once it's happened, and Hanna is sure it has here, it will happen again, and again and again. What was it that Jerry Hall said? A whore in the bedroom and a maid in the kitchen – something like that. Hanna has been that! She made sure she was everything he could ever want, and he has still strayed.

She has no choice: she must do something to keep him.

Leaving her things on the grass, she walks swiftly into the house. He'll be back soon, and she is a mess. She marches with purpose up the stairs and into their room, rushing through her wardrobe of dresses until she finds it. The green *velvet hip-hugging one she knows she looks a million dollars in.*

*She must keep all of this; she can't go back to the stark reality of life before. Part of the remit of the perfect wife is going out, drinking wine, and laughing at his jokes. Making him feel like a man. Letting him have sex with her. Because she's let that part of the deal slide recently. So, she must put the lipstick on. And those stockings he likes with the suspenders that made him groan the first time he saw them. She holds the dress up and stares at herself in the mirror. She'll look just the right amount of alluring. He will forget about that stupid girl once he lays his eyes on her. And if he doesn't?*

*Well, she'll just have to think of something else.*

I move my eyes away from the text, feeling a little sick.

'Felix!' I hear Emma cry from down below.

I ignore the rest of the chapter and move back to the window.

'Felix! Come down, have a coffee with me,' she calls, drying herself with a towel.

'Coming!'

I make my way down the stairs and out the back doors. Down to where she is lying on the lounger. She pats the cushion and I sit. She's wearing a bikini today with a knot at the front which binds her breasts snugly. She sits up, leaning over me, resting her chin on my shoulder. She smells like chlorine and sun cream.

'You tied me to the bed,' she whispers.

'You asked me to!' I quickly charge, expecting her to be cross.

She laughs lightly. 'It's fine. I did. Thank you.' Her hands snake around my chest, her lips graze my ear seductively. 'It's quite romantic actually, when you think about it.' Her voice is throaty, and my heart begins to thud in my chest. 'All tied up while I was fast asleep.' I feel a surge of something, something she's not allowed me to feel for a long time. Her hand moves down to my shorts, and I feel her fingers search towards my crotch. 'Almost like a fantasy.' Blood rushes, and I turn to face her, eagerly wanting to kiss her, feel her. I am excited by the idea she might let me.

But she laughs. In an instant she has pulled away. Her hands, gone.

She gets up, yanking the fabric of her sarong with her. 'I've got some admin to do,' Emma says, yawning, 'and then I'll take a siesta. I don't know why you put off working all day. I just can't relax until it's off my desk.'

'I'm not putting it off,' I tell her, frustrated at how quickly the moment passed. 'I'm just thinking.'

'Don't think too hard, you'll give yourself a headache!' she shouts as she floats back towards the house in a haze of opaque material.

I lie back on the sunlounger and look up at the wispy clouds slowly detaching from one another. I manage to endure the horrible swirling thoughts about Robyn for a few minutes, until the pull to dilute them with alcohol becomes too strong. I sit up, planning to go into the kitchen, but

133

see Emma's silhouette working at the table in there, doing whatever it is I should really be helping her with – emailing our film agent, or writing an article for a magazine. I decide against it. I can't bear her questioning looks as I open the fridge.

Instead, I walk down the lawn. Apparently, the orchard covers the right-hand descent of the hill, down to the row of houses we pass on our drive up to the bastide. I walk through the trees, the dry ground hard and lumpy, covered in curled-up dead leaves which crunch as I tread. About ten minutes in, I come across a low wall, which must be the boundary to the plot. The crumbling divide barely goes above my knees and is easy to step over.

I continue my wander, picking an apple, dusting it on my T-shirt before taking a bite. Sebastian, what is he going to do? He loves Ivy deeply; could he leave her? Sebastian is a good man; he would stay for the sake of the child and surrender to misery. He wouldn't do what I've done and cheat on his wife. He is a better man than me. But it must get worse before it resolves itself, otherwise where would the story be?

A cool breeze rushes past, giving off a tapping chorus of leaves. And then I hear something human – a soft cry. Is someone hurt? Another fox perhaps. No, it doesn't sound like that. Curiosity gets the better of me and I walk towards it, stopping when I see the source, and I hang back behind a tree.

Bodies. Against a trunk. Juliette's skirt is up around her waist and his trousers are down. I think it's that guy she was working in the bar with. Was it Marco? His butt is clenched as he moves into her body. Her chin up, her mouth open in pleasure. Her hands grabbing on to the skin on his back.

I swallow thickly. The details are rushing towards me, and it's impossible to look away. The way she's biting her lip to stop herself from shouting. The way her nails are digging into his flesh. His noises too, more guttural, a low animalistic growl. I've watched porn, sure, loads of it. But this. I've never watched like this.

I'm too scared to move. My fingers grapple with the trunk of the tree. I can't steal my eyes away. Sweat collects in my neckline. Her moans become rhythmical as if charging towards a crescendo. Finally, she cries out, her eyes burst open and squint into the sky. He falls into her neck, and she strokes his hair absent-mindedly as she regulates her breathing. Her eyes move to a more central position. They blink, staring in my direction. I slip back, and turn away, walking quickly. Did she see me? Did she?

I hear whispered words. Giggles. Laughter. Fun. Oh, yes, I remember that. The sound of a belt buckle as trousers are pulled up. She can't have seen me; she would have stopped. I would hear shouting in my direction.

As I pick my way back through the orchard, I can't get the heat of the scene out of my head. A throbbing stiffness in my crotch, and I press down on it, to quell the stirring. The image of Juliette's upturned face, and how she gripped on to her own breast. I imagine pushing her body up against a tree. Sliding my hand up her thighs into the pocket of wetness. I fall against a tree; I can't help but slide my hand into my shorts. So stiff. So in need of ending the longing.

'Felix!' Emma's voice rings up into the sky. *Shit.* 'Felix!' She's looking for me.

The glistening water of the pool spins at me through the branches. Emma is just there; I can see her colourful sarong through the thicket. 'Felix!' she calls again, trying to summon me. I hear her sigh as she gives up. She hasn't seen me yet.

I wait. Last thing I want is to walk out of here with a hard-on. She'll go back into the house soon. But to my dismay she sits on the lounger and takes a sip of wine, bringing a book to her face. I take a deep breath and wait for the urge in my trousers to calm.

A few minutes later I break free. 'Lovely walk,' I mutter as I walk past, quickly, wanting to get to the house. 'I might have a shower, I'm all sweaty.' I tug at my T-shirt to illustrate the point. I have that spoilt feeling straight after sex, like I'm covered in it.

She goes to reply, but is then distracted by something, and she looks over my shoulder. A laugh rises into the sky from deep within the orchard. Her eyes trail up me, thinking. She purses her lips, and stares. 'Felix,' she whispers. 'You were gone a long time.'

'Better get on with it,' I tell her as I rush away.

# CHAPTER SIXTEEN

It's the next evening and I've been sitting here for hours torturing myself in front of my laptop screen. I sit back in my chair. I go to add more but sit back again. I've been craning over this for hours, just to get these few words down. It's an okay scene. Sebastian has forced Hanna to see a medical professional about her anxiety, but she has refused to tell the doctor the truth about how she has been feeling and behaving, and he's frustrated when they leave. The walls are closing in. Sebastian feels like Hanna is one person at home, and a completely different version when she needs to put on a show, making it seem as if he's a controlling partner.

I tap my finger on the desk. I have no idea where to go from here. How am I meant to write with all this going on with Robyn? It's impossible. The timing is just terrible! My head is a jumbled mess and I slam the screen down and get up.

I am met by a delicious smell when I enter the living area. To my surprise, Emma is in the kitchen. The matching set of copper pans usually hung on the wall are on the hob steaming. Half-cut vegetables lie on thick wooden chopping boards. She has a tea towel over her shoulder and sweaty curls of hair are stuck to her forehead.

'What are you doing?' I ask, nearly laughing, as I pour myself a glass of whisky.

She swivels, knife in hand. 'I'm cooking dinner,' she replies, as if it is the most natural thing on earth.

'That's not like you,' I tell her, as I drag out a dining chair to sit on. Emma has set the beautifully battered table with a trio of little glass vases down the centre. After a few days in the sun, she has a light sprinkle of a tan across the bridge of her nose. But she looks beat, as if she is preoccupied. Must be the book. It always is.

There is a quiet knock on the back door. I turn, and see the outline of Juliette. Emma wipes her hands on her apron. 'I invited Juliette, I thought it was nice for her to have some company, and she was so kind to bring us up some fresh baguettes earlier.' I am startled. The last time I saw her she was in the throes of an orgasm. I can't help but heat up at the sight of her. I feel that sort of coy embarrassment the first time you see someone after a night of passion, even though it wasn't me at all.

'Come in!' Emma calls, smiling over at her.

'Oh, this smells *bon* – delicious!' Juliette says, walking through to the kitchen, admiring Emma's work. 'A *festin*! A Feast,' she clarifies for us.

'Please, take a seat,' Emma tells her, placing some cutlery on the table. 'You are right on time, I'm just serving.'

Juliette helps by setting the places before taking the seat

138

opposite mine. She smiles over at me, and I return it, feeling awkward. The atmosphere is confounded by an electric buzz that the women seem completely unaware of.

Emma carries out the plated food and sets it down in front of us. 'This smells *exquis*,' Juliette says, moving her face in front of the food and taking in the steaming aroma.

'I don't cook often, but when I do, I like to do it properly,' Emma explains. 'Please, dig in,' Emma commands, going back into the kitchen to get her own plate. She sits down and I pour the table wine. Emma's lips twitch.

'This lavender is lovely, Emma. Did you take it from the garden?' Juliette asks, touching the buds on the table.

'Oh, yes. The purple is so vivid, they are lovely,' Emma replies.

Juliette nods. 'It is very potent up 'ere. I make a great sleep aid with it.'

'You make it?' I ask.

Juliette nods. 'I learnt a lot about 'omeopathy from my mother.' I watch as she swallows the sadness of mentioning her mother down, quickly moving on. 'It is amazing what you can do with what you 'ave growing in your own garden.'

'Homeopathy,' Emma says, as if she finds the thought absurd. Emma is more into hardcore prescription drugs than St John's Wort. Her doctor is practically her best friend, and she sends him a Thanksgiving hamper every year to stay in favour. As a kid from Blighty, I still haven't got my head around the US medical system.

'Well,' Juliette says, 'I saw 'ow the work changed people. I wanted to learn 'ow to 'eal others too,' she states with simple grace that I can tell has riled Emma.

Emma nods. 'Sorry, I didn't mean to offend, I'm sure there must be something in it,' she replies, picking up her fork, a tight patronising smile as she takes a bite. God, she is hard work sometimes. Not everyone has to think what you think for you to like them.

'You think I am silly?' Juliette replies, and I'm impressed she hasn't let Emma off the hook.

'No. I just find some of that a bit wishy-washy. Not much science in there.'

Juliette raises her eyebrows and picks up my tumbler of whisky, which I hadn't quite finished before the meal. She holds it up to the light. 'This is whisky. It is made from fermented grain. And you are . . .' she pauses, lowering her chin, as if she is about to say something she shouldn't, and her big eyes track mine – 'drunk?'

I laugh. 'Getting there.'

'Yes.' Emma tuts.

'If a grain can chemically change your mind, your ability to walk, talk, for example, why shouldn't other natural elements change other parts of you, or 'eal you? Change your chemical make-up?' She places the glass down.

I nod. Juliette is something else. 'Yes,' I utter, in agreement. 'That does make sense.' I switch my gaze, feeling I've spent too long there, and check on Emma's reaction. It is hard to impress my wife, but I can see she is set between bemusement and fascination.

'Yes, well, we have often used home remedies in our books, poisonings – aconite, belladonna, the one you get from foxglove, I can't remember . . .' Emma looks into the air, thinking.

'Digitalis,' Juliette replies.

'Yes . . .' Emma says. *A truce*, I think.

Emma looks at Juliette's food, an undistinguishable twist on her lips, as if she has swallowed something rancid. Then she takes a sip of her wine. 'Well, I hope you are enjoying this concoction,' Emma says, her fork digging into her meal.

'*Oui* – you should join Pierre at the restaurant!' Juliette says. 'Very good for an American.' She tries the joke on Emma. But Emma just stares at her, with a vague smile which could be interpreted either way. Juliette quickly drops her eyes and continues to eat.

Women often find Emma off-putting. The way she isn't scared to look someone directly in their eyes, unashamed. They assume she is judging them, but often that isn't the case. She is watching every inflection, every movement. Every smile crease and confused gaze. Narrowing her eyes to remember every detail. Is that what she is doing now? Is that why she invited Juliette to stay for dinner? Is she taking notes for how to write Nancy? Or is that character based on someone else?

'What is your new book about?' Juliette asks between mouthfuls.

'It's about a woman on the edge, after her husband's infidelities,' Emma tells her. I sit up at this.

'Not quite. *Perceived* infidelities,' I remind her.

'Felix is refusing to write him as a cheater, I'm not sure

141

why.' Emma laughs. 'All part of the thrill when you write with someone else. Having to sidestep your own experiences and subconscious needs.' I shake my head slowly, the truth behind what she is saying yanking down on me.

Juliette is looking between us, confused. 'It sounds fantastic. I will read this one, I promise,' she says.

'Oh, Juliette, that is very sweet. But please don't feel like you have to,' Emma tells her. 'It's refreshing to hang out with someone who couldn't care less about all that.'

I let my cutlery clatter on my plate. I've finished the whole thing off. 'Oh, Felix, I'm so pleased you enjoyed it,' Emma says, reaching over and squeezing my hand. 'Is there anything better than watching your husband enjoy a meal you've prepared?' she asks, smiling warmly at Juliette. 'Just so rewarding.'

'It was absolutely delicious.' I choke slightly, the last of the red sauce slipping down my throat.

'I'm so pleased you both think so.' And she sits back, holding her hands together, her elbows on the table. A withholding smile. As if she knows something we don't.

# CHAPTER SEVENTEEN

Morning. I squint at the date and time on my phone. We've been in France just over a week, but it feels like a month already. It takes me a moment to find the strength to look through my notifications, with the idea that a horrifying piece of news could have pinged into my phone as I slept. Nothing about Robyn. *Yet*, my inner voice whispers, and I shudder. I see Emma's chapter nestled in between the fraff and I groan. Another day. Another chapter.

Morgansavage@infinitymail.com
15.07.2024
**Subject:** Book 9 – First Draft

### *CHAPTER THIRTEEN – HER*

*Hanna watches Sebastian and Nancy chatting through the opaque curtains. Once again, they are out there, finding a reason to talk. It is almost a daily occurrence. Do they also meet up behind her back when she thinks he's at work? Her stomach crunches at the thought of it. Sebastian is so close he can probably* smell her sweat, her rose-scented perfume. See the acne scar on her right cheek, and the cute little mole she has on her earlobe.

A few days later, he comes to Hanna with an idea. They are to have Nancy over for lunch to help Ivy settle in with her. As the fire grows within at the suggestion, he regales her with day trips they could take, the theatre productions they could see – once she's shaken off the worry of leaving Ivy. Apparently, she'd be able to 'relax and enjoy her life again'. What a stupid, stupid man.

Her fingers curl into her palms, her nails digging into the skin. Why is he so set on this girl being in their lives? He is obsessed with making her part of it. What is she to do?

The day of the supposed lunch, her phone rings. She doesn't recognise the number and rejects it. It can't be who she fears. They can't have found her. But the phone rings again and the smile freezes. She rejects the call hastily and brushes down her apron, twisting her neck until it clicks. Everything is okay. Okay. Okay. She realises her hands are shaking. She just needs something to distract her.

Hanna steps into the garden, and places Ivy next to her on the rug, but the little toddler gets up and totters around. Hanna digs a little, looking. Searching. Ivy joins her, getting her little hands mucky within the dirt. Then Hanna comes across what she was looking for. Luckily it rained a bit last night. She pulls a little writhing body out of the mud. Ivy goes, 'Ewwwww.'

'Worm, can you say worm?' But Ivy just giggles. Hanna puts about five wriggling bodies into the little ceramic bowl she brought outside, before picking up Ivy and taking her into the kitchen, placing her in the high chair. She takes the squirming worms over to the food processor and adds them in, before

144

*pouring a tin of chopped tomatoes too. Some delicious red
sauce. 'Yummy!' she tells Ivy. The little girl giggles. 'Yum, yum,
yum.' She rubs her tummy.*

*Later, during this forced lunch with Sebastian and Nancy,
there is nothing more entertaining than watching her
charming husband doing all he can to entertain this stupid
girl. As they chew on the delights of her cooking, telling her
over and over how delicious it is.*

*Hanna hasn't had such a good time for a very long time.*

I sit back on the large pillow and catch my breath. The
chapter has made me feel sick. No, more than that – repulsed.
The taste of red sauce from the previous night assembles in
my mouth. A full-frontal recollection of a piece of grit as I
chewed. The idea of a secret ingredient makes me want to
vomit. *No!* That is a ridiculous thought. Emma wouldn't serve
us worms. That's insane.

She must have got the idea of the red sauce from the meal
she cooked last night. Grew it in her mind, adding something
extra audacious.

I get up. Birds chirp in the distance. I have the urge to look
Emma in the eye, make sure that the words on the page don't
match up to my wife.

I make my way downstairs, and there she is, sitting on the
veranda, reading. Looking completely normal. She notices me.
'Morning, honey,' she says leisurely. 'Did you sleep well?' She
takes a sip of her coffee, and leans back, closing her eyes to
bask in the sun. I wonder if I am imagining the self-satisfied
smile upon her lips.

# CHAPTER EIGHTEEN

Once I've put it off as long as viably possible, and Emma's lips have begun to twitch as her eyes wander over to me irritably, I clap my hands together. 'I'll ... just get on with it then.' The door to the study looms ahead. I really don't want to go in there. But I can't see another way. So, I go inside and shut the door, taking a seat on the high-backed office chair Emma sent ahead of our arrival.

*Right, where were we?* I force myself to ignore the itch to procrastinate. *Where to next?* I look up at the Post-it notes. *S & N get closer – THEY NEED TO KISS – OR SOMETHING!* (she's underlined this twice). There is a new one that stops me in my tracks. I peel it off and it shakes in my hand: *Lamb to slaughter.* I swallow, remembering the conversation in the supermarket the other day. *She needs to die!*

I sigh, looking out the window at the luminous view as I think of the following scene. Okay, Sebastian's at work drinks, he's drunk, he knows he needs to get back to Hanna but is dreading it. He pays the tab for the entire group and they cheer – that's what Sebastian would do, he's a good guy. But he needs to bump into Nancy. Maybe she's at the same bar, also tipsy after a date. Maybe he offers her a lift back in his taxi.

And then they should kiss. Emma is right, it is what the story needs. I take a breath and begin.

'How's Hanna?' Nancy asks.

*Sebastian rubs an eye with his knuckle. What a question. 'I dunno. Good days, bad days. She isn't . . .' He sighs. He shouldn't be saying these things to anyone else. What happens in a marriage is private. But he's new in town, and doesn't have any long-standing relationships to confide in. 'I didn't know much about her background when we met, and she held off on a few things.' He thinks about all the prescription pills she hid from him.*

*He takes a drag of his cigarette and glances over at her. She looks full of sympathy. 'You must have been together for some time? Having Ivy and all.'*

*'Ah, no.' He pauses, another drag, enjoying the hit on the back of his throat. 'Ivy isn't mine. She was six months old when we met.' He must be drunk, telling her all this stuff.*

*'Oh,' Nancy replies, surprised. 'I'm sure it'll work out,' she whispers. Touching his arm. She stumbles. 'Gawd, sorry, I'm drunk,' she says, holding her head and giggling.*

*'You're so lucky,' he whispers out into the stillness of the night.*

*She snorts. 'Why?'*

*'You could literally go anywhere, do anything. I'd been desperate for something for so long and now I've got it, I've never been more miserable,' he confides.*

'Isn't that just being human? Never being satisfied?' she asks. Sebastian nods. She could never understand. No one does. From the outside he has everything. 'Wanna share a cab home?' she asks, already on her phone ordering one.

'Sure.'

A few minutes later a black Buick pulls up, and he opens the door for Nancy. 'Was that your boyfriend at the bar?' he asks.

'Kind of,' she replies. 'I mean, I'm only with Hank and Jolene for a few more months and then I'm meant to be going to Europe, travelling.'

'Have the best time. Really, drink every second up,' he advises. They sit in silence as the taxi drives down the freeway and makes the turning into their suburb and then onto their street.

They get out of the car. 'Bye then,' he says to her as they hover in the middle of the street.

'Night, Seb.' She waves as she heads to the house opposite.

Sebastian opens the front door. He's sure he can hear footsteps clambering up the stairs inside. But it's late, and he's drunk. He must have imagined it.

I sit back, staring at the jumble of words in front of me. No, they didn't kiss. I can't seem to bring myself to do it to him. I can't allow him to fall to my level.

I find Emma reading by the pool. She slaps the book down with a sigh when she sees me. 'Merrick's new one is brilliant. How irritating,' she says. Our arch rival, who has requested we read and endorse his next book. Pure torture. 'All okay?' she asks, referring to my chapter.

'Yep, I just emailed it over.'

I check my watch. It's late afternoon.

'Last night was nice, wasn't it? I feel sorry for that girl. She seems so aimless.'

'I don't know, Emma, she seems happy. Not everyone is bound by the same rules.'

She makes a sort of humph sound. 'She likes you,' she tries. *Oh, I see.*

'I'm sure she just likes the idea of celebrities being in the house. Besides, I'm just being friendly! Where is the harm in that?'

She gives me a cold hard stare.

'You invited her for dinner!'

'I was bored! She was standing there delivering bread, practically begging to hang out with us.' Then she lets out a laugh and the atmosphere changes. 'What could I do?' Her hand slaps my arm playfully. 'I'm just kidding. She's lovely! And she's been very helpful.' She looks at the time. 'Come on, better do this on the kitchen table out of the heat,' she says, looking over at me expectantly.

'Do what?' I ask.

'Felix, haven't you checked the diary? I made it shared for a reason, so I wouldn't have to chase you like your personal assistant reminding you of things.' I look at her blankly. 'We have a Zoom call with Max booked in. He said it was important. And you know how he hates these video call things.' I swallow. And quickly check my phone. My insides groan. I know exactly what we're discussing. *Shit*. She turns back and pauses when I don't follow her. 'Felix? What is it?'

'Emma, I need to tell you something.'

'Yes?' she asks, waiting.

'I know what the call is about.' Her eyes dart up to mine. 'It's about Robyn.'

Emma sighs. 'Robyn?'

'She's missing.'

'Missing?' She stares at me coolly.

'Max called me the other day, to tell me.' Her jaw tightens, probably trying to work out what this means for us. 'He says there is nothing concrete and she might have just wanted to get away from it all. I was going to tell you.'

'Why didn't you?' she says hotly.

'I didn't want to bring it all up again. I know how much the whole thing upsets you.'

'So, you were trying to spare my feelings?' Her voice spikes. Then she sighs. 'I was wondering when you were going to tell me.'

'You knew?' I cry.

'Of course I fucking knew! I called Max as soon as I saw it on Twitter.' I should have known she wouldn't have missed it. She probably has Robyn's name saved as an alert on the thing.

'Why didn't you say anything?' I ask, the wind knocked out of me.

'The real question, Felix, is why you didn't tell *me*. That poor girl . . .'

'Who knows what she had going on in her personal life. And we both know what a complex person she was,' I try, sticking to the script in my head.

'Felix, is there no end to the ways you can fuck up?' She looks at me, eyes staring at me in disgust. 'What you did to that girl . . .'

'I didn't do anything! She basically stalked me.'

'If you believe that, then I'm more shocked than ever at your ability to hide from reality.' She marches up to the house and I follow mutely, terrified that I am now having to confront this.

She gets her laptop and brings up the internet browser, clicking on the Zoom link. After a few seconds it connects and Max is there, sitting behind his desk. He looks sombre and worried, and I feel sick.

'Hello, Emma, and Felix.' Gone is his usual jovial tone. We are his bestselling authors; he is usually very pleased to see us.

'Look, this Robyn girl hasn't shown up anywhere. I figured it's about time we hashed this out. I think this is about to go big.' He sounds panicked, which is unlike him. He gets excitable when negotiating contracts but never flustered. He's too long in the tooth to let anything touch him, or so I'd thought.

'You said the police weren't taking it seriously,' I say. Emma glares up at me, her eyes misted with raw emotion.

'Seems like she packed a bag, which explains the lack of initial action. But none of her bank accounts have been touched, and her phone's gone silent. It's all a bit fishy.'

'Right. Well, I don't really understand what this has to do with us,' I say.

Emma turns to me. 'Because we are in the middle of fierce litigation with her, Felix. Because you took advantage of a young woman. Because she fell in love with you and then you messed with her head, and she lost her job.' She is angry and I fall back into the chair in frustration. 'They'll want to know everything that happened. That's what they do in these cases, anything in the girl's history. They'll be looking at any grievances. We'll be headline news before the week is out,' she spits.

Max is nodding. 'Look, I hate to break it to you, but chances are the cops are going to want to have a chat with you, maybe even both of you.'

'When was she last seen?' Emma asks, taking charge.

'The eighth,' Max replies. Emma is looking through our calendar. 'Why are you . . . ?' I ask, before realising. I snort. 'You can't seriously think—'

'Felix, I am just covering all bases. Right, that was the night before we left for France.' She freezes a moment, and looks over at me, shocked, before fixing her expression. 'We went to a party and came back to the apartment. We were together all night,' she says confidently. 'There were plenty of people there – photographers, the lot.'

Max nods along. 'I highly doubt they'd suspect you had anything to do with it, but it's always smart to be prepared.' He looks at Emma as if she is his star pupil in class and I shrink.

'It won't stop them running a story, it's too salacious for the papers to help themselves,' Emma says with a sigh.

'She could turn up any minute,' Max says optimistically.

'Yes, hopefully,' Emma says, still looking at me. 'But if she isn't paying for anything or using her phone, it doesn't look good.' Emma is well versed in police procedurals.

'Anyway, look. In a few days it could be nothing to worry about. How's the book coming along?' Max asks.

'It's coming. I'm feeling good about this one,' Emma tells Max.

'Good to hear. You've got this. This whole thing will blow over, and we'll have another bestseller to celebrate. You just needed to get to France and that beautiful house to thrash it out,' he says. I can see the twinkle back in his eye after the sombreness of our earlier discussion.

'We'll see,' Emma says dryly. 'I saw the numbers come in for number eight, Max – how did they let that happen?'

Max waves a hand. 'Emma, look, you know what it's like at the moment . . .' They begin a long, torrid conversation about the state of the publishing industry and I slowly move away to pour a drink.

Once the call is over, Emma stands up. 'Pour me one of those?' she asks, and I make her one. 'Emma . . . I . . .' I try.

'I know, you're sorry, Felix,' she says rigidly, moving away. Then she turns, peering up at me, almost scared. 'That night . . .'

'What?' I ask. What happened that night? I know I got very drunk at the book launch, and I must have passed out in the guest room. The next morning my bags were packed and by the door and I was rushed out to the car, wearing the same clothes. I swallow at the memory.

'You really don't remember?' She looks over, her eyebrow raised.

'No! I told you – nothing.' She nods, thinking, and I feel sick. 'Why?'

'Well, I wasn't with you the *whole* night, was I?' she whispers.

'What?' I ask, my voice rising slightly.

'You wandered off from the party, came back looking like a mess. I put you to bed. Where were you?'

I look at her blankly, having no recollection. I try. But all I can hear is a high-pitched strangled scream. 'I didn't go anywhere. One of the comms guys was talking my ear off and I had to get out of there. I went to the bar down the road and walked home,' I tell her, trying to sound genuine. I honestly have no idea.

She nods. 'Look, it's awful that she's missing. Probably just had a spat with her boyfriend or something. It's just a shame we're gonna get dragged into it.' She sighs. 'But it'll blow over,' she says confidently, trying to convince herself. Blow over. How many times can they say it? And why the hell can't I remember what happened that night?

154

# CHAPTER NINETEEN

I do not sleep well, and I turn over with a groan. I think I only managed to drop off around five a.m. On my nightstand is an empty glass ringed with red wine. I wipe my face and look down at my phone. My vision is blurry and my eyes feel dry and sore. What Emma said to me . . . Where was I? Why can't I remember a thing? The last remnants of the evening are a muddle of scenes from the party, talking too loudly, banging into people accidently as I tried to get to the bar, and then waking up in the guest room with a jolt. That's it. Where is the rest of it? I feel sick to my stomach. The shame is irrepressible.

I force myself to sit up and pause there, my head spinning. Urgh. I stare at my overturned phone, scared to pick it up in case terrible things linger there. The whole world pointing a finger at me, telling me what an awful human being I am, but unable to go public proclaiming my innocence. Cancelled. That's what I'll be after all this. A #MeToo nightmare. I swallow. This was all my own making, wasn't it? I let my head fall into my hands and I sob. 'Stop it,' I whisper to myself. 'Stop it!' I cry. I am stronger than this.

I force myself to pick my phone up and unlock the screen. My whole body is rocked in a sigh as I realise all that is there are just the usual notifications. I close my eyes with relief but then: *Not yet*, the voice in my head whispers, and I swallow. They are coming for me, I know it.

Waiting in my inbox is Emma's chapter. I freeze again, remembering her sour words and the silent treatment the rest of the evening. Maybe I can cheer her up, get her onside by reading her chapter and broaching a discussion about the next section. She'll like that. But as I read, my brow furrows. The words merge as I process what's there. Hanna has managed to get Nancy in her car, by offering a lift back from town. The words are a scatter gun of insane inner monologue.

*Hanna hums as she drives. There is a long road out of town that takes them to their little edge of suburbia. An outpost in the desert. Either side of them it stretches out as far as the eye can see. The first thing to do, in situations like this, is to befriend your enemy. Befriend and then break them down. That's what she's been taught.*

*'How long have you lived out here?' Hanna asks.*

*'A while. I was going to leave but then Hank and Jolene got in touch. I sat the kids a lot in the city, and they wanted a live-in so Jolene could take a promotion. I'm not sure how long I'll stay – I had been thinking of travelling come winter, but we'll see.'*

*'Going away?' Hanna asks, her hands relaxing.*

*'Well, it's a bit up in the air. I'm sort of dating someone.'*

*Hanna must force her head to stop still at this news, in its* desperation to twitch. She'd never imagined this girl to be so brazen.

Her grip on the steering wheel tightens. She can feel the blood thrumming in her ears, pulsating all around her. She did so much to get here. All that cooking and cleaning and all that horrible sex she pretended to enjoy. This perky young woman isn't going to take that away.

Ahead is a huge boulder of a rock. She passes it nearly every day. A blaring sound warps her ears. When she thinks of all she has done to have this life. Every manoeuvre – every midnight dash with clothes hurried in a bag.

For Sebastian. All of it to arrive here. Only for it to be taken from under her nose. By this slut.

Her heart pounds as the rock approaches. Closer and closer it comes. She could crash the car right into the passenger seat. Yes, Hanna may be hurt. But nowhere near the extent Nancy would be. She thinks of that pretty head, with her skull crushed in, brains seeping out onto the floor. And she smiles. Yes. She could cope with a few broken bones for that. She drives faster and faster. She can hear the smash of glass and the crunch of metal already – the idea of it has rendered her breathless. Yes. Yes.

There is something about a car crash – immediate, destructive. Deadly. Hanna likes the idea of a knife carving out a line across the young girl's throat. Letting the blood gush into a bath. Watching the life slowly career out of her once lively eyes. Watching as her flesh tears, her insides hanging out. Delicious. She shivers. But a crash. A crash would barely be her fault at all. It would be done in a blink of an eye. It would be magnificent.

*The rock looms ahead. 'Hanna?' Nancy asks, startled at their speed. 'Hanna?' She feels Nancy touch her arm, but this only coaxes her on. It is coming, it is coming. She thinks she can have an affair with her husband and get away with it? No. That is not going to happen. No one can have Sebastian. No one. He is hers. She fought for him to put that ring on her finger, every minute, every second of the day. 'Hanna!' Nancy screams.*

*'Mumma!' Ivy calls from the back seat.*

*Hanna's ears prick up with the sound of Ivy's little voice punching through her stream of consciousness. She'd completely forgotten all about Ivy in her car seat behind them. She bashes her foot against the brake and turns the car away from the collision. It screeches on the tarmac and comes to a shuddering stop.*

*Nancy is gasping for breath. The baby is crying.*

*How could she have forgotten? How could she have put Ivy in danger like that?*

I feel sick picturing Hanna in the car with Nancy. I've always read 'her' chapters with Emma's voice in mind. And I read that crazy stream of consciousness with her voice in my head. The frenzy of it. The paranoia. I often wonder what my wife is thinking. What if it's this?

*Stop.*

I sit back. I hold my head in my hands, almost wanting to laugh. I'm so lost in this, I am making myself ill.

*It's a story! A dumb story. This is ridiculous.*

I stand, holding the bedhead to stabilise myself before

158

walking over to the bathroom where I see my linen shirt tossed to one side. There is a little stain of puke on the fabric. Jesus. I don't even remember getting up in the night and vomiting. What is happening to me? Why do I keep blacking out?

I quickly turn on the shower and give myself a talking-to within the rising steam. Right, no more. I'm not going to drink anything for the rest of the trip. Not even a wine with dinner. That first drink only nails me to the cross. I won't make a big deal out of it or tell Emma. She'll only hold it against me if I fail. Which I won't. Not this time.

I turn the shower off and gingerly step onto the mat. I feel slightly better having washed last night off me. I tie a towel around my waist and walk back into the bedroom to where Emma has neatly hung my clothes.

'Felix!' I hear her cry from downstairs. Oh, God. What's happened? My heart beats into my ears. Maybe they've found her? I rush down the steps to where she is standing, her eyes lit up like fire. She shoves her phone into my hands.

I almost drop it on the floor when Robyn's face glares up and me. A newspaper article:

POLICE APPEAL FOR MISSING YOUNG WOMAN. Robyn Avery was last seen on the 8th of July. Her mother, Ruth Avery, 64, says her daughter had been having a difficult time since being fired from her dream job. She worked as a publicist for Blazing Eagle Books, one of the biggest publishing houses in the country, before being laid off. It is thought that some of her personal items had been removed, and the police are not ruling out that Robyn has simply relocated. But now Detective Morton is appealing for Robyn to get in touch as her phone and credit cards have not been used since her disappearance. He said in a statement this morning, 'Robyn, your family are very worried about you, please get in touch. If any members of the public have any information about Ms Avery's whereabouts, please call the phone number below, quoting the case number.'

'Well, it's out there,' Emma says, staring out into the garden. 'Fuck,' Emma spits. 'It won't take long before the dots are connected and we're the news. Felix, why do you always have to go and ruin everything?' She sighs. 'You're so selfish, I can't bear it.' She is looking around for something, and bangs open a kitchen drawer. Finding her pills, she lets two fall into her hand before swallowing them and breathing deeply to calm herself.

'I . . . I . . .' I try but the words won't come out.

I'm rattled to see it out there, in the proper certified press. Robyn, she's really, actually missing. All those lies I've told myself about her being away, she's . . . she's dead, isn't she? There isn't any other explanation. I cared about her, a lot. If things had been different, maybe . . .

I look at the photograph of her mother in the article. I wince at the memories. I remember now, Robyn would talk about her mother a lot. Robyn's father had recently died, and her mother wasn't coping very well without him. She'd go and see her every weekend she wasn't working. They were extremely close. That doesn't sound like someone who would just disappear into the night without saying goodbye.

160

The urge to drink hits me again.

If only she'd just dealt with the rejection better. Not got all clingy when it ended. It was barely anything! A bit of fun, for God's sake. We spent months and months dashing messages across, desperate to see each other. Yes, I enjoyed the attention. So what? If she could have just been like the others and shrugged it off and behaved like a normal human rather than getting all obsessed. She should have just got a new job and moved on, rather than taking it further and getting lawyers involved. *How petty, how pathetic! No, this isn't my fault.*

*What if she's killed herself because of me?* Blood drains from my face. *No, I won't be to blame.* A poor foundation of resilience! It gnaws at me all the same.

'I'm going to drive into town. I'd like to go to the store and buy the papers. Apparently, they sell *The New York Times* in the kiosk.' She looks over at me. She's pissed. 'You'll be fine here, yes? Getting on with your work?'

I rub my face. 'I'm not sure I can concentrate, Emma,' I mumble.

She walks over to me and slaps me around the face so hard and fast I take a step back. She looks at me, heaving. 'Fuck you, Felix. You don't get to play the victim.'

'I . . .'

She points a finger at me. 'You don't get to. I refuse to let you fuck this up even more than you already have. If anyone should be upset, outraged, confused, it's me. Okay?' She grabs her handbag and takes the car key out of the bowl. And I am left standing there, with the weight of the world pressing down.

# CHAPTER TWENTY

I hover at the entrance to the study, staring at my laptop in the centre of the desk. With a shaking hand I down the rest of my whisky. The alcohol sweeps through my system, giving temporary relief to the shimmering anxiety pulsating through my veins.

I walk tentatively over to the desk and take my seat. I sit motionless. I can't stop the thoughts. They are like drunk characters in a dive bar on loop, coming up to me slurring; coked up, spitting in my face. I open the screen and reread a few chapters of the book. It takes me ages; my head won't let me focus at all. But I must. If Emma gets back with my next chapter to read, she'll soften, I'm sure of it. And I need Emma on my side through this.

I look at what I've written about Sebastian's longing for a child.

Ivy. The infant in the book.

Authors often call their books their babies. How interesting Emma has created these characters. A husband and wife. With a child. A thought trickles through me, stabbing me in the heart. Sebastian isn't the real father, is he? No. He's impotent. That's what she is calling me, isn't it? Anger runs as I imagine the smirk on her face as she worked away at this. Thinking she is oh so very clever by emasculating me through our words. How she must have laughed playing this game with me.

I bang my fist down on the desk. I think about discussing this with her, shouting at her for being so evil, so callous and mean. But she would just turn it around on me. Calling me paranoid, a pathetic man with a bruised ego. Besides, she has this Robyn ordeal in her arsenal now.

*Fuck you, Emma Larson. Fuck you. I was a writer long before you typed one original word.*

I remember, a few dates in, she offered to read the manuscript I'd spent years writing. Sweat, blood and tears had gone into those opening chapters. And all she said was that it 'showed promise'. She hadn't, as I'd hoped, jumped around with excitement, telling me she'd submit it to all her contacts. No. She undramatically said those two words in a way that meant I couldn't possibly believe her. She thought it was rubbish, she made that obvious.

Later, she came to me with a new idea. Said she'd been working on something and needed my help. *Help her!* I'd thought. Well, she must think I had talent. That first book was born in a rush of excitement. The whirlwind process fooling me into thinking I was in love – I'm sure of it now. Were we ever real at all? She had the idea for the pseudonym and suddenly we had a deal. It was as easy as that.

Would I be a bestselling author without Emma? Probably

not. But would I have written something I could be proud of, with my name on it? Well, the jury is still out on that one, I guess. I daydream of breaking free – going it alone. But my confidence is broken into so many pieces, and I don't even think that's possible.

And now I am here. Trapped in this terrible marriage with our child, our brand Morgan Savage, keeping us stuck here. And all I want to do is run. But how can I leave? This is the thing that gives me stature, that makes me someone people look at with respect.

My phone rings. Emma. I sigh as I answer it. 'Hey, can you send Max the synopsis for book seven? He can't find it and my dumb phone won't connect to the internet. The film agent has requested it urgently.'

'Yes, sure, where is it?'

An annoyed pause. 'Felix, I emailed it for you to check over a few days ago.'

'Right, right.' Then I hear laughter in the background.

'Where are you?' I ask, swallowing.

'Oh, Juliette has bought me a drink. I said I'd give her a lift home.'

'Oh, right,' I reply.

'See you later!' she says. 'Don't forget to send the synopsis.' She hangs up on me.

My mind is instantly taken to the scene in the car with Hanna and Nancy, and I think of Emma driving Juliette home. Emma's stone-cold eyes as they turn a bend.

*Stop.*

*I'm being silly. Emma is just being nice!*

That night we left for France drifts into my ears, like a frenzied whisper. Hands grabbing at my face, trying to get them off me, my anger becoming more violent with every blow to my face. I get up and go to a small oval mirror hanging on one side of the room and touch the scratches by my ear. They've nearly gone now, the initial scabbing melted away.

I shake my head. Memories are mixing with the violence of our stories. Silly. I'm getting wrapped up in the plot of this book. It's time to channel this into something creative, show Emma I'm not the impotent bastard she has pinned me as. I'll show her!

I notice a new Post-it note. *Who is Ivy's real father? Is Hanna being followed?* And my jaw clenches. I feel completely bound by obligation, stuck in this, forced into doing something I can't bear. But what else can I do, other than write?

I need to give Sebastian's description of Hanna falling apart. The reader has seen inside her head, now they need to see how those around her are dealing with the fallout.

*Hanna has been acting strange since she got back from town. And by strange, Sebastian means stranger than usual. She looks crestfallen and replies to every question with an um or an err, like she isn't listening. She won't put Ivy down. Not even for a second, although it's obvious that Ivy would like to have a wander and play with her toys.*

*Her phone buzzes in the kitchen. It has a few times, but she's ignoring it. Sebastian picks up the phone and looks at* the number. No name attached. She quickly comes at him, snatching it from his hands. Turning the device off.

'Who was that?' he asks.

'No one. Just cold callers,' she snips back. 'They won't leave me alone!'

'Hanna. Are you okay, darling?' he enquires, stroking her back. She is now staring out the window, watching Hank and Jolene's house across the road. 'That was nice of you to drive Nancy back, I'm sure she appreciated it,' he tells her. That was strange too, he'd thought. He'd watched them get out of the car. And Nancy walked away without saying goodbye, her usual jolly spring missing. He'd noticed Nancy look back at Hanna, wide-eyed. Scared even. What had happened in that car?

'Has that van been parked there all day?' Hanna asks.

He walks over to the window to see. There is a dark blue van a few houses down, across the road. 'It looks like a window cleaning company, Hanna,' he tells her, noticing her wringing hands. 'It's got the logo on it and everything.' He points to the cartoonish illustration on the side.

'There aren't any windows being cleaned,' she adds. Is her voice shaking? She's blinking in a peculiar way, and her head is twitching slightly. He's starting to wonder, is the baby even safe with her?

'Maybe we should move,' she whispers, going back to her position by the window and staring out at the blacked-out windows of the van.

'Move?' he says with incredulity. They've barely got here, he thought the plan was to lay roots. 'Hanna, you really need to go and have a lie-down. Have a rest.'

*'Yes, I will soon,' she whispers, her wide eyes still fixated on the van.*

I push the laptop away and stand up, wanting to get as far away from the sodding thing as possible. I push the door so hard it bangs into the wall. I should rename the study the Cave of Doom. I look at the clock – four hours. Emma has been gone for a very long time. I try her number, but her phone is off. I can't help thinking about the poisonous thoughts in Hanna's head as she contemplated driving Nancy into the rocks.

I walk into the kitchen. The box of wine is still hanging out there, where I left it, on the kitchen shelf. I tap the top of the box, thinking. No. I wasn't going to get wasted today. If I start on that endless box of wine, it'll take the last few strands of sanity I have left. I spin myself around and go to the bookshelf in the living area.

*The Shining*, Stephen King. Yes. I haven't been in this world for a while. I turn and look at the box of wine again. It winks at me provocatively. I can't help it. I go over, take it under my arm and head to the veranda and settle down on one of the chairs.

And begin to read.

The sound of birds squawking wakes me. I open one eye, then the other. It's dark, and I sit up, confused. I rub my eyes and stretch as I look around for some sign of life. A noise inside and I realise she's back. 'Emma?' I call.

I cannot shake the feeling that something bad has happened.

The image of Emma in the car with Juliette. A sinister grin as she smashes the car into the side of the cliff.

The orange glow of the kitchen light is on, and I step inside. Emma looks up. And I feel only relief that she is back in one piece. Thank goodness. It seems Emma's isn't the only imagination that can run wild. 'Oh, hey,' she says. She's wearing her hair in one of those towel turban things. And has some fresh clothes on.

'Did you have fun?' I look around.

'Yes, was great to get out,' she breathes airily.

'Where is Juliette?' I ask.

She gives me a funny look. 'I dropped her home, of course,' she says with a shrug.

'Did you get a paper?'

'A paper?' She looks confused for a moment. 'Oh, no, the store was shut.' She seems subdued. Odd, in fact.

'I thought you said it was a kiosk?'

'Kiosk, store, whatever.'

'Well, you were gone a long time.'

She shrugs and says again, 'It was nice to get out.'

'You've had a shower?'

She raises her chin. 'Yes, very perceptive of you. I was all hot and sweaty, needed to wash it off me. What's with all these questions?'

'I'm just asking about your afternoon!'

She gives me an odd look. 'I need to dry my hair,' she says as she pulls off the towel. Her freshly washed locks fall to her shoulders. 'Grab a beer, I'll join you in a minute.'

*

168

I sit outside, biting my nail, watching the orchard, the gateway to the houses at the bottom of the hill where Juliette lives. I half imagine wandering down there to check she's okay. I chuckle to myself. The thought of it. Ridiculous! The story and real life are merging. I'm drunk, that must be it.

Emma would never hurt anyone. Yes, she is deft at letting it rip in her writing. But that's not *real*. I sit on a chair with the book, still unread. Sipping on the sixth glass of wine I've poured. Emma's right. This house is doing strange things to both of us. It is beguiling, haunting – with bats flapping their wings and squeaking into the tops of dark trees at night. Juliette will be at home, having dinner after a lovely afternoon with my wife in town. Nothing bad has happened. It's residue from this bloody Robyn stuff, seeping into my reality here. It's just another lovely evening in the south of France. Then why can't I shake this?

Emma joins me on the veranda. She has on a long light pink dress with buttons up the front. She looks soft. Feminine. Relaxed. I'm going crazy. *There is no great genius, without a tincture of madness*. Wasn't that the saying? That is all it is, I'm getting wrapped up in the story. Maybe good work can come of this.

'That's better,' she says, smiling, touching her newly blow-dried hair. 'What a lovely evening.' She stares at the view. I watch her, take in every inflection. 'I enjoyed your chapter, Felix. Great call with the van.'

'Thanks,' I say, pleased for a second.

'I bought some salad bits. And some meat.' She goes inside and brings back a plastic bag, dropping it at my feet with a ghastly slippery slap. It's one of those cheap blue plastic bags and inside is a bloody mound of meat. I swallow. 'Beef,' she says. With a glint in her eye. I am reminded of a scene in book two, where the murderer was finally caught, just before he was about to throw the sawn-up remains of a victim into the lake.

'Oh, great.' My voice comes out raspy and meek.

'Maybe you could fire up the barbecue?'

I notice a nasty red ring around her wrist and stop, jumping up to hold it in my hand. 'Emma,' I say, examining it. It's red raw. It looks painful. 'Emma,' I whisper this time, shocked. Did I do this?

She snaps it away, taking it in her other hand. 'Don't worry.' She looks up at me. 'I know you were just trying to keep me safe. Probably didn't mean to tie it so tight,' she adds with a grimace.

*Could I? Did I? Jesus.*

I rub my head. It's all a blur.

'Emma, I'm so sorry.'

'You didn't mean to,' she replies, grimacing. 'Felix, I just wanted to ask you something. Please don't get all worked up. I just have to know.'

'What?' I croak.

'You didn't . . . What I mean is, when you were out that night before we came here, do you really not remember anything?'

'What do you mean?' I watch her features, trying to work out what she is getting at. 'I do remember, I told you, I went to the bar.' I feel bad for lying but I can't backtrack now, can I?

She stares at me as if trying to find something. Then shakes her head. 'No, nothing. If that's where you were, that's where you were.'

'Emma!' I cry, shocked at what she is implying.

'Sorry,' she whispers. 'It's just that you've been blacking out so much, I was wondering if the same had happened that night. And we both know what you can be like when that happens.'

I shake my head. 'I can't believe you think . . . you think . . . It wasn't like the other times.'

She shakes her head. 'What about the time you . . . well . . .' She touches the side of her cheek. One night, not too long ago when I'd been out of it, we had a fight. Yes, I may have hit her – but she hit me first! I don't remember that either. She told me all about it the next day, almost relishing it.

'I apologised about that,' I tell her quietly, blood rushing into my cheeks. If my dad found out what kind of man I'd become . . . Oh, the idea of that makes me want to jump off that cliff myself.

'Sorry!' she cries. 'Sorry, sorry. I should never have asked.' She gives me a look that makes me queasy. 'If that's where you were, that's where you were.'

'Yes. It is,' I say quietly.

Then she pulls her arms around my neck and kisses me, a soft, passionate kiss. The closeness to her is overwhelming. 'Whatever happens, we'll get through it together. I'm sorry I snapped earlier.' She softly touches my cheek where she slapped me earlier. 'I'm sorry.' Then she laughs. 'God, what are we doing to each other? Can we start again? Let's just enjoy tonight, okay? Just us. Together, in this beautiful place. No one else for miles around. Let's just try and have one night where nothing else matters.' She goes into the kitchen, still caressing her wrist, and I feel terrible all over again.

'I'll get the salad going,' she calls.

I turn the gas on the large barbecue on the veranda. It clicks as the flame catches. Then I stare down at the blue plastic bag, and the blood splattered up the insides.

After my usual drinking fest on the veranda I stumble inside, the room spinning, the lights swimming in front of my eyes. I remember to lock the door, my hand fumbling around on the lock. I even drunkenly move the armchair across the back door. Just in case. I come across the note that was left when we arrived. It has Juliette's phone number on it. I try thinking of a reason to call her. A problem with the house, something I can't find. I get out my phone and dial the French international number. But then I drop it. *Silly Felix. Come on. Your wife did not hurt Juliette. She did not drive her into a rock or a tree or a building. That is ridiculous.* I've been spending far too much time in the murky underbelly of horror and death.

I get to the bedroom, holding the wall for support, and watch Emma sleeping from the doorway. So beautiful lying there. I walk over and lift her injured wrist and let it drop, instead selecting the untarnished one, and tie her firmly to the bed.

Then a thought stumps me, a memory of a hand as it tore at my face, screaming, crying. Where is that coming from? A horrible idea shimmies its way through me. What if Emma isn't the person I should be worried about in this equation?

What if it's me?

# CHAPTER TWENTY-ONE

Sun sprinkles through the curtain. Another day in paradise. But in this case, another day in this fucked-up marriage trying to write this insane book in this sinister house. I need to get back to New York, pronto. How will I cope with another month here? I crave walking down the street with a bustle of people around me. Dropping into our local bodega and chatting to the guy behind the counter about the crazy shit that went down in the alley behind his shop the previous night, while I chew on a bagel. I want to get dressed up in a new outfit and go to a high-society party and get wrecked with a beautiful young socialite.

I'm bored and freaked out. I'm not good at all this . . . this . . . nothingness. All this space to think and overanalyse.

I'm not in the mood to read about Hanna. Instead, I go downstairs, and head out to the garden. I see two figures through the glass – Juliette and Emma. Juliette, perfectly intact. Not a bruise or a cut on her skin. They're chatting, and Emma laughs at something she says. Yesterday was completely insane.

I need help.

Emma notices me. 'You look a mess, Felix,' she says good-naturedly. Then she turns back to Juliette.

'Thank you, Juliette, this is so kind,' Emma says, looking down at the book in her hands. 'Juliette has given me a poetry book. Isn't that nice?'

I smile and nod.

'Emma,' Juliette says. 'Would you like me to organise for the masseuse to come by? You were saying yesterday your back isn't good.'

'That would be brilliant,' she replies. 'Would you like one, Felix?' she calls over, in full organisational mode. 'Occupational hazard,' she explains to Juliette, caressing her neck.

'Sure.' I shrug. 'Whatever.'

Juliette walks away from us to make a call.

Emma turns to me. 'Felix, you really are deteriorating while we're here. Get it together. I don't want to have a go at you about the drinking, but it's getting out of hand. It will start to affect the book.' The book! She doesn't care about my health or happiness; she only cares about that sodding thing. 'We are about to have to do a whole load of firefighting and we need clear heads,' she advises.

'But . . .' I begin. She sits down on her lounger and picks up her phone. The conversation is coming to an end. 'You should get on with your chapter. I bet you haven't even got up to speed yet. This is a work trip, not a holiday.'

I don't get how she can just carry on as normal. She's a machine.

'I'll go make a coffee and get going.' And I troop back up to

174

the house to the Cave of Doom. The Hole of Death. The Cage of Worry. The . . . I'm too tired to think of any more.

Hot drink by my side, I pull open my laptop to read. My eyes skim the pages, taking in the important elements. Hanna destroys the SIM card in her phone – interesting. *It couldn't have been what she feared, it's not like she left any clues behind about where she was headed.* She is still obsessed with this Nancy: *she is the main problem now. She is out to get her husband; she can smell it on her, with every dosing of rose petal perfume she saunters past in. The smell is rancid, too sweet.* Emma has also written that Sebastian is going away for a few nights for work.

But it's the last paragraph that sinks me:

*The day before Sebastian is due to leave, Hanna goes into the basement and digs out the metal box with the padlock on. Sebastian thinks she keeps her grandmother's precious jewels inside it. But there is something far more priceless within. Gingerly, she takes out the key and opens it. Takes in a deep breath of excitement as she prises the top open to reveal the contents. She smiles. Her fingers shake as she plucks out the lock of hair, tied with a ribbon. She strokes the hair to her cheek, closing her eyes. Next, a tooth, yes . . . and a scrap of material from the dress she was wearing. And then her most prize possession – the bag, a little beaded thing with the outline of the state of Texas depicted below the clasp.*

*The doorbell rings. Hanna puts her precious things away, smiling to herself as she creeps back up the stairs, tugging on the light pull and closing the door.*

As I finish, I realise I am chewing my nail. It throbs with pain. What does Hanna have in store for Nancy? Is she going to hurt her while Sebastian is on this work trip? And all arrows are pointing to her having done something like this before.

Is Hanna a serial killer? Is this the book we're writing?

Usually, I get a kick out of how dark our books get, but here, this is having a rather adverse effect. Poor Nancy – a lamb to the slaughter all right.

How am I going to follow it? Sebastian is away. What should he do? My eyes search the corkboard for clues but there is nothing. *Come on, Felix, think, think.* I hear laughter floating dreamily through the window and stand, shoving my hands in my pockets as I watch.

Juliette is still out there. She's sitting on the sunlounger, with her back to Emma, who is doing something to her hair. I squint. A braid, I think. They look as though they're having a heart-to-heart. Speaking in whispers. Emma nodding and talking quietly as if offering advice. I can't help but feel peculiar. Emma is making Juliette her pet. *She is the enemy, and everyone knows what to do with those*, is what Hanna had said.

When she's done, Juliette stands up and twirls. Emma claps. I feel sweat creeping down my back.

I can't write. I can't think of how to move the story forward. I scratch my head, the blank page glowering at me, whispering terrible things about my abilities. I snap the laptop shut and give in.

I walk out onto the veranda, my palm above my eyes,

shielding them from the sun. 'You done already?' Emma asks, surprised.

'I need to get out and go for a walk or something,' I tell her, and she frowns. 'I might go into town, take a breather,' I say, with a sigh. Emma stares out at the view, her face a picture of disappointment. It's all I ever do, disappoint her. It's not fair that this comes so easily to her, she just doesn't understand.

Then she gets up and dusts herself off. 'I'll come too,' she says.

A stab of disappointment. 'You really don't have to.' I could do with a little time on my own.

'I'd like to. We can talk about the story, I can help. I'll go and get my things.'

Juliette stands there awkwardly, twisting her pendant between her fingers. 'How are things?' I ask her.

'Great! Your wife – Emma – she is so kind.'

I nod. 'Yep.'

She walks over to me and gets a little too close. I can smell that rose-scented perfume that sticks to the inside of my nostrils and refuses to budge. She steps closer, and I try very hard to keep my eyeline in the appropriate place. I get a flash of her tryst with Marco, her face as she orgasmed, and can't help but feel hot.

'Marco bought me this.' She shows me a pendant.

From nowhere, irritation hits me. 'Nice.'

A little cross with the smallest diamond I've ever seen set in the middle. Seriously, you'd need a microscope to pick that out. She looks delighted. Maybe she isn't as smart as I thought, getting bogged down by some young brat of a barman in the middle of nowhere when she should be out there, dazzling people.

'Well, that was nice of him,' I say, teeth sliding together. And then I realise, she is trying to make me jealous. That's nice. Isn't it? And I flash a smile, taking the pendant in my hand. 'Well, it's very sweet. I think I'd buy a rather larger gem if it were me,' I tell her throatily. Her eyes blink in shock. Did I get it wrong?

Emma walks out of the house, and I take a guilty step back. She pauses, looking between us. 'Juliette, that hairstyle really suits you. But then, you always do look so fresh,' she sings.

'Emma, you are one of the most stunning, elegant women I 'ave ever met,' Juliette replies quickly. 'I should get back.' She takes her bag over her shoulder. 'I might walk 'ome this way,' she says, pointing to the orchard, and we nod. 'Thank you for the advice.' She smiles at my wife.

'Thank you for the book, very thoughtful,' Emma replies. And Juliette walks back between the trees.

'Why are you suddenly all over her?' I ask Emma.

She smirks. 'What do you mean?'

'Usually, you are very dismissive of the women we have working for us.'

'Yes, Felix. And look where that's got me.' I give her a look, and she laughs. 'Come on, Felix, can't you take a joke any more?'

# CHAPTER TWENTY-TWO

The hot leather seats stick uncomfortably to the back of my legs as we drive into town. I shift around, and Emma notices my unease. 'Remember it's just a first draft. We'll fix it, we just need to get to the end.'

'It's not that. All this Robyn stuff has derailed me,' I confide.

She glances across. 'You need to put it to the back of your mind. We're in the public eye, there is always going to be something rearing its head. You need to learn to shut it out and compartmentalise. Focus on the writing, it's the only thing we can control,' she says swiftly, as if I'm weak and she is strong.

'Have you ever thought what would happen if we just didn't finish this book?' I can't believe I've said this out loud.

'What?' The car jolts to one side, and I grab the dashboard as she straightens out. 'Felix.'

I clear my throat. *Come on, I can have this conversation. We're adults, after all.* 'Maybe the reason we haven't been getting on is because we're working together. Maybe it's not good for our marriage. Maybe we need a break.'

Emma sighs. 'We're just having a rocky patch; all marriages have them. And after what happened last year, can you blame me for not being all roses and suspenders? Writing this book is the first step to getting us back on track,' she says with defiance.

*But it isn't working, is it? I want to tell her. We've scurried even further away from that hallowed track.* But I feel shut down. Deluded, that's what she is. Blinded by Morgan, as per usual.

'Why won't you even entertain the idea, Emma?' I ask. 'Okay, maybe not can it completely, but take a break. Take a few years off and find ourselves again. It's not like we can't afford it. Can't you see what it's doing to us?'

'What?' she replies harshly.

'That maybe Morgan isn't good for our marriage,' I state. 'You're so obsessed with the brand. The book dictates your mood and how you . . . how you . . . treat me.' There, I said it.

'Felix,' she breathes. I notice her fingers turning white squeezing the leather wheel. 'We need to finish it. If we don't, everyone will be disappointed. All the fans. The publishers. Max – especially Max. Come on. We're at a crossroads in our career, we're on a decline. We can't just throw in the towel. You'll feel better once it's done, trust me.'

I look out at the scenery as we pass. I'm in prison. 'Is it because you're worried we're nothing without it?' I ask quietly. 'That we'll be forced to look at each other and consider what we're even doing together?'

What has got into me? Emma's head jerks slightly, and I frown.

To my surprise, Emma pulls into a lay-by and shuts down the engine. Her hands are shaking, and she begins to cry. I don't think I've ever seen her cry before.

'Emma, Emma . . .' I lean over and console her. She wipes a hand under her nose. 'I don't want to hurt you,' I tell her tenderly.

'You've already hurt me,' she sobs, then places her hands over her eyes to shield me from her raging emotion, whispering, 'This is bullshit.' She sniffs, then turns to me. 'You think I can just take all your crap – all your partying, flirting, cheating – and hold everything we've worked so hard for together? Do you even understand how much I've been carrying for us both?'

'But you must stop punishing me for all that! Or what is the point of us being together?' I cry.

Her swimming eyes dart over at mine, her chin wobbling with emotion. Then she reaches a hand and strokes the side of my face, sniffing the tears away. 'You're all I've ever wanted,' she whispers. There is a sincerity in there, and for the first time in a long time, I believe her. She's hurt, and that's brought out this harshness. How can I break into it? How can I get the real Emma back? Maybe I'm wrong, and she hasn't been desperate for us to stay together for the sake of Morgan. Maybe she does actually love me. Could that be true?

'I just feel like our success has ruined us,' I whisper.

'Well, maybe if you'd kept your pants—'

I turn to her, furious. 'Emma, do not pretend you played no part in that. You can't be so naive to think I would have done any of those things if it weren't for the state of our marriage, your indifference, your ability to make me feel this big.' I hold my thumb and finger out an inch. 'You patronise me at every opportunity, you enjoy seeing me suffer after a night out. You never even seemed to care about the other women. Not once. Once! Have you asked me if I'm okay, or if I need help? I'm dying in here. You take every glimmer of self-respect away from me! You even took away my name, for Christ's sake!'

'So, I'm to blame?' she asks quietly.

'No!' I cry in frustration. 'We both are. What we've created between us, it's toxic, Emma. We need to go back to brick, have some therapy. Ask ourselves tough questions. Are you happy? Can you honestly tell me you're happy?' I stare into her moist eyes. She sniffs, and searches around for her handbag strap, and fishes out the bottle of pills, swallowing one without water.

'We're both self-medicating, Emma! Can't you see that?'

She bats a tear away, looking out the window before murmuring, 'You're right. When we get back to the city, let's get some help.' I'm so relieved, I feel like crying. 'But we're not stopping the book. After this one, I promise, we'll have a break, but I refuse to renege on the contract.'

I nod. Okay, that's a compromise, at least.

'I'm really, really glad we had this chat,' I whisper. 'I think it was overdue.'

She squeezes my hand. 'So am I.' She closes her eyes and leans towards me, resting her head against my chest. We sit there a moment, in the car, on top of a hill, miles from anywhere.

I begin to laugh. 'What is it?' she asks, sitting up.

I shake my head, wiping my face. 'I know it's crazy, and I've been drinking too much, but that Hanna character in the book . . .'

Emma sits up, smiling. 'Isn't she monstrous? She's my favourite character I've ever written.'

I laugh. 'Yes, she certainly is. And don't take this the wrong way, but she'd sort of started to merge with you in my head. The things she's been doing – started to make me . . .'

'What?' she asks, smiling in bemusement. Then realisation dawns, and she hits me playfully. 'I can't believe what you're saying.'

'Never mind. Never mind.' I laugh. Totally, utterly ridiculous.

We get into town. It's harder to park, far busier than I've ever seen it. 'Market day,' Emma says out loud, realising. In the distance a bell tolls the hour and there is an inviting, relaxed atmosphere. We wander down the tranquil streets, joining the slow-walking clusters in the square. Tourists mainly, carrying big straw bags and living out their retirement dreams picking out various artisanal goods. There are heaped tables of fresh produce, far removed from the trussed-up cellophaned food in mini-marts back home. People are laid-back, chatting to stall-holders as they hand over euros in the sun. I wander around admiring a stall selling leather accessories with a man offering to burn initials into the hide. There is an old lady hawking children's clothes made of white cotton and lace.

I realise I've wandered off and I look around for Emma and

find her eyeing up a long fawn-coloured linen dress. Pulling the fabric, imagining herself wearing it. I wonder how long she'll be. It's too hot, and I'm thirsty and tired.

My hangover sits in my stomach, and I start to feel ropey, all exposed like this. I wonder how Emma would react if I suggested a beer. I don't want to undo all the good feeling cultivated from our discussion in the car. I fan my face with the lip of my hat. Finally, Emma seems done.

'Let's have a coffee, talk about the next part of the book. We need a turning point, don't we, as we go into the second act?'

I nod, pointing over to a café. She gets out her phone as I try to get the waiter's attention. He is doing his best to ignore all the hand waving from customers looking perturbed.

'Get your laptop out, we'll make some notes,' she orders. I glance at my bag. It really is the last thing I feel like doing. 'This book, Emma. I . . .'

She taps my hand reassuringly. 'I'll fix it. We'll get there. This is the hard bit, the middle. We always struggle,' she says. Noticing this hasn't pacified me, she continues, 'Come on, honey, we'll get through this, we always do.' But I am unmoved, and she adds, 'I love you, Felix.' She hasn't said that in a long time.

'Why?' I croak.

'What?' she asks.

'Why do you love me? Sometimes I think you don't even like me very much,' I admit.

'Perfect doesn't interest me,' she says. 'I like mess. I like it when it hurts.' There is something about this sentence that makes me want to retch. I don't want that. I am so very tired of all this hurt.

'I'm nothing without you,' I tell her. 'But I need more. I need to feel more ownership. You know? Feel like I'm achieving something too when we go out there with something new.'

She tuts. 'Stop listening to the voice in your head. I couldn't do this without you. You are exactly fifty per cent of this. Haven't I said that over and over? You need to stop wallowing, Felix. This isn't me; this is on you.' And I feel deflated all over again.

'Right,' she says, clapping her hands together. 'Work. Actually, let's get those drinks in.' She stands up and waves, and the waiter comes rushing over. '*Un espresso et une bière, s'il vous plaît*,' she says, her American accent heavy. I go to get out my laptop.

'Oh, God,' Emma says, shocked. I look up. She's seen something on her phone.

'What?'

She hands it to me. The same photo of Robyn pops up with the copy about her being missing and emergency contact details. But then, a link. I grimace as I click on it. BESTSELLING AUTHORS TRIED TO KILL STORY ABOUT AFFAIR WITH MISSING GIRL. With a two-shot photograph of us both smiling. We look fiendish and smug next to this headline.

My whole body shrinks into itself. 'God.' I am suddenly very aware of our surroundings, and the people milling around. I self-consciously pull the lip of my hat down.

Emma is panicked. 'Jesus.' She presses a hand to her cheek,

185

the heat of the shock radiating. 'Felix, they could never find her. What then? Will this just go on and on?' Her voice trembles. 'Felix, this is a disaster.' She looks at me, horrified, and I feel the true impact of this whole saga. 'She was a really sweet girl . . . before' – she peers up at me – 'before she got obsessed, *like you said*.'

Why is she saying it that way? Like I've pushed all the responsibility of the fallout onto Robyn. That's not how it was, not at all. I take a sip of beer as soon as it lands on the table.

'If it wasn't me, it would have been someone else.'

'That poor girl,' she repeats, and I scoff.

'What?'

'Well, you've never said a kind word about her. You wanted her chased out of town. It was you, wasn't it, who told everyone not to hire her?' It makes sense now.

She leans in. 'What do you expect? You were carrying on with her, under my nose. While she worked at our publisher's. She came to our home! Travelled with us. And that whole time . . . that whole time . . .'

'It wasn't the *whole* time,' I tell her quietly. Even as I say it, I know it probably wasn't well advised.

'Oh, sorry! It wasn't the whole time. Just a few times, a couple of times. It's my fault probably, for catching you,' she cries, exasperated.

I look around. People are staring. I lean in to quieten her. 'Emma. It was a mistake. And I've apologised over and over and over. She went completely berserk when I broke it off with her. I told you everything. Everything! Don't pretend it

186

was a surprise. You knew the entire time; you didn't care as long as you had my pages and I turned up to whatever book event you needed me at. You couldn't have cared a jot until the reputation of the brand came into it.'

She sits back in her chair, her arms crossed. 'So, you think she went off the rails and is who knows where because of you? You sure think highly of yourself, don't you?'

I wipe my face.

'This Robyn stuff has nothing to do with us.'

I cross my arms in anger, and she sneers up at me.

'They won't give a shit, Felix. We'll be lucky to get out of this with a career intact.'

I raise my arms in the air. 'What happened to this will all blow over?' I cry, and she lets out a bitter laugh.

'Well, it feels a bit different when my face is slapped all over the internet!' She looks at me with daggers. All that closeness, gone. She gets up. 'I'm going back to the house; I need some space. I'm sure you can find somewhere out here to work. Maybe in a bar,' she spits.

'Fine!' I say, standing up. She's right, I could do with some space from her. And some whisky, too. The metal chair scrapes back on the cobbled stone as I pack my computer up. 'Make your mind up, Emma. Are you with me? Or against me?'

She shakes her head slowly. 'Screw you, Felix. You really have no idea what you are capable of, do you?' she says, with a hiss.

And with that, I storm off.

# CHAPTER TWENTY-THREE

My phone vibrates in my pocket every few minutes. The news broken, I suddenly feel very vulnerable. I should have gone back to the house with Emma but didn't want to give her the satisfaction. Damn my rash pride. It's still busy out, but the market rush is over, and people are leisurely heading home with their purchases as I dash past in a fluster, looking for somewhere to hide. Up ahead, I see the weatherworn sign for Juliette's bar as it sways in the breeze. I quickly hustle inside feeling safe within the quiet sanctuary. I pull up a pew at the bar and look around suspiciously at the few stragglers huddled on tables in corners finishing drinks.

''Ey, man,' Marco says, recognising me from the night we came in and spoke to Juliette. 'What can I get for you?' he asks.

'A beer would be great,' I order, and he nods.

'Coming up.'

I can't believe Emma's taken the car and left me out here on my own. What a cow. I feel like chucking the laptop across the room I'm so frustrated. Just when we'd found some middle ground, bloody Robyn had to go and ruin things again. When will this past mistake stop haunting me? I glug down the drink as soon as it's placed in front of me and make a signal with my hand for another. Marco dutifully obliges. He has no idea I've seen him with his trousers down.

It's so frustrating that I can't remember the night before we came to France. I must have gone to the bar, like I told Emma, and got a drink somewhere before staggering home. That's how my evenings usually pan out. It's just bothersome I can't remember it. And then there is that strange hollow echo of something I can't put my finger on. I touch my face, and feel the jagged edge of skin where the scratch had been. I must have fallen over drunk. That's how bruises and grazes usually appear.

For a moment I allow myself to daydream about what would happen if I was brave enough to pack up and leave my marriage. I could take my half of everything and make a new life. Become a teacher and settle in a small city. Meet a woman, another teacher perhaps? Buy a nice, suburban house and have some kids. The quietness of that life fills me up with something. I think of what Juliette said, about simply walking away from things that don't make her happy. What did she say as she left the night she came for dinner? Something hippy-ish about 'following your bliss'. I'd found it a little saccharine and idealistic at the time, but now I wonder if there is something to it. Writing this book is definitely not filling me with joy.

What have I gained from being with Emma and being part of Morgan Savage? An alcohol problem. Extreme anxiety. Money – lots of that. Were we never truly meant to be together, and the success of Morgan shielded us from that?

I down my drink. The thought of going back to the house chapter-less isn't helping. I decide to write any old shit and be done with it.

I yank up the screen.

Right, so, Felix is travelling to Chicago. I try to form a few words but the endless vibrations in my pocket distract me. I get out my phone. Max has called, three times. There's a message from a friend in the UK who loves to make snarky comments from his multi-million-pound penthouse in Battersea. My mum – *Shit, my mum.* I feel crushed.

*Sweetie, I've just seen the news. What's this all about? Where are you? Dad is worried, he doesn't understand x*

It hits me in the stomach. My dad would never cheat on my mum. They are the perfect married couple. They love each other, embarrassingly so. Kissing in public and never spending even one night apart in their forty-five years of marriage. They are always right there, next to each other. Complimenting, joking around. Staring into each other's eyes and reminiscing. No, of course Dad wouldn't understand. He would be disappointed with the man I have become. He would think about my brother, and how he would never have turned out like me.

Maybe I should have gone back when it seemed my dreams weren't going to materialise. All those arrogant assumptions I'd made on that plane ride over the Atlantic, my father's voice ringing in my ears: *There's a spot for you here when you come back.* He never believed I could do it. Never. I was going to prove him wrong. I'd imagined being welcomed into the New York literary scene with open arms, a publishing deal delivered on a silver platter, the first step to a remarkable literary career. The dream quickly dwindled following rejection after rejection. Even my old agent got sick of forwarding me bad news, barely even registering my existence after a while. 'We don't know how to market it.' 'It just doesn't have a big enough hook.' 'I enjoyed the chapters – but I just don't *love* it.' 'I can't see how it fits on my list.' Over and over and over.

I turn off my phone. Compartmentalise. *Come on. Rise above it.*

I think about Sebastian. How he'd deal with this. Well, he wouldn't have been in a mess of his own making. He is just a passenger in someone else's escapade, trying his best to do the right thing.

I stare at my screen. I should write about Sebastian going on this work trip, meeting up with old friends, remembering a time before Hanna. He'll get drunk to forget. Maybe an old flame is there, and he'll cry on her shoulder. Before I know it, my fingers are inching towards the keyboard, the thoughts distracting me from the hell of reality, and I find myself tapping away, lost in it.

*He stares out the window, thinking of a life without Ivy, never seeing that gorgeous face again. It would be like grief. Saying goodbye. But maybe he could meet someone else. Could he really do that? Say goodbye to that tiny girl he has watched grow? Who he has poured his whole heart into?*

I look out the window, imagining Sebastian arriving back in his old life. This place he used to call home. So relieved to be welcomed with open arms that know and care about him. The overwhelming relief to be away from the situation he's stuck in. Meeting up with friends who cheer when he walks into the room. Right, how can I move the plot forward? I take a deep sip of my drink. Sebastian makes me feel calm, like my brother used to. He has every attribute I wish I could embody.

*The table start talking about something else as he checks a message. He frowns. It's from Hank.*

**Did Nancy have plans to go out after sitting at yours? It's just that she usually lets us know if she's not going to be around, and her phone is off.**

*Sebastian frowns again.*

**I'm afraid I can't help – I'm away for work. I'll message Hanna and see if she knows anything.**

*Nancy arrived to sit for Ivy as he left for his flight. Hanna had a migraine and he refused to leave her in that state alone. And Hanna hadn't seemed to mind that the girl was coming over, for a change. It had left him feeling quite elated as he'd left for the airport.*

**Sorry to bother you. I'm sure she just forgot.**

*He shoves his phone in his pocket and turns to Laurie, who was his right-hand woman on the team and a good friend. Once Hanna arrived in the picture Laurie backed off considerably. He always knew his friend sensed something was off. 'Any other news I missed? Hey, whatever happened to Gerald?'*

*'I hear he's working over in Detroit. No one is sad about it.' She laughs.*

192

'Did Stella stay?' Sebastian enquires. Stella was Gerald's assistant, who Sebastian always thought was too good to be a junior member of the team.

'Nah, she left too. Was a bit weird that whole thing. She just didn't come in one day. Everyone assumed it was because she was loyal to Gerald, and she went back to Texas, or wherever it was she came from. Didn't even send an email. HR was pissed. It was around the same time you guys hit the road; you must have been too busy with the move to notice.'

'That's a shame.' Sebastian thinks of her. The way during her first presentation she blew them all away. She could have been a great asset to the team.

Plus, she'd really made something of herself, after running away from home at a young age. Wasn't she fostered in Texas or something? He remembers being very impressed she'd managed to pull herself together, without a family network to rely on. All she did was work; she didn't seem to have any friends outside of the office.

He thinks of the last time he saw her, at the Christmas party, just before they moved away. And that conversation they'd had by the fire escape. The dark shadow that fell over Hanna's face when she caught them together.

A few hours later and I look up. I take another glug of my drink; it hits the back of my throat and I cough. Wiping my mouth, I look at the screen. I'm quite pleased with it. I've set up a few things there for Emma to run with. And I'm pleased I picked up on that Texan thing with the purse in Hanna's souvenir box she laid out in the previous chapter. I'm elated. It seems Emma isn't the only one co-dependent on this stuff.

'Working?' Marco asks as he sets down yet another beer.

'Write drunk, edit sober.' He looks at me quizzically. 'Hemmingway,' I explain, and he jerks his head.

'Cool.'

I take out my phone and switch it back on. I try to stop myself, but I can't, and I google my name. Already two articles about Robyn, Emma and me. Twitter alight with conspiracy theories. My phone rings. *Max. Gah.*

'Why's your phone off, Felix? It's chaos over here,' he says, breathless. 'I tried Emma but couldn't get through.'

'She's probably on a whiteout,' I tell him. 'She's furious.'

'It's tomorrow's birdcage liner – we just gotta ride the wave. Once it's died down, I'm thinking maybe a grovelling apology – something about how marriage ain't perfect, and you got an intense working relationship to deal with. Might even add to the intrigue of your relationship – the passion, the creativity, you know?' I can hear him straining as he attempts to pacify me.

'Well, I just hope Robyn is okay,' I say.

'You got it, Felix. Let's buckle down and push through this together, then we'll be back on track in no time.'

'What are the publishers saying?' I croak. There is a pause.

'They're in the thick of it, Felix, fighting fires left and right. But hey, you two are their top-selling authors, they'll pull out all the stops to fix this mess. Once the truth about this girl's situation surfaces, that old affair will fade into the background.'

194

'So, we just wait?'

'Felix, there isn't much else we can do. But hey, at least we're not knee-deep in some high-stakes campaign. Although, it's all column inches. We may even see your backlist creep up again.' I shrivel at where his mind has gone. 'Just get through this, write the book, keep going. Thank goodness you're hidden away in France. By the time summer wraps, this'll all be a distant blur, and we'll have a book to show for it.'

'Yep,' I say, weakly.

'Hang in there, Felix. And get Emma to call me!'

I hang up the phone, rubbing my face. I should get back to the house. I pick up my bag to go.

'More?' Marco asks, gesturing to my empty glass, and I reconsider.

'Yep, just one more.'

'You're trending,' he tells me, showing me his phone. 'Nothing ever 'appens around 'ere.' He pats my shoulder. 'That's an – 'ow you say? – *accomplissement*?'

I am annoyed by the humour in his voice. 'A girl is missing. It's a shame this circus is distracting from that,' I say with a sigh.

'Shit, man, *pardon*. You see these things . . . l'*internet* . . .' He shrugs.

'You're Juliette's boyfriend, aren't you?' I ask.

He snorts a laugh. 'Juliette? Boyfriend? She is – 'ow you say? – a free spirit.' This news improves my mood slightly, and then comes the lick of shame. I down the drink.

'I better head back.' I pick up my bag and head to the glass frontage, looking out towards the square. My heart sinks as I notice a guy wearing a long-lens camera around his neck. Is he a pap? I watch him wander the circumference of the fountain. Then a lady wearing a visor stops to chat, and they hug. And I realise he's just some retiree on holiday. I'm jumpy. Still, I'm right to keep an eye out. It won't be long until they find us and send someone out to get a shot. That will be worth a lot of money. At least Emma made sure she didn't share our exact location on our socials. We've learnt our lesson the hard way doing that.

Marco joins me at the window and follows my gaze. I scratch my face anxiously. 'Journalists?' he asks. He seems to be enjoying having access to some international drama.

'Not yet,' I mutter back, still watching. God, if they get a picture of me looking how I do, and without Emma in tow, there'll be a feeding frenzy.

How am I going to get out of here? There isn't anywhere obvious to get a cab, and none of my apps work. 'Any chance I can call a cab from here?'

Marco laughs. But then considers my situation. 'Need a drive? If you no mind waiting, I can when I finish.'

I eye him up, unsure if I can trust him. 'Sure. Thanks.'

# CHAPTER TWENTY-FOUR

'What a shit show,' I say as we drive out of town in Marco's little red rust bucket. The air con is broken, and the windows are down. Our hair and shirts bellow and flap as we charge down the main road towards the turning for the *hameau*.

I want to believe Max when he says this will blow over. I just have this feeling that a bulldozer is about to flatten me, and I feel scared and claustrophobic, as if the walls are closing in.

'Being a *célébrité* must be crazy,' Marco says.

I nod slowly. 'Yeah.'

'Terrible,' he says, glancing over as he drives. This is a trick. If you moan about fame, people think you're an overprivileged, selfish prick. There is zero sympathy. 'Did you always want to be famous?' he asks, the sentence slow as he finds the words.

I think about the question. Yeah, I did. But you don't admit things like that. I wanted to do something that seemed impossible. Show my parents that they lost out by not treating me as a serious contender, and all the others who thought I'd most likely amount to nothing.

Another thought, from somewhere deep down in the pit of who I am. Something from the grainy echoes of my childhood. My brother once found my little book of short stories I hid from everyone when I was in that awkward pre-teen phase. I thought he'd ridicule me for writing – it didn't seem like something which would hold merit. But he told me I had something special; he looked up at me from that old ringbound notebook with this expression of wonder. *You're really talented, you know that, Fe?* I've never forgotten that.

'I just wanted to write,' I reply weakly. I wipe my face. 'It's all bollocks, they're just trying to sell papers.'

'You should sue,' Marco says, banging on the steering wheel, irate on my behalf.

'Yeah,' I reply weakly. Not sure I'd get very far with that one.

It's late by the time we pull up outside the house. Marco is a nice guy; he seems to have cultivated some sort of loyalty towards me, which is very sweet, although rather misguided.

'You want to come in for a drink?' I ask.

'It's okay.' He shrugs.

'Come on,' I push.

I could do with a drinking buddy on the veranda. Someone to protect me from Emma, who I'm sure will be itching for a fight. He could be the perfect deterrent.

'Cool,' Marco says, with another of his trademark shrugs.

As soon as I open the car door the sound of music infiltrates. I recognise the beat.

Talking Heads, 'Psycho Killer' – Emma's favourite – pumps

out the house and into the starry sky. I'd imagined Emma sitting, quietly seething, with her favourite book for comfort. But it sounds like she had other ideas.

I knock on the front door – 'Emma!' – but she can't hear me. I grin at Marco. 'Forgot my keys. Let's go around the back.' I regret asking Marco to come in for a drink now, but am unsure how to take the offer back.

As we go around the back of the house the music gets louder, and the sinking feeling in my stomach plunges further.

Just before I walk into the orange glow of the house, I get the sense that the scene that will greet me is something I should prepare for. The French chorus of the song spits in jittering slaps of sound, and I can't help but jut my head in time to the infectious beat.

I step inside, stop still, as my mind computes.

Emma dancing alone, eyes closed, with a glass of wine in her hand. The music is loud, far louder than she usually allows. She's wearing a multi-layered sheer patterned dress, which flutters evocatively as she twists and turns to the all-encompassing sound.

'Emma,' I call, taking off my bag, placing it by the door. Marco steps in beside me. A few empty bottles of wine are on the bar, and it stinks of cigarettes. 'Emma?' I shout. But she's so lost, I can't get through. I watch her toned body move to the music. I so rarely see her like this, it is quite fascinating to watch her get out of her head, the place she so firmly inhabits all the time.

Marco is staring, a distracted smile on his face. Emma's

eyes spring open; they are wild and sparkling. She's drunk.
She rarely gets drunk; she leaves that to me. The sight of it
spikes my nerves and I feel uneasy.

Then the door to the toilet opens and Juliette steps out. She
sees us and runs over, hugging Marco, and then me. I realise
she is wearing one of Emma's dresses. It makes me feel a little
uneasy, the way my wife has been playing dress-up with her
new friend. 'You're 'ere,' she whispers in my ear. Emma's eyes
fall upon us, and she loses balance slightly, then stops still,
staring. Our eyes connect.

How did we get here? We don't need to say anything at all.
All our deep cuts are bleeding, as we stand there watching.
The hurt, the pain. All of it.

Juliette breaks the moment. She is also drunk, and she
dances around us, trying to pull Marco in, and after coyly
refusing a few times, he finally picks Juliette up and spins her
around. She laughs. They seem so carefree and unburdened
compared to us.

The song ends and our song comes on. 'This Must Be the
Place'. Emma comes over and hugs me tightly, the smell of
alcohol on her breath making me blink. 'You're back,' is all
she says.

'You're drunk,' I manage.

'Juliette was here changing the sheets. We decided to have
a bit of a party.' She hiccups. 'I wanted to have some fun.
You're not the only one who gets to do that, you know.' She
is slurring, poking me in my ribs. Our argument and the news
headlines have caused a break in the matrix. She runs her

hand down my face. 'Why so sad, Felix?' she says with an exaggerated frown. I flick her hand away.

'The whole fucking world thinks I had something to do with this missing girl. That could be why,' I reply tersely.

I'm distracted by Juliette and Marco dancing, Emma notices. She leans in again.

'Did you fuck her?' she whispers in my ear.

I shake my head. 'Fuck you,' I reply angrily.

'I thought she was your type. Pretty, impressed with your *talent*.' She grins at me as her hand runs down my chest, working its way down towards my trouser leg. I flap her hand away.

'Get off.' I move, and she laughs, a loud cackling sound.

I walk over to the stereo and turn the music down; Marco and Juliette look over, disappointed. 'Sorry, guys, party is finished. It's been a big day; I think we need to get some rest.'

Juliette stumbles over. 'Felix! But we're 'aving a party!' she cries, arms in the air. Marco pulls at her, far more sober and with a better ability to read the room, tells her something in French and she nods in understanding.

'You're such a *party-pooper*,' Emma tells me. The use of British slang grates. 'Goodbye, Juliette,' Emma tells her as she trips over to the kitchen and pours more wine, looking over at me in a sour, hate-filled way.

I walk Juliette and Marco to the door. 'Thanks for the lift,' I tell him, and he nods, *no worries*, and gets into the driver's seat.

Juliette lingers. 'Ciao, Felix,' she says, leaning in for a kiss on my cheek.

Before she moves away, she whispers, 'Did you like watching?' And I freeze, a cold trickle of realisation down my back. She did see me in the orchard. Jesus. I swallow. I'm so shocked I don't have time to react before she runs off to the car.

I turn back into the house. The music is off, the house still. I find Emma pouring more wine in the kitchen, nodding her head to music which isn't playing.

'Emma, maybe you should slow down,' I tell her. She looks up at me, a frown forming.

'Are you kidding me?' The liquid slops around in her glass, red wine spilling out the rim.

'I thought you said you weren't meant to drink too much on those pills?' I say, repeating the same reason she uses to only have a glass or two.

'I'm fine! I just wanted to have some fun. Or is that not allowed? Am I just meant to lock myself away and write?' she slurs. 'You'd like that, wouldn't you? For me to just stay quiet.' She puts a finger up to her lips. It wobbles. 'Little Emma, doing all the work, all the admin, keeping everything rolling, so you can do whatever the hell you want!' She laughs. 'You've used me, Felix.'

'Emma, you're drunk, you don't know what you're saying.'

'Ha!' she spits. 'Sorry, Felix, I'd forgotten I'm not allowed.' Then she pauses, using the lip of the counter to balance herself. 'Did you want her all for yourself?' she asks, a dirty smile of resentment on her lips. 'Am I on your turf?' She walks towards me, her steps clumsy. 'Did you have her marked for your next adventure?' She flicks at the collar of my shirt. 'Was she to be your next *victim*?' she asks, wickedness shimmying in her eyes.

'Emma!' I cry. She's hurt and using anything she can to fling at me. 'What the hell does that mean?'

'You can't be so dumb that I have to explain it to you!' She bangs the flat of her hand on the counter. She looks ahead, takes a deep sip of wine. 'I never thought I'd end up like my mother.'

'Your mother? What the hell has she got to do with anything?' Emma's mother, Estelle, lives in New Jersey with her three Pomeranian dogs. She's as mad as a box of frogs. She has T-shirts printed with the covers of all of Morgan Savage's books emblazoned on the front and is front row at every book signing and event she can get to. Emma finds her embarrassing; she does not live up to her prestigious Sarah Lawrence-educated publishing brand at all. She never introduces her to anyone and leaves her hanging, so she just looks like an overeager fan in the corner. I always make sure I head over, give her a hug and take a photo while Emma talks to someone far more important, in her eyes. Estelle has put every hope, every lost ambition, onto her golden child. If anything, Max has been more of a parent figure to Emma. And she sure looks up to him like a father, as if she is desperate for that relationship with someone she deems worthy. Her perfectionism is always heightened when he is around. I think that's why these late deadlines and the writer's block has affected her so much. She hasn't been able to perform as the perfect pseudo daughter.

My own mother always gives me this painful look, like she loves me so much her heart might burst and can tell that no matter how many times I tell her otherwise, I've never truly been happy. She can see straight through the facade.

Emma takes a deep breath before launching into it. 'She just let things wash over her. Pretending nothing was happening while my dad tapped the ass of every skirt in town,' she spits. 'Never standing up for herself, sorting out mess after mess for him. She is pathetic. And so am I.'

'Oh, Emma, that's not fair,' I try.

'The only reason she left him is because he died! Otherwise, she would have just taken his shit for ever,' she cries, accentuating that last word. 'I promised myself I'd never be like her. That I'd do everything in my power to be somebody, even with all the crap that was dumped on me. He wasn't going to win. And here I am, doing exactly the same thing!'

I never met Emma's father. He died of a heart attack when Emma was in her early teens, leaving her mother with all his gambling debt, and Emma to fight her way to the top.

She's desperate for this argument; I can feel the rage rising from her like steam. 'You've been waiting for this, haven't you? This whole time, hoping you could bash me over the head with that. Because he's not here to punish. It's all you've ever wanted – for me to turn into him. You never trusted me! How do you think that makes me feel?'

She whips around. 'It's never you, is it, Felix? It's never your fault. Always someone else's. Isn't it time you took responsibility for your own mistakes? Without having us all running around to clear them up for you?' she screams. She grabs a vase off a sideboard and smashes it on the floor. I stare at the broken pieces. 'All I ever do is cover up your mistakes! You have no idea what I've shielded you from! And I'm sick of it.'

I need to cool this whole thing down; it's teetering on the edge of catastrophe. 'This argument is a huge waste of time. You think what you want, I have no control over that.' My voice is calmer, less vicious. I want to get rid of that crazed tint in her eye. 'Maybe we should leave, go somewhere else? This place . . .' I gesture around the room. 'We're not good like this, remote, alone. It's not helping anything. It was a bad idea. Let's pack up the car and head for Paris. We could leave first thing.'

'Paris? You want to go to the Louve or hang in St Germain looking like you're somebody?' She laughs callously. 'Felix, we are the number one most wanted for every paparazzi in France. You think we'll be safe in Paris? No,' she cries. 'We are meant to write here. I am not leaving until the book is done. We need to just shut everything out.' Her eyes land on the painting of the girl in the picture. Her voice comes out in a shaky wobble. 'Whatever our fate is, here is where we'll find it.' She casts her eyes around the house; she's so full of pent-up rage. She whispers, 'I love you and I hate you,' viciously. She picks up another ornament from the sideboard and smashes it on the floor. 'All I've done is give,' she cries. 'I've given you my body, my soul – and what do you do? You've broken every promise you've ever made to me.

'When I met you, you were nothing! A washed-up wannabe. Do you think you'd ever have got published on your own? Do you? I did that. I gave you everything you ever wanted. And you still treat me like a fool.' She puts her hands over her ears. 'I can't believe what I have done for you.'

'Emma, I . . .' I try. 'I love you, Emma, I've always loved you.' But she just stares at me. Anger built to a crescendo that's plateaued into quiet realisation.

'You have always cared about something else over me,' she whispers. 'Women, alcohol . . . I wasn't ever enough.'

I wipe my face. I shouldn't say it, but I can't help myself. 'All you've ever cared about is Morgan.'

'That is not true. It's you, Felix. It's always been you,' she whispers. 'And you've ruined everything.'

I shake my head. 'Fine. Wallow in how much you hate me. How much it is all my fault. See how that helps.' I grab a bottle of whisky and go out to the veranda, lighting a cigarette. And I proceed to drink my way through it, smoking cigarette after cigarette, until all the dark thoughts lodged in my brain are barely a whisper and I don't think about anything any more.

# PART TWO

# CHAPTER TWENTY-FIVE

Morning. My head. *Fuuuuuck me.* I grab it. A meat cleaver is lodged in there – that must be it. The pain. The agony. The sound of birds chirping is like nails digging into my ears, and all the bright morning colours bleed into my eyeballs and I can't open them fully.

The chaos of the previous day slides into my mind. The newspaper headlines. I groan. Emma drunk, dancing with Juliette and her whispering in my ear, *Did you like watching?* Then the fight. Jesus.

Please let this just be the worst hangover I've had in a long time, and it will shift away and something better will replace these terrible thoughts. It can't be as bad as I remember. It just can't.

I turn to the other side of the bed. It's empty. Emma is probably by the pool, drinking a litre of iced water and popping anti-anxiety pills. I find my phone on the floor by the bed. Its screen has a new smash through it. I must have dropped it last night. I can't even remember getting into bed.

I can't bear the thought of reading Emma's chapter. But it's an opportunity to see inside her head, and I want to know before I go down to her. I flick to my emails, but I can't find it. That's strange. In all the years we've been doing this she's never once neglected to send me her chapter at ten a.m. on the dot. Ever.

She must be in the worst mood imaginable to not have followed through. Snatches of the previous night ring in my ears. On the veranda drinking, something smashing to the floor and breaking into a thousand pieces. Emma berating me. The anger I felt towards her in the pit of my stomach, a fire lit inside. It reminds me of the night before we left for France. Patches of time unaccounted for. A violent occurrence I can't put my finger on. A blind state of confusion, and that same feeling of gnawing shame.

I walk to the window, expecting to see Emma in her bathing suit by the pool.

But she isn't there.

I pull a T-shirt on, and some boxers, not quite ready to deal with the wrath, but if I don't get a glass of water down me soon, I might pass out. Maybe it'll be the silent treatment? Emma is particularly good at that. I feel so heavy. So unbelievably worn out.

I head downstairs tentatively and stand in the living area. The house feels different, sinister even in this morning light. 'Emma?' I call. The door to the study is closed and I grab a croissant from the kitchen to soak up some of that pooling sour alcohol in my stomach, before peering inside to see if she's writing. But the room is empty. She is not tapping away behind the desk.

I look around at the mess in the kitchen, scratching the back of my head. Broken, smashed things all around. The hanging smell of rotten booze and cigarettes in the air. It's like walking into the remnants of a house party that got out of hand.

It is quiet. Too quiet. Some of the furniture is turned on its side, and I carefully bring it to its feet. 'Emma?' I call.

Emma doesn't like mess. I am surprised she hasn't tidied up in a frenzy of irritation. Maybe she is waiting for me to emerge, to show me how bad things really are.

The door to the veranda is open. Not fully, just a bit. I think of the metal bed frame. I don't remember the robe strap tied to it this morning. Did I even . . . ? I have no memory of fixing her to it. No memory at all.

The croissant falls out of my hand.

I quickly make my way to the back door. 'Emma?' I call out to the simmering view. A flock of birds rises from the closest tree.

My stomach plummets. I stumble forwards, rushing, lumbering across the grass and hiking over the wall in one swift movement. 'Emma!' I scream, careering down, running as fast as my aching legs can take me. Her voice ringing in my ears: *And for a split second she expected to open her eyes and be in bed . . . But instead, she just hit the floor.* My heart hammers in my chest.

Emma. Emma. Beautiful, extraordinary Emma. *No – you can't have.* My throat runs red as I call her name, again and again. The internal thrashing of desperation in my ears. I run to the cliff. *Did I forget? Did I forget?*

211

I run to the clearing that extends out to the sky and skid as I reach the top. I fall to the ground, hoisting myself so I'm lying on my front, face down, off the edge of the cliff.

I blink the wet moisture out of my gritty bevelled eyes. I blink and blink, the ground below coming in and out of focus. For a second my imagination brings me Emma's body heaped on the floor, limbs askew, lying in a pool of her own blood.

But there is nothing.

I turn onto my back, looking up at the sky. 'Emma!' I cry again. 'Emma!' Then I get up and rush around the side of the cliff, where you can pick your way sharply down to the bottom. I skid and slip, my impetus fraught with urgency. 'Emma!' I call and call as I reach the bottom.

But she isn't there.

I walk back up to the house, covered in dust, feeling foolish. I've cut my hand badly and the oozing blood is dripping off my finger and onto the ground. I feel shaken and confused, and I can't catch my breath.

I dust myself off, and sit on the step of the veranda and light a cigarette. She must have gone into town. I've completely overreacted. I sit there in that static state of shock after a bout of feverish adrenalin. I stub out my cigarette and head into the house. The sight of my reflection distracts me, and I stare. I look terrible. Covered in dirt, a smear of my own blood across my face. Jesus. What have I become?

I walk to the hallway and open the front door, looking out at the courtyard. The hire car is still there. Huh. Maybe she's pottering around the orchard lost in a book. She'll come back and laugh at me for imagining the worst and getting in such a state. She'll feel sorry for me, and we'll hatch a plan to work out this Robyn mess. She'll know exactly what to do and then we'll make up. She'll pull me into her arms, and we'll collapse into an impassioned embrace, grabbing at each other with an urgency that is hoarded for when we're close to the edge.

But the nagging feeling that she didn't write her chapter remains. She's just never done that. When she was sick with flu and could barely stand, she'd still written at the allotted time. She'd book flights around the schedule, not wanting to be distracted and miss her hallowed writing hour. That ring-fenced time is sacred, she says.

I look around. I should tidy. That way at least, when she does reappear, the berating I will get will be a little less ageing.

I grab a black bin bag from under the sink and begin to work. Chucking rubbish away, emptying ashtrays, lining empty bottles up on the counter. Sweeping broken glass and ceramics. We'll have to pay for the breakages. We can afford it, but I hope Emma didn't destroy any priceless heirlooms. I pull a chair back up and plump cushions on the sofa.

I hoover and mop the floors. Cleaning the kitchen, I wipe down surfaces and finally stand back to admire my work. I notice a smear of blood on the refrigerator. I walk over, touch it. It's dry. I look at my hand, which I plastered up before I began cleaning. Maybe I handled it? Yes, that must be it. I grab the all-purpose cleaner and spray, wiping the blood with a cloth.

Next, I tie up the black bags of rubbish and walk out the gates, to the main bins out front. As luck would have it, just as I do, a rubbish truck pulls up and I throw the bags in, waving thanks to the guys in the front. '*Merci!*' I cry, dusting my hands together as I walk back to the house. Perfect timing.

I admire my work as I pace the room, coffee in hand. Right, well, at least she won't be able to add that to her list of woes. Or use it to call me lazy and useless and . . . well . . . all those other things she pins on me. I take the coffee out to the veranda and sigh, my hangover making an exodus. Maybe today will turn out not too bad after all.

I check my phone again. But nothing from Emma. It's past two in the afternoon. Maybe she's taken that trip to the local farm or gone to that winery she was talking about. She's probably having a lovely time, a break from the intensity we've cultivated here. Good for her, she needs it. Maybe I should call? But she'd hate that. She'll say I'm checking up on her. She wants space, and I should give it to her.

I think about how we got here, rewind the tape. That first book we wrote; I'd never felt so alive. We were like giddy teenagers throwing it together without a care in the world. No high stakes, just fun. Partying, lovemaking, and the words just flowed, and we were free. Then she tapped Max, a contact she'd known for years in the industry, and he took us on, and somehow, a publishing deal hit the table. Well, an auction between the top five houses, and again, we couldn't believe how easy it all seemed when we accepted the highest bid. It all happened so fast, like a house of cards tumbling.

And before I knew it, I had everything I thought I wanted. My dreams were coming true. Emma was the great editor, so I didn't think much of it when that part of the process was placed firmly in her hands. *Let her fiddle*, I'd thought. *This is her territory, after all.* Besides, all those edits – the structural edit, the copy-edit, the proofread at the end – it sounded like a lot of grunt work and Emma relished it. I was just enjoying walking around being a 'published author'. More fool me, I suppose.

It wasn't until our launch party that I realised what Emma's 'fiddling' comprised of. I was laughing with a bookseller, selecting a gleaming new copy from the pile and flicking through the pages. My chuckle dwindled as I realised all my favourite parts of prose were gone, the red herrings more frequent, and the cliffhangers heightened.

I couldn't enjoy the party after that. Yes, I played my part. I gave a speech, I listened graciously to the rapt applause. Answered questions during the Q&A they'd put on. But inside . . . inside something had been chipped away at. Simile by simile, metaphor by metaphor. Gone.

That was when we had our first blowout argument. She called me selfish, egotistical. I got drunk and called her worse.

A crack had formed, and I had no idea how seismic it was to become.

And now I am here. A worthless drunk following Emma's coat tails. She's right, I have used her body and her mind. And I've desecrated them both. Rendered her unable to continue her writing. That's why she hasn't written today, isn't it? It's because of me.

*How do I fix this?*

*Is it fixable?*

I grab my copy of *The Catcher in the Rye* from the house – I found it in a vintage bookshop in Greenwich Village years ago, and have feverishly reread it many times. But lately, I've found reading tough, since all this happened. It's as though the great writers are taunting me with their genius, reminding me what a fool I am to even have tried. I get in the hammock tied between trees on the far side of the lawn, and try the first page, but nothing sticks. I place the upturned book on my chest, looking up at the blue sky, and the wispy, floating clouds.

I sleep. At first I think the noise that wakes me is Emma returning and I turn quickly to look. The movement knocks me from the hammock, and I fall, the ground hitting me with a painful thud. Fucking hammocks.

I stand up and look towards the house, expecting to see Emma standing there, leaning on the curve of the stone arch. But, I realise, the sound was just the back door knocking against the frame. A dull light has descended on the garden, the day is flagging, the sun is tired of this. So am I.

I walk up to the house. Is she back? I call her name. 'Emma?' But the inside of the house has the same cold, lonely feeling I was greeted with when I came down this morning. My hand still stings. And I wonder if Emma has any of those alcohol rub things to stop infections within her multiple carefully organised packing cubes she's obsessed with. I trudge up, one

216

step at a time, the muscles in my legs aching from the stresses of the last few days.

Her washbags aren't in the en suite. Huh.

I walk back into our room and realise her sarong isn't slung over the door, where it has lived for most of our stay. Her little embossed travel jewellery box isn't sitting on top of the antique drawers either. I turn and walk towards the wardrobe. I pull it open, and to my horror, all that is revealed is empty hangers jingling with the force of the motion. All her things are gone. I kneel on the floor and look under the bed for her black hard-shell case. But it isn't there.

It's gone.

Emma has gone.

# CHAPTER TWENTY-SIX

The first thing I do is get out my phone and try her number. It goes straight to her usual voicemail: *'Please email or call Max if it's urgent, I don't listen to voicemails.'* A note! She must have left a note. I rush down the stairs two at a time. But I cleaned, and everything is pristine, the kitchen table newly wiped down. Our things collected in straight little piles that I spoil in an instant looking for it. Nothing. Every surface sprayed and polished. Once I'd started, I couldn't stop. I've never scrubbed anything so well in my entire life. It was as if scouring this house clean would somehow mend the damage to my marriage.

I grab my cigarettes and head to the veranda, plopping down on the cool stone step and sparking up. Wiping my face, trying to compute what the hell this means.

Emma has left me. How do I feel?

Filled with dread and despair, panic. She is leaving me to deal with all this Robyn stuff on my own. I thought we were in this together. A team whatever happened, whatever I did. Because we have hurt each other, we would both pay the price, we would be there for each other no matter what.

But this is her saying no to all that. The imaginary deal we signed, she's torn it up, thrown it in the air in disgust and run away. Just when I need her the most. Is she saving her own skin? Removing herself from the scandal? Making me the fallout guy?

I'll call Max. I'm sure Emma will have got there first. And I need to get my story across otherwise he'll side with her. I scratch my head in a fidget, already fearing a losing battle ahead. Max knew Emma way before me. They are tight. He must know she has all the talent. But I must try. He picks up instantly.

'Felix! Jesus, finally. Are you okay?' Ah, he does know. I arrange the narrative before going in.

'Max, I—'

'Listen, they've got a few news crews looking for you. They've been using your Instagram posts trying to match the town you're in. So, for the love of all that's holy, stay put in the villa, all right? I'm swatting away calls left and right here. They still haven't found that damn girl and I've heard on the grapevine *The New York Times* is doing some digging into your past . . . erm . . . dealings.'

'What?' I breathe, startled. 'What do you mean, past dealings?' My whole body rigid.

'A few other girls have come out of the woodwork, Felix, you know, bandwagon stuff. They won't find anything. It's all heavily NDA'ed up. They're smelling a payout. It's not illegal to have an affair,' he scoffs. 'Half the country would be hauled up in court!'

'Listen, Max, I know Emma may have called but—' I begin to launch into it.

'Felix, the best thing to do is to hold a united front. Lay low, stay in the villa, wait it out. Is she there? Put me on speaker-phone. Is her damn phone broken or something? This isn't like her; tell her she's giving me a hernia!' And then it dawns on me: he doesn't know.

'She . . . she's just in the shower,' I stammer. 'I'll get her to give you a call later.' I'm not feeling fortified enough to tell him yet. He's dealing with enough; I can't bring myself to produce another problem to lay at his door. 'She can't cope with looking at her phone at the moment,' I explain. 'She's devastated.'

'Okay,' he barks. He's in troubleshooting mode. 'I gotta talk this through with her, it's not like her to ditch her head in the sand in times like this.' He sounds hurt. 'I'll get Jenny to book in one of those Zoom things for us.' I hear him shout his assistant's name and he hangs up. I swallow.

I stare at the phone in my hand. I should have told him, but I'm not ready. Maybe she'll come back. Besides, if he finds out Emma has left me, what if he sides with her and throws me to the wolves to clear a path for Emma's future success?

I stare out at the gorgeous evening view. I know it well now. The placement of the trees and the swallows that duck and dive. I've memorised the undulating high-pitched scream of crickets. I know that in about half an hour the last of the sun will leave the tips of those trees in the distance and a hazy darkness will fall lightly, growing in depth over time. I blow out a long stream of smoke. The copy of *The Catcher in the Rye* I'd tried reading on the hammock lies face down on the table, taunting me.

The book. Number nine. The book that didn't want to be written. That we've agonised over for months and months, and when we were finally getting somewhere, Emma has done the impossible: turned her back on a story. I never thought she couldn't finish once she'd started. The idea of it makes me sick. Like she's left me dangling in a noose and kicked the chair below away.

I imagine returning to New York solo. The thought turns my stomach. The questions. Am I now tarnished goods? The publishers will probably strike a deal with Emma and she'll become an instant bestseller in her own right – happier too, without me dragging her down. Maybe she'll even find the confidence to put herself centre stage for once, without having me there to hide behind.

A new thought. Do I even need to go back? I could buy a little cottage in the Springs up state, and sit on the beach, working on my great literary novel I've always talked about. Once enough time has passed, and they have forgotten, I could reappear on the scene with something, bigger, better, more original.

Maybe without Emma and her snarky comments, and the weight of having to fulfil a new Morgan Savage contract, I'll finally achieve my dream, rather than play a part in someone else's. Yes, that is what I'll do. Find my voice that has been stamped all over for so long.

Robyn will appear, that whole mess will be sorted out by Max and the publishers. I could make something of myself that's real, that's truly mine. Can I even do that? Maybe before, I just hadn't lived enough. I've now experienced great achievement and great loss. I've loved and despised. I've done dastardly things I'm not proud of. Maybe this is my chance to redeem all that. Be a better person. Find some pride and self-respect.

Sometimes for something new to begin, the present needs to be smashed into a million irresolvable pieces. Maybe, clever Emma, maybe she knew that. Maybe our breaking point has been reached. I see the face of that girl I met in the bookshop, her large glasses she hasn't worn since we found fame and got her eyes fixed. I wish I could go back to that day and start all over again. And never have met her at all.

I bang a fist against my head. Why won't it just stop? I am exhausted by the constant thoughts rushing through me, never giving me an opportunity to see things clearly.

I reach for the only thing I know will give me a moment to catch my breath.

# CHAPTER TWENTY-SEVEN

The wheels are off. I don't have anyone to stop me, and when I wake up the next day, I can barely remember getting into bed at all. I somehow manage to heave myself out of bed and have a shower, wiping the condensation off the mirror to see my reflection, giving myself a goofy, lazy smile. It falls into a grimace as my predicament rumbles between my ears.

I need a distraction from checking my phone every five minutes, and seeing what every Henry and Maureen are charging me with online. I can feel a message coming from Max, any minute, telling me he knows about Emma, and I've been dropped. It will be cold, and professional, and I will be left with the feeling of eerie nothingness, and I'm dreading it.

Because if Emma isn't with me, then she'll be dead against me. And that thought terrifies me. I know what she is capable of.

The doorbell rings, and I peer towards the entrance suspiciously. The door looms ahead as I realise it could be Emma! She's come back. She'll apologise and all of this will be forgotten, and we'll be united against all this ghastly business!

I walk quickly towards it, opening it slowly, imagining Emma's remorseful face as I bring back the door. But Juliette is standing there. '*Salut*, Felix,' she says cheerfully. Not Emma. Of course, I should have known. If there is one thing I know about my wife, it's that she's painfully stubborn.

'Juliette.' God, she is a sight for sore eyes. I've felt so alone. So desperately alone.

'*Pardon*, I don't want to disturb you,' she says. 'Are you working?' She peers over my shoulder.

'Ah, yeah. Sort of,' I lie. 'What can I do for you?'

'I'm just returning Emma's dress, and I left my clothes here, my jacket and my purse,' she says, holding a piece of fabric in her hand. 'I felt terrible, sick the next day. Was Emma okay? Your wife is crazy!' she says, laughing. 'Is she 'ere?' she asks. I'm unsure what to say and she gives me a curious look when I don't reply. 'I am sorry to 'ave bothered you. It's just that I really need my purse.'

I come to my senses. 'Yes, of course.' I begin to look around. 'I'm not sure I've seen it.'

She points to the coat rack. 'May I?' she requests, and I move aside so she can come in. '*Ici*,' she says, picking up the denim jacket. She feels around in the pocket. 'Phew!' She holds up the wallet.

'Oh, right. I think I must have assumed Emma left it. She has so many clothes it's hard to remember them all.' She stands in the hallway awkwardly.

'Do you want to come in? I'm not sure I've seen your clothes,' I say. 'A coffee?'

She stares at me, and I realise I must look a mess. She shakes her head. 'I wouldn't want to bother you.'

'Juliette, come in, have a coffee,' I tell her. She looks at me curiously. Has she been reading the rumours? Does she believe all those terrible things they are saying about me?

She smiles a little, and then a cheeky grin. 'Okay, but don't let Emma get me drunk again. I threw up all night.' She laughs, wiping her head. 'I 'aven't been that drunk for years.'

'Well, that's the thing. Emma ... Emma isn't here,' I tell her, as she walks through to the living room.

'Oh, yeah?' she asks, looking around.

'She's left me.' Juliette turns on the spot in surprise and gives me a pitying look. 'She's gone.'

'Gone?' Her eyes widen. She catches her bottom lip between her teeth. 'Where?' she asks.

'I don't know. She snuck out in the middle of the night. Back to New York? Maybe Paris? Who knows. She's taken all her things.'

Juliette lifts a hand to her mouth. 'Felix, I am sorry.' She shifts about, looking uncomfortable. 'Did you argue?' She looks up at me with those big eyes and I just want to tell her everything. I've been so alone through all of this.

I sigh. 'The last two years have been one long argument. It's been pretty bad,' I confide. 'I don't think we've ever taken it quite so far before. This news about the affair getting out, I think it was the last straw.' I sit down on the sofa and put my head in my hands. When I look up again, she's taken the seat opposite, and reaches forward, putting a comforting hand on my knee.

'I'm so sorry, Felix,' she says sympathetically.

'Don't feel sorry for me, I've been an awful husband,' I push back.

She shakes her head slowly, her eyes full of kindness. 'Oh, Felix, you are too 'ard on yourself,' she says with a sigh. 'Anyway, marriage is such an . . . archaic construct?' she says, looking at me, questioning whether she's said it right.

This makes me laugh in surprise. 'Really?'

'*Oui*. I don't think we were created to stay connected to one other person for life. It can bring out the worst in people – it can make us 'urt each other.'

I nod. She is so right. She understands me. This woman gets it all.

She stands up and looks around again, and wanders over to the fireplace, running a finger along the ledge, '*Oh là là*, so clean,' she says, inspecting her finger to see not a speck of dust.

'Once I started, well, I couldn't stop,' I explain. 'It was quite a party.'

'Will you stay now she's gone?' she asks, a lick of hope in there – or am I making it up?

'I'm . . . I'm . . .' I look around. 'I'm not sure. I think so. I haven't really worked out my plans yet. I don't know if I can face New York with everything going on. Maybe my American adventure is over, and it's time to start afresh.'

She walks over to the kitchen table and points to the open laptop. 'You are writing! Still the book?' she asks.

'Something else. Kind of.' I haven't written one word.

'Oh, I really shouldn't disturb you.'

I shake my head. 'Nah, it's all mulch at the moment,' I say, pointing to my head. 'Percolating.' Something is in there, but I'm not sure how to get going. Emma always used to start for us. I wipe my face. 'I just want Emma to call me, so we can talk. She doesn't seem ready,' I say, sadly.

'Oh, Felix, I am sorry.' Sympathy radiates.

'I just need to get my head around the fact we're just not right together. It's all for the best, you know?' I sigh, leaning back on the sofa, staring at the ceiling. 'I just feel too old to start again.'

'What?' She laughs. 'You're not that much older than me! You're not an old man.' My face heats up at the compliment. Then she tentatively asks, 'So, she just told you she was leaving and walked out the door?'

'She left in the middle of the night while I was passed out after the party. No note or anything.'

'Oh.' She scratches her cheek, just above that tiny pimple scar. 'But the car?' she questions.

I sit up. 'She must have taken a taxi.'

'Ah,' Juliette replies, with an uncertain look on her face.

'What?' I ask.

'I'm sorry, Felix, it's just that there is only one taxi driver around 'ere, and you need to book some time in advance. I'm sorry,' she tells me softly.

I realise what she is insinuating. It wasn't spontaneous, after all. Emma knew she was going that whole day as we drove into town, when she told me she loved me. It was all a lie. She'd already made up her mind, and forced the argument on us, so it had the most crushing effect and made me out to be the bad guy. What a cow.

'Who knows when it comes to Emma? I can never tell what goes on in that woman's head. I've been trying to work it out for years and have come to the conclusion that I just don't give a damn.' I sigh. 'Sorry.' I mustn't get wound up again.

'That's okay,' she replies quietly. The conversation has left a weight between us, and I take it upon myself to lighten it.

'Enough about all that. Tell me about you. What do people do for fun around here?'

She smiles. 'Swim in lakes, cycle around looking for trouble,' she says mischievously. 'Sometimes there are parties in the old monastery. Nothing like what you are used to, I am sure.'

'That seems a whole lot of fun to me,' I tell her.

She glances at me, wondering if she should say something. 'We should go for a swim in the lake. We could cycle there, this afternoon – if you don't 'ave much work to do?'

'I shouldn't,' I say, thinking about Max's advice. 'I'm under strict instructions to stay in the house.'

'I take you the off-road route – they'll never know. Come on, you need to get out of 'ere for a break.'

I really shouldn't. But then, if Emma is going to walk out on me like that, I may as well enjoy myself. 'Yeah, why the hell not? That sounds great.'

I could get used to this. A barefoot summer in France without having to step on eggshells constantly. Swimming in lakes, cycling down country lanes. Bliss.

But then an uncomfortable niggle. I think of what Juliette said about the taxi. I'll drop Emma a text. Just to ask if she's okay. Can't hurt. A carefully drafted message she'll reply to hotly but then I've done my bit and can relax again. This silence is making the whole situation feel far more sinister than it should. She obviously doesn't want to hear from me, probably doesn't even care.

But if I could just write something for her to pick up, look at, see there is a future without animosity. The last thing I want is an enemy right now, not with everything she has in her arsenal against me. She knows things I would hate to become public, and if she turned on me . . . well. The thought makes me shiver.

Maybe in time, we could even be friends. There'll be a lot of business we'll need to agree on and deal with, even if she never wants to see me again. It would be best if we could start this on the right footing. I get out my phone and draft a text.

*Emma. I'm sorry we argued. You know I love you, whatever the outcome of this. Can we talk, no pressure? F x.*

I reread it a few times. Yes. That is perfect. Nothing bitter or angry. I send it.

Emma and I have been a lot of things. Darkness followed us around. But maybe, just maybe, we could end this in a healthy way. Be one of those couples people talk about, who become friends after divorce. Once the news of my affair has died down, we could write one of those 'consciously uncoupling' articles in *The New Yorker* and our backlist would be on fire. Emma will like that. I'll suggest it later down the line. Once we've got over the initial shock of this.

# CHAPTER TWENTY-EIGHT

The sun hits our backs as we ride down the lane. I feel younger than I have all decade. The breeze drifts through Juliette's long untamed hair as we weave in and out of each other, laughing. God, this feels good after the darkness I've been wrapped within the last few days.

Juliette's brakes squeak as we come to a stop by a tree. She stands her bike against the trunk and reaches up for an apple, picking it off and handing it to me. She gestures for me to take a bite and I do. And she smiles as I nod in appreciation for it. Bloody delicious. All of it. We get back on and ride beneath the dappled light under the trees.

I realise, for the first time in years, that I don't feel the need to find oblivion. I thought I'd been attempting to blot out my feelings, but maybe it was Emma I was trying to blot out. She'd completely invaded my every thought and feeling. I ride, and we swerve in and out of each other's tracks, pressing forward, Juliette laughing at me as I race her. All those problems knocking at my door, they don't feel so close right now.

We come to a little path off the road, and she ducks into it without notice, forcing me to apply the brake. The bike skids to a stop and I topple over. I lie on my back, winded, looking up at the trees. Juliette's face replaces shining leaves, her hair dangling from above, and she holds out a hand to help me. I take it.

I walk the bike through the path and balance it by hers. She pushes me playfully, before running ahead, daring me to chase her. And I do. By God, I do. It's all I've wanted to do this whole time I've been here, if I'm honest.

'Come on, Felix, you first.' She points to the lake. It is utterly gorgeous. A dreamy enclave with trees shielding the world. The sky blue, the water a clear green.

Juliette comes over, and forcibly jimmies up my T-shirt. I laugh and try to fight her off, but she isn't having any of it. 'Fine,' I say gruffly, whipping it off and running down the jetty before bombing in with a 'Weeeeee!'. The cool water hits and I come to the surface, gasping. She is standing on the wooden planks above, grinning, before removing her dress and performing a perfect arrow dive. She comes up for air, swiping her hair back and wiping the water off her face with a grin. She swims up next to me, splashing water in my direction.

My smile wavers. A slam of a memory careers into my face like a slap. Isn't there a scene like this in one of our books? A couple swimming in a lake the day after their wedding. A murderous stranger in the reeds who slips into the water unnoticed and grabs the woman from below, holding her under, while her husband is taking a leak. When he returns, she is floating in the water, with nobody around.

I swallow as I stare at Juliette's perfect head. My fingers are itching to grab it from above and push her under. Like those intrusive thoughts you get at the top of a building, whispering for you to jump. Every inch of me is telling me to dive forward and push that heart-shaped face beneath the cool water. I can practically feel her fighting against the pressure of my hands to get out. Hear suffocated screams as she swallows water and finally gives up with a shuddering stop.

'Felix?' Juliette questions.

I shake the fantasy out of my head. 'I need to get out,' I croak, as I swim back to the jetty and pull myself out.

We lie back on the grass verge. She turns, stomach down, and begins to pick at the grass. 'Are you okay?' she asks, noticing my mood change.

I scratch my head. 'Yeah, I should get back,' I tell her.

'Felix,' she says, disappointed. ''Ave I not done a good job of distracting you?'

I shake my head. 'Juliette, sorry. This was really kind of you but . . . I'm not who you think I am.' I push myself off the grass and pull my T-shirt on and begin to walk back to the bikes.

''Ey!' she calls, trying to keep up with me, as she grabs her things. 'Felix!'

I turn around. 'Sorry. You really should stay away from me. Haven't you read what they're saying in the press? My wife hates me. The world hates me. Maybe they're right to.'

She just stands there. 'I don't 'ate you,' she says quietly. 'Emma is a complex person, isn't she?'

I nod. 'The most complex person I've ever met.'

'She was behaving strange in the car back from town,' she mutters.

'What?' I ask, strained.

'She got this . . . peculiar look in 'er eye, and I was calling her name over and over, and she just went faster and faster.' My mouth opens at this piece of news. 'It is why I came over the next day. She asked me to, so she could apologise. I bought her the book because I thought it might 'elp her.'

'I wish you'd told me this before.' Jesus, the scene in the car. I wipe my face in shock.

Juliette laughs. 'I wasn't sure . . . It was so strange. It was like she was someone else.'

A shiver runs through me.

She steps forward. 'I don't believe what they say. Emma, she was in charge. She was – 'ow do you say? – playing with you,' she whispers.

Yes, she's right.

'She wasn't very nice to you, always picking at you.'

I thought I was the only one who noticed. I look down, ashamed.

'Sometimes I worry I've turned into a monster,' I whisper. The guilt, the shame, the negative voice in my head constantly telling me terrible things about myself. Who even am I? Are these feelings real? Or was it just Emma manipulating me into this monster? My resentment towards her builds. I try to swallow it down.

'I wasn't always like this,' I croak. 'I loved her. We went

233

through a lot together.' It all happened so fast. It was good at the start. Emma changed. There was a power dynamic and it consumed me. 'And then . . . well.' I sigh. 'I cheated on Emma – which I'm not proud of, and it caused a lot of other things to happen.' I swallow at the thought of Robyn and the legal dispute – and now her disappearance. 'The consequences were brutal. The anxiety about it getting out and ruining this business – and Morgan is a business, a brand – the anxiety that what I did could hamper that . . . Well, I haven't dealt with anything very well.'

'A brand?' She stifles a snort. 'It all seems silly to me.'

'I'm sure it does to you,' I reply, slightly irritated at her dismissal.

'Felix, just give up.' She lays her hand on my shoulder, and looks directly into my eyes. 'See? Doesn't that feel good? Just to let go?' I feel my whole body relax when she says that.

'You think it's all so simple.' I watch her scrunched-up nose and the freckles splattered lazily there.

'Maybe it just is?' She looks across at the lake. 'After what 'appened to my mother, it made me realise I am never going to trust someone else with my 'appiness. And I'm not going to wait for it to find me. It's inside me, not out there or tied to anything else. It's already here, if I make the decision to take it.' She has her hand on her chest and looks so radiant as she tells me this.

'Don't you ever get lonely? What about companionship?' I ask her.

A smile spreads. 'I never get lonely.'

I am surprised as my cheeks heat up. A vision of that day in the orchard, and she didn't seem to care that she saw me as she whispered it into my ear that drunken night. There must be a reason she's brought me out here to this remote location.

'Wise Juliette,' I whisper, my throat tight with longing. I can't stop looking at those plump quivering lips. I should lean in, kiss her. Finally touch that smooth, perfect skin. I step towards her, moving the hair from her face, and she smiles up at me coyly. My fingers close around a lock of her hair, and I have the distinct urge to yank it clean off her scalp. I blink rapidly, and let go, stuffing my hands in my pockets. That scream that has followed me around since we left for France echoing in my ears.

She looks up at the afternoon sky. 'I should get back. I have a shift at the bar, they'll be wondering where I am,' she says softly. No idea about the slippery thoughts I've been infected by. Where are they coming from? And why do they feel as though they've been hiding in plain sight this whole time?

We cycle back down the lanes to the house. The day is cooling and there is a tinge of dull light in the sky. I'm scared of being alone again with my undulating thoughts.

I wave Juliette off at her cottage and make my way back up the hill to the main house. Reality hits me as I wheeze and gas up the hill, having to walk the last fifty metres. I pause at the top, looking across at the view. My God, it's beautiful here. I get out my phone and take a photo. The colours are stunning this time of day, and I decide to stick it up on the Morgan Savage account that has two hundred thousand followers. That will annoy Emma. I usually don't get involved in such things. But I post it, so she can see I'm still here. Totally fine. Not crumbling with the shock of her departure. *I'm not missing you*, I want the photo to whisper. Quite petty really. But I want her to know I'm not about to crawl back, pleading for forgiveness, this time.

Maybe I want her to react. Maybe I want to provoke her. She'll message me irritated that I'm posting and giving the cacophony of twitterers a fresh pass to discuss our plight. I can almost hear the tapping keyboards as they debate what the photo could mean. Ha.

I slide over to my old account that I haven't used for years. There are photos on there from when we first met, sitting around dining tables laughing. Then I remember the message I sent her, and I double-check I haven't missed her reply. It hasn't even got through to the recipient. Has she blocked me? For fuck's sake, Emma, do we have to be immature about this? This is so . . . *her*. I feel like flinging the thing on the ground in frustration.

I go back into the deathly quiet house and pour a glass of red on the veranda. I daydream that Juliette comes back to the house under darkness. Knocking on my door and kissing me. No. The last thing I should do right now is begin an affair. If Emma were to find out . . . I shudder. Juliette just feels sorry for me. I'm probably entertainment. An anecdote she can tell her friends. That scandal-hit writer she befriended once.

It is strange without Emma here, even though her presence made me anxious a lot of the time. I was constantly waiting for her to blow up at me and remind me I'd done something shameful. I've realised something while she's been gone. It was easier to be the man she assumed I was than wait for her to accuse me of it. There was less exasperation in that.

I stare at the glass of red and the almost full bottle next to it. I shouldn't drink any more. I need my sleep. If Emma is about to launch into battle, I need to be in the right state of mind to fight. But I can't stop myself. The bottle empties quickly, and I turn back into the house for another.

# CHAPTER TWENTY-NINE

The harried sound of birds rallying their peers wakes me. I barely remember staggering into bed. I get out, groaning. A new bruise is on my leg. Did I fall over? Up the stairs? No idea. I force myself up and stumble over to the window, the curtain waving in the breeze. *Come on*, I think to myself, *I need to do something to get me out of this fug.* I glance back at the bed, the pull to stay there wrapped up in the sheet hiding all day strong. *No, come on.* What could I do to distract myself? Read my book in the hammock, maybe cycle into the village, have an espresso in the square? No. I shouldn't do that. Maybe I'll finally take the cellophane off that moleskin notebook I bought at the airport and write some notes for my new book. The length of the day seems cumbersome, long and empty.

I grab my phone from the bedside table. My emails are teeming with ignored notifications, and I open the app to quickly run through them. Requests from journalists, threads of emails from our team we've been CC'ed into. But there I see, at ten a.m. on the dot, I received an email from Emma. A cool breeze passes through me as awareness dawns.

I thought this was over. I thought we weren't doing this any more. What the hell is she playing at?

Morgansavage@infinitymail.com
21.07.2024
**Subject:** Book 9 – First Draft

### *CHAPTER SEVENTEEN – HER*

*Hanna looks at the photoos, her teeth pressed together, A pain in her heart. A collagel of ten pictures one his friends has posted of Sebastian's night out in the city. What a time!!!!! The firt is of his old gang around the table at what looks like a high ballin' sushi restarant. Hanna knows all these faces this group all tried to pull Sebastian away from her when they first started dating. She knew what all thought of her – golddigger. A single mother on the hunt for a free ride. They did not aprove from the off and she feel their judgy eyes on her at every event she was forced to attend.She stares at Laurie – oh, she hated that one!!! She felt as if this woman could see right through her. The next shot is of the gang on the sidewalk. Grinning like a basket of chips, the lot of them Blurry-eyed. Then there she is again. Laurie, that BITCH, with her arm around Sebastian. She feels a viscel urge to dive into the photo and pull out her hair. Hanna gasps, unable to get air intoher lungs. He's been cheating on her. Disgusting illicit sexxx in hotel bedrooms, room service breakfasts with mimosas. She squeezes her eeyes shut, anger cutting her in the very pit of* her stomache. How could he do this to her when she's literally given him everything? Hanna's ears begin to rang, and she covers them. Her head jerkss with stress.

'Mumma!' Ivy calls and Hanna turns on the TV, placing her in the travel cot in the living room to keep her safe while she attends to oter business. She looks around. The place is a STINKING mess since Sebastian went away. She hasn't cleaned washed or done anything she usually focuses on obssively. The dishes are pilled up and there are childrens toys strewn across the floor. She isn't up to her usual standards. She has had too much going on

The doorbell rings, and she looks in the mirror. She has a smudge of red lipstick on her face. She quickly leans forward and swiptes it away.

'Why hello, Hank,' Hanna says, smiling as broadly as she can manage as she opens the door.

Hank's thumbs are circling each other. 'Sorry to bother you, Hanna. I was just wondering if you'd seen Nancy?'

Hanna does her best to look concurned. 'Nancy? she questions.

'Yes, we haven't seen her since she sat for you. I've been messaging you, haven't you seen?'

'Oh goodness! Sorry, my phon!e, it's broken. What a worry. I'm afraid I haven't. She said she was going into town for a date or something?'

Hank strokes his chin, his browb furrowed. 'I see. I'm sure it's nothing. I'm sorry to have bothered you.'

'Mumma!' Ivy calls.

'Such a lovely age,' he mutters. 'Enjoy every second,' he says wistfully. 'It doesn't last for ever.'

'Will do, Hank. Have a lovely day and I do hope Nancy comes home son. she's just having too much fun and has forgotten to let you know.'

He turns, pondering. 'Yes, yes, I'm sure you're right.'

She closes the door and turns back into the house. What a lot of fuss ovr a stupid missing girl. She smiles to herself.

'Jesus, Emma,' I mutter. How could she? That last line – *over a stupid missing girl* – is incredibly insensitive, what with everything going on with Robyn at the moment. Plus, it's a mess – not like her at all. Full of feverish typos. She is obviously not herself, probably boshing those pills to get over all the stress. Maybe she's carried on drinking since the night she left. I don't want this story to have an end. It's done and so are we. This book represents everything that is wrong with our marriage. And I don't want any part of it.

I email Emma back. I must put a stop to this.

*Emma. Look, can you call me? You've disappeared off the face of the planet and I'm worried about you. We need to talk. It may well be we need to accept we're not right for each other. Maybe you were right to leave. But please can we talk about this? I couldn't give two sods about this book. By all means write it yourself. But do me a favour and leave me out of it. Have your final Morgan Savage – complete the contract – but I'm done. I'll always love you and want the best for you. I know*

*that it's hard for you to say goodbye to everything we've built,*
*as it has been part of our lives for so long, but it's time to let*
*go.*

I pause. At least I know she's safe. I think of her in our sweeping multi-level apartment in its prime Manhattan spot. I actually feel sorry for her, sitting there, maddened by all this, with only this insane story for company. Living in a fantasy world that she can keep this going. I'll have to go over there and grab my stuff when I get back. I add another few lines.

*I'm going to stay here, in France, for the rest of the summer*
*and will then probably go back to the UK. Feel free to pack my*
*things until I organise for a shipping company to freight them.*
*Happy for you to keep the apartment. You worked hard for it.*
*Get some friends to come over, try and rest. Be kind to yourself,*
*Emma. F x*

There. I've showed willing. More than willing. I'll get my half of the cash we've made and start a new life. I wonder about her motives for sending the chapter. Maybe I've been too kind in that note. Was she attempting to reel me back in? Expecting me to be so terrified of losing Morgan too that I'd go running back to her, whizzing off my chapter just to keep us together?

Well, I'm not playing her games any more. Maybe the realisation that that isn't happening will finally break her. Emma isn't as strong as she makes out, and she is fallible too. She'll have to go through her own process to get over all this, but it's not my problem. In time, she may even be relieved. Not straight away, but time is a healer, and besides, the best thing you can do after a separation is to steer clear of each other for a time.

I'm going to be mature about this. Our marriage was toxic, but our break-up doesn't have to be. And if she is falling apart, this is my opportunity to rise from the ashes with sanity. At least that way I'll manage to claw back a little self-respect.

I chuck my phone on the bed, feeling the poison seeping from it. I'm an idiot to think Emma could just walk away. She is loyal beyond anything. But her loyalty can easily turn into obsessive ownership.

She likes keeping things she's had for years and years.

I make myself comfortable at the table downstairs, with my laptop in front of me. I press the power button, but nothing happens. Urgh, how annoying, I must have left it running last night. I have a vague flashback of tapping away in my drunken state. God knows what I wrote on it. I can't remember a thing. It will have all been rubbish. I get up and grab the notebook I bought at the airport, and a pen.

Right, so, where was I? A coming-of-age story, yes. That's what I want to write. *The Catcher in the Rye* for my generation. A young man's arrival into his adult life after a rough start. Yes. *What? Where? When?* The questions pop. New York City – is there anywhere else that can make a man of you? The street lights, the steam rising from manhole covers on freezing winter days. But then I think of my own experiences there, the constant noise in my head as I went from party to party. *You don't belong here*, it would whisper. No, I don't want to write a love letter to New York. I'm not ready for that.

I look around at the still beauty of this place. Here. I could set it here. Is my character working in the depths of rural France? Maybe caring for an elderly relative? What about end-of-life care? That is fascinating – both extraordinary and prosaic. So much in there that I could say about the human condition and regret. Being by someone's side as they leave this planet, and in that same moment you're figuring out who you are, and your own path.

Yes . . . there is something interesting here. All that lost hope. You begin with dreams that get brushed aside to make way for the realities of life, and realise that life isn't an exciting adventure. It is hard, and mundane and often painful, even when you have everything you thought you wanted. And then you die, and there is a raft of poor old sods with shining, hopeful eyes, ready to take the same course.

I get a flash of exhilaration. An idea! An idea that I've had all on my own. Pride swells in my chest. I can already feel the first line of the first chapter bubbling away. Felix Larson shall have his name on a book. Yes. Not just one half of a team, but a writer in my own right. I feel like standing on the edge of the cliff and screaming.

It is later. Much, much later. I have written lines and crossed them out. Tried bullet points and spider diagrams. By the afternoon I've started drinking. And slowly, I move the notebook away, feeling defeated. I listen to the piercing noise of the whining mosquitos that comes in rolling waves. It feels insidious and inescapable. I cannot help myself; I end up doom scrolling the unravelling drama back home.

There is a new news clip that is doing the rounds with the lead investigator. 'Yes, we are looking at all avenues and would certainly like to speak to the Larsons,' he's said. My stomach ties in knots. How ridiculous! How could they think such a thing? Then an email from Max:

*E & F, police have been in touch. They know you are away but would like a phone call or Skype in this first instance, purely for intel and to strike you off the list. Am holding them back. But might be better just to get it out the way?*

I try to remember that night before we left for France. I wouldn't hurt someone, would I? I've been in punch-ups before – in my school days, and the odd bar argument I may have taken too far in the heat of the late-night blur with emotions heightened. Fights with Emma have got out of hand, but they often ended with passionate sex too. I look down at my hands, thinking of the urge I had to push Juliette's head under the water.

Is there another side to me I've never admitted to?

I see a figure in the trees. My whole body freezes before it melts. Juliette. She waves cheerfully. '*Salut*, Felix!' she calls, smiling. I stand up too quickly, hitting a knee on the table. *Ouch. I hope she didn't see that.*

I wave back. 'Juliette,' I reply, trying not to sound too joyous to pull back a little dignity. She ambles up the lawn.

She's wearing a strappy short white cotton dress, and she looks angelic. 'Do tell me to go away, but I was bored at 'ome and, well . . . I had so much fun yesterday.' She looks at my notebook and laptop all set out on the table. 'But I see you are busy,' she looks nervous then. 'I leave you to it.'

'No!' I cry, too keen. Damn it. And I put my hands in my pockets, shifting about. I cough, and in a softer voice say, 'I could do with an adventure. Besides, I've cracked something this morning, so deserve a break.' She looks impressed. 'Quite a big thing really: the basis for a new book,' I add.

'Wow!' She grins. 'That's excellent, Felix!' She smiles sweetly at me. 'I thought I could show you the castle. It's on the edge of town. 'Ave you been?'

I shake my head. I remember seeing a decaying structure hanging on the hill above the town. I'd much prefer to go back to the lake and watch her take off that dress. 'I'm not meant to go into town,' I remind her.

'I just rode through it, completely empty! 'Onestly, Felix, it's like a *ville fantôme* – a ghost town. You'll be fine.'

She makes me feel as though I'm being overly cautious, and besides, I just want to spend time with her. Get out of here and away from this constant noise in my head.

'Sure,' I tell her. 'That sounds perfect.'

I can't help it; I'm drawn to this woman.

Just like all the other girls.

# CHAPTER THIRTY

I get into the car and Juliette slides into the passenger seat next to me. 'All set?' I ask and she nods. I try the ignition, but it doesn't catch. 'Weird,' I say, trying again – but nothing. I sigh. Great. 'I'll have to call the rental place.' This is the last thing I need. Where did Emma put all the paperwork? She usually deals with this stuff. I lean over Juliette, to get to the glove compartment, but it's empty. Bugger.

'*Mon dieu*,' Juliette says. 'We could cycle?'

'It's so hot today,' I mutter, looking up at the rich blue sky. My weather app told me it would hit one hundred and four Fahrenheit this afternoon.

'Oh, Felix, you are a – 'ow do you say? – a woosh.' She looks over at me with those big eyes and I melt.

'I think the correct term is wuss, actually,' I reply, laughing.

I'm drenched by the time we arrive. Can barely breathe, in fact. The hot air sticks to my lungs and I can't filter it. I need to give up smoking. I add that to the list of improvements for the next chapter of my life.

My exhaustion only seems to amuse Juliette, who laughs at the state I'm in. We ride through town, over to the other side, where I've not been. She is right, it's deserted today. I feel slightly hidden riding along, with my cap and sunglasses on. We cycle up a wall-lined road, and I use all my energy to make it to the top, my thighs burning with the exertion. The sight of Juliette happily, and very easily, conquering the elevation forces me on, and I refuse to get off and walk. Once at the top, we get off at the crumbling entrance, and I pile my bike on top of Juliette's on a nearby post. I look at our bikes, embracing each other, and feel a pull of something.

Juliette's hand strokes the wall as she turns inside the ruin. This castle is not what I was imagining. It is a ghostly labyrinth, skeletal remains of what used to be a grand building. No one else is here. She was right, we have it completely to ourselves.

'Wow! This is . . . amazing,' I tell Juliette.

'*Oui*. Isn't it? It's a medieval pilgrimage site. Many years ago, worshippers would come from all over Europe to visit. Come on, Felix,' she says, taking my hand, and soon we are lost within the maze of weather-beaten stone. I love having my hand in hers, and I'm happy to just follow her as she tugs me around this ancient place. Finally, we come to a cut in the wall where a window would have been, hundreds of years ago. The view below is stunning – it reaches straight into the valley with the town below.

'It's so quiet,' I say, looking out at the stillness. A lone rusty van, that looks like it's made from corrugated metal, trundles down a road in the distance. 'How can you bear all this . . . space?'

She shakes her head. 'I like it. Back 'ome everything reminded me of my mother. She didn't want to leave our little house and go into hospital. I'm glad I 'ad that time with her before she . . .' She looks at the floor. This is good, I can use all this in my new book. 'And after I wasn't needed any more I packed a bag and vowed never to stay too long in one place. I want to experience all of it – the quietest corners and the busiest thoroughfares. I don't want to be trapped by the idea of a 'ome. I've never stayed long in one place, all these years.'

I think back to the apartment I'm leaving in New York. I never felt like it was my home, though. Emma found it, furnished it, told me where I could and couldn't put things. I always felt like a visitor.

Juliette settles back against the stone wall to one side of the gap. 'See, I told you you'd like it 'ere. Now, are you going to tell me about your new book? Is it about me?' she teases.

'Ha! No.' I'm not prepared to tell her that the story about her mother may have sparked it. 'If anything, it's about me,' I reply.

'Of course it is!' she cries. 'Narcissiques, aren't you all? Writers?' She grins.

And I nod. 'Yeah, probably.'

I am distracted by some movement, and I look up to see a couple. They are about my age, flanked by a few young kids who look sweaty and annoyed. 'Raven, stop that!' the father cries as one of the little tykes picks up a few stones and chucks them over the wall. The mother looks tired, and I watch as she removes her sunglasses and wipes the sweat from under the dark circles of her eyes. She looks up and sees us and stops in a jerk. I know instantly she knows who I am, as she gets that blink of recognition in her eyes, and a desperation to turn and nudge her partner, who is already berating a child. 'For God's sake, Raven,' he is shouting, grabbing their arm and yanking them away from the wall. I see her fumble for her phone, which is dangling from a cord around her neck.

'We have to go,' I whisper to Juliette, walking towards the entrance. Why did I leave the house?

'Felix?' she asks, confused. 'Why—'

I move away, glancing back, just as the woman whispers over.

'We have to go,' I repeat. Juliette rushes behind me, and I feel her hand hold mine, and I don't brush her off. I glance back at the woman, just as she takes out her phone and snaps a picture. *Shit.*

We walk quickly back to our bikes. I grab mine to get on, but it almost falls onto the ground, my hands are shaking so much. I feel it then. A million eyes on me, watching. I begin peddling as soon as I can. 'Felix!' Juliette calls, mounting her bike and following me.

What am I doing? Flirting around with this beautiful woman while another is missing, and my wife has left me. 'Felix!' Juliette calls, racing to catch up. I am behaving exactly how Emma would have predicted. All I am doing is proving her right. What if that woman loads the photo online, or sells it to a newspaper, and Emma sees it? Oh, God. Oh, God. I cycle through the pain.

Hanna pops into my mind, and her obsessive compulsion to hurt the young woman her husband encountered. I wouldn't

250

write him as a cheater, even though we both knew that is what Emma wanted. I wonder if in the final draft, she would have altered that, to suit her narrative better. I think of Robyn, missing. And I shudder.

We cycle back to the *hameau*, and I drop her at the cottage. 'Bye,' I say. She crosses her arms self-consciously, and I'm acutely aware of the drop in pressure between us. She is spooked, and so am I. If I'm honest, I hadn't given much thought to my actions, so wrapped up in the attention of this beautiful woman. How I've enjoyed the distraction. I am selfish. I'm exactly what Emma says.

'Oh, Felix.' Juliette sighs. 'You look so sad.' She steps forward.

'I shouldn't be doing this,' I whisper, turning away from her.

'Doing what?' she asks.

'You know. Spending time with you. I should be trying to sort out the mess back home instead of finding a thousand things to distract me.' I'm annoyed that I was so easily persuaded out of hiding for such a frivolous activity. This is everything that is wrong with me, looking for some gratification to numb the pain of reality. I need to stop this. I need to grow up. 'I should never have left the house,' I say bitterly.

Juliette looks at the floor, her cheeks tinged red. Shit, now I've upset her.

'I just thought you seemed like someone who desperately needed a friend.'

I feel terrible. It's not her fault. She just doesn't understand the absolute clusterfuck of a situation I'm in. My life is on fire

251

and the whole world is waiting with bated breath to see how it'll turn out.

My eyes fill up then. And I turn and swallow, so she can't see. A friend. I don't have many of those. I've behaved terribly, let them all down.

'Okay, well . . . Ciao,' she says sadly, heading home. I feel awful.

'Juliette, wait,' I call towards her, and she stops and turns her head.

'Will you come to the house with me? I . . . I don't want to be alone.'

She looks almost hopeful, and it breaks my heart. 'Are you sure?' she asks quietly.

'Sorry, look. I'm a dick. You've been so kind to me and the stress of all this . . . well, it's got to me. Just a drink? So, I can apologise for being so ghastly.'

A slow nod. 'Okay,' she replies tentatively.

'But you have to make sure I don't get trashed; this is the new Felix!' I say, attempting to sound confident in that sentiment.

I swallow. Alcohol and a beautiful woman. What could possibly go wrong?

'You know, they can all go fuck themselves.' I blink, attempting to pour us more wine. I miss and some dribbles down the side of the glass and onto the marble countertop. I use the bottom of my T-shirt to wipe it off. Juliette laughs. 'It's dirty anyway!' I explain. Now what were we talking about? We've been back a couple of hours and I'm drunk. It feels good to have someone who nods in understanding and sympathises rather than ridicules. I wander back to where she's relaxing on the sofa.

Gesticulating, I continue, 'You see my dad . . . my dad, he wanted me to be someone else. He could never be proud of me. Never! Because he simply wants something from me that just doesn't exist. Bestseller? Pffff . . . he'd be more impressed if I installed a boiler.' I feel like I'm slurring. I blink, trying to regain control of my senses, but the room merely undulates in front of my eyes.

'So, your dad isn't a nice man?' Juliette asks, looking over at me.

My shoulders slump. 'No . . . no. He is. He just has a set idea of how things should be, and I don't fit into that template. Never have.' In the back of my head, I know what I'm doing, that thing that happens when I'm drunk and feeling sorry for myself. I become the victim in the tale, to anyone who'll listen.

Juliette is lounging on the couch, her hand extended to the low table where she absent-mindedly rings her finger around the edge of the glass. 'At least your dad was around for you,' she says quietly. Fuck, I've been on a self-loathing quest and have been locked in a one-sided conversation.

'What was your dad like?' I ask.

She shrugs. 'Not really sure. My parents weren't married, it was more of a liaison. My mum was left to look after me with no 'elp. It was 'ard,' she says with a sigh. ''E's tried with me since, but I'm not sure I can ever forgive 'im for that.'

'Shit, that's terrible.'

'She had a 'ard life because of it. Three jobs, no money. Me.'

'How the hell is that even allowed to happen?' I say hotly.

'I don't think she wanted anything from 'im after the way 'e treated her. 'E ran back to his family and pretended we didn't exist.'

I realise what she is saying. She is the product of an affair. I don't understand why she's being so kind to me, then it clicks into place – some fucked-up daddy complex. Do I remind her of him? I think about something that happened, a few years back. I slept with someone, and she got pregnant. She was very conflicted, but I managed to get her to terminate after a very stressful three weeks of deliberation. There was no way she could have the baby. It would have made what happened between us real and I had to keep it back there – in my fantasy life. The one that didn't really exist. Not in the real one with Emma and our brand of books. I told Max, who helped me organise the paperwork to keep it all under wraps. Emma doesn't know about that one.

And here Juliette is. The product of something like that. It makes me feel wretched. I take another drink. 'And you don't hate him?' I ask.

She ponders this. ''Ate? No, I don't 'ate him. It's more . . . complicated than that. I don't want the best for 'im either.' She laughs.

There is a humming sound and Juliette picks up my phone from the coffee table in front of her. 'You 'ave twenty missed calls,' Juliette says. It's been on silent for the evening.

I wipe my face. 'Who cares?' I tell her sluggishly, trying to believe it.

'It's ringing again.' She holds out the phone.

And I walk over and take it. Max. 'Give me a second,' I tell her, moving onto the veranda, answering it.

'Felix, can you pick up your damn phone as soon as I call? This is unbelievable. Put me on to Emma immediately. I must speak to her.' He's pissed off. 'Tell her I don't care if she's imploding, she needs to put on her big girl pants.' He tsks. 'This isn't like her. Did you get my email? The cops want to interview you. It's starting to look like you have something to hide.'

I blink. Emma still hasn't spoken to Max? Her wonderful gatekeeper she'd do anything for. That doesn't sound right. 'Has she still not been in touch?'

'No.' I feel a sweep of unease shuttle through me.

'Max . . . I need to tell you something.'

A stagnant pause. He can tell I'm about to lay a new problem at his door. I can't bring myself to break the news.

'Emma has left me,' I state.

Silence, then, 'What the hell are you talking about?'

'I mean, she's packed up and left me. Has she not been in touch with you at all?'

Max is flabbergasted. 'No, I've had nada. I've been forwarding her emails and asking her to get in touch but assumed she's too upset and leaving me to deal with it.' I can hear his teeth grinding.

'Max, you know we haven't been good for a while.'

'Felix, are you drunk? You're slurring.' He sighs. 'This was the summer to fix things. What the hell has been going on?'

'It was just never going to work, Max. Us here. Nowhere to hide.'

'But you love each other. The passion and creativity in you both, it's magnetic, anyone can see that. You belong together, Felix,' he presses. He has no idea what he is talking about.

Exasperation builds. Max is just looking out for himself. He's nervous his biggest authors are imploding and his twenty per cent amounts to a big wedge, probably more than his other authors combined. He never cared about our well-being. If he had, he'd have suggested a break to sort myself out, not forced this hellish writing retreat upon us.

'Max, I'm sorry your cash cow has dried up, but I can honestly say, if I want to keep my sanity, I cannot go anywhere near that woman again. She is the reason I kept fucking up, over and over. The way she treated me, the way she used me . . .' My voice is rising.

A pause. He can hear the finality in my voice. 'Listen, Felix, you know I only want the best for you – both of you.' *Ha.*

'Morgan Savage is over, Max. It's done. We'll pay the money back; it's not like we can't afford it. And I'm writing something new anyway. Something better than Morgan. More meaningful.' I tense after I say that, already imagining him rolling his eyes. He'll be thinking, *That's not what the readers want. That's not what the market wants. Morgan Savage is a sure-thing money spinner.*

'Well, let's just get over this mess before we can start thinking about launching new titles,' he says weakly. 'I'm more concerned that Emma has left. Is she doing okay?'

I place my hand on a wall, to stop myself pacing. I need to stand still for a moment to process this.

'I assume so. But I haven't spoken to her exactly. Crazy cow took all her things and left in the middle of the night.'

A pause. 'I'll try and reach her again,' Max says. 'I'll check in and let you know.'

Just then, Juliette walks out and hands me a glass. ''Ere you go.'

'Thanks,' I knee-jerk reply.

'Who was that?' Max asks.

'It was . . . no one. Nothing.'

'Felix, have you got someone there with you?'

'No. It's no one. It's just the girl who helps around the house,' I tell him. Juliette gives me a look of understanding and slips back inside.

'Felix, it's late evening there! If you've been doing anything other than trying to get hold of your wife, I can't tell you . . . I can't tell you what I'll do,' he says, his frustration peaking.

'Max, Max . . . It's not what you think. Honestly.'

'Felix, if you go near that girl . . .' he warns hotly.

'Max, calm down. Look. Emma is fine! She's been sending me her chapters. She's angry and out for revenge and thinks the silent treatment will do that. You know what she can be like.'

'I can get Jenny to book some flights, get you back on home turf, if you'd like? Maybe being out there . . . maybe we should get you back.'

'Are you crazy?' I ask. 'They'd stalk me – I wouldn't be able to—'

'Felix, listen. Behave yourself, okay? No more girls. I can't tell you how bad that will look with all this Robyn stuff going on.'

'Of course,' I scoff. 'Look, I'll call you tomorrow, okay? Tell the police I'll speak to them.' And I hang up the phone, turning back into the house.

Juliette has put some music on. She's drinking whisky and looking at the books on the shelf. One is in her hand, and she turns it to read the back. I walk over and turn it back over, to see the cover. '*Rebecca*,' I tell her. 'Have you read it?'

She laughs. '*Non*. Is it good?'

'One of the best.'

'What is it about?' she asks.

'It's about a young woman who marries a widower and moves into a grand stately home. It has a great twist. You should read it.'

She places it onto the shelf. 'If you think it is good, I will read it.' She takes a large gulp of her drink and I do the same. The strong spirit shimmies down my insides.

'The girl that is missing. Did you love her?' she asks me, eyes wide.

The room is spinning. The memories of Robyn flood my mind. I take another sip, trying to quell them. 'I didn't love her, no. I liked her, a lot,' I tell her. 'I'm not sure I am capable of love.' It's hot in here. I feel like I can't breathe.

She steps towards me. I blink away a scene in our fourth book. A woman with a broken-down car and zero phone service knocks on the door of a farmhouse, desperate for help. She has no idea that the lone man who greets her left a string of nails specifically to snare her. She is nervous but thinks this is her only option. He lets her in willingly, a kindly face plastered on. As soon as she emerges in the room she senses something is off. But she thinks, *Quick, make the call, get out of here.* She is relieved as the call rings through and she hears a voice, *'How may I help you today?'* from the local tow truck service. But before she can reply, his itching bare hands clutch her neck, and the phone falls to the floor.

My hands shake, and to my surprise, tears collect in my eyes. What is happening to me?

'Ah, Felix,' she whispers. 'Is it Emma? It will be all right.' And she hugs me. I allow my hands to fold around her frame, and I gently stroke her back. But then, I feel the urge to move them up towards her neck. To feel the full strength of my power with this woman here, alone. Who am I? What the hell happened that night?

What have I done?

I push her away and step back, a stricken look on my face as the dark thoughts crawl into my mind. 'You should go,' I tell her.

'Felix, what?' she questions. 'I don't understand.'

'Please, Juliette, please. You need to go. You shouldn't be here; I am a bad man. My wife was right to leave me.'

Confused, she whispers, 'Felix?' Her hand rises upwards, as if trying to cup my cheek. But I push her away, with too much force, and she stumbles back and trips.

She stares up at me from the floor, her eyes wide and scared. She scrambles up, and rushes towards the door.

'Juliette!' I call, but she doesn't even turn around. The door slams with a deafening thud. And I am left standing there, staring at the shaking palms of my hands.

# CHAPTER THIRTY-ONE

I wake up at the kitchen table, my head resting on my forearm, my computer open, just out of reach. My head hurts, and music is playing through the 1970s speakers in the living room. I stand up, stretching my neck to one side. It's painful and sore. I turn off the amp and the sudden silence is eerie. All I can picture is Juliette's terrified face as she looked up at me from the floor. I hold my head. That crying, sobbing sound, the feeling of someone grabbing at me, scratching my face. And I shudder.

I pick up my phone and message Juliette.

*I'm really sorry about last night, I didn't mean to hurt you. I'm just under so much pressure right now. Thank you for being so kind to me x.*

Then I read a message from Max:

*Still can't get hold of Emma, her phone seems to be off. Might be in the sky. Are you sure she didn't leave a note? Worried.*

I frown. But then I notice something else on my screen. Another chapter from Emma. What the hell is she playing at? I thought I was firm enough the last time.

Morgansavage@infinitymail.com
22.07.2024
**Subject:** Book 9 – First Draft

### *CHAPTER EIGHTEEN – HER*

Hanna has been staring at the wall since puting Icy to bed. Shessiting on the sineing room chair, just staring at the qall.. Sebastian messages wwarler.

**Flight cancelled. Having o fly to vegas and then rent a car. See you soon x**

She lnpws he is just buying time. He doesn't want to come heme to her. Thoughts circulate. The madness undaulating line waves. As soon as she was out of the picture he jumped on his next cvitim. How predicatble.

Her land shakes as she picks up her phone. She can' put it off any longer, she has reached the end of the road now. If she could turn back the clock a few says, she might hacw a choice, but not now.

'Hello,' she wispers, swallowing.

'I was wondering when you'd call,' the voice replies.

'I . . . I . . .'

'You've done it again, haven't you?' It sighs. 'I told you you would. But you always say it's different this time. Look at what happened in Chicgo. You really thought a fresh start would have helped? I knew the second you took off this would happen.' A sigh.

Hanna sniffs, wheepiong into the pphne.

A sinister whisper asks, 'Have you been careful?'

'I think so.'

'Is the baby okay? She is all that matters;'

'She is perfect,' Hanna says, thinking of the child upstairs. She would never do anything to harm her.

'You shouldnt have taken her.'

'I'm sorry – I thought it was for the best.'

'You know it wasn't, Hannaa,' the voice replies, weighted in emotion. 'But look, you know I'll always be there for you, right?' Hanna sighs, yes, she knows. It was all just a a dream wasn't it? the two point five and the picket fence. They were never meant for her. she treid and tried to git herself into that hole but she was the weong shape. Always has been, alwys wil be.

'How much time do wehave?'

'Aroud twelce hours. Her has to pay – he has humiliated me.

'You think I'm going to let anything bad happen to you? Come on, you know me better than that.' Happa shatys to cry. 'Dopnt worry, I'm here now. I have always been here watching from afar. I'll come as quickly as I can. I'll clean it all up for you, like I always do. Don't I?' A pause. 'Pack a bag Hanna – I'm cumming for you. Don't do anythig stupid. Okay? Don't let him win.'

Hanna;s lips twitch – 'I can[t believe I've done ti again.'

'Don't do anything stupid,' the voice repeats. Before hangig up.

She ,oves to the kitchen and take the surgical gloves out of their packet and focires her fginers into the the tackey tubber.

262

*Next, she carefully take the kitchen knofe off the pile of
dirty dishes by the sink; the last person to use the knife aws
Sebastain. Then she turns toward basement door her eyes
blazeing with anicipation.*

*He should never have sheated on her with Nancy –
fornication out side marriage is fisgusting, revolgting. Doesn't
he understand the wmtioional damage, the societal harm this
kind of pain caiuses? And he has taken every opportunity to
fo it. this is all his failt if he has just treated her better, none of
this would be hapfening. Its his turn to suffer.*

*HE HAS TO PAY.*

I swallow. The words smash into me. I've never seen her
writing like this. So uncontrolled, so unedited. So full of frenzy
with no care to go back over to correct any of the numerous
mistakes. Where is she? What the hell is going on? And the
horrible snarky words she has used to describe Sebastian – it is
as though she is spitting them directly in my face. I don't get
it at all. She's left me – why continue to use this character to
verbally bash me over the head with it? For once, it's not me
that needs help – it's her. She is coming across as deranged.
In my rash, frustrated state, I bash out a reply.

*Emma, you left in the middle of the night without even
discussing your plans with me. I don't know how I can get
this through to you. I'm not in love with you any more, and I
doubt you are in love with me at this point. We were terrible
together. Please leave me alone. No more of this nastiness. We*

*were toxic together – look what our relationship has done*
*to both of us! It's time to move on. To be honest, right now I*
*would be happy if I never saw you again. Stop emailing me.*
*Get some help through the rough patch. I'll sort everything*
*through my lawyers.*
*Felix*

I don't even bother with a kiss. She wants to push me. Well, *honey*, I am going to push back. I'm not the emasculated loser you walked out on. My free will has re-entered the room and is far from turning back.

Guilt trips me up then. The castle and the family the previous day. How will Emma feel if she sees that photograph of Juliette and me together? She'll be smug, probably. Maybe she'll use it to get more of the pot when we wrestle with dividing our assets. Damn it! Why did I leave the house?

I need a distraction. And I need to get away from my bloody phone. I'll go for a walk and think about the first few scenes of my new book. How to set up the new world I am going to plunge my readers into. The first ever Felix Larson novel. The idea of it makes me feel giddy. *Come on, Felix. Keep going. Ignore the noise.*

I wander down the lawn, and into the orchard, and find the path that meets the cliff. I pick up a stick and begin to swipe shrubbery left and right, thinking of my main character. What shall I call him? Winter – a summer-set novel with a main character called Winter. No, that is pretentious as fuck. What about Nathan? That's a strong edgy literary name. Right, first decision made. See, this isn't all that hard.

Nathan, in France for the summer, looking after an elderly aunt, who is dying. No, an uncle, known for his bad temper. Nathan's just finished school, and he's been charged with his care for the summer. That's nice. It can get teary at the end when the uncle redeems himself and dies. Everyone loves getting emotional as they close a book for the last time. Get a reader to cry and they are more likely to rate it five stars. Yes, no jumps or twists, just pure emotion.

I come to the cliff and stop, taking in the hazy view, the heat melting the last few low-hanging clouds. I take a photo to remember it. I'll have to put a cliff in the book. That would be good. Maybe it could be symbolic. How? Not sure yet. I make a mental note. I walk around the edge of the cliff and back towards the trees, whipping the bushes absent-mindedly with my stick. Enjoying the freedom in my head to explore a new idea without the usual confines of Emma as the gatekeeper.

I allow myself a daydream. Of having a book out the same month as Emma. Larson versus Larson – that would be a splash. The bestselling co-authors become adversaries. *The New York Times* will lap it up. Twitter will ignite! I imagine my book reaching the top spot and Emma's clinging on to the last position. Oh, wouldn't that be good? I smile. But first, I need to write the thing. If I manage two thousand words a day, I'll have a book by Thanksgiving. *No, stop it.* I shouldn't get ahead of myself. I promised that I wouldn't rush. This will be a slow process of cultivating something with more clout than ever before. And it will take time to get it right. I'll write it quietly. Maybe a few years will go by, with people thinking I'm washed up. And then bang! I'll reappear with a smash hit.

Yes. That's what I'll do.

I continue my walk, whipping the ground with my stick as I proceed. A million futures ahead out there, waiting.

But then, I notice something that doesn't look like it should be amongst the rocks, grass and wildflowers, slumped against a tree. I narrow my eyes and stop.

My stomach plummets. No. It can't be.

I tentatively step forwards and use the stick I'm holding to push back the long strawy grass from it. I stop very still, my breath scant, blinking to make sure I'm not hallucinating. But I'm not.

Sitting there, brazenly, is Emma's black hard-shell suitcase.

# CHAPTER THIRTY-TWO

My heart is hammering and my hands are shaking as I yank at the strap and pull it in front of me. Falling to my knees, I unzip it and open it flat. All her things are there, bunched up and chucked in as if in a rush. I sit back on my heels, my head in my hands. This doesn't make any sense.

I move my hands from my face, hoping I've made it up, but it's still there. I lean forward and pull out an item, holding it up. The scrunched material comes loose in my hand. I'd imagined Emma in the apartment overlooking Central Park. Hanging these very shirts and pushing dirty items into the laundry bag ready to be picked up by that pimpled boy who arrives in a branded electric minivan, *LaundryGuys*. But this shirt, the pale blue linen one she likes very much, isn't hanging in our closet, after all. It's here, in her abandoned bag. But why wouldn't she have taken her things?

If her belongings aren't in New York, what if she isn't there either?

The world I've been building in my head – Emma leaving on a plane, hating me from afar – is gone. And I am in an entirely different place. Dread lingers. But the emails – she's been sending me chapters. She must be fine. Right?

I stay there, kneeling on the spot, for a timeless period of confusion. Threads of thought that just don't tie up.

In the end, I zip up the case, and carry it back to the house. I place the bag on the kitchen table and reopen it, having a more thorough check. All her things. Her washbag, and expensive make-up too. Her little jewellery box. It's all here. Then I see something worse.

Her pills. I hold the bottle up, with her name on the label. My God, she wouldn't have left these, would she? She barely lets them out of her sight.

I pace around before taking out my phone and trying her number again. It doesn't connect. Maybe she was so angry she decided to start afresh and buy new things. Could she possibly hate me so much she couldn't bear to wear these clothes again? No, that sounds completely barmy too. I grab a glass of wine and sit down, the case in front of me. Open. Oozing her things. What do I do? I drum my fingers on the table.

But the book – she must be writing it from somewhere?

I decide to call the concierge of our building in New York. 'Good afternoon,' he says.

'Hi, Trent, it's Felix Larson here.'

'Good afternoon, sir. How can I help you?' he says, very professionally, even though he's seen me stagger through the communal hallway many a time. I once fell asleep on the floor by the lift, and he phoned up for Emma to come and get me.

'Listen, Mrs Larson had to cut our trip short, and I think

she's lost her phone or something. Can you let me know when she arrived back at the apartment?'

'Sorry, Mr Larson. No one has been in your apartment since you both left for France.'

'Right . . .' I say, baffled by this news. 'Okay, that's fine.'

'The night you had a friend around,' he adds pointedly.

'A friend?'

'Yes, sir.'

'Who was the friend?' I ask.

'Sorry, sir, I'm not sure, we had a temp on. It was just noted in the log when I came in the next morning.'

'Right . . .' I say again, swallowing. Who could that have been? Emma doesn't really have many friends she'd invite over when I'm in that sort of state, and she didn't mention it the next day. But we were in a rush to make the flight, I suppose.

'Do you think you could let me know if she arrives back?'

'Yes, sir, I can ask her to give you a call,' he says stiffly, letting me know he's not going to do any spying on my behalf. He always did prefer Emma. 'Sorry, sir, I've got to go. The men are here fixing the CCTV system; it's been down for two weeks. It's caused us quite a headache, let me tell you.'

'Thanks, Trent.' I hang up the call, before he can get into a boring monologue about the state of repairs. Who on earth was at our apartment? All I remember is the quiet car journey to JFK where I was scared to make a sound, in fear of inciting an argument. I drum my fingers on the table again. What should I do?

I stand, pacing around the living room. My laptop winks

at me and I grab it, and reread the last chapter sent. *This is all his fault. If he just treated her better, none of this would be happening. It's his turn to suffer.*

It is by far some of her worst writing. What if she's trying to tell me something? What if the only way to get her to engage is to write my alternate chapter? There's a stabbing feeling in my stomach. I hate the thought I am being drawn back in. But what if it's the only way to get through to her in this muddled state she's in?

### CHAPTER NINETEEN – HIM

*Sebastian has a tight feeling in his chest. A feeling that he needs to get home, that something terrible has happened. Hanna hasn't replied to his messages, and he knows how strangely she's been behaving recently. What if she has hurt herself? What if she has hurt Ivy? He should never have gone on that work trip. What was he thinking? He just needed to get away so badly, he needed to feel normal again – just for a few days.*

*He has a notification on his phone, his barely used Instagram account. Laurie has tagged him in a load of photos, and every time he is notified of a new comment, he is compelled to have another look. He flicks through them, a distant smile which is lost as soon as he sees Hanna's name – she's 'liked' the pictures. So, she does have her phone, and she's ignoring him. He knows Hanna was threatened by Laurie. Scared of her almost. She didn't even give her little digs, like she managed for the more inferior members of the team, like Stella.*

*The flight to Vegas is packed. He's hemmed in between two huge guys, and he can barely move his legs. The Wi-Fi isn't working, so he can't check his messages, which is adding to the distress. It's the longest five hours of his life. All he can think about is Hanna's odd plastered-on smile. And the robotic way she has said, 'I'm fine,' recently, and stared at him with those vacant eyes. And those strange phone calls she refused to answer. Who was she scared of?*

*Hanna. Please be okay. I'm sorry. I just want to know you're okay. Please, please let the first thing I see when I get off this flight be a message from you, telling me you're all right. That's all I want. If we ever meant anything to each other, just let me know you are okay. Please.*

With shaky fingers I paste it into an email and send it via the usual address before sitting back. Then I realise I slipped into the first person at the end. I'm pleading with Emma for her to contact me – passing through the fourth wall and onto the page. I stare at my phone, waiting. Counting down the minutes for a call that never comes.

# CHAPTER THIRTY-THREE

Later, I sit on the veranda. I push away my laptop with the blank screen, where my new book is supposed to be surfacing. I am in a confused state of shock. My head is so compounded by this new information it is numb, and barely a whisper of a thought can permeate through it.

My phone lies there, lifeless. I keep checking it, but never anything from Emma. Why did she hide all her things, only to continue the farce of the book? The question turns over and over.

By the evening, I am drunk. I feel maddened. I have no idea what to do with this. Tell Max? The police? But I can't seem to bring myself to do it. What will they think?

The doorbell rings – Juliette! A swell of relief. She'll tell me there are no bad feelings between us and help me pick through this mess. She will tell me I'm not the terrible person I think I am. She'll console me and make me feel better.

I open it quickly and am surprised when I'm not greeted by her luminous face and that drifting smell of roses. But an angry Marco who grabs me by the throat and backs me into the closest wall. *Shit.*

'You!' he cries, holding me tightly by the scruff of my neck.

'What?' I gasp. He's taller than me, younger and stronger. 'Give me some room,' I wheeze, trying to push him away.

'You bastard. She upset. What you do? You sleep with her, no?'

'Hang on . . .' I try, unsure how to temper this beast lost in a whirl of rage. He breaks away. 'Marco, I swear, it's not what you think at all,' I splutter out.

He's heaving, overwhelmed with emotion. What I see within the anger is misery. I go towards him. 'Marco,' I try, patting his arm, which he shrugs off. 'It's not what you think.' *Not for the want of trying*, the voice in my head whispers.

'Juliette say your wife gone to New York, she leave you.' His moist eyes stare me down. 'And now she upset. Won't talk to me. You think I don't know what you done?' He walks past me, into the house, knocking my shoulder as he passes.

'Honestly, this isn't what you think.'

'I come 'ere for the summer, and suddenly she is there – wants me. And then just when I think . . . she is letting me . . .' – he's frustrated and can't find the right words – 'you arrive. Before her, I never had to chase. But she different.' He sniffs. 'She is special. *Magnifique!*' he says bitterly, looking across, full of hatred, and something else – resignation.

I don't know what else to say. 'It's not what you think,' I repeat.

His jaw clenches. Then he nods sadly. 'How can I rival with a *célébrité* from New York?' The thought makes him look desolate. 'Is this why your wife left?'

273

'No!' I cry.

'You think I don't know what they say? That you a drunk who uses young women for play.' His words twist uncomfortably in his mouth as he finds the correct ones.

I am winded and I stammer, 'They don't understand – they've got it all wrong.'

'If you 'urt Juliette . . .' he says, with a finger pointed directly at me.

'I have never hurt anybody!' I cry out. But the scared look on Juliette's face rips into my mind, and I hold the back of my neck and fall against the wall. All the other faces pop in there too. The other women – how they looked so sad, so angry with themselves, and me, for believing my lies. Tear-stained cheeks. Devastated shouting. Feelings hurt – no, worse than that, destroyed.

'She was always too good for me,' Marco whispers. Then he storms into the living room. I sigh. it doesn't look like I'm going to get rid of him quickly. I follow. He spins around. 'She talked about you both. All the time. She was *obsédée* with Emma.'

'Obsessed?' I question.

'She told me things,' he adds, delighted he has the power to make me uncomfortable.

'Things? What things?' I ask.

A smile spreads across his lips then. Oh, so he is out for some sort of revenge. 'You tied her to the bed at night. She 'ad marks.' He gestures to his wrists. 'Juliette thought maybe kinky sex. But then she told me about the other night . . .

Something 'appened. What was it, big writer?' I feel that sickly surge again. Is that what Juliette thought? They've got it so wrong. 'It all seems like a – 'ow do you say? – pattern.'

Marco paces in the living room area. If he's going to beat me up, I wish he'd just get on with it.

'Look, it's all just a misunderstanding,' I explain.

'A lot of misunderstandings for one man, *non*?' He peers up at me, a slight smile that he's got one over on me. Part of me respects him for coming over here like this.

I walk to the kitchen. 'Look, let me make you a drink, we can talk about this, man to man.' I open the fridge. When I don't hear a reply, I turn around.

*Shit.*

He's by the kitchen table, looking, staggered, at the open suitcase. He reaches into it and pulls out a piece of rich red fabric. And then a bra. He is looking at them curiously, and then back at me. A new expression on his face spreads. Something bad. Why didn't I put the bag away? In my drunken state, I didn't even think of it.

'These are your wife's?' he states.

A banging in my chest. I clear my throat. 'She left in a hurry,' I croak. Marco takes out her make-up bag, shaking his head, and then looks over and stares darkly at me. His eyes running over my five o'clock stubble, lingering at my plastered-up hand. He drops the make-up bag and begins to back away.

'No, Marco!' I shout, rushing towards him, as he bulks to the hallway and towards the front door.

He leaves it open, striding towards his car. He pulls at the door, but before getting in he turns back. 'You fucking crazy, man. Where is your wife?'

'I . . . I don't know.' My arms hang by my side, and I hope he believes the sincerity in my eyes. But he just shakes his head, disgusted.

'If you go near Juliette, I kill you, understand? I kill you!' And with that he gets in, revving the engine so the car skids into action. The little pebbles in the drive fly into the air as he zooms away.

I swallow, thinking about him parking up at Juliette's house and telling her what he's seen. This is getting very bad indeed. I turn slowly back into the house.

*Please, Emma, please have messaged me back.*

# CHAPTER THIRTY-FOUR

Emma has not messaged me. The case is sitting there, stressing me out. In the end I close it behind an antique corner cupboard and lock it, sliding the key into my pocket. I try to pretend it isn't there – but I can hear the deceit beating through the chipped wooden door.

Then I stalk out to the veranda, a bottle of wine clutched in my hand and any thoughts of writing expelled from my mind. I try phoning Emma again and again. But nothing. I stare into the night sky, my eyes barely blinking.

My phone rings and I dive for it, willing her name to pop up on the screen. But I sigh. It's just Estelle, Emma's mother. The last thing I feel like doing is talking to her. The conversations regularly turn in nonsensical tangents that baffle me. The pieces of tittle-tattle she thinks I have use for. But maybe she will have heard from Emma? Yes. I answer.

'Estelle,' I breathe.

'Felix, how are you?' she enquires. Estelle has always been nice to me. She is one of my biggest fans, after all. If there is anyone I can charm into understanding what I'm going through, it is her. I very much doubt Emma would have chosen to confide all her secrets in her mother at a time like this. But I can imagine her collecting people to side with her, and I just won't have it. Estelle must hear my side before that happens. Emma can be cruel to Estelle, and she takes it, but she is very aware of her daughter's dark side. She sees me as Emma's saviour, and deems me the true talent behind Morgan Savage. Something that has always irritated Emma rotten. *Stupid woman*, she'll whisper under her breath.

'Ah, you know. Surviving,' I say, with a sad chuckle.

'Oh, Felix. The papers all love some garbage to yack about,' she says in her nasally New Jersey accent. 'It all seems quite far-fetched! Like something straight out of one of your books. I know you would never cheat on Emma, how absurd!' I smile. *Yes, Estelle. Yes.* But then, I know the truth. My smile falters.

'You've spoken to Emma?' I ask.

'No, that's why I picked up the phone. I can't get hold of her, and Barb from down the road wanted a signed copy of . . .'

Oh, so she hasn't been in touch. I guess I'll have to break the news. 'Estelle, I'm so sorry to have to tell you this, but Emma has left me.' I sigh, the worn sigh of a long-suffering husband.

'What?' The word comes out in a bark. 'But . . .' She wobbles, in shock. I can imagine what she is thinking. All she does is rave about our marriage, our books, to anyone who'll listen. It gives her status in her little community, and she'll be unpicking what this will mean for her.

'Felix, I'm sure it is just a spat. You creative types—'

'I'm sorry, Estelle, but we haven't been good for a while, and out here with no distractions it all sort of came to a head.'

'But she hasn't called me,' she says quietly, torn. 'When did she leave?'

'A few days ago.' How long has it been? All the days seem to have merged into one. 'I'm sure she'll be in touch. She hasn't been answering my calls either. I'm sure, I'm sure . . .' I start, then my eyes linger on the locked cupboard where all her things are hidden away. My dirty secret. One I cannot fathom the reason for.

'Where'd she go?' she asks stiffly. Then in a more high-pitched tone, 'Did she take her pills?'

'Her pills . . . Estelle. She left in the middle of the night. I assumed she went back to New York, but I just spoke to our concierge, and she hasn't arrived back. She may have gone straight to the house in Amagansett – but I can't reach her. She could have also flown to Phoenix.' Oh, yes, I wonder.

'Phoenix?' she questions.

'Our new book was to be set there. For research.'

'But, Felix, I don't get it. You're writing your new book in France.'

'We were,' I tell her.

'Did you have an argument?'

I think back to the drunken night. The terrible things we said to one another. They all mix up with the night before we left for France, the disturbing screams for help I cannot place, and I shudder. The way Emma had packed us all up

279

and hurried me out of there, refusing to look me in the eye. I sigh. 'Estelle, things haven't been right with us for a while.'

Silence.

'But why isn't her cell connecting?' Estelle asks again, quietly. I hear a yapping in the background from one of her dogs. They quickly go quiet. She'll have slipped a treat out of her pocket and the ghastly thing will be licking it off her hand. 'And you were in this house, in France' – *Fraaance*; the way she says it irritates me – 'all on your own. Pretty rural, huh? Could there have been some sort of intruder?' she asks, her love of crime fiction forcing her to jump to the conclusion.

I sigh. 'Look, I know she's okay, because she is sending me her alternate chapters,' I explain. 'I'm as much in the dark as you are.'

'She's still writing?' she asks, confused.

'Yes, the book,' I tell her. 'The new book,' I repeat, frustrated already. 'Estelle, as I said, she's emailing me. We don't need to jump to any conclusions.' Giving her my most calm and stable tone. I must be the voice of reason here.

*God, Emma, call me. I can't cope with another one of these inquisitions.*

'She's probably in a hotel in Paris eating caviar. She's still writing, as I said, so she is fine. We've been under a lot of pressure, I'm sure she just needs a minute to catch her breath. The whole thing has been quite stressful if I'm honest. I thought she'd fallen off a cliff at first. I thought I was losing my mind.'

'A cliff?' she mutters. 'What the hell are you going on about?'

'Here, on the property. She started sleepwalking.' As I

babble on, I realise I am overcomplicating this. 'Look, it's just one of her games, I'm sure of it.'

'A game?' I should have just kept things simple; I've only confused her. 'Felix, you need to find her,' she says fearfully. Why is Estelle, who is usually so malleable, suddenly being so tricky? She barely knows Emma at all. She's always desperate for her daughter's attention, but Emma ignores her, mostly.

'I'm sure she'll get back to me today so don't worry. I'll call you as soon as she does.'

'Yes, please.' She is silent for a moment. Then a thought occurs. 'The email account you share to send each other chapters?'

'What?' I reply, in a stammer.

'She's been emailing you with the address you use to write your books?' Her voice comes out in a tentative whisper. Of course, our biggest fan would know that. Our quirky writing ritual is emblazoned as a novelty across nearly every magazine spread. 'The email address you share the password to?' she says, fearfully. Her dogs begin yapping again and she furiously tells them to shush.

'Well, I'm not writing the bloody things!' I shout.

'Huh, well.' I can hear what she is thinking all the way over here. She thinks I've hurt Emma, and if Estelle, who finds me deeply charming – her handsome, talented son-in-law – could think that, what is everyone else going to assume? 'And that girl is missing . . .'

'I've got to go, Estelle; I'm sure Emma will be in touch very soon.' I quickly hang up, my stomach in knots.

281

I pace around the kitchen as darkness falls, drinking, thinking of Emma laughing at me from wherever she is. I feel like I'm playing a game I never agreed to. Maybe I should go to the police. But then I think of Marco's dark face when he saw Emma's things, and the bandage on my hand. And the conclusions Estelle chalked up so quickly. No. I need to find Emma first. Otherwise, well . . . otherwise. What? I wish I could see Juliette, but I'm too scared that Marco has got to her. That beautiful light feeling of joy as we cycled to the lake is a distant dream.

I didn't think I could hate Emma any more than I already did. *All you can control is the work.* Emma used to say that a lot. I think of the themes in the book, a marriage in breakdown, accusations of affairs. Ivy between them, one in ownership, the other a fraud. But this person on the phone, who was that? The only way to find out is to get to the end, where all the threads tie up.

She wants to write this book. Fine. I'll finish it for her. I grab my laptop and begin to type.

### CHAPTER TWENTY – HIM

*Sebastian is covered in sweat as he drives, the freeway sprinting past as he speeds through the five-hour journey. Still nothing from Hanna. He can tell this is bad. His insides are squeezing at the thoughts of dread pummelling him. Where is she? Why isn't she answering his messages? Why is she causing him this much pain?*

His teeth grit together when he sees a cop car, and he slows down. He gets a message and Siri asks him if he'd like it read out through the car system. 'Yes!' he shouts, strangled by urgency. The message is read by Siri's robotic voice. 'Message from: Laurie Work. Hello, darling – lovely to see you last night. Come again soon, whenever. Forgot to say about Stella – it was pretty wild. The last night anyone saw her was the night of the Christmas party. Didn't her and Hanna have that squabble? Anyways, get home safe.'

Siri: 'Would you like to reply?'

'Fuck,' he whispers under his breath. His whole body goes rigid. No. It can't be. Hanna wouldn't . . . But who knows what she is really capable of.

Finally, the suburb is in sight, and he screeches along the road. A flood of relief and trepidation hits him when he finally turns the corner into their street. He leaves the car door open as he runs towards the porch.

'Hanna!' he calls as he unlocks the door. 'Hanna! Ivy!' He runs upstairs but there is no sign of anyone. His chest heaves with panic. He comes downstairs, panting with emotion, and then he stands very still. He turns on the spot. The house, usually so clean, is a total mess. Hanna would never leave it like this. His eyes zone in on the basement door, which is ajar. 'Hanna?' he calls, his throat tight.

But there is no answer. He steps tentatively towards the basement entrance, his hand outstretched and shaking. Bracing himself for what could be down there.

But before he can open it, someone on the other side pushes

it forward. *'Hello, Sebastian,' they say with a wicked grin, their teeth covered in blood.*

There. Emma loves it when a chapter is left on a cliffhanger. She'll be pleased with me for that. She won't be able to help herself but finish it, the compulsion too strong. And I like the way I've looped it back to Hanna, that whole Stella thing. *See how you like it.*

*Ha! I did what you wanted, bitch. Not one, but two chapters for your stupid little project today. Now come out from wherever you are hiding.*

'You win!' I shout. But no one is listening.

I am all alone.

# CHAPTER THIRTY-FIVE

I wake up in the living room and groan. I twist my legs off the sofa to get up, but my feet hit something, and the sound of glass bottles toppling pierces my throbbing head. There is a weight of something on my chest, and I look down. My laptop. I sit up and place it on my lap, tapping the space bar to wake it, but the battery has gone. I have no idea what I was doing on it. God, I hope I didn't drunkenly message anyone last night. That's the last thing I need. I discard it next to me, and look around, to get my bearings. My blurred sight slowly lifts as I place what's happened.

My phone! Emma must have called me! She must have. I stand up – too quickly; stars hang loosely all around. I blink them away before searching, trying to locate it. But it isn't in its regular spots. I jump onto the sofa and throw off the cushions, feeling around in the underbelly of the fabric. Something hard hits my fingers and I pull it out the back. I stab at it, trying to wake it up, but it's run out of battery too. I groan. Dizzy, I look for the charging wire, jab it in, and then check the time on the antique clock on the wall. Wow, it isn't even ten yet. I'm usually fast asleep. It must be the large glass doors and the bracing sunlight. I swallow.

Emma's chapter will be the final one, the one that will explain what happened before the story even started, and what it all means. Who this cloak-and-dagger person is that Hanna has been speaking to. What are her motivations for doing these hateful things? If this story is all an analogy for Emma's anger towards me and my actions, maybe that means there'll be clues about where she has gone and taken Ivy – or our career – with her.

At ten a.m., all will become clear, I am sure of it. The phone lights up, having gained just enough juice to power it.

I bite my nail; my leg shakes with adrenalin as I wait on it. Nine thirty-five. Nine forty. I stand quickly, to pace, and make myself a whisky, willing the time to go faster. But it does nothing but slow it down.

Nine fifty. Jesus Christ. Who knew time could be so slow? *Come on, come on.*

My phone rings. Bloody Estelle! What the hell does she want? Maybe she's heard from Emma! Yes. Finally, this nightmare will end.

'Estelle!' I say hopefully. 'Did she call you?'

'Felix.' My name has never sounded so cold. 'Felix, I have to let you know about something.' She coughs. What is it? Has Emma told her about the affair I had with Robyn? Does Estelle hate me now? 'I called up the overseas citizens services yesterday. I know you might think that's overboard. But Gloria in my book group reminded me about it from the Detective

Clarke anthology . . .' I listen as she witters on about her various friends and their amateur crime-book sleuthing, who have whipped her up into a frenzy. 'It's who you're supposed to call if a relation goes missing abroad. They get the local—'

A light ringing starts in my ears. 'Estelle, you didn't?' I whisper, swallowing.

'Look, I'm sure you're right, and she's just holed up in some fancy hotel, but it just seems mighty strange. Very strange indeed.'

'And asking all your friends for their opinions is also strange,' I snip back. And she falls silent. 'Emma is just playing games, Estelle!' I cry. Why doesn't she get it?

'Playing games!' she scoffs. Her voice is harder than I've ever heard it. 'She isn't as strong as she makes out, you know!' Ha. As if she'd know.

'The emails!' I remind her.

'Felix, are you trying to talk me out of looking for my daughter? Because that's sure what it sounds like.' She appears to have been galvanised into action by all this gossip and assumption.

'No! Of course not. I want to know where she's got to as much as you.'

'Felix, something's up. I can feel it in my bones. If you've laid a finger on my daughter . . .' And she hangs up the phone.

'Fuck!' I shout, chucking the thing across the room before coming to my senses and running in the direction I threw it. The crack on the screen is larger, and a fragment of glass has fallen out. I look at the time. Nine fifty-nine. One minute until the answers will all flood into my email account. What if she doesn't take the bait? No, she has to. The answers are coming.

Ping! A notification comes flinging into my mobile. Yes! Her email. Now, what the hell has she been playing at? She'll have to come clean in her next chapter. I half expect her to run through the door laughing at me: *Suuurprise!*

I stab at the email icon quickly.

Then the doorbell rings. I ignore it, pressing the screen, trying to open the bloody emails. But the cracked screen has other ideas. It just won't work. Fuck's sake, why didn't I charge my computer? Frustration is building and I whip around, wanting to scream.

The doorbell goes again, and I let out a strangled sound of annoyance. 'Fuck off,' I whisper under my breath. 'Go away, Marco.'

But then a regimented banging starts. '*Monsieur! Monsieur, ouvre la porte!*' I freeze. It isn't Marco at all but the police. No! Bloody Estelle. I really need to read the email. I know now, the answer is right here, in my hands – isn't it? It must be. It must . . .

'Monsieur, we will take the door down, if you do not answer.' I try and try, but I cannot get the screen to play ball with my tapping.

How is this happening? How? My reflection catches in a mirror, and I stare at the exhausted man in front of me. I stink of booze. I look guilty as sin. I stare out at the open door to the veranda. I could run. I could take my phone and run out that door. But I know what that would look like. No one would understand. I am stuck between a rock and the hardest of places. I have no choice, do I?

I force myself to walk down the hallway. I stand at the closed door willing myself to open it. I place a shaking hand on my face – this can't really be happening, can it? Please God. Another regimented bang. '*Ouvre la porte! Police!*'

'Okay, okay, I'm coming!' I call out.

I open it to find two police officers, in uniform. One of which I know. He's the man I met in the square, who was reading one of our books. He raises an eyebrow when he sees me. 'Monsieur Larson,' he says dryly, giving me the once over.

I try a smile. It feels phoney. '*Bonjour*, officers. *Pardon*, I was sleeping.' I scratch my head as if to illustrate the point.

'Monsieur, I am Capitaine Dupont. This is my colleague, Lieutenant André. We were hoping we could ask you a few questions about your wife?' He pauses to think, placing a hand on his chest in apology. 'My English is . . .' He lifts his hand and performs a so-so. 'We have been notified she's missing. May we enter?'

'Yes, yes, of course.' I open the door wide, and they troop inside. I grimace at the state of the place through their eyes.

The capitaine looks around, before turning back to me with a wide smile. 'I remember you from the square. The book.' He knows I deceived him that day. He already thinks I'm a liar.

'Sir, apologies, it felt wrong of me to introduce myself at the time.' His smile is almost as fake as mine. I get it: he's pretending to be on the back foot to build a sense of camaraderie between us. But I see the traces of accusation in his

289

eyes. I remember what he said in the square – *It's always the husband* – and my heart shrivels.

He uses a finger to stroke down his dark moustache as he nods at this. He has dark hair and deep crinkles in his smile lines. His eyes are blue, and his eyebrows are thick and bushy. He reminds me of my father. I have a sudden longing to be back at home in London, under the security blanket of my vast, tight-knit family that I used to find so suffocating and parochial.

'Come on through,' I invite them, trying to be as welcoming as possible. Surely they must see that I, a nice, polite, British writer, would never harm his wife? *I'm innocent, I haven't done anything wrong*, I remind myself. But I feel guilty and can't shake it.

How is one meant to behave if they are innocent? I can't work it out. I rest my hand on the wall, trying to look relaxed. Not managing it very well. 'Can I get you a drink?' Capitaine Dupont's eyes fall on the empty bottle of whisky on the table, and the discarded wine bottles on the floor. There is the low-hanging haze of cigarette smoke lounging just above their heads. They look at one another knowingly.

'*Non, non. Merci.* We've been told your wife hasn't been seen for a few days and is, erm . . . uncontactable. We've been asked to have a look into the situation, by her mother. She is very concerned,' he says, watching carefully, trying to gauge my reaction to this.

'That's right – Emma isn't here. She left me,' I tell him. His colleague is poking around, looking at the clusters of antiques.

Was I wrong to let them in? I swallow as he snaps on some blue rubber gloves. I sure as hell know that isn't a good sign.

'Do you know where she is?' Capitaine Dupont asks, taking out a notebook and pen.

I dig my hands into my pockets. The tips of my fingers fall on the key to the cupboard, and I swallow. 'I don't know. She took off in the middle of the night. Our marriage . . . we decided to call it a day.' I scratch my head and gesture to the state of the room. 'I haven't taken it very well.'

'I see,' Capitaine Dupont says, noting this. The other one continues to sniff around. Are they allowed to do that? But I've invited them in, haven't I? I try to think back to all the police procedural elements in our books, but my brain is a fog. And besides, Emma always relished that kind of research far more than me. 'So, she just left in the night. Poof!' He makes the gesture with his hand, making the idea of it seem ridiculous. 'Your car is outside; did you have another one?'

'Nope, just that one. It is broken, though.' I tut. 'Bloody annoying.'

'Broken?' Another thick eyebrow is raised. 'So, one couldn't leave, even if they'd wanted to?' I stiffen, realising what he is implying. He makes another note. I frown. 'Monsieur, how did she get off the grounds? You are quite remote?'

'I think she called a taxi,' I tell him, shrugging. 'She must have been planning it all day, seeing as you need to call in advance.' Capitaine Dupont translates this to the other one.

'*En taxi?*' the lieutenant replies. They speak a while. The name Francisco is dropped in.

'What date was this?' Capitaine Dupont asks.

'Erm . . . it was . . .' I try to remember but all the days blur into one. 'I think the last time I saw her was the night of the eighteenth, so, um . . .'

'It is the twenty-third today. So, your wife has been missing for . . . five days.' They stare at me, heads to one side. Five days. That does seem like a while. They think I've killed her. That's what they think. I swallow.

The younger one, Lieutenant – I can't remember his name – takes out a mobile phone and makes a call, while Capitaine Dupont just stares at me, smiling with mock sympathy. The call is in French, and I don't know who he's speaking to. '*Oui, oui – merci – au revoir.*'

The lieutenant tells Capitaine Dupont what happened in French, who then turns to me and explains. 'Francisco, the only taxi driver around here, did not pick up an American woman the night of the eighteenth. In fact, he did not pick up an American lady at all, recently.'

I shrug. 'Maybe she got someone to give her a lift? She is incredibly resourceful. I'm sorry, officers, but I really don't know.' I try walking towards the front door, hoping they'll follow. But they don't. 'I would really like to be left in peace. The last week has been rather challenging, as I'm sure you can imagine.'

The lieutenant tries the door to the cupboard, shaking it. But it does not budge. 'Do you have the key?' Dupont asks, motioning to the cupboard, to where Emma's things are hidden.

'I . . . I don't think the owner wanted us to use that cupboard,' I reply, my mouth dry. 'We weren't given a key.' The lie came out quickly, I barely had a moment to decide whether to utter it. He nods slowly, watching me carefully. Then turns to his colleague and says something in French, which he then repeats for me. 'We will have to wait for the warrant to come through.' Warrant. *Fuck*. Why did I lie?

'Have you had any contact with your wife since she left?

'Yes.' Great, I can answer this one. 'We were writing a book together, here, this summer.' I can't help the lick of pride in my voice, but they remain unimpressed. 'I have emails from her.'

'*Oui*. The emails.' Dupont says slowly, considering it. So, Estelle's theory has filtered down, I see. I wonder why they're asking me all these questions if they've already talked to Estelle and taken her guileless detective work to heart.

'You write thrillers, do you not, monsieur?' Dupont asks. 'They are *très bons*,' he tells his colleague, and I can't help but smile. But then he says, turning back to face me, 'Very bloodthirsty.'

I scratch my jaw. 'It's all part of the genre . . .' I reply. I'm too winded by all this to go into it. I just want to find out where bloody Emma has got to.

'Lots of murder,' the capitaine says flatly. They stare back at me.

I swallow. 'Well, there isn't going to be another book. Without our marriage, there is no Morgan. Morgan is dead.' I immediately regret how I've phrased that.

293

'Dead.' Dupont repeats. 'But she has been emailing you, you say? Have you been replying?'

I cough. 'Yes, I was trying to get her to contact me.'

'But Morgan is . . . dead?' They both stare. They look at me as though I'm insane.

Am I insane?

'Monsieur, I believe the authorities in the US would like to question you about a missing girl, and now you seem to have lost your wife. And you are saying Morgan . . . is dead.'

'I . . . I didn't mean it in the physical sense! He's not real – he's a fictional character that only embodies something when we write!' I try, exasperated by myself. 'And we are no longer writing so he cannot be alive. It was a metaphor – sort of.' They look as lost as I feel.

'But you have been emailing each other chapters since she left?' He looks confused.

'I was just trying to get her to contact me,' I say through gritted teeth. 'Look, Emma gets heavily invested in the work. Once she starts a story, it is difficult for her to let go. She . . . she's angry with me. That's all. She'll come around.'

'So, you had a fight? The night she left?' Dupont asks, his pen ready to scribble this down.

'Who doesn't argue with their wife?' I try a laugh. It sounds strangled.

'Monsieur, my wife has never gone missing,' he says simply. I fall silent. Dupont points to my bandaged hand with his pen. 'How did this happen?'

'I hurt myself looking for her.' I wipe my face. 'There is a cliff on the side of the property. When I woke up and she was gone I was worried there'd been an accident,' I explain. 'Look, she'll be in the US by now—'

I am stopped mid-sentence. 'Monsieur Larson, the airport registers have been checked, and your wife did not leave the country on the eighteenth of July. Or the nineteenth or twentieth – or any day since.'

I feel like I have forgotten how to breathe. My chest is tight, and uncooperative. 'What? Well, she must still be in France! Paris most probably – I'd check the Ritz.' I try to laugh again; they stare at me oddly. The image of her in a red velvet booth eating her favourite langoustines pops into my mind. God, she must be enjoying this. The perfect storyline for the death of our marriage.

'The investigators in the States are checking with her bank. So, I'm sure we'll find out where she is shortly, if she is still . . . around.' I know what he means by that, and I swallow.

'She'll be around, Capitaine. She'll be laughing about all this, and I can only apologise about all this wasted time. Terrible of her, really. Causing all this fuss.'

Dupont nods sadly. 'Well, we hope so. Because the likelihood of her being alive, with no money used, no flights . . .' They stare at me; I know exactly what they are getting at.

I feel winded. 'I know what you are insinuating!' I say, then I force myself to calm down. 'Look, I want to know where she is as much as anyone else.'

'You don't seem as though you are particularly worried, or have been looking for your wife,' Dupont says, motioning to the smoke-filled room. 'You haven't spoken to us before now. That is odd, *non*? Five days later.'

'Of course I'm worried! I practically scaled a mountain looking for her! But then I realised all her things were gone.' I swallow again, my eyes sliding to the cupboard. 'And she began emailing me. So . . . I knew there was nothing to worry about.' They look at each other. 'I did not kill my wife!' I implore. 'She is fine!'

Dupont nods to the lieutenant and he takes out his walkie-talkie. Dupont turns to me. 'Monsieur Larson, we are just waiting for the paperwork, but will be looking around the grounds, and the house shortly. Could you please make your way onto the veranda while we wait for the search team? We'll be taking you to the station shortly for a voluntary interview, if that is okay with you, of course.' I nod, dumbfounded. 'Super,' Dupont says, with a smile.

What the hell is going on? Where is Emma?

# CHAPTER THIRTY-SIX

I fiddle with the key to the cupboard in my pocket. I should just give it to them, have a chance to explain. *Here you go, sorry about that. I found the case a few days ago and wasn't sure what to do about it. Sorry, I decided to hide it behind a locked cupboard.* No, that doesn't seem plausible. They'll never understand.

I feel my phone vibrate in my pocket. I go to retrieve it, but remember all eyes are on me. I point to the downstairs toilet. 'May I?' The officer looks at the capitaine for permission and he nods. I hastily pop inside and look at the screen. Max. Thank God. I try to open the call; luckily this mechanism seems to be functioning.

'Max,' I say in a whisper.

'Felix, what the hell is going on? I've just spoken to Emma's mother, who is irate.'

'I wish I could tell you,' I say wearily. 'The police are here; they're searching the place for Emma. Or signs of Emma.' I rub my eye with a knuckle. I wonder if they would let me have a drink. We're in France, after all.

'Felix, listen up. This is going to break wide open, I think.

Can you just level with me, man to man – did you have any part in this?'

How can he ask me such a thing? 'Max, I can tell you, hand on my heart, this has nothing whatsoever to do with me. Emma's fine! She's been sending me emails.' I keep my voice low, my hand cupping my mouth to direct the sound into the receiver.

'Yeah, well, Estelle told me about that.' He coughs. 'There is something else.'

Something else? 'What is it?' I whisper.

'It seems Emma has been skimming off a considerable amount of money from your shared account. Every year, it amounts to over five million pounds – funnelling it into some untraceable overseas account.'

'What do you mean? Skimming off?'

'The cops seem to think she was creating some sort of nest egg. Apparently, in domestic abuse cases, people often create a sum of money they can use if . . . if they need to make a break for it. A financial go-bag type of thing. Did you never notice?'

Silence. 'What?' I whisper. 'No, I . . . you know I leave all that stuff for Emma to sort out. Max, you must believe me. I haven't harmed a hair on her head.'

'Felix, this is tough for me, you know how much I respect you. But were you ever violent towards Emma?'

I feel like I've been punched in the stomach. 'Violent?' I hiss. 'No!' A laugh escapes me at the ridiculousness of it.

'This isn't funny,' Max states.

'Max, this is utterly bonkers! Honestly, I haven't done

298

anything wrong. Yes, I know I had my . . . my . . . faults. But I would never physically hurt her. I loved her.' I did. In our own way, I truly did love her. He doesn't respond. Even Max doesn't believe me.

'We should never have come here, Max. Why the hell did you send us to the most remote house you could find? It's insanity! We were hanging on by a thread and you go on Airbnb and find a haunted bloody house on a remote hill for us to write in? Are you crazy?'

'It was . . . well, Emma wanted to. I did mention to her I didn't think it was the smartest move, but she told me you both had your heart set on it.'

There is a swift bang on the door. They want me to come out. 'One minute!' I call.

'Felix, I'm sure this will all get straightened out. Make sure you get your phone call when they . . .' My God, he thinks they're going to arrest me. 'Look, I want to be clear with you, Felix: if this is what it looks like, I'm off. You listening? You won't be hearing from me any more.'

'Max,' I wheeze. My friend. Well, okay, more Emma's friend. But he's been with us through thick and thin. 'Please . . .'

'The cops are on their way to your apartment. Estelle is meeting them there. She is beyond consoling, Felix.'

I'm barely listening as I think how I look in all this. Guilty. Guilty as sin.

Just like all the men in our books.

I finger the key in my pocket, and begin to take it out. I'll open the door and hand it to them. They are detectives, I'm sure they'll get to the bottom of all this. The sense of dread that this could be my last few hours, or minutes of freedom, is palpable.

Then something the doorman said hits me, about someone coming to the apartment the night before we went away. Nancy in the book – missing – and the tin in the basement with the lock of hair Hanna gently caressed to her cheek. Sebastian racing to find out what was down there – is it Nancy? Or could it be Hanna and Ivy? Who is in that basement?

My God, what happened the night before we left for France? The violent memories, the screams, the crying, the begging. Oh, God. No. Did I have something to do with Robyn after all? Yes, in our books we've slaughtered many. But none of that is real. Is it?

And if I did that, then could I have harmed Emma? I think of all the drunken nights, and the chapters I was getting the next morning. Could I have been the one writing them? Programming them to be sent at ten a.m.? I do that often, programme emails in the evening to be sent first thing when I know I'll be asleep. Emma taught me how to do it once.

An image appears of me tapping away at my laptop in the early hours, and all those messy chapters that came through. Could this have all been me? Am I completely disillusioned like the character in that book, *Shutter Island*, that Emma loves so much? I feel it, I do.

'Max!' I cry. 'Max you have to tell Estelle not to go to the apartment.'

'Why, Felix?' He sounds incredulous.

'Max, you have to phone her, tell her!' I implore.

'Tell her what, Felix?'

'Not to go into the basement.' The words wheeze out.

'One sec, Felix, Jenny's got something urgent.' I hear some voices talking. And then the sound of the television in the background turning on. 'Motherfucker,' Max whispers as the phone disconnects.

# CHAPTER THIRTY-SEVEN

'Monsieur, we will be departing for the station now, to formally question you.' Capitaine Dupont comes through to the veranda where I've been waiting, a shaking wreck. He's been on the phone for some time, and the mirage of affability has diminished faster than a New York minute. He looks increasingly serious and morose.

'Can I finish my cigarette?' I ask, taking a long churlish drag. But the look on his face causes my bravado to clatter onto the floor. He must be thinking, *Let him have that last cigarette as a free man*. I can't take it. I can't take this man assuming the worst of me. I'm a good person. Aren't I? I want to cry on his shoulder. What has become of me?

'We just came here to write a book,' I croak feebly. He stares me down; he's imagining what I've done to Emma. I am seized by the feeling of guilt, and I can't bear it. People like me! I'm a nice guy! 'I swear, I haven't done anything to her,' I plead, but even I am unsure.

He looks down at the broken phone I'm clinging to. 'Monsieur.' Then he makes a snip of a whistle sound and beckons a colleague over, pointing to my phone, and they hand him a plastic evidence bag. Flapping it open, he says, 'We'll need to take that, if you don't mind.' I hand it over, staring pitifully as he bags up the lost chapter. What is in it? If I did write it, do I know more than I think? Is there another side to me that unlocks a door to some other reality that I am completely unaware of?

The harrowing sound of Max's voice as he ended the call clings on. He's always been Emma's guy, Emma's confidant. But we were mates, weren't we? As we rode the wave of success. Yes, he grew weary of my excess and problems I dumped at his door, but that is part and parcel of agenting, isn't it? I think of him watching the rolling news. Was there a black bag on a gurney trolleyed out of our building to a waiting ambulance? Is that what he saw? Or did Jenny, his young PA, whisper it into his ear?

I have no idea how the apartment was left. I just remember being bundled into the car and Emma handing me a Gatorade. The evening before we'd been at that book launch at a warehouse in the Meatpacking district. I began to feel groggy, I felt as though I was about to spiral, and could feel my conversations getting out of hand. I needed to duck out early before I did something stupid. I remember that much. But what happened in that apartment while I was blacked out? Who came to see me and why can't I remember? Did I do something?

Then another thought comes that causes me to swallow down the putrid taste of bile – could Emma have covered something up for me to save Morgan Savage? Is that what she has been keeping from me?

My stomach twists in knots.

I think of how Emma appeared out of nowhere and made all my dreams come true. Beautiful, clever Emma. I would be lying if I said all her contacts weren't a lofty bonus within my attraction. And all I had to do was love her. Right? That was the deal, wasn't it? But our love turned into a horror show, just like our books. It was me, wasn't it? I ruined our marriage with my fragile ego and my petty regrets.

She'd shout at me, 'Well, just bloody write it then!' when I bemoaned my literary dreams of writing something meaningful, away from the cheap tricks and bloody violence of our books. But my head would chip on negatively about my ability; I simply wasn't talented enough. So, I stewed and made mistakes. Acted out.

But it couldn't have turned me into this. Could it?

I think back to the night Emma left, after Juliette and Marco were here. Another drunken haze, that similar sick feeling of minutes unaccounted for. All I can cling on to are the chapters. She must have been writing them. It's madness to think otherwise!

An officer ushers me into the house, just as the blade-slapping sound of a helicopter materialises above. I squint up into that melting blue sky, the stunning view torn apart by this hovering vehicle. 'Monsieur,' the officer says, waving me along with more urgency.

The hugeness of the story I am embroiled within hits me.

'Is she . . . is Robyn dead? In New York. Did they . . . did they find her?' I ask him, my voice barely there at all. But he doesn't reply. 'I'm innocent,' I try. The sound comes out strangled.

I look through to the kitchen. They're closing my laptop left on the kitchen table. Had it run dry from a frenzied night of writing? Was I in some sort of maniacal trance?

I watch as the sleek piece of hardware slots into the bottom of an evidence bag. How bad have my blackouts been? I've had so many over the last few years, I've become used to waking up with no recollection. Emma said I was like Jekyll and Hyde.

I look down at my hands, and for the first time I have no idea what I am capable of.

*Am I mad?*

I turn to look at the garden one more time. Sniffer dogs are leading the charge into the orchard, another pack going the other way, towards the cliff. I'm nudged, more aggressively, and I trip as I make my way inside the house. I am told to wait, and I stand there, my vision coming in and out of focus. I notice something strange about the wall. It takes me a moment to realise what it is. The painting is missing. It should be right there.

The girl with the book.

'Monsieur,' the officer says, and I follow him to the door in a daze, looking back one more time in case I imagined it. But it's gone.

I'm soon distracted as the front door opens to the court-yard. I'd heard some bustle from the back garden, but this is beyond what I'd imagined. Every American media outlet must have jumped on the phone, sending all their regional contacts here as soon as they caught a whiff of Emma's disappearance. Suddenly it's not just a missing girl with a tenuous link to the Larsons. It's a missing wife and a dead body. This is huge. I can see limbs hanging through the gates. Like in a zombie movie, reaching out, trying to get the best shot.

A rain of camera flashes. 'Felix!' they shout. 'Felix, where is your wife?' The helicopter above compounds the intense drama and chaos of it all. 'Did you kill Robyn Avery?' the next one shouts.

The police are aggressive now with the tense atmosphere permeating from the shouting crowds, and my head hits the lip of the door with the haste with which I'm bundled into the back seat of the car. Bodies clunk against the vehicle's side as we drive past the reporters, and I'm too shocked to have the foresight to hide my face. They rush to cars and onto motorbikes, and the cavalry fills the once idle road.

I look over as we pass Juliette's cottage. There is a police car outside. She is standing on the steps, talking to a woman in a uniform, as she hugs herself, looking sad. Her eyes rise to see us pass, and she freezes, her lips parting in shock as our eyes connect for the briefest of moments. She'll be telling them all about the suitcase Marco saw, and how last time I'd seen her, she was knocked to the floor.

And the noose around my neck tightens with every terrible thought.

# CHAPTER THIRTY-EIGHT

Finding an English-speaking lawyer at short notice must have proved tricky as I've been stuck alone, waiting in a room at the station, my head buzzing, for longer than I would have liked. The clock on the wall moves at a snail's pace, and four hours have felt like a week. I'm jittery, rinsed and aching, my body desperate for alcohol. I've not gone this long without a drink for a very long time.

I've been trying to unlock that night before we left for France. The hazy memories make me feel sick. As I sit with my head in my hands on the plastic chair in the corner of the room swaying, I try to let my mind truly wander back through it. The cries and the screams, the cat-like whip of nails to my face. Am I a monster? Please, let this be a bad dream. Emma will appear any minute. *Gotcha!* Unless . . . did I kill her?

Emma was so businesslike the next morning. Focused, like she was going through some sort of protocol. Get me in the car, get through departures. Tick, tick, tick. Were we actually fleeing the country?

The door is opened, and a thin man in a very poorly fitting

suit slots between the gap. He has a worn leather briefcase and a coffee stain on his shirt. 'Are you from the embassy?' I ask, my eyes begging him.

'Mr Larson, I am your lawyer.' He has a British accent; this makes my shoulders fall with relief. 'I relocated here from Britain twenty years ago so that should simplify things . . . erm, slightly.' He uses a cotton hanky to wipe his nose.

'Did Max send you?' I ask hopefully.

He shakes his head. 'Max?' So, he's rejected me. Fear grips. I should call my parents, but I just can't bear to hear their anguish.

'I need to speak to someone from the American embassy. I'm an American citizen.' He just places his briefcase on the small table in the corner with a sigh. 'Mr Larson, you are about to be questioned by the police. There are many inquiries taking place, and the authorities are coming over from America, about the matter there. I would like you to be patient. Is there anything you'd like to tell me before we proceed?' He looks at me expectantly, as though he has already made up his mind. My own lawyer thinks I'm guilty without having barely said two words to me.

'Can I check my emails on your phone?' I ask urgently, ignoring his question. What's on that last email? I have to know. If I did author those chapters, who did my subconscious put in the basement? Nancy, Hanna and Ivy? *All the people I've killed.* I feel like dragging the skin off my face with my nails.

His eyebrows shoot up. 'No, Mr Larson, that is not possible,' he tells me with a sad shake. 'It is against policy.' Great, of course I get laden with a bloody paper pusher.

'Come on,' I plead. 'You're my lawyer, you're on my side, there is something in there I need to read that'll help . . .'

'If you're attempting to meddle with evidence . . .'

'I'm not! I swear. I just want to read something,' I plead.

'It is not allowed,' he says swifty. 'Now, Mr Larson. Would you like to tell me what happened to your wife and how you'd like to proceed?'

I sit there, ruminating. How can I explain? How can I tell this person something that sounds crazy, even to me? Especially as he is fixed on the same ending as everyone else. I must have done it, but how? I couldn't have, no. I sob. A tear runs down my nose and onto the floor.

'I didn't kill my wife,' I say, my voice cracking as I bang my fist on the table.

He sniffs. 'Sir, I advise at this stage that if you intend to plead not guilty, you should answer with no comment during the interview.' He thinks I will tie myself in knots trying to cover myself, and it'll only harm my defence. 'Now, there are some differences with the legal system here, which I can run through with you.' He begins to laboriously go through it, but my mind is too busy to hear. I sit back in the chair, my hands running up and down my thighs with the stress of it all.

I have nothing to hide! Do I? I want them to find Emma. I choke a cough.

'I need to talk to them. Explain.' The lawyer looks bored. I wonder how many men he has defended after a wife's demise. I wonder what the statistics are on the outcome of those cases. Not good, one can only assume. And I'm sure they are usually right. Is he correct here? I look at my shaking hands in front of me. What have I done?

The door is opened, and a guard beckons us out of the room. '*Ils sont prêts*,' he shouts.

'They are ready,' my lawyer translates. We are moved through narrow dark corridors to an interview room. A table, two chairs either side. We've described these rooms in our books. We even visited a station once, for research. I never imagined I'd one day be involved in my own interrogation scene.

I sit in one of the chairs, my lawyer next to me. Capitaine Dupont and the lieutenant are in front of us. The loud beeping sound of the recorder makes me shudder, and the customary caution script is read out, and then in English too, for my benefit. 'Monsieur, we would like to know where your wife is. Her family is in great distress. Can you help us with that?'

'I don't know where she is,' I croak. The detectives look at each other, and smirk. My lawyer flicks his pen on his notepad, annoyed I have gone against his advice at the first possible juncture. 'What happened in our apartment?' I ask quietly, trying to seem as though I am innocently enquiring, but it doesn't come out that way.

Capitaine Dupont folds his arms. 'Monsieur Larson, we would like to ask you a few questions about your time here, and the whereabouts of your wife. The investigation in New York is another matter – for now.'

'When did you last see Madame Larson?' the lieutenant asks.

I wipe my face, resigned to it. 'The night of the eighteenth of July. We'd all been drinking, a few of the people we've met here were at the house. After they left, we had an argument, and then she took off in the middle of the night while I was asleep. The first I knew of it was the next morning. I know how this all looks but . . . I honestly can say this really has got nothing to do with me.' I look up at them. They are unimpressed with my explanation.

'And how did you know she'd left you? Weren't you worried something more sinister could have taken place?'

'Well . . .' My mind goes back to that morning, running down to the cliff. 'All her things were gone,' I mutter listlessly, and swallow.

Dupont nods. 'Right. Now, you've said you had an argument, and she left.' He pauses, and leans in. 'What was the argument about?'

I shift in my seat. 'Nothing. It was stupid really.' I'm too scared to bring up Robyn, because that's what it was about, isn't it? About the missing girl and the newspapers connecting us to it.

'And did you not think it was strange that nobody could contact her by phone?'

I sigh. 'I told you, all her things were . . . gone.' I shift about again. 'And she was emailing me.'

They give each other a look. 'Yes, I see. From this email address you share the password to.'

I sit back on my chair. This is infuriating. 'I didn't write her parts.' The conviction in my words is gone. Even I am unsure of it now. I think of myself tapping away at night, writing

311

my new book but having nothing to show for it. 'How could I have been writing them while I was asleep, for God's sake? She always sends them at ten a.m. – as long as I've known her,' I say, throwing my arms in the air. 'It wasn't me.'

Dupont pulls a few papers from a pile by his side. 'Our technical man has looked through a few of the chapters you say are from Emma. You said earlier that you could never have sent them, as you were asleep at ten.' He uses a pencil to circle the time stamps. 'Apparently it would be practically impossible to send an email at exactly ten o'clock in the morning. And more than once?' He clicks his tongue. 'Improbable.' The graphite of his pencil leaves dots around the zeros of the time stamp to illustrate the point. He flips the page to show the next 'Her' chapter from a few days ago. It has the same time stamp – 10:00:00 – on the dot. He looks at me with a self-satisfied smile. 'I am told the only way for this to happen would be if they were scheduled.' I swallow. I see exactly what he's doing, he's debunking my claim completely. 'Do you have anything to say about it?' he asks, leaning towards me. 'Because it certainly looks as though you were attempting to make it look as though she was sending them at her usual time.'

I shake my head and shrink into my chair. 'Someone else must have been doing it.'

He nods. 'We are looking into the IP address and will be able to confirm shortly whether they came from Villa de la Falaise.'

'Good. Well, you'll find her then,' I say, my conviction failing, my heart drumming in my chest.

'Okay, the next question.' He takes out a photograph from

a file. 'Monsieur Larson, can you explain this? We found it in a locked cupboard in the house.' He pushes a photograph of Emma's case, open, with all Emma's things displayed. My lawyer shifts nervously and I sit back in the chair, winded.

'I . . . I found it.' I sigh. 'Look, I found it on the grounds a few days later, but I'd been receiving emails, so I knew she was okay. I knew it would look . . . dodgy.'

'Hmmm . . .' Dupont is not convinced. 'At this point you still didn't call us. Were you not worried about your wife?' He pushes another photograph, a close-up of her pill bottle. 'You think she would have left without her medication?'

'They are anxiety drugs, not daily dose sort of things,' I explain.

'Monsieur, these are anti-psychotic drugs. You definitely need to take them every day, I've been told.'

'Anti-psychotic . . .' What? 'Look, I found the bag, I freaked out and hid it. I'd spent the last few days in contact via email so wasn't too worried.'

'Yes, the emails, you said,' Dupont replies staunchly. 'There is something else.' He pushes more photos into the middle of the desk.

They are photos from our Instagram account. Pictures of Emma she'd had me take, and a couple of selfies. I lean in to have a closer look. I glance back up at him questioningly, for an explanation. Then Dupont places the end of his pencil on her wrists. There they are – the red-raw rings. Only noticeable if you knew what you were looking for. My mouth drops open. My body feels as though it has been funnelled through with freezing water.

'We have questioned the owner of the property, who told us that Emma said you'd been tying her to the bed. Was she trying to escape? Is that why you damaged the car, monsieur?'

'Escape?' I whisper. No, that isn't right at all.

I shake my head. 'No – no! This has all been blown out of proportion. She was sleepwalking – she asked me to, so she wouldn't fall off the cliff like the young girl. She asked me! She asked me to!' I say, frustration building. They look at me, baffled. Emma had, hadn't she? That is what happened, right? My head is a mess. I can't think straight.

'Young girl?' They look at each other. 'What young girl?'

'Years ago, that is why the house is haunted. You must have heard the story, know of the case?'

They look at me as though I am mad. '*Non*, monsieur, we have not heard of this case.'

'And this.' Dupont pushes a photograph of me from the day at the castle. My angry face blustering back at the photographer, holding a woman's hand, her slender arm only on show. 'Who were you with here?'

'Just a friend,' I say, swallowing. They look between each other, eyebrows raised.

'You hold hands with all your friends, Monsieur Larson? And so soon after your wife leaves you?'

'No . . . no . . . you don't understand.' My hand shaking, I pick up the photograph of Emma, with her injured wrists. 'The owner told you?' I frown. 'We never even met the owner of the house,' I whisper.

Dupont frowns. 'Madame Brewer.'

314

'Brewer,' I repeat. I have never heard the name. All the emails about the rental were sent to Emma, after all. 'I have no idea who that is.'

'Juliette.'

'Juliette? Juliette didn't own the property. She worked there.'

They look at me, a little bored now. 'Monsieur Larson, are you drunk?' They discuss something in French.

My lawyer leans in and whispers, 'They are deciding whether you need a mental health assessment.'

'I am completely sane,' I shout, banging my fist down. But I'm not really sure.

'Madame Brewer also told us that the morning after Emma disappeared you deep cleaned the entire house, and timed it perfectly with the refuse collection. Is that true?'

*Oh, God.*

'No . . . no. That's not . . . We had a party. The house was a state, I thought Emma was just out, I thought I was helping.' But I realise how ridiculous it sounds. What a mess. What a huge terrible mess.

My eyes dart between them. They think I'm mad. A sex-hungry killer. Deranged. A psychopath. Emma left, didn't she? She left the house, right? I didn't do what they think I did, surely?

'Tell us, Monsieur Larson,' Dupont sings, realising I'm close to breaking point. 'Where is your wife's body? Tell us where you hid it. Give her mother peace.'

My head in my hands, all I can do is repeat, 'I don't know,' over and over, swaying slightly.

'Do you drink a lot, monsieur?'

My eyes squeeze tight with the pain of it all, and I stammer, 'Too much, probably. I'm going to stop, though; I've had enough of it all. First chance I get.'

'Do you sometimes get angry when you are drunk?'

'No! Well, sometimes, but not . . . I wouldn't *kill* someone.' I swallow thickly.

'Do you often get obsessed with younger women? Especially when they don't concede to your advances?' He pokes further.

I sit up at this. This is just not fair, not at all. 'No, no! That's not right at all. If anything, they get obsessed with me!' Dupont ignores this and continues bating me.

'Was Juliette your next victim?' he asks, tapping on her photograph. 'She tells us you knocked her over, and she had to run out of the house to get away.' He pushes a piece of paper over. On it is the message I sent her the next day: *I'm really sorry about last night, I didn't mean to hurt you. I'm just under so much pressure right now. Thank you for being so kind to me x.* 'You apologise for hurting her,' he states simply.

I sit up, enraged. 'What? No! That was an accident. This is madness!' I cry. I rub my sweaty hands up and down my thighs, the anxiety reaching tipping point. 'You've got this all wrong. I do drink a lot. You would if you were married to my wife!' More eye bulging. That was the wrong thing to say. I try a calmer, more stable tone. 'Look, it must have got lost in translation somewhere – maybe Juliette got the wrong end of the stick when talking to Emma,' I try.

Dupont snorts. 'Juliette is Canadian. So, I am not sure about this language barrier thing . . .'

I stop then, my whole body slacking. 'Canadian?' I breathe, winded.

'*Oui*, she is from Quebec, originally.'

I try to work it out. I'm so confused. 'So, Juliette owns the house?'

'She has owned it for the last six years.' I can't piece together what is going on. Everything is swimming, dancing in front of my eyes. I realise I never asked where she was from, I just assumed it was France. It would never have occurred to me it could be another French-speaking country.

'Do you know where Emma is, monsieur? It is better if you just tell us now.'

'This is madness! I couldn't have . . . I couldn't have.' I get up out of my seat and rush to the door, banging wildly, suddenly feeling the terror of incarceration. I am grabbed from behind and pushed back into the chair; it slides across the room with the strength of the action. And I don't know what else to do other than cry.

'I don't understand,' I sob. One of them smirks at the other.

'Monsieur Larson. We understand there is another murder investigation happening in your home country. You are also the prime suspect in that case.' Prime suspect, *also*. Dear God. 'Your wife is missing, with many, many factors linking you to it. You, in fact, killed your wife and attempted, very poorly, to make it look like she had left you. She was terrified of you, wasn't she, Monsieur Larson? You had been tormenting her for years.' He bangs his hand on the table.

'No!' I shout. 'You don't understand. This isn't—'

'You sabotaged the rental car, didn't you? So, your wife couldn't leave.'

'No!' I slam my hand on the table.

'You made her life hell, didn't you, Mr Larson?'

'No!' I cry. 'If anything . . . she made my life hell!'

Why has Juliette turned on me like this? Unless . . . Emma did ask me to tie her to the bed, didn't she? My head can't work it out. I didn't tie her up for another purpose, like Dupont is saying, did I? But those nasty dark red rings on her wrists tell another story altogether.

It's all a mess. One huge mess. Hanna, Nancy and Sebastian. Hanna, Nancy and Sebastian.

And the person on the phone.

Could it be Ivy's real father? But who . . . ? I scratch my head. Is there someone Emma has been hiding from too? If Ivy represents Morgan, then . . . No – I'm in a muddle. This can't be.

Dupont reads something out that sounds official, that I assume are my rights. 'Monsieur Larson, the *magistrat* has agreed we have enough evidence to arrest you in connection with the disappearance of your wife. We believe you murdered and hid her body. I believe another case is being brought against you, and we are liaising with the principal officers of that case to coordinate these matters. Do you understand?'

'This wasn't me,' I whisper again. But it is futile.

The detective gives me a bored look. I am a drunk, a wife beater, a snake. And he's caught me. This crime, on the world stage, press buzzing around, and he has caught me.

'And there is the other matter, the email you wrote last

318

night. A confession, *non*?' A smile curls up the ends of his lips. He looks like a fucking cheshire cat.

'What?' I whisper. My eyes search the table in front of me. The photographs and then the neat pile of emails that make up our ninth book. What is in that final chapter? I move my hand towards the pile, but he drags the papers away from my reach.

'Monsieur, I would reconsider, if I were you. Tell us the truth, the judge will look at your predicament far kindlier,' he advises.

'Please, please can I just read the chapter,' I choke, pleading.

Someone comes into the room and whispers in Dupont's ear. He nods. 'We will have to continue this later.'

I stand up. 'You can't do this!'

'Monsieur, on the contrary, we have a very strong case.'

I turn to my lawyer. 'If you don't want to be sacked on the first day, get them to let me read those papers,' I hiss over at him. He blinks at the power behind my request, and then sighs before speaking fluent French to the officers who are already halfway out of the door.

Dupont turns to me, laughing. 'You want to reread your work?' They all laugh. 'You writers . . . are all *fous*,' Dupont says. 'You can stay in here and read it with your lawyer present if you really must. And then you will be taken to your cell.' And with that he follows his colleagues out of the door. My lawyer sighs and makes himself comfortable on a chair with his phone.

I cling to the papers in my hands. It's in here. The answer to this riddle is hidden inside. I have it. I have the final chapter. I fall to the floor, shuffling through them, trying to find the final chapter where all the threads tie up, like it does in all our books, and it'll all finally make sense. It must! Whatever they have thought they've read, there must be answers. The conclusion will be in there and I'll be able to untie this mess. Emma wouldn't have been able to resist it, I am sure!

My whole body is hot with anticipation that this cliffhanger will finally be resolved. My hands shake as I shuffle through them, and they all mix together out of order. I spread them out on the floor, looking at the dates and chapter numbers frantically.

Finding it, my eyes fall onto the sheet, blinking rapidly. It isn't a 'her' chapter, after all. Heat builds within me and the paper shakes in my hands as my pupils track the sentences and lines.

Morgansavage@infinitymail.com
23.07.2024
**Subject:** Book 9 – First Draft

### *CHAPTER TWENTY-ONE – HIM*

*Sebastian unlocks the door to the basement. Feeling that calmness he gets, just before he does it. He's done it before. Look at Stella, back in the city. It was easy.*

*'Sebastian?' Hanna says, looking up from where she's been asleep on the floor. 'Please, let us out. You can't keep us locked*

*down here for ever.' The sound wakes Nancy, her cheeks red
from crying. She clings to Hanna, scared. 'Sebastian?' she
whispers fearfully.*

*Sebastian smiles. 'Hello, girls,' he grins. Ivy is clinging on
to Hanna. He just needs to get his precious girl upstairs, and
then he'll go get that knife he saw in the kitchen and do it.
Then he'll strap her into that car seat, and they'll drive to a
new city, and this will all be a bad dream. Until next time,
of course. Because there will always be a next time. There is
something inside him, and he just can't help it. He likes the
vulnerable women, the trusting ones. The ones that fall apart
without their medication. The ones who'll rely on him, thinking
he's the good guy, until they are stuck, and he's safe to show
his true colours.*

*He's feeling very tired after that flight. He's pleased he had
the foresight to dig that grave.*

*There is no way anyone will ever find them.*

*THE END*

I scream, banging my fists on the floor. This doesn't make
any sense – it doesn't even follow the story! It's total hogwash!
'Why would I write this?' I scream at my lawyer, who looks
at me, bored. 'It doesn't make any sense!' I shout. I grip on to
the paper, pointing at him, trying to get him to read it, but
he has little to no interest. I fling it onto the floor. 'It doesn't
even follow the story!' I scream, my throat raw. 'What about
the person on the phone?' I cry, incensed. 'It was clear that
Hanna did it! Surely they have to see that?' He looks at me as

though I am completely barmy. I move my hands around the floor searching for another page, something that ties up those loose ends. Emma would never have let a red herring dangle so visibly. But maybe Emma didn't write it? Maybe it was me? Could it have been me?

I fall to the ground, my head in my hands, and I sob.

# PART THREE

# CHAPTER THIRTY-NINE

## FRANCE. SOMEWHERE NEAR THE SPANISH BORDER

'Emma, relax, we'll be there soon,' Juliette tells her from the driving seat. 'They aren't even looking for us!' she reminds her. Emma stuffs a lock of dark hair behind her ear. She's still not used to her newly cut bob and dye job, and being out in public for the first time in nearly a week has been more overwhelming than she'd expected. Every time another car has driven past, she's looked the other way. She feels exposed and vulnerable, and she just wants to get out of this country.

She sits up in her seat as they pass a sign. '*Espagne!*' Juliette cries. 'See I told you this was the right way.' Emma rests back in the chair, relieved. Certain people didn't stick to their side of the bargain, and they thought they were driving aimlessly, lost. She scratches her chest, which is red and blotchy from all the stress.

A map would be handy. She closes her eyes for a moment, imagining crossing the border. Hoping that the fake passports work, and that the police haven't cottoned on. She fears they may suddenly appear as they attempt to drive through it, sirens blaring. But if they, by some miracle, make it through, the plan is to get a ferry over to Gibraltar and drive into Morocco, finally boarding a flight to Panama. She'll be able to breathe a lot easier then.

'Well, we got lucky with that turning,' Emma replies, lowering her face as a lone car shuttles past. 'We should have bought a phone, this seems crazy,' Emma says, dragging her nails against her chest.

'You try an international escape route without satnav. We're back to basics, remember?' Juliette says. 'We can't leave a digital footprint. Trust me, I know. I had to do all that off-grid research, remember? That plot twist in *Meghan's Wrath*, with the dad?' She reminds her. Her French accent has completely vanished, replaced by Canadian. Although fluently bilingual, she was never as resolutely Quebecois as her mother. And now they're leaving France, she no longer needs to lean on her Gallic heritage to play the part.

'I thought you said you had everything prepared,' Emma says, through her teeth. They've been clashing most of the journey about the missing piece of vital kit. 'Who drives through four countries without bringing a map?'

Juliette's eyes leave the road and she casts a weighted stare. 'I did my best, okay? While you were busy watching RHOBH reruns some of us were out there laying the groundwork, and keeping an eye on your wayward husband.' She sighs. 'If you're going to keep on about it, you can find another ride.' Emma shakes her head in disbelief. Juliette relents and tries to calm her. 'You need to relax. Once we're off the continent you'll feel better. We're almost there, I wish you'd chill out.'

'I just prefer to have everything accounted for,' Emma continues. She would never have forgotten the map, had it been on her list. 'It makes me nervous that we've forgotten something else.'

Juliette is getting rather tired of her whining. 'Emma, we did it, our plan worked. Exactly as we plotted it. That drunk grifter will be behind bars for life.'

Emma stares over at the messy woodland whipping past. Juliette is right, everything is going to plan. But then the bright colours of the painting on the back seat catches her eye in the mirror, and she huffs. As soon as they stop, she's going to stick it in the boot away from prying eyes.

'You shouldn't have taken it,' she tells Juliette, for the third time.

'What? The painting again? You think I'm going to leave behind the last picture my mom had me sit for before she died? Are you crazy? That thing has been in every home I've had since I left Quebec.'

'It's just risky,' Emma says, wiping her eye. She's exhausted from sitting in the dark, waiting for the cue to leave. The anticipation and the never-ending circular motion of her mind. It's been a living hell. Harder than she ever thought it could be when they'd discussed it. She jumped with every sound, assuming the game was up.

Juliette laughs. 'Darl, after all the years we've been writing together – we've crossed every T and dotted every I, and this is no different. We've never, not once, let a plot hole slip.'

Emma nods, but then a new thought panics her. 'Are you sure he didn't see you in the house?'

Juliette shakes her head, getting quite tired of her fluctuating neurosis. 'I told you, I waited until he was passed out and used my key to get in, and set the emails to send from his computer.' She pats her hand reassuringly. 'You were right, he couldn't help but get completely wasted every night. He behaved exactly how you said he would. The cops will be able to prove he sent them.'

Emma nods. This should make her happy. 'He is so predictable.'

For a split second she feels sad about everyone assuming Felix is a stone-cold psychopath. And of course they will, he is the mastermind behind those bloodthirsty Morgan Savage books, isn't he? *Ha.* The sadness doesn't stick around, and a smile spreads across her lips. This is what he deserves: his perfect ending.

'The sleepwalking thing worked well. What an inspired idea,' Emma tells Juliette. 'I wondered where you were going with that story when we first turned up. Good work.' She massages her wrist, still sore from using a rough piece of rope to ligature them. Binding them tightly and chafing the skin down. It hurt. But the pain felt good.

'You're the one who ran with it. Never knew what a great actress you are, Em. You missed your calling.'

'Urgh, never. Actresses are the worst.'

Emma wipes her forehead. She's had so many balls flying in the air these last few weeks, and the constant patter of anxiety that's ebbed and flowed has left her body weary. Not long now, she just needs to tie up these final loose ends and rip herself from this torrid co-dependent relationship she's been stuck in all these years. With Juliette.

The money is in an overseas account in Juliette's name, and she needs to get it for herself. She smiles across at her accomplice. 'You're right. Nearly there.' Her emotions cannot get the better of her when the finish line is in view ahead. 'Sorry to have kept on about the map. I know the last few days have been tough,' she tells her softly. And Juliette grins at her supportively and shrugs: *No worries.*

Emma turns back to look out the window with a sallow smile. She's lucky Juliette is so unquestioning of her motives and has no idea of what is truly in store. Because Emma doesn't plan to share a cent of that money. It's hers. She's done all the hard work. Those Morgan Savage bestsellers would still be idling nonsense on Juliette's old hard drive if it weren't for Emma seeing them for what they could be.

Besides, Emma had to live the deceit every day, while Juliette had zero responsibilities out here in the sticks. She can't comprehend how tough it's been on her. And besides, she is a total liability. Emma isn't risking a future attached to her. Look at what happened in France. She was meant to lay low. Fine, have a few flings, but amusing herself with a job in a bar? Emma couldn't believe it when they turned up and that was sprung on her. Juliette loves a heart-to-heart, and God knows what she was spinning to all the customers every day. It doesn't bear thinking about.

Besides, Emma simply doesn't need her any more. It was one thing when the books needed to be delivered, on time, year after year, the chapters sent through every morning without fail. But that isn't in the equation any longer.

'Once we're set up, we can start writing together, like we used to, no one reading a word of it, just us, together.' Juliette grins lazily at the thought.

'Yes, we sure can.' Emma nods, not meaning a jot of it. She never wants to be in such proximity to this woman ever again. She's actually looking forward to it: putting a full stop on Juliette for ever.

'I wonder if he's worked it out yet,' Emma says, thinking of Felix completely baffled, on the worst comedown of his life.

Juliette snorts. 'Who, Felix? Doubt it. I thought you said he'd been blacking out every night for the last year. He probably thinks he did kill you!' She laughs.

'He deserves it,' Emma says with misty eyes. The back end of this has been harder than she could have imagined. Maybe she does have more of a conscience than she thought. 'He deserved everything.' Nobody betrays Emma and gets away with it, she reminds herself.

'Oh, Emma, cheer up.' Juliette knows Emma better than anyone. 'He was a great find, to start with. If he hadn't wrecked it,' she says, her eyes still concentrating on the road.

Emma thinks of the first time she saw Felix, standing in

the bookshop all those years ago. Looking so contrived, with that book in his hands he was barely reading, more involved in watching the door to see who was coming in. She had the manuscript in her bag eating away at her, whispering that she couldn't let this story go to waste, but how? How would she publish it? The perfect book that would surely be a bestseller but was destined to never see the light of day, because of whom she'd written it with.

'Will you miss France?' Emma asks. Juliette's beloved house on the cliff is soon to be lost for ever.

Juliette ponders this. 'I always wanted to spend time there, get back to my roots. Feel close to her, you know? But I couldn't have stayed for ever. The timing was right. I'm just glad that some of the money went into experiencing the town my mom grew up in. On to the next adventure, Em!'

'I'm glad too,' Emma says warmly. 'I still love the idea that Felix had absolutely no idea that the bulk of the novels were written in the very house he was sitting in.'

Juliette cackles at the thought of it. 'He stole my spot on the veranda! It's a darn shame we didn't get to finish the ninth book, it would have been sublime once you'd finally got your hands on it.'

'Yeah, I'm kind of pissed I'll never get the chance to work on Hanna.' Emma already had a hundred ideas about the story. Oh well. It was all just part of the scheme to wind Felix up and make him question everything. And it worked, too well. He was on the cusp of madness; he just needed a little more to push him over the edge.

She sighs. 'It was a great premise Juliette, another stroke of genius. I don't know how you did it book after book.'

Emma watches her take the compliment. Juliette's always been the picture of modesty when it comes to missing out on the accolades attached to the novels. She's never seemed to mind that she couldn't take the praise. She did it for the love of writing, and the cash. Emma has been syphoning off money from the books for years and putting it into an untraceable account for Juliette. It was the deal they'd concocted. The money paid for the house in France, with far more stashed away in the account. An impressive fee for continuing to write the lucrative books with Emma.

She has a lot of respect for Juliette. But there isn't another way, she must go. It's too much of a risk to let this thread hang – and although Juliette is smart, Emma knows she's so very stupid when it comes to her loyalty to her partner in crime.

The best team there ever was. With the perfect beard to hide the truth: Felix.

Emma glances over at the woman who has traced the line of her life so violently. Her life would be completely different if they'd never met. She wonders if she'd have gone back to New Jersey after college. It was as if, when their eyes connected that first day at Sarah Lawrence, Emma felt like she'd come home. Although, this home was a building with a gas leak, and it was always going to blow. It was just a matter of time.

The writer's block Emma had wasn't Emma's. It was Juliette refusing to type another word until she came out to France to be with her. No, it wasn't writer's block; it was blackmail. Yes, Emma could edit – she was a master at moulding an idea into something edible. But the ideas, she was nothing without Juliette's staggering, inexhaustible melting-pot mind. But after eight books, Juliette was feeling ignored and relegated. Emma had managed to put her off for the last few books, but Juliette was sick of the excuses, and threatened to stop writing completely unless she came to France for the summer. That first hug when Felix wasn't looking was suffocating. Emma knew then, she wouldn't be able to bear her in this next unfamiliar chapter.

The original plan was to go out to France, galvanise Juliette into writing the next book, and placate her for the foreseeable. Keep the Morgan Savage money train rolling and all the balls in the air.

She knew Felix would be none the wiser. He is so completely self-absorbed, so consumed by himself – it was painful to watch, really.

But then a subplot reared its head, and the plan needed a redo.

Robyn.

She scratches her chest again. The past year she's felt as though she was freefalling – Juliette on her back constantly, and then all this litigation stuff she was attempting to stamp out. She may have been taking too many prescription pills to deal with the stress of it all. Her control over the narrative she'd clung on to was slipping.

Felix's run of affairs was to prove their undoing. He'd

pathetically tried to keep them a secret. The problem was, he was so drunk half the time he was running rings around himself trying to remember all his lies. He just wasn't smart enough to follow through and get away with it.

Besides, Emma has all his passwords. She knew exactly what he was up to. For the most part, she felt these girls had what was coming. They knew he was married, after all. Think you can steal my husband? She almost enjoyed watching all the waifs and strays with tear-stained cheeks. Felix would never leave her; he had too much to lose, she could count on that.

But Robyn was different. She just wouldn't let it go. Maybe she took it too far getting her dismissed, and then ensuring that she couldn't get hired. She underestimated her. She did not go quietly.

The truth is, in the end, it was never about Felix. Robyn uncovered the truth behind Morgan Savage, about Juliette. Emma couldn't believe she could be so stupid when she realised she'd forgotten to change the password for their Instagram. Robyn had taken over the account during their last press tour. An oversight she's paid for. Usually, Emma deletes messages from Juliette's anonymous, faceless account, but she forgot, and a heated exchange over a book title was left, which made it obvious that another person was, in fact, writing the books with Emma.

Robyn turned up at the book launch the night before they were to fly to France for the summer, and cornered Emma. At first, she thought she could handle it, like she handles everything. Just stamp the fire out with her usual quick thinking and steely doggedness. But then Robyn paraded those screen grabs in front of her with the deliciously smug look of revenge in her eyes. She wanted to ruin Emma, just like Emma had decimated her burgeoning career. And she certainly had the wares to back up her plan.

Money – that was what this girl wanted, she thought. Emma's mind had whirred, trying to work out how to fix it. She just needed to get her somewhere private so they could thrash it out. She told her to meet at the apartment later, and she'd simply write a cheque. Everyone had a price. The pieces of the puzzle came together as she dropped a few too many of her pills into Felix's drink. He couldn't know about this. If he found out about Juliette, it would push him over the edge, and give him power in the dynamic, and she was sure as hell not letting that happen. And although it pains her to say, she needed Felix too.

Robyn seemed pleased with the invitation. It would be fine; a deal would be thrashed out while Felix slept through it. Done and dusted before their early morning flight. And she could lie back and relax in the sun while Juliette wrote book nine with Felix dithering around the plot, thinking he was having something to do with it.

Then once they were back in the city, she could take the first draft and turn it into a pitch-perfect Morgan Savage novel. Oh, she relished those days, when it was just her and the writing. Everything went quiet in her head when she had a plot to work through.

The meeting with Robyn sadly did not go to plan. She

arrived giddy with power, a rucksack slung over her shoulder planning to sweep her mother away on a surprise vacation once this dirty business was over. Emma offered her money but to her dismay Robyn switched, enjoying the power she had over this woman who used to terrify her so. She tore up the offer, and laughed at her. Laughed! The stresses and strains of the last year amplified in Emma's ears as she listened to Robyn's delight at having boxed her into a corner. And Emma cracked.

Seeing red, the knife on the kitchen counter found its way into her hand. And before she could stop herself, Robyn was splayed out dead in front of her. Oops.

She had to think quickly. The blade she was clutching, the blood on the floor. A flight to catch.

But she'd pulled off trickier plots in her time.

She'd heaved Robyn's lifeless body down the steps to the basement and cleaned up, badly. Forensics wouldn't have a problem uncovering a murder scene, but to the naked eye, it looked all right. She swapped the knife with an identical dirty one from the sink Felix had used.

Then she stood over a passed-out Felix, hatred congealing around her. He did this. He'd turned her into this! The first slap barely stirred him, but she couldn't stop. She despised him for what he'd turned her into, loathed every cell in his body. All this anger and frustration boiled over and she smacked him, hit him, scratched him, howled and screamed it all out.

He was so out of it, he barely put up a fight, and couldn't

even open his eyes, his pathetic hands trying to bat her off. It was farcical really. It wasn't until the next day she realised he had no idea it was her at all. Later, she'd toyed with him, pretending there were hours he was unaccounted for, and she'd enjoyed listening as he stumbled through a lie about going to a bar. It only confirmed he had no memory of her that night whatsoever.

Standing there, with a dead body at her feet, heaving with exhaustion from the frenzied knife attack and dragging her from the kitchen, her mind went to work, plotting a new course for the summer. The end of which has now beautifully played out. Felix will be another male character stuck behind bars. And Emma can just slip into the ether with all the stashed money – yes, her final scene will be that well-trodden sequence depicting a yacht and a cocktail.

Emma Larson will go down in the history books as one of the great authors of her generation, and a victim of her barbaric husband. She can live with that. There was no way Felix was going to destroy her legacy. She didn't do all that hard work just to become a laughing stock.

She gained much pleasure from the idea of a fictitious death, almost as though she was morphing into one of those characters she'd co-penned.

Now, she just needs to get her hands on the money. But, of course, she's been hatching a plan for that too. Then for the first time since becoming entwined in all this, she'll be able to breathe. The notoriety and fame never sat well with her – she didn't enjoy all the photos and the questions. She felt exposed, as though her true self was going to bubble over at any moment, and everyone would see what she'd been attempting to hide her whole life. The dark side of her.

The only person who knows that girl is her mother. Estelle took her from appointment to appointment as a child, and she was on medication from the age of seven. But her mother knows what she is capable of. She knows all the dark, twisted things she would do for kicks as a kid.

Juliette turns to Emma. 'Do you suppose Felix actually thinks he killed you?'

Emma opens the mirror and checks her hair as she replies, 'He's been blacking out for years. It would irritate me so much I'd make up little things to stress him out.' She laughs a little then. 'He'd always buy it, was a trembling wreck for a few days, full of shame, and then he'd get trashed all over again.' She looks at her nails. They're all chipped, and it's making her uneasy. Such a mess. 'The truth was, he'd just fall asleep. Always the same, a slurring wreck and then, like clockwork, bam, fast asleep. Against the wall, on the floor – he wasn't picky.' She shakes her head in amazement. 'Anyway, it doesn't matter what he thinks. All that matters is they have the proof to back up the theory, and he sure does look guilty. Especially with that final chapter. Besides' – she grins conspiratorially at Juliette – 'he isn't smart enough to work it out. He'll probably plead guilty with all the confusion and self-loathing,' Emma says. 'I gave him everything he ever wanted. All he had to do was appreciate me.'

'I can't believe you've let go of him,' Juliette replies, amazed.

'He deserves everything that's coming to him,' Emma says hotly.

Juliette shakes her head, a sly smile drawn across her lips. 'No, I don't mean him. I meant Morgan.'

Emma sighs. Yes, that is tough. 'The sales have been lagging. Yeah, sure, I would hope that this new one would have turned things around. But maybe the timing was right anyway.'

'Oh, Emma, I'm so looking forward to it, just us. We can do whatever we want!' she says, banging joyously on the steering wheel. 'Do you remember that first semester at college? We were terrible, Emma. Or should I call you *Felicity*?' she laughs, tapping the fake passport sticking out of her back pocket that she managed to procure from a local drug dealer. 'Just us. For ever,' Juliette adds, glancing over at Emma, who feels a prick of repulsion at the prospect.

What Juliette doesn't know is that Emma has acquired another fake document. One with Juliette's real name on it, only with Emma's photo. She'd ordered it on the dark web as soon as they got to France, just as backup. A plan B is always a good idea. But there isn't a doubt in her mind: when she enters that cool air-conditioned bank in Panama, she'll use the identification to get the money out of Juliette's account. The thought of it sewn into the lining of her bag calms her. She can't do it here; she'll wait until they've hit Morocco. In the desert maybe. Yes.

'It was clever, making Felix believe he'd hurt that girl while he was blacked out,' Juliette mutters. 'I'll never forget your voice when you called me afterwards to tell me what you did. You sounded . . .'

'Don't say it,' Emma whispers.

'You sounded like you again,' Juliette says, enjoying it. Emma's heart beats a little faster. Murder. It was as if she'd been in training for it all these years. The ease with which it happened only confirming her true identity.

Juliette notices the agitation this comment has caused, and squeezes her hand. 'You'll feel better once we've crossed the border. Besides, they're looking for you in the dirt, not on the road.'

Juliette clicks the indicator, and Emma turns to her questioningly. 'Sorry, but I need the bathroom. There is an *aire de repos* rest stop coming up,' she says, pointing to a little sign with a WC and a picnic table depicted on it.

'What?' Emma's head whips up, annoyed. 'But we're so nearly there.'

'You want me to get out the car and go pee at the border?'

Emma groans. 'Okay, let's be quick. I just want to get the hell out of here.'

'I'll be two secs,' Juliette says, pulling into the layby and jumping out the car. Emma watches her walk, with zero urgency, through the WC door. Emma bites her nail; she'll feel less anxious once she's on the plane to Panama. She almost feels sorry for Juliette, who has no idea she'll be dead long before the appointment at the bank.

Every stage of her carefully plotted plan has worked so far, and there's no reason to think the denouement won't go off without a hitch.

She thinks of Felix, destined to spend eternity behind bars

for crimes he didn't commit. But he gave her no choice. If he hadn't taken her for granted and been just a tiny bit more grateful for what she'd given him, they'd be in a very different place.

She thinks back to the day of Morgan Savage's inception. She had no idea that the decisions made would lead them to this.

She stretches, and glances at the digital clock on the dashboard. Juliette has been gone a good ten minutes. Emma's itching to get out of here. What could be taking her so long? With a sigh, she takes off her seat belt and opens the car door. She gets out, and stretches, looking around. Just as the sign showed, there are a few picnic tables on the grass, beyond which are tall trees. Then a few metres along by the road there is a cube of a building, with a boys' sign one side, and a girls' on the other. The forest setting is pretty. She supposes families on holiday stop here for a break, and to eat their soggy sandwiches and run off a bit of steam.

She opens the door of the female bathrooms, expecting to see Juliette leaning on the sink to get a better look at herself in the mirror. But it's empty, and the stall doors are unlocked and open. It's quiet and still, with only the sound of a lone dripping tap.

'Juliette?' she calls. The solitary word echoes around the deserted space.

# CHAPTER FORTY

### A LONG TIME AGO

'Emma,' Max says, gesturing her to a seat in his office. She glances around the room, stuffed with papers, the windows of the building opposite their view. She tries to ignore the feelings of intimidation as her eyes run along the pictures of numerous bestselling titles framed on his wall, spanning his forty-year career.

'Max, it's great to see you.' She has no idea why he's called her in. He hasn't submitted a new novel to her recently. And if they're catching up about publishing gossip, it'd be over a glass of champagne somewhere he deemed glamorous and fun, like Balthazar.

Max is one of the stalwarts of the literary scene in New York, and her peers are amazed she has him on speed dial. 'Thanks for coming in. Heard things are going well for you,' he says, and Emma gets a little flush of pride that he asks after her. His assistant places a coffee on the glass table next to her seat. Max shoos her out the room with a hand. 'Close the door,

Jenny,' he tells her as she leaves. She nods compliantly, used to his brisk ways.

'I'm good. Under the weight of about fifty books I'm meant to have read. Editing three manuscripts simultaneously.' She laughs. 'You know, I could do with a bit more sleep, but I'm loving it.'

'Ah, yes. The life of an editor. I'm glad it lives up to what you'd hoped when you first told me about your ambitions. Not many can hack the pace.' He smiles in a fatherly way that causes to Emma sit up in her seat.

'Well, I have you to thank for that.' Emma grins. 'If you hadn't pulled those strings to get me onto that training programme . . .'

Max makes a gesture with his hand, swiping the thanks away. 'You gotta stop thanking me for that. I knew you were hungry for it and wouldn't let me down. Besides, it was a pleasure, after . . . everything.' He coughs into his fist. 'But, on that subject.' He walks around his desk, picks up a manuscript, and walks over and hands it to her.

Oh, this meeting *is* about a book, Emma realises. This is all very clandestine. It must be a celebrity, she assumes, excited by the prospect. 'What is it?' Emma asks.

'Take a look,' he encourages.

She opens the pages and recognises it instantly. No, not a celebrity. She wrote this, with Juliette. She didn't want anyone to ever see this. It was meant to be a secret.

'My daughter sent it to me. She told me you've been writing books together all this time.'

343

Emma smiles coyly. 'It's silly really. She was bored in that place, and she sent me a few bits and pieces and, well, I guess I couldn't help myself.'

'Like pen-pals.' Max perches on his desk, looking down at her admiringly. 'You know, I've always appreciated how you've stayed in touch with her, even after what she did.'

'She wasn't in her right mind,' Emma says. 'And she was my friend,' she adds quietly. A friend with a dad with ties to the industry she was desperate to crack in Manhattan no less.

'Yes, well. Many others wouldn't think that way. You've been good to her. More empathy than most in the situation. At least we managed to get her into the mental facility and not jail.'

'Well . . . I know she would never have hurt those girls if she'd been well,' Emma tells him resolutely.

Max nods, staring out the window. His face becomes softer, in a way she's not seen before. 'I was unhappy with how I treated Juliette and her mom, I wanted to make it right somehow. I'm not proud of what I did. She was a brilliant secretary, and I acted like a jerk when she told me she was pregnant. I hope she understood, I was scared out of my mind my wife would find out. I thought I could just forget the whole thing and move on. I was younger then. I had three kids under five running around and a busy working life. The stress got to me, and I behaved badly. I've always regretted it.' He sighs. 'You always pay for things in ways you can never imagine.'

Emma doesn't know how to reply. She's never seen this more vulnerable side to Max. She's heard Juliette's side of

344

this story. Her estranged father stepping in and paying for her college tuition here in the States, after hearing of her great talent from her dying mother in Canada. Juliette had confided in Emma about her complicated feelings for her father.

Max turns quickly. 'But this novel. It's tremendous. You both have a real gift.'

'It's just a game we play. It started in college. It's silly.'

Max won't have that. 'Emma, I cannot get this book out of my head. It is sheer brilliance, with her writing and your editing skills – you're a match made in the fucking celestial gates, Emma. It's gotta be published.'

Emma's mouth hangs open. 'But Max, Juliette . . .'

'I know, I wouldn't ever dream of trying to get her published after what she's pulled. But you, Emma, don't you think this book deserves to be out there, to be read?'

'They'll find out,' Emma says quickly. The last thing she wants is to be tied to Juliette and the horrific crimes she was tried for.

'But how? Juliette has her mother's name, there is no connection between us publicly, I've made sure of that. Besides, we'll publish under your name. I'll talk to her, she'll get it. And we can make sure Juliette is renumerated for when she gets out. She's doing well there, I'm told. It can be a nest egg for her future. Besides, without you to give her direction, to plot . . . this work would be garbage. You know that.'

'Max, I'm not sure.' Emma feels heat run up her neck. The idea of putting herself out there is terrifying. No, she leaves the limelight to her authors.

'Emma, this will be good for her! Give her some direction. Besides, I'm sure my behaviour impacted her state of mind. Let me have this. Let me get this book published with your name on it. It's all I've got to give her,' he adds, looking out the window distantly.

'Can I think about it?' Emma whispers, the weight of what she owes this man for her own career heavy. She wouldn't have got that first foot in the door without the letter she wrote him, after she'd finished college, asking for advice and reminding him all she knew about his secret daughter.

'Of course.'

Emma walks down the street, stopping in a little café before heading home. As they make her coffee, she stands at the counter wondering how many calories are in a Danish, and whether the six a.m. Soul Cycle class would offset it. Suddenly, it begins to rain, as if a shower has been turned on, and she turns to watch as people outside run for shelter cursing, while others struggle in the deluge to open umbrellas.

A man strides up to the door and opens it, dusting the water from his blazer with a lopsided grin. She watches in fascination as he laughs and jokes with the cashier.

He's British and charming. She notices a copy of *The Catcher in the Rye* in his hand. How pretentious, Emma thinks.

Once he has a coffee in his hand, he leaves, shouting, 'Ciao! Got to get back to the ol' novel,' over his shoulder.

'Good luck!' they call, giggling.

Emma listens in to the all-female baristas' conversation.

'Same book every day,' one sniggers.

'He'll be back in here with some girl he's picked up in the bookshop in about half an hour. We should time it,' they laugh.

'Sorry to be nosy; is he a writer?' Emma asks.

'He wishes! He lives upstairs, always here on his laptop telling us about this great novel.' They giggle. The barista elaborates. 'I went on a date with him when he first moved in. Bad idea. All he did was talk about himself. Totally deluded!'

'I'm going to take this to go,' Emma says, smiling, and they shrug and pour her coffee from a mug into a cardboard cup.

The manuscript in her bag feels unwieldy. The book. The book she wrote with her friend. Emma worked on it behind a desk in her apartment, while Juliette worked on it in her room at the psychiatric unit upstate.

Her friend, who'd tried to poison half the sorority house when they wouldn't admit her. Either of them, in fact. They weren't the right sort to have membership. Apparently. They weren't pretty enough, or peppy enough, or didn't have enough money. It wasn't fair. And if there was anything Emma hated, it was injustice. And worse than that? Injustice against her.

But what Max doesn't know is that Emma helped Juliette do it. She, in fact, came up with the idea: digitalis from foxglove into a bowl of punch.

No one died, unfortunately. They were just very ill. Hospitalised. One of them was in a coma for two weeks.

Juliette's fingerprints were found. If anything, Juliette deserved that time in the psychiatric hospital for being so careless.

Juliette never told anyone about Emma's part in it, and Emma was confident she wouldn't. Emma had taken her under her wing that first semester. She was so malleable, and useful. They promised each other if either of them got caught, they'd protect the secret with their lives. Emma is unsure whether she'd have stuck to her side of the bargain. Probably not.

She'd cultivated that friendship tightly, once Juliette confided in her about her father, the great literary agent from New York. Emma didn't have anyone like that to open doors for her when she finished college and moved to the city.

And then, after the incident, she made sure she publicly distanced herself completely, batting off the friendship as surface level after the fact to everyone at Sarah Lawrence. But not to Juliette, or her father. To them, they were bosom buddies and Juliette believed she was lucky to have such a loyal friend.

She leaves the café and shields herself from the rain under the awning. The next one over is a bookshop and she peers into the frontage. There he is, pretending to read a book, a smirk of misplaced ego on his face.

An idea forms. If she had someone else to share the burden of the manuscript with, she would be safe. If it was a charming man she could hide behind, yes. That would make her feel far more comfortable. She could push him into the limelight, and she could sit in the shadows working on the books with Juliette, letting him take all the heat.

Besides, men in this genre are taken more seriously. Think

of Stephen King, Harlan Coban, Lee Child – they were never going to languish on a mid-list. Yes, if Emma had a partner, someone she could elevate, that people would assume was the talent of the pair, it would blow them off the scent of the true identity behind Morgan Savage. And there is money in this book, she can smell it.

Yes. If he takes the bait, and is what she thinks he is, this could work out very well, indeed.

She pushes the door, the tinkle of the bell goes, and the story of Morgan Savage begins.

# CHAPTER FORTY-ONE

*FRANCE. SOMEWHERE NEAR THE SPANISH BORDER*

Emma stares into the empty room. Jesus, Juliette, this was meant to be a quick dash. Where has she got to? She looks around, panic growing. The feeling that something isn't right shuffles through her. 'Juliette?' she calls again. But nothing. She walks past the stalls and checks each one. When she comes to the end of the row, she sees something at her feet and bends down to pick it up. Juliette's red hair scrunchie. She squeezes it in her hand as she rises to her feet. Next to her is another exit, out the back, and the door is ajar.

Frowning, she pushes it open.

All that is behind the door is trees. 'Juliette!' she calls, with the scrunchie squeezed in the palm of her hand. 'Juliette!' she calls again. Has someone taken her? Felix? No, that is improbable, he is behind bars.

She wanders in to the first row of trees. 'Juliette!' she calls. Silence, and her shoulders fall.

Then relief floods as she hears her name. 'Emma!' She sounds strangled, or in pain. 'I'm down here. I'm hurt.'

'What the hell?' she mutters under her breath as she makes her way towards the sound. Still unable to locate her, she walks further. 'Juliette, where are you?' she tries. Trees blur past with every stride.

'I'm here!' she hears again.

'What the hell are you doing?' she shouts.

'Sorry – my ankle!'

Emma rushes further through the trees until she comes to a clearing. Where Juliette is standing. 'What are you playing at? This isn't the time for a fucking stroll in the woods.'

Then she feels a shudder of something in her stomach. Her ears black out and she feels as though someone has turned the volume down. She blinks. That's strange.

'You took your time,' she says dryly. Something isn't right. Emma clutches her stomach, and Juliette looks at her watch. 'Just a few more minutes.'

'What have you done?' Emma manages. Juliette would never betray her, would she? Juliette did time for them both, staying quiet all the while, for God's sake. She even promised to go on the run with her, when really she could have left the incident behind. With Felix arrested, and Juliette's involvement in their working relationship hidden from sight, she would never be considered as a suspect in any of this.

But then it dawns on Emma. Maybe she was never in control. Maybe her devotion was merely a ruse. Has there been another ending in the works this whole time?

'Just a few more minutes.' Juliette moves from her position, and Emma realises she is standing in front of an open grave. Her knees buckle as the pain rushing through her insides amplifies. 'I was worried you'd blow back there and I'd have to carry you.'

Emma's mouth goes dry, understanding. 'What is it?' she croaks, her mind wandering back to the beginning of the car ride, and the cup of matcha Juliette had so kindly made her for the journey. How considerate, she'd thought.

'Don't worry, it'll be quick,' Juliette responds. She gestures to the hole in the ground proudly. 'I came out the other day and prepped everything. It's deep,' she says, leaning on the stick of a shovel. 'No nasties will get ya.'

Emma groans with pain, falling onto her back and looking up at the sky, blinking. Her whole life rushes past. The exhaustion from for ever striving, and here she is, lying in the middle of the woods on the side of the road about to die. A tear slides from her eye.

'Why?' Emma asks. It's painful to even talk.

Juliette kneels down next to her. 'I had to get there first.' She holds out something to show her. It takes Emma's eyes a moment to focus on the item. Emma sees it then, the picture of herself, next to Juliette's name on the identity document. The one she had forged to get the money out of the bank account. 'You should have thought of a better place to hide it. I found it the other day – I checked through your things, just to make sure we were on the same page.' She sighs. 'Sewn into the lining of your handbag? That was my idea for concealment, remember? The second book, it's all there in black and white.'

352

She holds Emma's shaking hand and lifts it up to her lips to brush a kiss against it. 'You understand, right?'

Emma does understand. And funnily enough, she realises, her first emotion isn't anger, it is pride. Emma mumbles something, but Juliette can't hear her, and she leans down to catch the mumblings. 'We were good, weren't we?' Emma croaks. Her teeth begin to chatter, and she feels as though she is being submerged by a tidal wave.

'Better than good. We were the best,' Juliette tells her, nodding as she moves some hair from Emma's beautiful fading eyes.

Emma hears her get up, and next, there is the sensation of being dragged by the feet. Bump, bump, bump, as her body is pulled across the dirt and then a final slip as she's yanked feet first into the hole in the ground. Bang. Her head hits the floor.

Lying in the earth, the first pile of mud lands on her numbing body. She smiles to herself, the soft smile of resignation. Thinking to herself that if she'd been wrestling with this plot, it is true, this is the far better ending.

# CHAPTER FORTY-TWO

*A FEW YEARS LATER*

Max takes another sip of the straight gin he ordered as soon as he arrived at the five-star hotel. He looks around, delighted at the view. A calm lapping sea in the distance, and palm trees dotting the coastline. An infinity pool a few metres away. There is a lazy, relaxed atmosphere he isn't used to. If he is away with the family, he'll be found on the phone in a back room, much to the annoyance of his wife. But this is work, really. He just needs to grit his teeth through it, and leave this whole messy business behind. He was a fool to get wrapped up in it in the first place. It was all some stupid misplaced guilt for what had happened all those years ago. Sleeping dogs and all that.

He hears the click of heels.

Max turns, sees her, before getting out of his seat. His Juliette. 'Darling,' he calls as she rushes into his arms. 'Daddy!' she cries. It makes his insides shrivel.

'Juliette, how good it is to see you.' He points to a chair.

'Come, sit.' He looks around, nervous about being in public like this. But Juliette has assured him, they are safe here. It's been almost two years. Nobody is looking for her anyway.

'It's so good to see you too,' she says, leaning in. Max smiles, trying hard to hide the grimace. He didn't want to come, but her emails were getting rather strange. And the last thing he wanted was for this to bubble over into his real life.

'Well, it's all blown over, hasn't it? I reckoned it was time to book a little trip to see my daughter after all this time.' They sit at the table together and Max clicks his fingers for service, and someone comes rushing over. 'She'll have a cocktail. What's good?' he asks, pointing to the menu.

Juliette shakes her head. 'I'll have a coffee actually. Black.' Max nods stiffly, and the waiter departs.

'Well, to be honest, I had no idea Felix had it in him. He was a prissy puppet, no idea what was going on past his own nose. But a killer?' He watches Juliette's features; he's had a feeling there is more to this caper but can't work it out. Those girls, they were the smartest cookies he'd ever met. And for Emma to die at the hands of someone like Felix, and Juliette to walk away unscathed ... He smells a rat, but daren't unpick it in case he ends up entwined in the whole damn business, and he'd rather back off as quickly as possible.

He looks at his daughter, this woman he barely knows, who frankly terrifies him. He coughs the discomfort away. He doesn't need to fear Juliette. They are on the same team. He is the one who set up Morgan Savage. He made sure she was well compensated for all her efforts. Felix had no idea about the money either. Max couldn't believe it when he quizzed him over it in France – not a clue. What grown man doesn't have a handle on his finances? No, Max has done right by her, after all. She appreciates that. She wouldn't have invited him out for a visit otherwise. Maybe pestered is a better word.

He sighs at the glorious view, happy that it's over. Felix locked up for decades; he'll probably be long dead if he ever makes it out. Max is on the edge of old age, and can retire on all that Morgan Savage gold, the royalties of which never seem to dip, the infamy of the case making his twenty per cent a huge mound of cash. He barely has any other authors now. He doesn't need them. He is rich beyond his wildest dreams. His children – his *real* children – and his grandchildren will never need to worry about anything ever again.

And all because of a torrid affair he had with his secretary thirty-odd years ago.

Maybe some mistakes end up as happy accidents, after all.

Bianca, his youngest, is getting married in a month, and insisted on some high-balling affair in Montauk of course. It's going to cost him over a hundred grand. The money isn't going to stop coming in. And besides, it's made her so happy.

'Well, I just thank God you managed to come out of it unscathed. Had I known Felix was so dangerous, I'd never have let them come out to the house.' Max smiles. 'You know, before Morgan Savage came along there had been a time where I was seriously thinking of throwing in the towel. A tax bill I couldn't pay nearly finished me. Thank God for you, and your very clever books. The spike in sales has been phenomenal.'

'Right, the itinerary for our holiday,' Juliette says, clapping her hands together.

'Itinerary?' Max scoffs. 'Honey, I think we should just lay low. I have some paperwork I must catch up on.' The last thing he wants to do is traverse the island with Juliette in tow. No, much safer in this sanctuary.

'Oh no, nothing like that.' Juliette slides her hand across the table, putting it on top of Max's. He looks at it, feeling the creeping sensation of dread. 'More of a business agenda, rather than an itinerary really.'

'Oh, honey, let's not talk business, we're here to relax,' Max says, taking a sip of his drink and shifting uncomfortably.

Juliette sighs. 'Sorry, *Pop*, we're not here to relax,' she says with a wicked smile. Max's eyebrows rise as Juliette removes her laptop from her bag. 'We're here so I can fleece you,' she reveals, with a flourish. Turning the computer around, he sees his bank homepage asking for passwords and usernames.

'But . . .' he splutters.

Juliette taps his hand again, before nudging the computer closer. 'All of it, Daddy, I want it all. Now and for ever more. Otherwise, guess who is coming out of the woodwork?'

He looks at her, aghast. 'You wouldn't!'

'How would Bianca, Allegra and Lucia feel knowing there is another sister you've hidden all these years?'

Max stiffens. 'They'd get over it.' He's not getting played.

'I think it's time everyone knew who Morgan Savage really is, don't you?' He goes a sickly, pale green and stares at the computer screen.

'It'll probably sell even more books,' he shoots back. He's played hardball before.

Juliette sighs. 'But Daddy, what will they do when they find out you hounded all those poor girls out of pressing charges against Felix? Pretty damming, don't you think?' She clicks open a folder, showing all his emails. 'This is blackmail, isn't it?' she asks innocently, pointing at a rather vicious attack on a young woman's character. She must have hacked into his account. All his emails . . . He dreads to think what is hidden in there. He turns slowly, staring in disbelief at his own flesh and blood.

Juliette knows she's snared him. By the time she's finished with this horrible excuse for a man, he'll barely have a penny of that Morgan Savage money to his name, plus the rest.

She glances up at the sapphire sky. Winking. If her mother is looking down on her now, she'll be very, very pleased indeed.

# EPILOGUE

The stooped back of the inmate cowers above the lined notepad at the desk in cell C193, his fingers black with ink. His lips move and he mutters as he writes, trying to ignore the irritating sound coming from the radio. His new inmate is a particularly imposing muscled man who towers above him by at least a foot, and over the years he has learnt not to moan in the early days of living together, before a sort of impasse is reached. Besides, he's got very good at tuning out noises after a decade within the walls of Baumettes Prison in Marseille, where he is to serve the first part of his sentence, before he is extradited to the US to serve the time owed there. He'll be an old man by the time he gets out, unless he dies first, and with the muck they serve him, that may well happen.

Someone screams a few doors down, and Felix barely bats an eyelid. There is something far more engrossing happening in front of his eyes. To the left of the small desk in the tight space is a pile of one hundred lined notebooks. All drafts of his book. The first twenty were piss poor. But something within him is compelled to continue – he can't stop. This draft, this is the one! The adrenalin is pulsating, as he pushes it over the line.

*The End*, he scrawls, standing up, the hugest weight lifting. It is as though he is having an out-of-body experience. He's done it! He's finally done it. He whoops, laughing, turning around with shining eyes. 'I did it!' he cries. *'Je l'ai fait!'* He grabs his cellmate around the shoulders and hugs him. The man just snorts, and pushes him away. *'Lâche-moi, connard!'* the man with the face tattoo shouts, spit flying, and then he begins laughing at him. That sort of deranged laugh Felix hears a lot of around here.

But this is no bother. Felix raises his arms as he circles the tiny room. He's done it. He's finally done it. Eighty thousand words, and even though he's the only person who's read it, he knows it's the best thing he's ever written. It's the only thing that's kept him buoyant all these years.

But the moment shifts. It's like it was never there at all. His arms hang back down, as though he's been stung. And he stares at the open notepad, and the carefully looped scrawls. The reality of where he is: the bunk beds with the inch-thick plastic mattresses, the graffiti-lined walls, the smelly toilet and the window that won't open, allowing stenches to permeate every molecule.

He coughs and steps back to the desk, and ceremoniously closes the notebook, adding it to the pile before picking up one of the brand-new pads his mother sends him, and scraping off the cellophane, crunching the plastic up in his hand.

And he sits down, picks up his pen, and starts all over again.

# ACKNOWLEDGEMENTS

This book was so much fun to write, mainly because I have such a talented, enthusiastic, hardworking team behind me. Thank you to everyone at Quercus Books. My editor, Katherine Burdon, whom I highly rate as a creative, always makes my work about ten times better than it should be. Thank you, Ayo Okojie, on publicity, Jess Harvey on sales, Charlotte Gill on marketing, and Lorraine Green for your excellent copy-editing skills. Lisa Brewster, for another exquisite cover. Getting a book to market is a massive team effort, and I appreciate everything you all do.

Teresa Chris, thank you for all your guidance and passion. And to Rachel Neely for everything subsequently – I'm very excited to continue my work with you.

Thank you also to Graham Bartlett for helping me with all the police procedural and legal elements of the story; any errors are my own. To Pierre Viger for checking over my French, as mine is truly awful. And to the excellent Benjamin Blaine for sitting in my kitchen with a cup of tea while I barked the plot at him, hopeful that the kernel of a story at least made sense to someone outside my head. Thank you for helping me work out what I was trying to say. Thank you to my friend Bridie Woodward for answering all my questions about New York and for having me stay in your apartment overlooking the Williamsburg Bridge so many times in our twenties.

This book is about ambition and expectation and setting it

within the publishing world was a treat after the last five years and four books. It is a love letter to it all – but of course, it wouldn't be one of my books without some added horror and dread. Felix and Emma seemed to burst through into my consciousness, and I relished writing them.

Huge thanks to the friends who encouraged me: Lottie Dominiczak, Lucy Francis, Kate Hubert, Sophie Nevin, Candice O'Brien, and my wonderfully supportive writer friends: Lizzy Barber, Charlotte Duckworth, Katie Khan, Liv Matthews, Kate Maxwell, and Charlotte Philby. Thank you so much to all the authors who read and endorsed early copies of this.

My mum and dad have never discouraged me from following my dreams, however precarious they may be – thank you. I had no idea how difficult parenting was before I became one, and I wholeheartedly use this platform to apologise for all the heart attacks I gave you in my formative years in the hope that karma may bypass what is rightly coming my way.

Thank you to my sister Juliet for feverishly reading early copies of my books. To my family – I have no idea what I've done to deserve you. Dan – the life of an author's other half is pretty thankless – thank you for putting up with my low moods when projects aren't going my way and celebrating the highs with aplomb. Lola and Jude, you are my favourite little comedy duo.

Finally, and most importantly, thank you for picking up this book to read. And to all the booksellers, book bloggers, and champions of books who've spent time selling, writing reviews, and posting my books online. If you enjoyed this book, please consider leaving a review. I love reading them; they spur me on for whatever I write next!